W9-CLW-637

Pulp Fictions

PULP FICTIONS

HARDBOILED STORIES

EDITED AND INTRODUCED BY
Peter Haining

BARNES
&NOBLE
BOOKS
NEW YORK

1997 Barnes & Noble Books

Printed and bound in the United States of America

ISBN 0-7607-0430-9

97 98 99 00 01 M 9 8 7 6 5 4 3 2 1

QF

CONTENTS

6 CONTENTS

INTRODUCTION

At first glance there is little connection between the tawdry office blocks, sleazy hotels and dimly lit bars of downtown Los Angeles and the quiet, leafy suburb of Dulwich in South London, yet in the colourful legend of hardboiled fiction they are inextricably linked. For it was a classical scholar from Dulwich College who, as a man, was to capture in story form the wisecracking, colloquial style of the LA citizens' language and give crime fiction its most renowned private eye. His name was Raymond Chandler and his character was Philip Marlowe.

Although Chandler was an American born in Chicago, he was brought to England as a child and educated at Dulwich which, despite all the fame he later achieved in his homeland, made him a lifelong anglophile. This man, who relished the hexameters of Latin and Greek, is nevertheless best remembered for pioneering the use of the metaphors that are now regarded as characteristic of hardboiled fiction.

'He pawed my office with his eyes,' Philip Marlowe declares on one occasion, and then says of a visitor, 'His tie had apparently been tied with a pair of pliers.' And who would relish meeting a man described thus in Chandler-speak: 'His smile was as stiff as a frozen fish'?

For years, Chandler's links with Dulwich were scarcely known. Although he retained fond memories of the public school, founded more than 350 years ago, which he attended between 1900 and 1905, the establishment for its part did not even list 'Pupil 5724' (his college number) in its volume of famous old boys. The error was to some degree redressed in 1988 when some enthusiasts of the author's work, knowing of the connection, decided to mark the centenary of his birth with an exhibition of memorabilia. It was only then that the influence of Chandler's education was seen in the character of Philip Marlowe. Where else could the private eye's ability to quote the classics have come from? More striking still was the college's association with the famous sleuth's name—a name so English-sounding that for years readers had puzzled over its possible origins. The answer again lay at Dulwich, for in the early 1900s when Chandler was a pupil, the college boasted six houses: Drake, Grenville, Raleigh, Sidney, Spencer and . . . Marlowe.

Even more recently, evidence has emerged in the form of a typewritten letter purchased as part of another crime writer's effects, revealing Chandler's love of England and his desire to return here after the death of his beloved wife in December 1954. The letter was written by the English mystery novelist Nicholas Bentley, proposing that Chandler should be allowed to join the exclusive Garrick Club in London. It is dated June 1955 and is addressed to a Mr George at the club:

> I wonder if you would care to sign the book at the Garrick Club in support of Raymond Chandler, whom I have just proposed and whom Malcolm Muggeridge has seconded. Chandler has come over to stay in this country indefinitely, I think with the idea of ultimately settling down here, and would very much like to join the Club. Unfortunately he is not known personally to more than a few members, so if you would feel inclined to sign the book on his behalf, I am sure it would be a great help.

There can be few more poignant letters about the still mourning and lonely Chandler than this one, with its suggestion that he wanted to leave the country that had made him famous and spend his remaining years in England. But *why*? Nicholas Bentley's missive suggests more than it explains and surely offers a mystery worthy of Marlowe's talents.

Like so much of the lore and legend surrounding hardboiled fiction, there are still many stories to be unearthed not only about the authors, but also about the pulp magazines in which they appeared—so called because they were printed on cheap, untrimmed wood-pulp paper, octavo size, and stapled inside a slick paper cover printed in garish colours. Few copies survive of these magazines, which rapidly yellowed and fell into fragments, while many of the writers are now no more than names on the pages, having disappeared completely, either by choice or design, when the industry folded in the 1950s. Some of the authors, like Chandler, survived to make the transition into the permanency of book form, to be followed by recognition when the true scope of their achievement was realised: the creation of the first truly original American style of detective fiction. It is these men and the spirit of their forgotten colleagues that have been the inspiration for today's upsurge of interest in, and new contributions to, the hardboiled genre.

The hardboiled dick is now as much a part of American folklore as the frontiersman and the cowboy, and like most heroes his exploits are often exaggerated. Indeed, his seemingly limitless capacity for drink, and his amazing ability to recover from beatings, blows to the head, and knife and gunshot wounds, coupled with his need for only an hour or two's sleep at night, are almost superhuman. Certainly no ordinary mortal could match him. A similar view might be taken of some of the tough cops and gangsters who provided the other main elements in the genre.

But what made these almost caricature-like figures so popular? The answer, I suggest, is not too hard to find. The first of the hardboiled dicks were born in the age of disillusionment in America that followed the First World War, when there was intense frustration among many people about the way organised crime, in the shape of high-profile mobsters and hoods, was taking control of the big cities, their politicians and civic officials, and filling the streets with speakeasies, gambling joints and vice-spots, all packed with low-life. The private eye who emerged in pulp fiction was an almost romantic figure, bent on a crusade against this cancer in society, although he had none of the finer feelings for language, took immediate action (usually brutal) and was dedicated to the preservation of justice. No matter the cost to his limbs—or anyone else's, for that matter!

The explanation for today's new wave of interest in this kind of fiction has a similar origin, I believe: many people, especially the younger generation, feel an equal sense of frustration and disillusionment towards society and their grim prospects for the future. As Ian Penman wrote recently in *The Independent* about Jim Thompson, his hero among the pulp writers: 'He has grabbed our moral imagination: providing— and provoking—strong passions in a lily-livered time; a time which perhaps thinks do-goodery can wash the elemental guilt from our hands, when the persistence of evil is clearly inescapable.'

In another article, in the American magazine *New Republic*, a leader writer attempts to define the current hardboiled genre—American Noir, as he calls it—of which Elmore Leonard, James Ellroy and Quentin Tarantino are the leading exponents. It is, he concludes, 'the moral phenomenology of the depraved or ruined middle class'.

It is not, however, my intention to indulge in a sociological study of hardboiled fiction, but merely to introduce what I believe to be a representative selection of stories by the most influential writers in the genre spanning the last three-quarters of a century. Reading through the precious copies of the pulp magazines that still exist, to find stories that have not been reprinted before or else are not easily available, has been, for me, a return journey to a treasure chest I explored earlier, before the current boom in hardboiled fiction. Twenty years ago I assembled the first collection published in Britain of material from these magazines, entitled *The Fantastic Pulps* (1975) and now out of print, to be followed a year later by a facsimile reprint of stories from one of my favourite pulps, *Weird Tales*, complete with the original text and illustrations. Only the paper quality and packaging—in hard covers— were an improvement on the original. In 1976 I also compiled *Terror! A History of Horror Illustrations from the Pulp Magazines*, and in 1977 *Mystery! An Illustrated History of Crime and Detective Fiction* which included numerous covers and interior illustrations from the hardboiled pulps, including *Black Mask, Detective Fiction Weekly, Dime Mystery* and so on. It was the publisher of those two volumes who invited me to compile this new anthology.

Thanks to the collectors and enthusiasts of pulp fiction on both sides of the Atlantic, who generously helped me with those earlier books and have risen to the challenge once again for this volume, a considerable number of the stories by the early exponents of the hardboiled genre have been saved from the oblivion they would undoubtedly have suffered if left in the pages of the original pulp magazines. And what a loss it would have been—these unique stories with their mixture of rapid-fire action, violence and cynical humour, and especially the wisecracks which Raymond Chandler, Dashiell Hammett and their fellow writers turned into an art form. Indeed, I shall always remember the words of one Chandler fan who supplied me with some rare copies of his favourite writer's stories to consider.

'I don't read Chandler for the story,' he said, with a smile that spoke of hours of pleasure, 'I read him for the *cracks*!'

Peter Haining
Boxford, Suffolk, 1996.

HARDBOILED DICKS

Cases of the Private Eyes

TORCH NUMBER

James Ellroy

Although the hardboiled school of writing gave the world the tough cop and the mean gangster, it is best remembered for the two-fisted, gun-toting, cynical yet dedicated sleuth, whose territory was the big cities and whose appetites for drink and dames were equal. And with a renewed passion for the genre among readers on both sides of the Atlantic, the hardboiled dick has once again reappeared in the work of authors whose inspiration can be traced back to the pulps where his career began. Spade Hearns is typical of this new breed: a tough private eye who works the mean streets of Los Angeles and is, in all respects, the spiritual son of the immortal Sam Spade. He is the creation of James Ellroy, self-described as the 'Mad Dog of Contemporary Fiction' yet regarded by the American GQ magazine as 'our Premier Crime Novelist'. Whichever may be nearer the truth, Ellroy bestrides the crime genre as an outstanding writer and larger-than-life character.

More than one critic has written that the life of James Ellroy (1948–) has been every bit as bizarre as that of his (usually) ill-fated characters. Born on the fringe of Hancock Park in Los Angeles, he is the son of a freelance accountant who worked in the Hollywood studios, was an incorrigible womaniser and once told his son he had slept with Rita Hayworth. His mother was a promiscuous alcoholic who was found murdered with a nylon stocking around her neck when he was just ten years old. James himself dropped out of school in his late teens, went on the streets, and was thirty-five times arrested for petty crimes. He also became addicted to drugs and alcohol. To get by he slept rough or broke into houses, and was swiftly writing his own death warrant when he discovered crime fiction in the pages of Raymond Chandler's books and found a purpose in his life. In 1975, he says, he gave up drinking and, two years later, drugs; then he began writing and his first book, a detective novel, Brown's Requiem, was published in 1981. A series of police procedurals followed about the detective Lloyd

Hopkins, but it was with The Black Dahlia *(1987), which explored the low-life crime and moral depravation of Los Angeles complete with its police corruption, racial bigotry and sexual perversions, that he leaped to fame and almost literally reinvented the hardboiled novel. Further blockbuster works, including* The Big Nowhere *(1988),* LA Confidential *(1990),* White Jazz *(1992) and, most recently,* American Tabloid *(1995), have confirmed his position of pre-eminence. Like his fiction, James Ellroy is a big, intimidating-looking man who speaks in a gravelly voice and wears Hawaiian shirts. He has a caustic sense of humour and relishes being outrageous when he is interviewed or signing copies of his books. When I met him during a visit to London to promote* American Tabloid, *I felt unnervingly as if I was in the presence of Spade Hearns. The meeting confirmed, if I ever needed confirmation, that he was the only writer who could start off this opening part of the book, devoted to the hardboiled dick.*

*   *   *

Before Pearl Harbor and the Jap scare, my living room window offered a great night view: Hollywood Boulevard lit with neon, dark hillsides, movie spots crisscrossing the sky announcing the latest opening at Grauman's and the Pantages. Now, three months after the day of infamy—blackouts in effect and squadrons of Jap Zeros half expected any moment—all I could see were building shapes and the cherry lamps of occasional prowl cars. The ten p.m. curfew kept night divorce work off my plate, and blowing my last assignment with Bill Malloy of the DA's Bureau made a special deputy's curfew waiver out of the question. Work was down, bills were up, and my botched surveillance of Maggie Cordova had me thinking of Lorna all the time, wearing the grooves on her recording of 'Prison of Love' down to sandpaper.

> Prison of Love.
> Sky above.
> I feel your body like a velvet glove . . .

I mixed another rye and soda and started the record over. Through a part in the curtains, I eyeballed the street; I thought of Lorna and Maggie Cordova until their stories melded.

Lorna Kafesjian.

Second-rate bistro chanteuse—first-rate lungs, third-rate club gigs because she insisted on performing her own tunes. I met her when she hired me to rebuff the persistent passes of a rich bull dagger who'd been voyeur perving on her out at Malibu Beach—Lorna with her swimsuit stripped to the waist, chest exposed for a deep cleavage tan to offset the white gowns she always wore on stage. The dyke was sending Lor a hundred long-stemmed red roses a day, along with mash notes bearing her *nom de plume d'amour*: 'Your Tongue of Fire'. I kiboshed the pursuit quicksville, glomming the tongue's Vice jacket, shooting the dope to Louella Parsons—a socially connected, prominently married carpet muncher with a yen for nightclub canaries was prime meat for the four-star *Herald*. I told Louella: She desists, you don't publish; she persists, you do. The Tongue and I had a little chat; I strong-armed her black bodyguard when *he* got persistent. Lorna was grateful, wrote me the torch number to torch all torch numbers—and *I* got persistent.

The flame burned both ways for about four months—from January to May of '38 I was Mr Ringside Swain as Lorna gigged the Katydid Klub, Bido Lito's, Malloy's Nest, and a host of dives on the edge of jigtown. Two a.m. closers, then back to her place; long mornings and afternoons in bed, my business neglected, clients left dangling while I lived the title of a Duke Ellington number: 'I Got It Bad, and That Ain't Good'. Lorna came out of the spell first; she saw that I was willing to trash my life to be with her. That scared her; she pushed me away; I played stage door Johnny until I got disgusted with myself and she blew town for fuck knows where, leaving me a legacy of soft contralto warbles on hot black wax.

Lorna.

Lorna to Maggie.

Maggie happened this way:

Two weeks ago Malloy co-opted me to the DA's Bureau—the aftermath of the bank job was running helter-skelter, he needed a man good at rolling stakeouts, and a citizens' committee had posted extra reward gelt. The B of A on North Broadway and Alpine got knocked off; two shitbirds—Caucasians, one with *outré* facial scars—snuffed three armed guards and got away clean. A score of eyeball witnesses gave descriptions of the robbers, then—blam!—the next day a witness, a seventy-three-year-old Jap granny set for internment pickup, got plugged—double blam!—as she was walking her pooch to the corner market. LAPD Ballistics compared the slugs to the pills extracted from the stiffs at the bank scene: match-up, straight across.

Malloy was called in. He developed a theory: one of the eyewitnesses was in on the robbery; the heisters glommed the addresses of the other witnesses and decided to bump them to camouflage their guy. Malloy threw a net around the three remaining witnesses; two square johns named Dan Doherty and Bob Roscomere—working stiffs with no known criminal associates—and Maggie Cordova—a nightclub singer who'd taken two falls for possession and sale of marijuana.

Maggie C. loomed as the prime suspect: she toked big H and maryjane, was rumoured to have financed her way through music school by pulling gang bangs, and played it hardcase during her two-year jolt at Tehachapi. Doherty and Roscomere were put out as bait, not warned of the danger they were in, carrying DA's Bureau tails wherever they went. Malloy figured my still-simmering torch for Lorna K. gave me added insight into the ways of errant songbirds and sent me out to keep loose track of Maggie, hoping she'd draw unfriendly fire if she wasn't the finger woman or lead me to the heisters if she was.

I found Maggie pronto—a call to a booking agent who owed me— and an hour later I was sipping rye and soda in the lounge of a Gardena pokerino parlour. The woman was a dumpy ash blonde in a spangly gown, long-sleeved, probably to hide her needle tracks. She looked vaguely familiar, like a stag film actress you were hard for in your youth. Her eyes were flat and droopy and her microphone gestures were spastic. She looked like a hophead who'd spent her best years on cloud nine and would never adjust to life on earth.

I listened to Maggie butcher 'I Can't Get Started', 'The Way You Look Tonight,' and 'Blue Moon'; she bumped the mike stand with her crotch and nobody whistled. She sang 'Serenade in Blue' off-key and a clown a couple of tables over threw a handful of martini olives at her. She flipped the audience the finger, got a round of applause, and belted the beginning of 'Prison of Love'.

I sat there, transfixed. I closed my eyes and pretended it was Lorna. I forced myself not to wonder how this pathetic no-talent dopester got hold of a song written exclusively for me. Maggie sang her way through all five verses, the material almost transforming her voice into something good. I was ripping off Lorna's snow-white gown and plunging myself into her when the music stopped and the lights went on.

And Maggie was ixnay, splitsville, off to Gone City. I tried her dressing room, the bar, the casino. I got her vehicle stats from the DMV and got nowhere with them. I slapped around a croupier with a junkie look, got Maggie's address, and found her dump cleaned out lock, stock and barrel. I became a pistol-whipping, rabbit-punching, brass-knuckle-wielding dervish then, tearing up the Gardena Strip. I got a half decent lead on a ginch Maggie used to whore with; the woman got me jacked on laudanum, picked my pocket, and left me in Gone City, ripe prey for a set of strong-arm bulls from the Gardena PD. When I came off cloud ten in a puke-smelling drunk tank, Bill Malloy was standing over me with glad tidings: I'd been charged with six counts of aggravated assault, one count of felonious battery, and two counts of breaking and entering. Maggie Cordova was nowhere to be found; the other eyewitnesses were in protective custody. Bill himself was off the bank job, on temporary assignment to the Alien Squad, set to rustle Japs, the big cattle drive that wouldn't end until Uncle Sam gave Hirohito the big one where it hurt the most. My services were no longer required by the DA's office, and my night curfew waiver was revoked until somebody figured a way to chill out the nine felony charges accumulated against me . . .

I heard a knock at the door, looked out the window and saw a prowl car at the kerb, red lights blinking. I took my time turning on lamps, wondering if it was warrants and handcuffs or maybe somebody who wanted to talk dealsky. More knocks—a familiar cadence. Bill Malloy at midnight.

I opened the door. Malloy was backstopped by a muscle cop who looked like a refugee from the wrong side of a Mississippi chain gang: big ears, blond flat-top, pig eyes, and a too-small suit-coat framing the kind of body you expect to see on convicts who haul cotton bales all day. Bill said, 'You want out of your grief, Hearns? I came to give you an out.'

I pointed to the man-monster. 'Expecting trouble you can't handle?'

'Policemen come in pairs. Easier to give trouble, easier to avoid it. Sergeant Jenks, Mr Hearns.'

The big man nodded; an Adam's apple the size of a baseball bobbed up and down. Bill Malloy stepped inside and said, 'If you want those charges dropped and your curfew waiver back, raise your right hand.'

I did it. Sergeant Jenks closed the door behind him and read from a little card he'd pulled from his pocket. 'Do you, Spade Hearns, promise to uphold the laws of the United States Government pertaining to executive order number nine-oh-five-five and obey all other federal and municipal statutes while temporarily serving as an internment agent?'

I said, 'Yeah.'

Bill handed me a fresh curfew pass and an LAPD rap sheet with a mugshot strip attached. 'Robert no middle name Murikami. He's a lamster Jap, he's a youth gang member, he did a deuce for B and E and when last seen he was passing out anti-American leaflets. We've got his known associates on this sheet, last known address, the magilla. We're swamped and taking in semipros like you to help. Usually we pay fifteen dollars a day, but you're in no position to demand a salary.'

I took the sheet and scanned the mugshots. Robert NMN Murikami was a stolid-looking youth—a samurai in a skivvy shirt and duck's ass haircut. I said. 'If this kid's so wicked, why are you giving me the job?'

Jenks bored into me with his little pig eyes; Bill smiled. 'I trust you not to make the same mistake twice.'

I sighed. 'What's the punch line?'

'The punch line is that this punk is pals with Maggie Cordova—we got complete paper on him, including his bail reports. The Cordova cooze put up the jack for Tojo's last juvie beef. Get him, Hearns. All will be forgiven and maybe you'll get to roll in the gutter with another second-rate saloon girl.'

I settled in to read the junior kamikaze's rap sheet. There wasn't much: the names and addresses of a half dozen Jap cohorts—tough boys probably doing the Manzanar shuffle by now—carbons of the kid's arrest reports, and letters to the judge who presided over the B&E trial that netted Murikami his two-spot at Preston. If you read between the lines, you could see a metamorphosis: Little Tojo started out as a pad prowler out for cash and a few sniffs of ladies' undergarments and ended up a juvie gang honcho: zoot suits, chains and knives, boogie-woogie rituals with his fellow members of the 'Rising Sons'. At the bottom of the rap sheet there was a house key attached to the page with Scotch tape, an address printed beside it: 1746¼, North Avenue 46, Lincoln Heights. I pocketed the key and drove there, thinking of a Maggie-to-Lorna reunion parlay—cool silk sheets and a sleek tanned body soundtracked by the torch song supreme.

The address turned out to be a subdivided house on a terraced hillside overlooking the Lucky Lager Brewery. The drive over was eerie: street-lights and traffic signals were the only illumination and Lorna was all but there with me in the car, murmuring what she'd give me if I took down slant Bobby. I parked at the kerb and climbed up the front steps, counting numbers embossed on doorways: 1744, 1744½, 1746, 1746½. 1746¼ materialised; I fumbled the key towards the lock. Then I saw a narrow strip of light through the adjoining window—the unmistakable glint of a penflash probing. I pulled my gun, *eased* the key in the hole, watched the light flutter back towards the rear of the pad, and opened the door slower than slow.

No movement inside, no light coming towards me. 'Fuck, fuck, fuck,' echoed from a back room; a switch dropped and big light took over. And there was my target: a tall, skinny man bending over a chest of drawers, a penflash clamped in his teeth.

I let him start rifling, then tiptoed over. When he had both hands braced on the dresser and his legs spread, I gave him the Big Fungoo.

I hooked his left leg back; prowler collapsed on the dresser, penflash cracking teeth as his head hit the wall. I swung him around, shot him a pistol butt blow to the gut, caught a flailing right hand, jammed the fingers into the top drawer space, slammed the drawer shut, and held it there with my knee until I heard fingers cracking. Prowler screamed; I found a pair of Jockey shorts on the counter, shoved them in his mouth, and kept applying pressure with my knee. More bone crack; amputation coming up. I eased off and let the man collapse on his knees.

The shitbird was stone cold out. I kicked him in the face to keep him that way, turned on the wall light, and prowled myself.

It was just a crummy bedroom, but the interior decorating was *très outré*: Jap nationalist posters on the walls—racy shit that showed Jap Zeros buzz-bombing a girls' dormitory, buxom white gash in peignoirs running in terror. The one table held a stack of Maggie Cordova phonograph records—Maggie scantily attired on the jackets, stretch marks, flab, and chipped nail polish on display. I examined them up close— no record company was listed. They were obvious vanity jobs—fat Maggie preserving her own sad warbles.

Shitbird was stirring; I kicked him in the noggin again and trashed the place upside down. I got:

A stash of women's undies, no doubt Bad Bob's B&E booty; a stash of *his* clothes; assorted switchblades, dildoes, french ticklers, tracts explaining that a Jew-Communist conspiracy was out to destroy the world of true peace the German and Japanese brotherhood had sought to establish through peaceful means and—under the mattress—seventeen bankbooks: various banks, the accounts fat with cash, lots of juicy recent deposits.

It was time to make Shitbird sing. I gave him a waistband frisk, pulling out a .45 auto, handcuffs, and—mother dog!—an LA sheriff's badge and ID holder. Shitbird's real monicker was Deputy

Walker T. Koenig, currently on loan to the County Alien Squad.

That got me thinking. I found the kitchen, grabbed a quart of beer from the icebox, came back and gave Deputy Bird an eye-opener—Lucky Lager on the *cabeza*. Koenig sputtered and spat out his gag; I squatted beside him and levelled my gun at his nose. 'No dealsky, no tickee, no washee. Tell me about Murikami and the bankbooks or I'll kill you.'

Koenig spat blood; his foggy eyes homed in on my roscoe. He licked beer off his lips; I could tell his foggy brain was trying to unfog an angle. I cocked my .38 for emphasis. 'Talk, Shitbird.'

'Zeck—zeck—order.'

I spun the .38's cylinder—more emphasis. 'You mean the executive order on the Japs?'

Koenig spat a few loose canines and some gum flaps. 'Zat's right.'

'Keep going. A snitch jacket looks good on you.'

Shitbird held a stare on me; I threw him back some of his manhood to facilitate a speedy confession. 'Look, you spill and I won't rat you. This is just a money gig for me.'

His eyes told me he bought it. Koenig got out his first unslurred words. 'I been doin' a grift with the Japs. The government's holdin' their bank dough till the internment ends. I was gonna cash out for Murikami and some others, for a cut. You know, bring 'em to the bank in bracelets, carry some official-lookin' papers. Japs are smart, I'll give 'em that. They know they're goin' bye-bye, and they want more than bank interest.'

I didn't *quite* buy it; on reflex I gave Koenig's jacket pockets a toss. All I got was some women's pancake makeup—pad and bottle. The anomaly tweaked me; I pulled Koenig to his feet and cuffed him behind his back with his own bracelets. 'Where's Murikami hiding out?'

'Fourteen-eleven Wabash, East LA, apartment three-eleven. Bunch of Japs holing up there. What are you gonna—'

'I'm going to toss your car and cut you loose. It's *my* grift now, Walter.'

Koenig nodded, trying not to look grateful; I unloaded his piece and stuck it in his holster, gave him back his badge kit, rounded up the bankbooks, and shoved him towards the front door, thinking of Lorna accompanied by Artie Shaw and Glenn Miller, the two of us enjoying Acapulco vacations financed by Axis cash. I pushed Koenig down the steps ahead of me; he nodded towards a Ford roadster parked across the street. 'There, that's mine. But you ain't—'

Shots cut the air; Koenig pitched forward, backward, forward. I hit the pavement, not knowing which direction to fire. Koenig slumped into the gutter; a car sped by *sans* headlights. I squeezed off five shots and heard them ding metal; lights went on in windows—they gave me a perfect shot of a once-rogue cop with his face blasted away. I stumbled over to the Ford, used my pistol butt to smash in a window, popped the glove compartment, and tore through it. Odd papers, no bankbooks, my hands brushing a long piece of slimy rubber. I held it up and flicked on the dash light and saw a paste-on scar—*outré*—just like the one eyewitnesses at the bank job said one of the heisters had.

I heard sirens descending, blasting like portents of doomsday. I ran to my car and highballed it the fuck away.

My apartment was in the wrong direction—away from leads on Maggie into Lorna. I drove to 1411 Wabash, found it postmidnight still, blackout black—a six-storey walk-up with every single window covered. The joint was stone quiet. I ditched my car in the alley, stood on the hood, jumped up, and caught the bottom rung of the fire escape.

The climb was tough going; mist made the handrails wet and slippery, and my shoes kept slipping. I made it to the third-floor landing, pushed the connecting door open, padded down the empty hallway to 311, put my ear to the door and listened.

Voices in Jap, voices in Jap-accented English, then pure Americanese, loud and clear. 'You're paying me for a hideout, not chow at two-fucking-a.m. But I'll do it—*this time.*'

More voices; footsteps heading towards the hall. I pulled my gun, pinned myself to the wall, and let the door open in my face. I hid behind it for a split second; it was shut, and Caucasian-san hotfooted it over to the elevator. On tippy-toes, I was right behind him.

I cold-cocked him clean—wham!—grabbed his pocket piece while he hit the carpet and dreamsville, stuffed my display handkerchief in his mouth, and dragged him over to a broom closet and locked him in. Two-gun armed, I walked back to the door of 311 and rapped gently.

'Yes?'—a Jap voice—from the other side. I said, 'It's me,' deliberately muffled. Mutters, the door opening, a jumbo Buddhahead filling the doorway. I kicked him in the balls, caught his belt mid-jackknife, pulled forward and smashed his head into the doorjamb. He sank down gonesville; I waved the automatic I'd taken off the white punk at the rest of the room.

What a room.

A dozen slants staring at me with tiny black eyes like Jap Zero insignias, Bob Murikami smack in the middle. Arkansas toad stabbers drawn and pointed square at my middle. A Mexican standoff or the sequel to Pearl Harbor. Kamikaze was the only way to play it.

I smiled, ejected the chambered round from my pilfered piece, popped the clip, and tossed both at the far wall. Jumbo was stirring at my feet; I helped him up, one hand on his carotid artery in case he got uppity. With my free hand, I broke the cylinder on *my* gun, showing him the one bullet left from my shoot-out with Walter Koenig's killers. Jumbo nodded his head, getting the picture; I spun the chamber, put the muzzle to his forehead, and addressed the assembled Axis powers. 'This is about bankbooks, Maggie Cordova, Alien Squad grifts, and that big heist at the Japtown B of A. Bob Murikami's the only guy I want to talk to. Yes or no.'

Nobody moved a muscle or said a word. I pulled the trigger, clicked an empty chamber and watched Jumbo shake head to toe—bad heebie-jeebies. I said, 'Sayonara, Shitbird,' and pulled the trigger again; another hollow click, Jumbo twitching like a hophead going into cold turkey overdrive.

Five to one down to three to one; I could see Lorna, nude, waving bye-bye Hearns, heading towards Stormin' Norman Killebrew, jazz trombone, rumoured to have close to a hard half yard and the only man Lorna implied gave it to her better than me. I pulled the trigger twice—twin empties—shit stink taking over the room as Jumbo evacuated his bowels.

One to one, seven come eleven, the Japs looking uncharacteristically piqued. Now I saw my own funeral cortège, 'Prison of Love' blasting as they lowered me into the grave.

'No! I'll talk!'

I had the trigger at half pull when Bob Murikami's voice registered. I let go of Jumbo and drew a bead on Bad Bob; he walked over and bowed, supplicant samurai style, at my gun muzzle. Jumbo collapsed; I waved the rest of the group into a tight little circle and said, 'Kick the clip and the roscoe over.'

A weasel-faced guy complied; I popped one into the chamber and tucked my Russki roulette piece in my belt. Murikami pointed to a side door; I followed him over, a straight-arm bead on the others.

The door opened into a small bedroom lined with cots—the Underground Railway, 1942 version. I sat down on the cleanest one available and pointed Murikami to a cot a few yards over, well within splatter range. I said, 'Spill. Put it together, slow and from the beginning, and don't leave anything out.'

Bad Bob Murikami was silent, like he was mustering his thoughts and wondering how much horseshit he could feed me. His face was hard set; he looked tough beyond his years. I smelled musk in the room—a rare combo of blood and Lorna's 'Cougar Woman' perfume. 'You can't lie, Bob. And I won't hand you up to the Alien Squad.'

Murikami snickered. 'You won't?'

I snickered back. 'You people mow a mean lawn and trim a mean shrub. When my ship comes in, I'll be needing a good gardener.'

Murikami double-snickered—and a smile started to catch at the corners of his mouth. 'What's your name?'

'Spade Hearns.'

'What do you do for a living?'

'I'm a private investigator.'

'I thought private eyes were sensitive guys with a code of honour.'

'Only in the pulps.'

'That's rich. If you don't have a code of honour, how do I know you won't cross me?'

'I'm in too deep now, Tojo. Crossing you's against my own best interest.'

'Why?'

I pulled out a handful of bankbooks; Murikami's slant eyes bugged out until he almost looked like a fright-wig black. 'I killed Walt Koenig for these, and you need a white man to tap the cash. I don't like witnesses and there's too many of you guys to kill, even though I'm hopped up on blood bad. Spiel me, papasan. Make it an epic.'

Murikami spieled for a straight hour. His story was the night train to Far Gonesville.

It started when three Japs, bank building maintenance workers pissed over their imminent internment, cooked up a plot with rogue cop Walt Koenig and a cop buddy of his—Murikami didn't know the guy's name. The plot was a straight bank robbery with a no-violence proviso— Koenig and pal taking down the B of A based on inside info, the Japs getting a percentage cut of the getaway loot for the young firebrands stupid enough to think they could hot-foot it to Mexico and stay free, plus Koenig's safeguarding of confiscated Jap property until the internment ended. But the caper went blood simple: guards snuffed, stray bullets flying. Mrs Lena Sakimoto, the old dame shot on the street the next day, was the finger woman—she was in the bank pretending to be waiting in line, but her real errand was to pass the word to Koenig and buddy—the split second the vault cash was distributed to the tellers. *She* was rubbed out because the heisters figured her for a potential snitch.

Double-cross.

Bad Bob and *his* pals had been given the bank money to hold. Enraged over the deaths, they shoved it into Jap bank accounts, figured the two whiteys couldn't glom it, that the swag would accumulate interest until the internment was adios. Bob stashed the bankbooks at his crib and was soon to send the white boy fronting the getaway pad over to get them—but he got word a friend of his got greedy.

The friend's name was George Hayakawa, a vice-warlord in the Rising Sons. He went to Walt Koenig with a deal: he'd get the cash for a fifty-fifty cut. Koenig said no dealsky, tortured the location of the bankbooks and the address of the hideout out of Hayakawa, snuffed him, chopped off his dick, and sent it over in a pizza delivery box. A warning—don't fuck with the White Peril.

I pressed Murikami on Maggie Cordova—how did she fit in? The epic took on perv-o overtones.

Maggie was Bad Bob's sister's squeeze—the femme half of a dyke duo. She was the co-finger woman inside the bank; when Mrs Lena Sakimoto got shot to sukiyaki, Maggie fled to Tijuana, fearing similar reprisals. Bob didn't know exactly where she was. I pressed, threatened, and damn near shot Murikami to get the answer I wanted most: where Maggie Cordova got 'Prison of Love'.

Bad Bob didn't know; I *had* to know. I made him a deal I knew I'd double-cross the second Lorna slinked into view. You come with me, we'll withdraw all the gelt, you take me to TJ to find Maggie and the money's all yours. Murikami agreed; we sealed the bargain by toking a big bottle of laudanum laced with sake. I passed out on my cot with my gun in my hand and segued straight into the arms of Lorna.

It was a great hop dream.

Lorna was performing nude at the Hollywood Palladium, backed by an all-jigaboo orchestra—gigantic black men in rhinestone-braided Uncle Sam outfits. She humped the air; she sprayed sweat; she sucked the microphone head. Roosevelt, Hitler, Stalin, and Hirohito were carried in on litters; they swooned at her feet as Lor belted 'Someone to Watch Over Me'. A war broke out on the bandstand: crazed jigs beating each other with trombone slides and clarinet shafts. It was obviously a diversion—Hitler jumped on stage and tried to carry Lorna over to a Nazi U-boat parked in the first row. I foiled Der Führer, picking him up by the moustache and hurling him out to Sunset Boulevard. Lorna was swooning into my arms when I felt a tugging and opened my eyes to see Bob Murikami standing over me, saying, 'Rise and shine, shamus. We got banking to do.'

We carried it out straight-faced, with appropriate props—handcuffs on Bad Bob, phoney paperwork, a cereal box badge pinned to my lapel. Murikami impersonated over a dozen fellow Japs; we liquidated fourteen bank accounts to the tune of $81,000. I explained that I was Alien Squad brass, overseeing the confiscation of treasonous lucre; patriotic bank managers bought the story whole. At four we were heading south to TJ and what might be my long-overdue reunion with the woman who'd scorched my soul long, long ago. Murikami and I talked easily, a temporary accord in Japanese-American relations—thanks to a healthy injection of long green.

'Why are you so interested in Maggie, Hearns?'

I took my eyes off the road—high cliffs dropping down to snow-white beaches packed with sunbathers on my right, tourist courts and greasy spoons on the left. Baby Tojo was smiling. I hoped I didn't have to kill him. 'She's a conduit, kid. A pipeline to *the* woman.'

'*The* woman?'

'Right. The one I wasn't ready for a while back. The one I would have flushed it all down the toilet for.'

'You think it will be different now?'

Eighty-one grand seed money; a wiser, more contemplative Hearns. Maybe I'd even dye a little grey in my hair. 'Right. Once I clear up a little legal trouble I'm in, I'm going to suggest a long vacation in Acapulco, maybe a trip to Rio. She'll see the difference in me. She'll know.'

I looked back at the highway, downshifted for a turn, and felt a tap on my shoulder. I turned to face Bad Bob and caught a big right hand studded with signet rings square in the face.

Blood blinded me; my foot hit the brake; the car jerked into a hillside and stalled out. I swung a haphazard left; another sucker shot caught me; through a sheet of crimson I saw Murikami grab the money and hotfoot it.

I wiped red out of my eyes and pursued. Murikami was heading for the bluffs and a path down to the beach; a car swerved in front of me and a large man jumped out, aimed, and fired at the running figure—once, twice, three times. A fourth shot sent Bob Murikami spiralling over the cliff, the money bag sailing, spilling greenbacks. I pulled my roscoe, shot the shooter in the back, and watched him go down in a clump of crabgrass.

Gun first, I walked over; I gave the shooter two good measure shots, point blank to the back of the head. I kicked him over to his front side and from what little remained of his face identified him. Sergeant Jenks, Bill Malloy's buddy on the Alien Squad.

Deep shit without a depth gauge.

I hauled Jenks to his Plymouth, stuffed him in the front seat, stood back and shot the gas tank. The car exploded; the ex-cop sizzled like french-fried guacamole. I walked over the cliff and looked down. Bob Murikami was spread-eagled on the rocks and shitloads of sunbathers were scooping up cash, fighting each other for it, dancing jigs of greed and howling like hyenas.

I tailspinned down to Tijuana, found a flop and a bottle of drugstore hop, and went prowling for Maggie Cordova. A fat white lezbo songbird would stick out, even in a pus pocket like TJ—and I knew the heart of TJ lowlife was the place to start.

The hop edged down my nerves and gave me a *savoir faire* my three-day beard and raggedy-assed state needed. I hit the mule act strip and asked questions; I hit the whorehouse strip and the strip that featured live fuck shows twenty-four hours a day. Child beggars swarmed me; my feet got sore from kicking them away. I asked, asked, asked about Maggie Cordova, passing out bribe pesos up the wazoo. Then—right on the street—there she was, turning up a set of stairs adjoining a bottle liquor joint.

I watched her go up, a sudden jolt of nerves obliterating my dope edge. I watched a light go on above the bottle shop—and Lorna Kafesjian doing 'Goody, Goody' wafted down at me.

Pursuing the dream, I walked up the stairs and knocked on the door.

Footsteps tapped towards me—and suddenly I felt naked, like a litany of everything I didn't have was underlining the sound of heels over wood.

No eighty-one-grand reunion stash.

No Sy Devore suits to make a suitably grand Hollywood entrance.

No curfew papers for late-night Hollywood spins.

No PI buzzer for *the* dramatic image of the twentieth century.

No world-weary, tough-on-the-outside, tender-on-the-inside sensitive code of honour shtick to score backup pussy with in case Lorna shot me down.

The door opened; fat Maggie Cordova was standing there. She said, 'Spade Hearns. Right?'

I stood there—dumbstruck beyond dumbstruck. 'How did you know that?'

Maggie sighed—like I was old news barely warmed over. 'Years ago I bought some tunes from Lorna Kafesjian. She needed a stake to buy her way out of a shack job with a corny guy who had a wicked bad case on her. She told me the guy was a sewer crawler, and since I was a sewer crawler performing her songs, I might run into him. Here's your ray of hope, Hearns. Lorna said she always wanted to see you one more time. Lor and I have kept in touch, so I've got a line on her. She said I should make you pay for the info. You want it? Then *give*.'

Maggie ended her pitch by drawing a dollar sign in the air. I said, 'You fingered the B of A heist. You're dead meat.'

'Nix, gumshoe. You're all over the LA papers for the raps you brought down looking for me, and the Mexes won't extradite. *Givesky*.'

I forked over all the cash in my wallet, holding back a five-spot for mad money. Maggie said, 'Eight-eighty-one Calle Verdugo. Play it *pianissimo*, doll. Nice and slow.'

I blew my last finnsky at a used clothing store, picking up a chalk-stripe suit like the one Bogart wore in *The Maltese Falcon*. The trousers were too short and the jacket was too tight, but overall the thing worked. I dry-shaved in a gas station men's room, spritzed some soap at my armpits, and robbed a kiddie flower vendor of the rest of his daffodils. Thus armed, I went to meet my lost love.

Knock, knock, knock on the door of a tidy little adobe hut; boom, boom, boom, as my overwrought heart drummed a big band beat. The door opened—and I almost screamed.

The four years since I'd seen Lorna had put forty thousand hard miles on her face. It was sun-soured—seams, pits, and scales; her laugh lines had changed to frown lines as deep as the San Andreas Fault. The body that was once voluptuous in white satin was now bloated in a Mex charwoman's serape. From the deep recesses of what we once had, I dredged a greeting.

'What's shakin', baby?'

Lorna smiled, exposing enough dental gold to front a revolution. 'Aren't you going to ask me what happened, Spade?'

I stayed game. 'What happened, baby?'

Lorna sighed. 'Your interpretation first, Spade. I'm curious.'

I smoothed my lapels. 'You couldn't take a good thing. You couldn't take the dangerous life I led. You couldn't take the danger, romance, the heartache and vulnerability inherent in a mean-street-treading knight like me. Face it, baby: I was too much man for you.'

Lorna smiled—more cracks appeared in the relief map of her face. She said, 'Your theatrics exhausted me more than my own. I joined a Mexican nunnery, got a tan that went bad, started writing music again, and found myself a man of the earth—Pedro, my husband. I make tortillas, wash my clothes in a stream, and dry them on a rock. Sometimes, if Pedro and I need extra jack, I mix Margaritas and work the bar at the Blue Fox. It's a good, simple life.'

I played my ace. 'But Maggie said you wanted to see me—"one more time", like—'

'Yeah, like in the movies. Well, Hearns, it's like this. I sold "Prison of Love" to about three dozen bistro belters who passed it off as their own. It's ASCAP'd under at least thirty-five titles, and I've made a cool five grand on it. And, well, I wrote the song for you back in our salad days, and in the interest of what we had together for about two seconds, I'm offering you ten per cent—you inspired the damn thing, after all.'

I slumped into the doorway—exhausted by four years of torching, three days of mayhem and killing. 'Hit me, baby.'

Lorna walked to a cabinet and returned with a roll of Yankee greenbacks. I winked, pocketed the wad, and walked down the street to a cantina. The interior was dark and cool; Mex cuties danced nude on the bar top. I bought a bottle of tequila and slugged it straight, fed the jukebox nickels and pushed every button listing a female vocalist. When the booze kicked in and the music started, I sat down, watched the nudie gash gyrate, and tried to get obsessed.

THE EGYPTIAN LURE

Carroll John Daly

The 'founding father' of all hardboiled dicks was Race Williams, a
fearless, cynical, impatient, aggressive and even brutal man who at a
stroke became the archetype of all his kind. Described as about 30
years of age, almost six feet tall with brown hair and black eyes, he
had previously worked as a newspaperman, insurance investigator,
undercover man for the racing commission and police detective in
New York, Chicago and California before setting up as a private eye.
Regarded at first as a kind of 'lone urban cowboy', Race could be
sentimental about women in trouble; but although he was on the side
of the law in fighting gangsters, crooked politicians and criminals of
all kinds (including many evil foreigners whom he viewed as a threat
to the political welfare of America), he still had an uneasy relationship
with the police. Throughout his career, officers of the law were forever
warning him about the reckless way in which he gunned down suspects
without so much as a second thought. He was deadly accurate with a
revolver, once firing two guns simultaneously and only making a single
hole in the forehead of his target. Williams made his début in the May
1923 issue of Black Mask, the detective story magazine which was the
first home for hardboiled fiction, in a case entitled 'Knights of the Open
Plain' in which the villains he pursued were members of the Ku Klux
Klan. Soon, however, he was at work in the more familiar territory of
city streets . . . and detective fiction would never be the same again.

Carroll John Daly (1889–1958) was a somewhat unlikely figure to
have created this milestone in crime fiction. A mild-mannered, theatre-
loving man who had worked his way up from film projectionist to owner
of the first cinema in Atlantic City, he had taken up writing purely as
a diversion. In his suburban home in White Plains, New York, he began
turning out crime stories of fast-paced action, packed with violence and
little characterisation. They were quite unlike anything being written
by Daly's contemporaries and were eagerly seized upon by readers

looking for a new kind of thrill in crime fiction. Among his earliest creations—all of whom narrated their adventures in the same terse, clipped language that has since become such a mark of the genre— were Vee Brown, a revolver-carrying avenger who loved composing music, and the awesome Three Gun Terry Mack. But it was Race Williams who captured the public imagination. And although Daly produced his work at such speed it was regularly criticised by editors for being crude and sloppy, his manuscripts were never rejected. Indeed, with the passage of time a legend grew in publishing circles that the name of Race Williams on the cover of a magazine could increase the circulation by anything up to 20 per cent—a fact which contributed to making Daly one of the highest-paid writers of his era as well as the acknowledged creator of an enduring prototype. 'The Egyptian Lure' is a typical Race Williams adventure from the March 1928 issue of Black Mask *and has not been reprinted since that date.*

* * *

The zero night blasted a biting wind through the narrow streets of the lower city. But no dust or dirt, or the smells of the filthy streets came with it; they were embedded in the thick black ice that filled the gutters. Clear, crisp and biting—like the country air—the breath-taking wind cut into my face. An occasional scuttling, scurrying figure hustled from one doorway to another, or beat its way uncertainly along the pavement.

Once, beneath a dull light, a harness bull eyed me through watery lids. Half stepping out to block my passage, he thought better of it and waving his arms across his chest hurried along his beat. I knew the thought that ran through his mind—if he could drag in a drunk he could get warm while he was booking him. And I didn't blame him much. Still, that was the difference between him and me. I had business to attend to, or thought I had, and the old mercury could slip right out the bottom of the thermometer before I'd duck out on a job. The name of Race Williams stands for service.

Less than an hour ago, a boy had brought me an envelope full of money and there was a note requesting that I show up at a tough night-club as soon as possible. It spoke of trouble, and that I was taking my life in my hands, and had all the earmarks of an obituary column— without the place of my interment. It was just typewritten, and no name signed to it. But money talks, and here I was slipping along through the night to the 'Egyptian Lure'.

Now, I'm not exactly a child in arms, and I know there's a few hundred loose-thinking gunmen who'd be glad to try a pot shot at me. So the idea of a trap was not entirely from my mind. But I wouldn't disappoint the boys anyway. If they're willing to pay for a shot at me, why discourage the practice? Besides, there isn't any way to judge beforehand what's good business and what's bad. People that hunt me out aren't apt to be giving references. They're in trouble when they think of Race Williams. I'm a court of last appeal. Not exactly a private detective, though my licence so labels me. But the gilt letters on my office door spell—CONFIDENTIAL AGENT.

But—back to the street and the winter night and the temperature that was out to break all records. I found the 'Egyptian Lure'. It wasn't hard for me to locate the little door. I know the underworld well, and all its dives, and this place a blind man could find. Someplace below the street level, the tin pan notes of an over-ripe piano were clanging feebly against the insistence of a trap drum.

My eyes are accustomed to take in a picture quickly, and I got one that made my right hand slip to my overcoat pocket as I reached the dark, ill-smelling hallway which gave entrance to the so-called 'night-club'. For a figure had slipped back into the adjoining doorway, and two others had disappeared in the alleyway across the street.

Maybe there was nothing alarming in that, and maybe there was. It might be simply the big-hearted boyishness that makes one gangster wait to playfully knock over another, or it might be a reception committee for me. But if they intended to plug me from the darkness, they lost their chance almost the very second they had it. I'd swung through the outer door and was in the blackness of the hallway of the 'Egyptian Lure'. The next moment I was doing my stuff on the inner door—four, three and one—which was the regular knock of the preferred sucker list. If you didn't know the rap, a little shutter went open while you were looked over. They hated to lose a dollar in that joint. It was easy to get in if you had any money—harder to get out if you had any left. If you wanted a card of introduction, most any taxicab driver could furnish it.

The door opened slightly and I shot my foot within. I was fortunate as I stood in the dim light. The old bird on the door was a stranger to me.

'Just one—just one,' he muttered, as I slipped a bill into his hand. 'You're joining a party?' And he tried to stare into my face that was hidden by the slouch hat and turned-up collar.

'Just one.' I nodded at him. 'But I'll make a party of it before I leave.' And while he was thinking that one out I swung into the cloak-room, jerked the gun from my overcoat pocket to my hip, and parked my coat with the attendant. Then I turned, shot back my shoulders and stepped down the three steps into the dance hall.

The proprietor, a big oily Greek, labelled Nick, recognised me almost at once. His cheeks puffed, his eyes bulged and after rolling them around a bit he tried to smile as he finally led me to a little table in a dark corner of the room.

The whole room was a dismal affair, for that matter. Shaded, dirty lights, which were meant to give the effects of the soft Egyptian night, might have registered with that gang. But to me it looked more like the dingy, dirty cellar of old Madison Square Garden when the circus was in town. The paintings on the walls were a scream. Emaciated little camels rubbed noses with mangy lions and a dark-skinned warrior in gaily coloured robes overshadowed the pyramids, while a Pekingese dog in the background turned out on closer inspection to be the Sphinx. The atmosphere and the odours didn't have a whole lot on the Zoo, but it suited the crowd. Perhaps, after all, I don't know my geography and the smells of Egypt.

The proprietor bent over me.

'On pleasure, Mr Williams?' He tried to make his voice simply solicitous, but an anxious, alarmed note crept into his simple question. 'If you're not,' he added significantly, 'I'll have to speak to Joe.' And he jerked a thick thumb towards the huge bulk of the bouncer, who lounged behind the orchestra.

I laughed up at him—I couldn't help it. If I said I was there on business, he'd quit. This bird had seen me in action once before, when he was a waiter over on the Avenue. He knew if Joe tried to put me out of a dump like that, he'd put me out in a cloud of smoke. It may be pride on my part. But to be chucked out of there wouldn't help my business any nor my reputation. I'm not a mussy guy, you understand—but I don't lay down to have my face trampled all over either. Just one rule for the lad who starts a row with me. He must be prepared to finish it. I don't go in for horseplay.

But there stood the owner, Nick, ready to take my order—and when I gave it to him his face fell until his chin hung down on his chest.

'Bring me a split of White Rock,' I told him. 'And be sure the cap's tightly on. I carry my own opener.'

The hurt expression of his fat face, when he thought I'd questioned the honest intention of the house, lifted when I slipped him a five-case note—which was good pay for the water, but not too much if the cap was securely fastened. No—I didn't suspect the joint, but I hate to put anyone in the way of temptation.

'Now—beat it. You're blocking the show, and I'm all for a light fantastic evening.' I waved him aside.

And the show was on—such as it was. Five or six girls were shaking themselves loose from their clothes upon a small platform. There was the leading lady, who had seen her best days before McKinley was shot. But she had an arm on her like the sturdy oak and, so, could swing a mean chair if trouble started. Also her capacity for bum liquor could probably be rated in tank car lots. And that was a big asset. I daresay, through eyes of gin, her calcimined face looked like the Madonna's.

The younger ones were hand-picked and awkward. But the faces and figures stood out even through White Rock. Hard, speculative little faces, maybe, but pretty—that is, with a sinister sort of beauty. And I saw the one on the end.

She was two steps behind the others and about a note and a half off key in her song. Her eyelashes were blacker, her cheeks redder, and her golden curls the cheapest kind of a wig. Yet, she stood out. There was a fearful tightening of her lips and a ghastly grimace to the way they slipped back into what was meant for a smile. But the impression she left was that she didn't belong, and her flashing eyes searched the room with both fear and hope. A deadly terror one moment, the next a ray of hope. Her eyes told the story—nothing remarkable in that. I'm not especially gifted in reading faces, but hers was like an open book.

But I wasn't there to give the dames the up and up. I looked over the customers, and it was a queer crowd. Down near the stage were a half dozen college boys. At the next table a little pickpocket from the Avenue kept smiling at Nick, the proprietor, in an attempt to leave the impression that he was there simply on pleasure. Then, a flashy party from uptown, with high society stamped all over their dress shirts, and middle class stamped on their loud coarse mouths. There were a couple of stick-up men, spending the proceeds of their last haul—tipping lavishly and letting the crowd know that they were liberal guys. Yet, it wasn't hard to pick them out. Some I recognised, some were just stamped with the type—you can't miss them.

And I saw the two men who came in shortly after me—swarthy, dark fellows they were. Neither conspicuously dressed nor shabbily dressed. They were quiet, watchful men who, too, drank White Rock and eyed the performers with an absorbing interest and a certain sense of satisfaction that could hardly be built up on charged water. They neither applauded nor waved to the girls, but whispered occasionally to each other and nodded in apparent agreement. Instinctively, I knew that with these men my mission was connected.

The dance was over and the girls hopped from the platform and scurried about the room—greeting friends, acquaintances and strangers alike. It was a free and easy party. It was the girl on the end, with the tricky blonde wig, who came from the stage last. Uncertainly, she glanced about the smoke-laden room, then started down a narrow aisle between the rows of tables. I didn't watch her especially—I watched the dark men who now sat with their heads close together; their eyes upon the table, as if they made it a point to impress upon the performers that they did not desire their company.

It happened quickly, and I doubt if a single one in the room saw the motion. Even I, watching closely, could not be sure. But it seemed as if the blonde-wigged frail slunk close to the opposite tables as she passed the two men. It seemed, too, as if a thick brown hand shot out, closed upon the girl's wrist and pulled her to the table. Anyway, one thing was certain. She was sitting between the men and their grave demeanour had departed and they were laughing and talking and calling loudly for something to drink. In a dazed, uncertain, fascinated way the girl sat between them.

And I had something else to occupy my mind. A sharp-featured little performer had suddenly flopped into the seat beside me.

'How about a little drink, dearie?' A hand was laid upon my wrist. I shook her off.

'Beat it, kid,' I told her. 'I'm waiting for another Moll. She's jealous and has long nails.' That would save a long argument, and abuse for being a cheapskate. I know these dives and I know these women.

She laughed hoarsely, drew back slightly—and I heard her whisper, 'Race Williams.'

It was my turn to reach for her wrist now. Things were going to open up and the bank notes in the envelope be explained. I don't forget faces and this dame's map was strange to me. She wasn't sure, so she whispered my name.

'You want me?' I half pulled her closer. 'I'm Race Williams—you sent for me?'

'Not me! That girl over there,' she nodded vigorously towards the girl who sat between the two men. 'The one with the Wops.' And if her words were not elegant they were at least expressive. Certainly those boys looked her description.

'She didn't know you—didn't dare ask who you were. I picked her up on the street three nights ago. She's scared of something, and I told her of you. She's dough heavy and I think those lads are looking for a split. Anyway she wants to chin with you, and she was afraid those Wops would try to stop her. My Gawd! they're giving her the walk now.'

And they were. They had jerked suddenly to their feet, with the girl between them. They didn't exactly drag her, and she didn't exactly go willingly; her feet sort of lifted and scraped alternately. But it didn't attract attention, for the two men leaned over her from either side, and they were laughing and talking as they hid her face behind their bobbing black heads.

She didn't scream and she didn't hold back, or if she did it wasn't noticeable. But there was my bank roll, being dragged off by two strangers.

'What's her name?' I asked the girl by my side quickly.

'Bernie—' She stopped a moment. 'Just Bernie, I guess. She's a good kid, and—'

But I didn't hear any more. Bernie had sent for me; Bernie had paid for action—and Bernie was going to get it. I snapped to my feet and turned towards the steps which led to the cloakroom.

I was just in time, for the men ahead with the girl between them ignored the cloakroom and were willing to brave the zero night without coats. Hardly thoughtful, for the girl's flimsy lace dress was built for the banks of the Nile. Of course, the cloakroom attendant made no effort to stop them. He had passed the stage where anything was strange to him.

One quick glance I took back over my shoulder, then stepped out quickly, shot past them, and turning stood before the trio in the dull light of the hall, between the cloakroom and the inner door.

'Why, Bernie.' I cocked one eye and played a lad with half a jag on. 'I thought I spotted the back of your neck. Not going, without having a drink with your little friend.' And then seeing the bewildered look in her eyes as she stared vacantly at me, I added, 'Thought you said you'd see me here tonight—said it, or wrote it, or something.' And this time I thought I got my wink over. At all events, the fear went out of her eyes—they shone once in that quick sparkle of hope

I'd seen on the platform, and she tried to speak. But no words came—
her mouth just opened and closed, and her lips clicked with a dry
snap.

'You'll pardon—my friend.' The big swarthy fellow attempted to
push me aside. But the odds were against him. The hall was narrow,
and besides, I'm not so easily pushed. 'The young lady is our friend.
She feels not so well, and we are taking her home.'

'What—Little Bernie not well?' I still blocked the passage. 'She
must have some medicine—got some real fine old stuff,' I babbled on,
reaching for my hip. It was a hard game for me to play. Neither of
these fellows knew me, and it might be to my advantage later on if
they still thought me simply a drunk. Again—if the game was big
enough and desperate enough and they suspected that I was not really
talking through a bottle, an attack might come suddenly. It was in my
mind to stick a gun into each man's ribs and bid them bye-bye. If there
had been the slightest suspicion in their faces I would have done that
little thing. But it was early in the game and I didn't want to misplay
my cards. The smaller of the two men spoke for the first time.

'Get from before me.' And though there was no suspicion in his face,
there was a threat in his words and in the hand that crept beneath his
jacket.

'Little Bernie—going out in the cold—without no flannels.' I stammered on but I watched that hand, and I saw the knife before ever he
raised it. I don't know if he intended to slip it between my ribs or if
he was just going to threaten me with it. And I didn't wait to find out
what was in his mind. My hand shot up; metal cracked against a protruding chin, and as they say in the movies—'the Italian sun went
down'. The hall was narrow; he was close to the wall; and he did his
stuff like a gentleman, slipping easily and softly to the floor.

There wasn't any use to fool after that. Somehow Bernie got a kick
out of real action—fear or hope, or just good judgement. Anyway, she
came to life, snapped out of the mechanical doll act, and with a quick
jerk busted loose from her gentleman friend. That bird hesitated between
following her, looking after his friend, or settling with me. 'He who
hesitates is lost' may have its exceptions but this lad wasn't one of
them. His face went through all the tricks of a pantomimist, right up
to the point where he decided to pull a gun. And then I gave him the
well-known rush—just a double grip and a swing about, and he was
picking them up and putting them down in the most approved style.
There are times, I suppose, when I do go in for light comedy. Since

the popularity of the night-clubs the 'bum's rush' has come into style again.

The door man didn't hesitate. He may have thought I was the bouncer; his action may have been an involuntary one, but when he saw us coming towards him like that, he knew of but one thing to do. And he did it. He threw open the door, nodded at my final shove, and muttered something to himself as he closed the door again and slipped the lock home. The thing couldn't have come off better if we had had a dress rehearsal.

I turned back to the hallway. There was Nick, the proprietor, and he was shaking Bernie by the shoulders and demanding an explanation of the recumbent attitude of the paying guest upon the floor.

'Leave the kid alone.' I jerked Nick's hand roughly from the girl's shoulder. 'She's my girl friend. I came here to see her tonight. We want to talk. That bozo,' I pointed at the lad I had given the snore, 'wanted to go bye-bye with her.'

Nick's face started to show slight signs of intelligence. Besides, a couple were coming up the steps from the dance-hall, and the bulldog face of Joe, the bouncer, had appeared in the background.

'What's it to be?' I whispered quickly to Nick. 'A quiet evening or a riot? Make up your mind.' And I tapped my pocket significantly.

And Nick acted. He was all business and no mistake. His face cracked into smiles as he jerked out a hand and pulled a curtain, which hid the form upon the floor from the approaching couple.

'It is so, Mr Williams,' he finally said. 'Bernie is a lovely girl,' and he pinched her cheek. 'Perhaps you would wish a little drink with her in a private room.' He rubbed his hands together, patted me on the back, stepped to the people who were getting on their coats, and, after signalling Joe the bouncer, broke into loud laughter at some crude joke. But he kept the guests busy for the time it took Joe to slip behind the curtain.

Distinctly I heard feet scraping across wood, and a door slam. A moment of silence, and the curtains parted and Joe was in the hall again. He eyed me in unconcealed admiration.

'You must have slapped him an awful wallop.' He shook his head several times. 'He's as stiff as a mackerel.'

I simply nodded and smiled as I slipped the brass knuckles back in my pocket. Why give away the secrets of my trade?

Bernie stood trembling against the wall; the proprietor, Nick, was standing beside a little door which he held open. I took the girl by the arm and half led, half carried, her towards the narrow flight of stairs behind the open door. The smirking Nick winked and grimaced as we passed and slowly mounted the stairs. There are certain things I don't like, and the temptation was strong to give Nick a side swipe along his thick lips. But business must come before pleasure, and I might be able to use Nick before the night was over. Anyway, the door closed, and his fat, sensuous face was shut out.

'Come, Bernie,' I said, 'brace up—you're safe now.'

'Oh—oh,' she sobbed, and—'oh' again. And although there was deep feeling and great emotion behind the sobs, it sort of left me flat.

If she couldn't talk or walk very well, she was able to direct me along the dim narrow hall above to a shabby little private room. It took her a few minutes to get herself together, but finally she swung around, came towards me and opened up. If she couldn't talk before, she sure got off a chestful now.

'You came.' She busted right into a jumble of words. 'I knew those two men—recognised them, but, like a little fool, I didn't think that they'd know me. They only saw me once, and with the paint and wig and—But you were just in time.' Little hands crept around my neck, a blonde wig twisted itself upon my shoulder, and Bernie was telling me what hot stuff I was.

'Lay off the sex stuff,' I told her, as I pulled her arms away, and she sort of shot back and jerked her wig from her head. And Bernie was pretty. A little soap and water applied to that face would make her a knock-out. And I guess she saw the look of approval in my face. For she started in to do the vamp act again. A pitiful sort of effort it was, with the ghastly smile I had seen on the platform. Bernie wasn't bad— she was good. There was the sparkle of youth to her eyes that fear hadn't killed yet—a sparkle that no number of beauty doctors can put in the eyes of a soul that is bad. Bernie just hadn't met the right kind of boy friends—that was all. So I'd put her right, on the time she was wasting.

'Yes, you're pretty, Bernie.' I looked straight at her. 'Maybe beautiful—and I daresay you have a bagful of cute tricks. But put them back in the bag. You have sent me money and I have come to help you. You might be cock-eyed and have a hare lip and an ear or two that had been gewed up by a gentleman friend. It wouldn't make any difference. You've paid cash for service—you're going to get it. What do you want?'

Her hands were half in midair and hung there until I finished, then they dropped to her side. The lips ceased to quiver; the black eyes widened slightly as she weighed my words.

'You will help me—regardless?' she finally asked.

'Regardless of what? Those boys downstairs?'

At the mention of them the fear shot back into her face again. 'Will you—can you get me out of this place?'

'Absolutely,' I told her, and meant it.

'These are desperate men—they would have taken me by force tonight—they would have killed you without hesitating. They would kill you without thought.'

'But they'll give considerable thought to it after they make the first attempt.' I smiled down at her. And then, 'Why didn't you call out when they led you from the room tonight? You were too frightened?'

'Yes,' she said quickly, and then—her cheeks whitening beneath the rouge—'Partly that; but I was afraid.'

'Of what?'

She hesitated; and I cut in again.

'Of the police, Bernie?' I asked.

And this time she jerked back against the table.

'How did—you know that?' she stammered.

Mind reading? Maybe. But I simply smiled. People who don't fear the police for some reason or other, don't want me. Bernie very easily could have hollered herself in a cop or two most any time, yet she hadn't. And the answer, of course, was that she didn't want one.

'It is true.' She finally cocked her head up half defiantly. 'But I am not bad—or if I was it was for a good purpose—an all-compelling purpose. You will not help me?'

'There are laws and laws,' I told her. 'I have my own ethics and I am my own judge of right and wrong. But I'll do this for you. I'll see you safely away from here. I won't help you beat the law, without knowing the facts—but I'll help you beat this gang you fear.'

'How much must I tell you?'

'As little or as much as you please.'

'How much must I pay you?' She hesitated.

'You have paid enough for that service. If you want to open up later, why—'

'I want to tell you now,' she cried suddenly. 'I don't want you thinking I'm bad. My mother was an Italian, but I am an American. I was born in this country. My father died—my mother sang upon the stage. There was money from my father, and I went to a convent in

Italy. Then from a doctor I received word that my mother was sick and might die. I had little money, but enough—so I went to Naples to sail for New York. And there I was robbed—there, with the boat about to sail, I was without money—and my mother dying.' She wiped away a tear—real stuff, too—and continued:

'There I met a lady to whom I confided my trouble. She helped me— arranged my passage—but I must do something for her. So I became bad. I smuggled in some diamonds. I knew it was wrong; I knew that I shouldn't—but I did it. My mother was dying. That is my crime. That is my secret, for which I pay money to hide. My guardian helped me. And then I began to fear him and think that perhaps he had so arranged things. And he used my money, and his eyes burned when they watched me, and once, when I would run away—but enough—'

'Who is your guardian, Bernie—and what is his name?' I asked her.

'I think—all that I shall not tell. I only wish to run away and hide myself. From time to time I can send him money, and he may be satisfied and leave me alone. But I have seen him talk friendly with one I considered my enemy—one who received money to keep my secret. The tall man below, whom I have heard called Ferganses—the one you put out the door. You see, I fear him; I fear my guardian; and I fear this government that would punish me for my crime, for they did not know and would not understand my desire to see my mother. But my mother had died before I reached New York.' And she started in to turn on the water works again.

'You have money, Bernie—much money?'

'It is considerable. I could stand it no longer. I ran away, but I did not know where to go. My guardian had sent me to the bank, and I drew out a large sum of money and left. Then I was afraid—and I met a girl who was kind and brought me here. They must have suspected— sought me out. This girl spoke of you, and I sent for you.'

I could have laughed, but I didn't. Bernie's face made it all ring with sincerity. Poor kid—no doubt this guardian was behind the whole show and played the fear of the government up in her imagination. It wouldn't be hard—Bernie had 'convent' written all over her. To her it was a horrible crime. It was certainly lucky that Bernie got me instead of some private detective who'd prey on her fears and take most of her money to straighten things out with the government. But I don't play the game that way. I'd soon put her wise that her fears were groundless. I know the ropes and I know men, and I know a good fixer.

'Bernie,' I started—and stopped, swung about suddenly and flung open the door. It was with considerable effort that Nick, the proprietor, saved himself from pitching forward upon the floor.

'Well—' I jerked him erect. 'Why the Little Bo Beep act?'

'You—joke,' he stammered—caught his breath and faced me with a scowl. 'I should go for the police,' he snapped suddenly. 'If I had known why you came here, Race Williams, and what trouble you would bring my house, I—But you must go at once—I will help you.'

'Why must we go?' I watched that shrewd, fat face with its mean, snapping little eyes.

'Because him you thrust out has returned. He demands that this girl come to him. He is of your disposition, and threats.'

'Why not send for the police?' There was one thing certain about Nick—he'd take care of himself.

'I do not desire the police here. This is an honest club; but people lie about it, and the reputation must not get too bad. Besides, then I would make an enemy of three divisions—the police, these people who seek the girl, and you.'

I understood that point of view all right. Certainly, Nick and the police would have little in common. As for me, perhaps he was right there, too. Bernie and I didn't seek the cops. But the others; if I went with the girl they wouldn't be any too friendly towards Nick. And he straightened that point out before I could put the question to him.

'Come—I wish for peace,' he shot in on my thoughts. 'You take her out the back way. I want not to see her face some more. Then, you are satisfied with Nick; then these strangers can be convinced that she did not linger here, but went at once. But hurry.'

'Can we get out the back without being seen?'

'It is so. When I am notified of raids, it is through the alley in the back that the guests leave. Shall I show you?'

And I guess he could. These people were strangers to Nick's place—they would not know of the back way. Or would they? But I shrugged my shoulders. Bernie and I would do our stuff out the rear entrance. The next move was up to them. If those fellows couldn't shoot any straighter than they talked, they'd regret their lack of education.

Nick led the way down the long hall to the rear of the building. He was in a hurry and nervous. Guess he must have remembered that bit of gun play on the Avenue, when he was a waiter. Another thing—Nick was the sort that could see a nickel a mile, and here he was helping me show a clean pair of heels to Bernie's little playmates without asking a cent for it. That wasn't like Nick, and I chuckled inwardly. It all went to show how anxious he was to see the last of me.

Yet, with all his anxiety, he was prepared to see that no time was lost. Over his arm was swung a heavy, hooded cape for the girl, and he had also brought my coat and hat.

We passed some place back of the music, took a quick twist, and stood in a dark, cold little vestibule. Outside, the wind whistled and the zero night crept between the cracks, and through the dirty, musty glass above the door were the outlines of buildings—the lower city's tenements. Here and there was a small patch of the blue sky reflected behind the sharp brightness of half a dozen stars. The night was as clear and bright as it could be without a moon.

I slipped into my coat and jerked on my hat. Nick threw the cape about the girl's shoulders and pulled the hood well down over her head so that it hid her face. It was too or three sizes too big for her, but Nick explained that—as if he had thought the whole thing out.

'Others leave hurriedly by this little door,' he said. 'Sometimes wives, with detectives, come seeking divorce evidence—and we have such a hurried exit of a couple. So, if they suspect this way, they cannot be sure. If you desire you can look and see if it is safe—then be gone.'

Not half bad advice that. I turned to Bernie.

'You stand here.' I pulled her close to the door as I carefully jerked it open and slipped out into the stone yard behind. Then I shut it, all but an inch. 'If you hear anyone coming or get afraid of anything let out a holler,' I cautioned her. 'Don't be afraid to scream. We're only going quietly for the sake of dear old Nick. I won't be far.' So I gave the kid's hand a squeeze of encouragement. It was cold, and trembled in my grasp.

And I didn't go far; the night was clear enough. There was just a few feet to the little alleyway between two fences, and this alley led down to the yard behind. I couldn't be sure, but I thought that I made out a door between the two fences, in the back. Not a soul in sight— no place in the alley for a man to hide. Several places in the square of yard, though, for it was a dirty litter of barrels and boxes. It would have taken a half-hour to look behind all of them, and while you were looking behind one a hidden enemy could pop up behind another. No— I wouldn't waste the time. It would take just a few seconds to rush Bernie the distance to the alley, which was protected on both sides by the high fence. Nick had, no doubt, built that extra height of board fence for the convenience of suddenly departing guests.

One more quick glance I took down the alley—and turned, listening. There was no sound but the dull hum of the music and the scraping of feet across the dance-hall floor. I looked towards the door—it was still slightly open—and the music stopped. Not a sound in that vestibule, so I finished my 'look-see' in the alley. The coast was clear. I didn't waste any time getting back to Bernie.

The girl was there, leaning close to the door and back against the wall—dimly I made out her figure, the size of it triply accentuated in the wrap and the hood which hid even the whiteness of her face. And Nick—nervously his feet were pawing the ground, and his breath was coming in great sucking sounds.

'Listen, Bernie—you must brace up now. You are safe.' I encouraged the girl, who leaned against the wall. I think that she nodded, but it was too black there to be sure. But she did not speak.

'Tell me if you can walk it—' I started, and stopped. Footsteps were in the hall behind us. There was an angry voice, a quick curse, and a sudden pound against the wall—as if two men struggled.

But I didn't hear any more. Nick had jerked open the back door, and once again Bernie broke into life. She grabbed suddenly at my wrist and dragged me after her into the night—and I didn't have to guide her. She must have had real fear of these people, and she knew how to go, too, for I had hardly time to jerk a gun into my hand before we were in the alley and beating it down the straight stretch between the two fences. It just goes to show that you don't know women. I'd have been willing to bet, a minute before, that she would blow up and I'd have to carry her.

She held my hand now, and hers wasn't cold any longer. It was warm and moist, and her legs didn't sag—they were real speedy. She seemed to know, too, where the gate was and how it opened, but perhaps she had come that way before—perhaps the girl who had spoken to me at the table wised her up to all the little ins and outs of Nick's establishment. But what did it matter? Here we were in a straight line for the street beyond. And even then she didn't pause. A taxi was passing. The driver saw us reach the sidewalk, flung open the door—and we were in. Certainly she had all the luck, if it was simply luck.

That taxi being there was more than luck—at that time of night. It was almost like an act of Providence—and I believe in Providence as much as the next fellow, maybe—but I don't believe in Providence furnishing taxicabs at two o'clock in the morning. Yet, if the taxicab was there to inveigle us into it, what good would that do the swarthy gentleman and Bernie's kindly disposed guardian? There was only one man on the driver's seat, and his back was towards me. Surely he wasn't childish enough to think that he could run off with me.

'Where to?' the driver said, slipping into second. And then added: 'You got a lucky break. I got your message right. You can count on me any time, Boss,' he finished, with a touch of pride.

Now that didn't sound like a trap. Of course the taxi had been arranged for. But by whom? Nick? Yes, I suppose so. Nick certainly did things quick and thoroughly.

'Nick got you all right.' I fell in with the driver's spirit as I told him to slip along uptown.

'I don't know if it was Nick.' The driver shook his head. 'I just come back from a trick and got the message out front.'

And that was that. I turned to the girl, who had started in the vamp stuff again. She clung to me like a drunk to a lamp-post when I tried to push her away, and when I asked her where she'd like to go she simply grunted. Yep—grunted, is right.

'You're safe now.' I gave her a pat on the back and told her to lay off the parking business, and as I turned my head I got a whiff of her breath—and it startled me. It reeked of whisky, and I hadn't noticed that before—but I wouldn't in the cold. And, boy, I got a real shock, for I suddenly remembered that Bernie had clung around my neck in the heat of the private dining-room and that she didn't gag me with her breath then. And surely she hadn't tanked up in the moment I—And I knew. I pushed the girl from me, roughly knocked down her arms and jerked her head up. We passed a street lamp, but I didn't need one. I knew even before I glanced into that map. The girl in the taxi with me was not Bernie. I had been taken in like a child.

I don't cry over spilt gin—and I don't holler when I'm hurt. I just had the driver pull the car to the kerb, and I flung open the door.

'Get out!' And when she didn't move fast enough I picked her up and sat her on the pavement. I knew now why this girl made such good tracks down the alley, and I knew why the hand was warm instead of cold. Should I have been suspicious? I should have. For I had had one real opportunity to suspect that things were fishy, and that was Nick's not asking for a hand-out. He always wanted money for every little thing—why not a big one like this?

It was all simple—so simple that I nearly boiled over. There had been another girl and another cape. A hand over Bernie's mouth—and another girl in her place. Just a matter of seconds, and while I was looking down that alley there were many. It only goes to show you how much we misjudge human nature. I didn't think for a moment that Nick had the guts to double-cross me like that. And I had been proud because he was so anxious to get rid of me. 'Pride goeth before a flop' must have been written for me.

But the girl on the sidewalk was putting up an awful squawk, and the taxi driver was turning in his seat and looking at me reproachfully.

'Drive on,' I told him, and there must have been something in my voice that made him realise I meant business. The girl, too, seemed to understand, for her tough little face slunk from view as I slammed the door. And if it hadn't—well, I like to pose as a gentleman, so we won't go into the probable damage to the taxi when that door swished through the air.

This time when the driver asked me 'Where to?' I had a definite point of destination.

'Back to the "Egyptian Lure",' I said simply.

Oh, I've often blown about my sense of humour, but I didn't laugh then. I just sat back in the cab and thought, and my thoughts were not pleasant. At least, they shouldn't have been pleasant—but I think I got some satisfaction over the little surprise I promised Nick.

And Nick would tell that story around, and Race Williams would be the laughing stock of the Avenue! Good enough. They could have their laugh—that is, all of them but Nick. But most of all, my pride was hurt—and I had paraded my courage and confidence and ability before Bernie. Where was my boasted service now? And Bernie's money was in my pocket.

Was she in actual danger? Was she back with her guardian or still at Nick's? But I didn't believe she was still at Nick's. Then why was I going to Nick's? I tapped the driver on the shoulder.

'Pull up for a minute,' I said, 'and don't disturb me. I'm going to think.' And if he got a laugh out of that last crack, he got it to himself.

Why was I going to Nick's? That was the question I had to answer. If it was simply for private vengeance, then I was wrong. My duty now more than ever was to Bernie. Nick had double-crossed me. But why? Money? Certainly. Was Nick in the game all the way through? No— the coincidence would be too great for that. He didn't know the reason, and he didn't know the men, maybe. He worked as he always worked— blindly, on the size of the bank roll. But perhaps he knew where Bernie was. Oh, they wouldn't tell him, and he'd deny it to me. But I knew

Nick—he'd look for more money in the game, and he'd probably try to follow the car that Bernie went away in. And if he succeeded he'd tell me—maybe he thought he wouldn't, but he would. There wouldn't be a cent in it for him either. I have most persuasive ways. I set my teeth grimly—ten minutes before, I'd strutted before Bernie like a game-cock; now—I tapped my gun. I'd find Nick and stick that forty-four down his throat, even if he had Joe the bouncer and all the other waiters in the establishment ready for me.

'Drive on,' I said to the chauffeur, and this time our destination hadn't changed much. I was still going to the 'Egyptian Lure'—but I'd stop the car around the block and get out. Nick had taken me in like a child—well, I'd play the child's game and make this visit a surprise party.

'Listen, Big Boy,' I told the driver as I slipped a few yellow-backs into his hand, 'this is for telling a bed-time story—any you wish. I want to know if Nick's at the club. If he isn't, I want you to tell me when he gets back. If he asks about me, strike him for a tip; tell him I got out of the cab and raised hell, and left you. I'll wait in the doorway around the corner.'

'You'll freeze to death, mister.' He shook his head.

'Not me—' I told him. But if I had added that I was so hot that the perspiration was pouring down me, he wouldn't have believed it. Anyway, I was hot under the collar.

I didn't threaten this lad with what I'd do to him if he put it over on me. He wasn't that sort of a bird. I simply promised to double the fistful of jack I'd given him if he made good. There was no use in my going to the 'Egyptian Lure' if Nick wasn't there. And if he was out snooping on Bernie's little playmates, it was ten to one he'd ring up to find out if I'd come back before he returned.

Perhaps Bernie needed me at once. Perhaps Bernie was in danger. Yet I could not afford to hurry things. I must give Nick a chance to get the information I needed. Of course, it might be possible to work back over the ground and track down the two swarthy boys who had grabbed Bernie in the restaurant, and so find her. But that would take time. No—for a bit I must move cautiously—cautiously, until I was sure—and then strike. I clenched my teeth tightly. What a fine mutton-head I had been!

The taxi had gone. The little narrow street was empty, and the hallway I shivered in, a dismal, cold, damp place. Twice I looked out, but there was no sign of a taxi, but the third time the street was not entirely deserted. Down the block a figure dashed from an alleyway, looked up and down the street—then, turning, ran quickly along the sidewalk in the opposite direction from my hiding-place.

For a moment I stood there watching the fleeing figure. But there was nothing odd in that. A criminal? Maybe. The lower city is full of them. A derelict—a poor, homeless creature of the night? Probably; just frightened out of a sleep in a rubbish heap. And I got a glimpse of those broad shoulders and a fleeting vision of his face as he passed beneath a street lamp.

It jarred me erect and out on to the sidewalk. Imagination? Maybe. The thing was on my mind, of course. But the man who sped down the street was strangely like the swarthy man whom I had helped out of Nick's some time before; the man Bernie had called Ferganses. As I say, maybe it was a mind picture; certainly there was little else under my hat. Anyway, I was out of that doorway and speeding after him.

Whether he was my man or not made little difference. He heard me, or saw me, almost at once—for his head darted quickly back over his shoulder. There was a brownish-white face in the darkness, and he increased his speed. Whatever his purpose, it wasn't an honest one.

The chase was hopeless from the beginning. He was around the corner before I was half-way down the block. I heard the throb of a racing motor—the grinding of gears, and when I reached the corner the street was deserted. Maybe a car had been waiting for him—maybe he had disappeared in any of the numerous tenements—and maybe, again, he was not my man at all. But if he was, what business did he have in the alley a few houses down from the hallway where I had parked?

So I retraced my steps. The run had done me good; warmed up my body and cooled off my head. I'd have a 'look-see' in that alley. And it was like most other alleys of the lower city. Garbage-cans piled along the sides and the little yard in the back—cans that might stay there until a sensitive nose from the health department drifted by.

There was a printing shop in front and the rear yard was full of boxes. I looked up at the tenement windows above—all dark. Yet I dared not use a light, and there was no moon. I stumbled over the thing before I saw it. A foot—a human foot, with the shoe protruding from beneath some boxes.

I'm not easily thrilled or shocked and I am entirely without nerves—but I'm willing to admit that I got at least a kick out of that foot. There wasn't enough light to tell me if it was the foot of a man or a woman—

just the dull outline of the shoe and the feel of the ankle as I kicked it. And my heart did a jump—neither of fear nor horror—sort of a conscience twinge of remorse. For I thought of Bernie and the fear she felt.

I knelt on the ground and removed the boxes from the body. It wasn't Bernie. The figure was too bulky and the clothes were a man's—black, but for the generous expanse of white stiff shirt. One hasty glance at the windows above and I jerked out my flash. Just a single instant the bright rays lit on that stiff white-bosomed shirt and the patch of red with the handle of a knife sticking from the centre of it. There was a pudgy hand, too, with fingers clenched across the body. Then the sharp brilliancy rested on the face—pasty, greasy white, with wide, staring, sightless eyes. Enough is enough, and sometimes too much. When I jerked myself to my feet I knew that I wouldn't get any information from the lips of Nick. I had planned vengeance on the poor, money-grabbing Greek—now, that was forgotten. Nick had double-crossed me. To the old proverb, 'The way of the transgressor is hard,' might be added another line—'also speedy'. They don't come much deader than Nick.

I experienced no sense of satisfaction that Nick had paid the price. It only made me feel just how badly I had erred—how real were the fears of Bernie—and just what danger the poor kid must be in. But why had they killed Nick? What had he learned? Did he know who this guardian was? Had he followed the man and found out? But all that would take time. Then what—had the guardian himself come to the 'Egyptian Lure'? Had he approached Nick earlier in the night? But all that was only guesswork. One thing was sure. Nick had tried to follow them, and Nick had been caught and killed and probably dragged into the rear yard.

Had he gained any information—had he—? And I flashed on the light again, for I remembered seeing Nick's hand and the tightly closed fist when my flash first went to work. It took real force to open those fingers, but I did it and got out a piece of paper. It was crumpled into a tiny ball. I slipped it into my pocket. Then I turned quickly and left the alley.

I didn't wait for my taxi driver to return. I didn't need the information that Nick wasn't at the 'Egyptian Lure' and I wasn't afraid that the taxi driver would mix me up with this bit of murder when it was discovered. Not him. His kind don't talk. His life was hardly an open book and wouldn't stand investigation. If the police did connect him with Nick and his business the night of the murder—well—I shrugged my shoulders. It wouldn't be the first time I had come under an official investigation, and I guess it wouldn't be the last.

I was five blocks away when I spread open that bit of paper. And there was something in it. The enemy was right in suspecting that Nick had followed them for a purpose; but they were wrong in suspecting that he used his head. Nick always had a bad head for figures. But there were numbers written on that sheet of paper. And I didn't need any Sherlock Holmes to tell me that the numbers were the licence of an automobile—the automobile that Bernie was carried off in. I felt a little better as I shoved the paper back in my pocket. Bernie was going to see me strut my stuff again—and this time we were going to get action.

I didn't have much fear that the licence number would be a fake one. They didn't know that I was in the case until Nick told them—if he did. The enemy had just tracked Bernie down and intended to drag her from her hiding-place. They didn't suspect she had consulted anyone, and there was no reason for them to believe that they would be watched or followed. That had all come later. They were gentlemen who met unexpected problems when they came to them—met them thoroughly and efficiently. As a witness to that efficiency was the cold, dead body of Nick stretched out in the alley yard.

The next day I had the desired information about that licence. There was a real kick in the foreign label of the lad who owned the car. Doctor Antonio Maderia. It made me rub my hands together. The name was certainly in tune with Bernie's story and the two gents who had tried to drag her from the night-club. Now, we'd have a slant at the bird with the fancy moniker and see if he'd like to teach me any playful tricks with a knife.

Doctor Antonio Maderia hung his hat in a brownstone front well uptown. There was a sign in the window that modestly designated his profession and pointed out that he saw patients by appointment only. Well—I didn't have any appointment, but then—I didn't intend to be a patient.

A female chirped as the door opened.

'You have an appointment with the doctor?' And I drew a bit of a shock at the trim little maid who answered the door. I didn't exactly expect to be greeted by a lad with a blackjack in one hand, a gun in the other, and a knife between his teeth. But I did expect to find a lad who could hold his own in a fight.

She frowned; told me that the doctor was busy over some work, but finally, when I was persistent, agreed to take in my card. I made no bones about that card—there was no necessity for Doctor Maderia to peek through a hole in the door to see who was asking for him. I'm not ashamed of my name, and RACE WILLIAMS stood out like a sore thumb in the centre of the white pasteboard. This doctor would grab himself off an eyeful and no mistake.

Only a minute or two I waited in the hall before he came down. He was a tall, rangy bird, with sharp features and uncertain eyes that were sunk far back in his head. They were dull sort of eyes but for the steel-like points in the centres of them, and he sort of bent his head forward and looked up at me, tapping the card nervously in his hand.

'Mr Williams,' he said at length, 'we will talk in here.' And I followed him into a little room off the hall. Before he shut the door he pulled up all the shades, flooding the room with light. Then he turned again and looked at me, and looked at the card.

'"Confidential Agent",' he said after a bit. 'You are a detective then. You are not going to tell me that something has happened to Bernie.'

Now, you'll admit that was a good start—the opening words of a man who has nothing to fear. But if it was a monkey wrench he was trying to toss into my works, it missed the machinery. I eyed him placidly.

'Yes—' I looked him straight in the eyes. 'You are her guardian, I believe.'

'In a way—in a way.' He tapped his fingers upon the chair. 'Nothing legal, you understand. She was alone and abroad. Her mother—well, I knew her. She was of my country and she asked me to look after the girl, before she died. She is of age, of course. I have tried to advise her at times.'

'She lived here with you?'

'Yes, that is so,' he said, after a moment's hesitation. 'She lived here with me.'

'And you helped straighten out her mother's estate?'

'There was little to straighten.' He smiled. 'Stocks and bonds and a savings bank account.'

'You charged her for such service, of course.'

'But, no.' He shook his head. 'There was really nothing to do. I have enough for my own needs—and her inheritance was trivial.'

'She told me it was considerable.' I fired the statement straight at him.

'So—' He stroked his chin with long, thin fingers. 'Perhaps it was to her. And now,' he broke in before I could fire another question, 'you have come here, taken up my time and questioned me. May I ask just why I am indebted to you for this visit?'

'I have come,' I said, 'to see Bernie—where is she?'

And he was on his feet at once.

'Ah—' His eyes flashed far back in his head. 'So you waste my time. I tolerated your presence, Mr Williams, because of the girl. I thought you brought information. Now—you would question me. I have helped her and advised her, and she has repaid me by leaving my house suddenly—three days ago. What, might I ask, do you know about her?'

And I quit beating about the bush.

'I know enough to know that she's in trouble. I know enough to know that she fears you. And I know that you threaten her with a secret. And I know that she left your house in fear, and that you followed her and found her and carried her away. And I know—' I stopped suddenly and raised my right hand that was sunk deep in my overcoat pocket. 'I also know,' I said very slowly, 'that if the lad who is so carefully opening that door behind you don't close it again, there'll be a mess on the carpet.'

And the door closed with a click—and Doctor Maderia's face whitened. I had struck my first blow.

'The maid—' he stammered, as he turned towards the door.

I stretched out a hand and stopped him.

'It's no use, Doctor.' I took advantage of my first blow and followed it up quickly. 'I don't know the whole game, but I know enough of it. The girl did wrong—probably inveigled into it. How you worked it is not my business. How to prove it on you is not my business. I'm here only in the interest of Bernie. Produce the girl—cut the blackmail, and the dead body of Nick is up to the police. Otherwise—' I finished with a shrug. 'They burn 'em in this state.'

The doctor's back was half to me, but I could see the side of his face, and he was weighing the possibilities. At length he turned—and the whiteness was gone from his cheeks. He was the calm, dignified physician who had entered the room a few minutes before.

'You confuse me, Mr Williams.' Again those long, delicate fingers swept over his face. 'And I do not know exactly how to answer you—your accusation can hardly be ignored. I am hesitant—undecided whether I should simply show you the door and let the police take care of the whole muddle.' He paused a moment—then, 'I am willing to discuss the matter further. You have seen the girl and she has spoken to you. May I understand just what she had told you? Certainly she has had trouble—and we must make allowances. You have discovered Bernie's secret and you wish to be paid for silence.'

And I just laughed that one off. But if he wanted the cards laid on the table I'd lay them for him. And I did. I told him I had seen the girl. I told him that I knew she had smuggled in rocks. I told him how Nick had died, and I told him of the piece of paper in Nick's hand. And he listened to the evidence like a learned judge.

'You have made quite a case against me, Mr Williams.' He smiled. 'But it seems to rest on facts that are weak. If the police had found that licence number I would have something to explain, perhaps. And if the girl was to tell her story again I would have something to explain. But since the police did not find the paper and the girl does not come forward to tell her story, things are rather awkward.

'Bernie committed a wrong. I have helped her hide it. Another held her secret. Blackmail has been paid—and then she ran away. That is my story to you and my story to the police. Not a pleasant one—I admit I have been foolish.'

'And you deny that the girl is here or that you know where she is?'

'Absolutely.'

'And if I wish to search the house?'

He frowned slightly, and then:

'I do not think that under the circumstances I would deny you that. And I think that I shall tell you a few facts. Perhaps, then, you will believe that I have been wronged. Bernie is weak of character. I believe that when her mother died she was without funds and in Italy. A young Italian whom she met offered her her passage in return for smuggling in diamonds. We will give her credit for wishing to see her mother before she died. Her secret was discovered. A man followed her to this country and blackmailed her. She confided in me. I advised seeking lawyers—but, no. She paid, and I assisted her. At least I could hold their demands in check by threatening to tell the police. Personally, I had little to fear. Somehow, Bernie got the illusion that I was helping them. But—there, you do not believe me. She ran away. I have not seen her since. And the car, which number you have, she took with her.'

Bull? Probably. But he had one advantage over me. My threats were useless. If I went to the police, what would become of the girl? Her smuggling didn't amount to near-beer. I could straighten that out. But this doctor knew where the girl was and was keeping her a prisoner. What then? The thing behind it all was big enough for him to go in for murder. Since you can't electrocute a man more than once, why should he hesitate about shoving Bernie over? She'd make a tough witness against him. Still, my game wasn't to roast this duck; my game was to save the girl.

It was in my mind to shove a rod into his mouth and threaten to blow him off if he didn't tell me where the girl was. But it couldn't work out that way. Somehow I had the impression that I was sitting on a keg of dynamite and a couple of kids were playing around the fuse with matches. And there was his invitation to search the house. Was Bernie there? No! If I thought she was I'd have searched the house, even though I believed he might have a half-dozen gunmen parked above. But it wouldn't help Bernie any to have me walk upstairs and get my roof shot off at the top step.

No—I thought it better to fall in with his humour and try to trip him. I'd turn a back flip and take the attitude that after all maybe he was a very wronged man. And I did.

'I only know what I'm told, doctor,' I said brusquely. 'You can't blame me for investigating the girl's story—especially since she disappeared. Now—her mother is dead; did you happen to meet this mother as the attending physician?'

And that was a crack he hadn't expected. I scored again. His face did a few quick colours, but he answered without hesitating.

'I was called in by her physician.'

'And his name?' I pulled out a little pad, like a stage detective.

'Doctor Robinfall.' His eyes were narrowing.

'And who signed the death certificate?'

'Enough!' And now there was no mistaking his attitude. He was rattled; his poise was gone; his long fingers shook. He was a murderer and a crook; it was all written on his evil face. I hadn't had much doubt before, but now I was sure. Oh, I envied the Central Office detective then. The time was right for a signed confession. A police officer's duty is to the law, and he wouldn't need to worry about the girl. My duty was to the girl, and I had to worry about her.

I followed him as he staggered to the hall. And I gave him the final blow as he stood trembling and pointing at the big front door. There was murder in his heart and in his face—but I watched his hands and advised him once to keep his right further from his pocket. He was a loathsome, slimy thing—fear, stark terror, in his face. I had guessed his secret—his first crime, that would connect him with all the others. Protected as a doctor, he had killed Bernie's mother.

'What are you going to do—what are you going to do?' he kept saying over and over as we stood by the door.

'You must produce the girl at my office at six o'clock tonight.'

'And—what of me?'

'If she is safe—and things are satisfactory, you'll have twenty-four hours for a get-away.'

'She'll die—die—die,' he slobbered like a jibbering idiot, 'if you—you get the police.'

But I only smiled over at him.

'At six o'clock,' I told him, as I backed out the door.

'And if I don't?'

'I'll get an order to exhume the body of her mother.' And as I finished, the door closed. But his white face, with the hollow cheeks and the sunken eyes, still stared through the glass. You've got to admit that the old head sometimes works, as well as lead. But I didn't strut, and I didn't pat myself on the back. I'd await results.

Now, my methods are open to criticism, and perhaps some may think I should have stuck to this bird and made him lead me to the girl. And I thought of that, weighed the possibilities, and decided against it. For he was not the only one in this game. There were the two swarthy gentlemen with the trick names, one of whom had croaked Nick. Surely they would have something to say about the girl being turned loose. One of them had committed murder—both of them were in the game deep enough to fry at Sing Sing. Where the dead body would be evidence enough against the doctor, the live Bernie would be evidence against them.

Besides, there was always the possibility of a trap. Of course the girl was not in the house. Doctor Maderia wouldn't know that the girl had never told me his name nor address. He would be expecting me, but he wasn't expecting what I'd bring up about the girl's mother. That was luck. He'd killed her and planned to milk the daughter's bank account dry. It was a pretty game—worthy of a lad with more guts than Doctor Maderia. When the show-down came he blew up. He thought only of himself. My only interest was the girl. The doctor would give his little playmates a story that might bring results.

As for the doctor slipping away on me, he couldn't do it. Two of the sharpest shadows in New York would be on his heels. He'd soon know that, and feel the fear of the hunted criminal. He'd have to produce the girl. Just a few hours stood between him and the road which leads to the electric chair.

At six o'clock, almost to the dot, he walked into my office. And he was alone—and he was a wreck. I almost felt like taking him for a tour of the country, as a living example that crime doesn't pay.

'You've double-crossed me—you've betrayed me. They are down by the door now. They've been following me.'

'So you wanted to beat it. Where's the girl?'

'Those men are not—police officers?'

'Not a chance.' I shook my head. 'They know nothing about you—just obeying my orders. Now—what of the girl?'

'I couldn't bring her,' he told me. 'Don't—don't,' he cried as I reached for the phone. 'Everything that you accuse me of is true—except that I am but a tool. Ferganses planned things. I had stolen money. I was desperate. I was in debt. The girl is very rich yet. But I will lead you to them—to her. Ferganses' pal, Farro, was in the house when you came. They plan a final coup. It is for me to cash the cheque because I am known at the bank. They will torture her to sign, but I will lead you to the house—to them—to her.'

Could I believe him? Was he a great actor or an awful bust? I'd have to chance it. There was no doubt that the girl was in grave danger. Still, I didn't intend to play any Goldy Locks for the three bears. If this lad would double-cross his friends, he would double-cross me at the last moment. There was just one person he'd play straight with. That was—himself. I knew his kind. Like a prize fighter who is hot stuff when he's winning, but who hollers 'foul' at the first real crack in the bread-basket, such was the doctor. When he was hurt he squawked.

'What's the plan?' I asked him.

'Listen—' He rubbed his hands together. 'I have been most careful. I told them that you suspect, and I told them also that you want the girl. But I saw I was at fault there. And I saw, too, that suspicion was entering their heads. Ferganses I spoke to on the phone. Farro, at my house. To them there is no advantage in giving up the girl. And they tell me to tell you that she dies if you go to the police—but if you let her pay them the money, then she can go.'

'How will they arrange to get the money? The bank will be suspicious of large amounts.' And I eyed him closely.

'That is for me to arrange.' He gulped. 'The bank knows me. I can do it. You think perhaps it is best?'

'No. I don't think perhaps it is best.' I stood over him as he crouched there in the chair. 'The girl goes free tonight—or you burn. You knew that—what else have you planned? What is this idea of leading me to them?'

'That could be done.' He nodded vigorously. 'I am to see them tonight—to get a cheque from the girl. So I could bring you to them. But they are desperate men—you might have to kill Ferganses.'

'That's agreeable,' I told him.

'And me—I go free. You remember your promise. They do not deserve consideration from me. They did not trust me. It was not until the girl saw them that she doubted me. It is their own fault. If they had played the game I would not—'

'That's right.' I agreed with his attempt to tell himself what a real guy he was.

He came to his feet and clutched me by the arm.

'You will not have me arrested? I shall have my chance to leave the country if I do this thing? You are a brave man—you shoot quick. You will come on them from behind. They will fight, and you will kill them.' And he got to rubbing his hands again.

'Where are they keeping the girl?'

'In Jersey. I will lead you to the place—we will drive there together.'

'Just where, in Jersey?'

He smiled, in what he considered a knowing way.

'Just where?' I stretched out a hand and took him by the throat. 'You don't think you can fool me any longer!' And, indeed, I was growing impatient. I thought of Bernie; of her youth; of her childish simplicity; of her bringing-up in a convent, and now being in the hands of those two cut-throats.

'I don't dare tell you yet—because I am afraid you will tell the police. Don't—*don't*!' he screamed, as my fingers closed the tighter about his thin neck. And then, 'I will tell.'

And he did. Just beyond Newark. Did I believe him? I didn't know and I didn't care. I was heartily sick of this detective business. It isn't in my line. What I need is action. What I generally get is action. If it was a trap, all well and good; my guns were loaded and oiled. If it was shooting the boys wanted, they were welcome to it.

Some may question my right—my ethics—in letting him go if I saved the girl. And I'll admit there's room for argument there. But I must play the game as I see it. After all, it's my business and I must run it my own way. Besides, there was the possibility that he wasn't on the level, and I might have to slip a bit of lead into his miserable carcass anyway. And that was a thought worth imparting to the crouching dog who seemed to think of nothing but his own safety.

'You understand the situation thoroughly,' I said to him gravely, for I was not fooling. 'You are to lead me to the girl; you are to lead me so that my coming will be a complete surprise to these pals of yours. You will always be ahead of me—never behind me, and my gun will cover you. You could lead me to a trap where I would be killed. That is possible, but not probable. But it is impossible that you could live. At the first sign of suspicion I'll put a bullet in your back. Don't labour under any delusion that I'm too high-hat and nobleminded to shoot a man in cold blood. You know my record. So—we understand each other.'

His cheeks whitened and his eyes sank the deeper as he nodded, but back in his head might be the hope of betraying me. He felt, maybe, that his time would come. He felt, perhaps, that Ferganses would not be taken alive, and while we shot it out would come his chance. And I smiled to myself. Just before any shooting started the good doctor would be tapped bye-bye with the barrel of my gun. Not a pretty thought, maybe—but, then, I don't go in for pretty thoughts.

As we waited for a later hour to depart the doctor's spirits grew brighter and he began to look on me as his partner, and confided in me. It seems that he didn't trust these other men, anyway, and that he had intended to double-cross them in the long run. From his story they had gotten a few thousand from the girl. It was his idea to take the money in easy stages, but his friends were all for quick action. He didn't exactly tell me that he had killed Bernie's mother—signed the death certificate and framed Bernie in Italy, but he didn't need to. He was all rotten—and more than once he hinted at the pile of jack I could make if I helped him out.

I wasn't mad and I didn't fly at him. I just smiled to myself. If he made a false move and I plugged him, I'd have an easy conscience. Let him think he was a bright boy and encouraged him to go on—and I found out how Nick had gotten his. Nick had been paid earlier in the evening to let the two swarthy lads cart out Bernie. But at that time he knew nothing, and he hadn't suspected I was in the game until he saw one of the Italians lying in the hall. But Nick double-crossed me for the money that was in it then and the blackmail he felt certain would follow. And Nick had run quickly around the corner and seen Doctor Maderia's big car with the doctor in it, with the chloroformed girl and the whozzle-headed lad I had cracked. But Nick hadn't seen the swarthy Ferganses, who had dropped behind for the purpose of seeing if Nick would attempt to follow.

And that part of the story, I guess, was true. Doctor Maderia said that Nick reached for a gun and that there was a fight, and he drove on, picking up Ferganses around the corner later. That was the first time he knew that Nick was dead. Whether there was a fight or not did not matter. Certainly Nick was dead.

They had driven to Jersey, left the girl there with Ferganses, and the doctor had returned to New York with the other lad, called Farro. That was his story—and it was true enough, I guess. At least, as near the truth as would ever come out. But the more the doctor took me into his confidence the more I distrusted him. Was he just trying to make me less cautious—telling me everything, yet telling me nothing that I really didn't know already?

Of course I got Bernie's last name and all about her mother and her father, but why go into that? I would not give her real name, anyway, so we'll just continue to call her Bernie. That I had frisked the doctor and copped all his hardware is hardly necessary to say. But I had.

The doctor was to be at the house in Jersey at one o'clock; Farro had left for the place early in the day. The doctor was booked to start at twelve, so I thought we'd better start at eleven.

'You'll drive,' I told him, as we stepped into the car.

'But I don't know how. I give you my word that I shall make no attempt to—'

'Stick your hands behind your back then,' I said, swinging him around.

'What—what are you going to do?'

'Put the cuffs on you. Come! Make it snappy.'

And that was enough. He didn't fancy having his hands bound behind him, and he learned to drive in jig time.

'I drive a little—but not well,' he stammered.

'I'm not particular—jump in.' I opened the door of the car for him.

And we were off. That was the doctor's first attempt to put it over on me. Or was it? But it didn't matter. I didn't intend this to be a pleasure trip. I was expecting most anything to happen. Bernie was about to receive her delayed service.

Doctor Maderia booked the trip across the Hudson River at Forty-second Street, so I decided to cross at One Hundred and Twenty-fifth. Not that I was just obstinate—but I thought it more conducive to long life and the pursuit of liberty to pick my own route. So we left the ferry at Fort Lee and wound our way up the big hill. And the doctor forgot that he was a novice and drove remarkably well.

But as we shot off towards Newark he got nervous—twice he shifted gears on a hill that a car like mine would race over at forty. There was something on his mind besides his hat, and at length he came out with it.

'Mr Williams,' he said suddenly, paying due respect to my age and dignity with the 'mister', 'I didn't tell you all the truth—the house is not near Newark—rather, up by Englewood.'

'Yes?' I fingered the gun in my lap. 'You're sure this time?'

And he nodded.

'Because,' I went on, 'we must reach the house by twelve o'clock. If we don't—' I shrugged my shoulders. 'Well—Doctor, you'll be a most distressing corpse.'

If it was a joke he missed it, for he was turning the car and we nearly backed into a ditch.

'I am not going to double-cross you,' he gulped. 'I lied because I feared you might break faith with me once you knew the truth, and arrange for the police to come. But now—I shall drive you straight there.'

'You must suit yourself,' I said icily as I snapped out my watch. 'You have until twelve o'clock.' I didn't say any more. I didn't need to; he understood me. And, after all, there was a certain amount of reason for him lying to me at first. I had thought of the police, of course. I never use them if I can help it, but I would use them if I thought it was for the benefit of my client. But here—once the police came into the case—Bernie would go up. Another murder wouldn't bother these lads. Unfortunately, you can only electrocute murderers once.

We passed through Englewood and back towards the Hudson River. There, just at the top of the Palisades, we turned and followed a fairly good highway—shot into a side road and he stopped the car.

'It is only—a few—hundred yards further.' His lips quivered and the words trembled like a popular 'mammy' song.

'You suggest that we walk?' I asked.

'It is best.' He stuck close to me as we left the car. 'This Ferganses—he is a killer. You must shoot without hesitating—in the back, if possible.'

'Fine—we'll ask him to turn around, then.' But my levity didn't cheer up the doctor. His legs were trembling in his pants and his teeth chattering. Maybe it was the cold, and again maybe it wasn't. But I stuck my gun in his back, jerked him erect and told him to lead on. So we started. My own safety lay in the doctor's love of life. He was walking with death, and he knew it.

It's funny, too, what an effect a gun has on the physical as well as the moral attitude of a man. When the doctor's feet would sag and his body slink closer to the ground, I'd just press that gun forward and up he'd come again with a sharp jerk.

So we left the little road, and, with the doctor still doing his jack-in-the-box trick to the sudden prods of my gun, we crossed a wooded field, slipped through the busted part of a barbed-wire fence and saw the house.

Bio, black and ominous it loomed in the moonlight. And then a light—a wavering, flickering flash that came from a room in the upper storey. And it was gone almost at once.

And now we were close to the house.

'How do we get in?' I asked.

'We can use a cellar window—unless you want me to go, alone, by the door and trap them into conversation while you enter.'

There was a laugh in that.

'We'll try the cellar window,' I told him. 'Which side is the best?'

'There is one on this side—and one on the other. But the room above the window on this side is where they will be. You cannot see a light because it is heavily shuttered. Both cellar windows will be locked—you'll have to break one.'

'We'll try the other side—lead on, MacDuff.'

He stopped dead as we reached the back of the house.

'I can't—go—another step—with that gun—against my—back.' And his teeth punctuated each word like a buzz-saw.

And, indeed, he seemed in bad shape. Luckily, the grass was soft and deadened his staggering steps. I had only pushed the gun against him for the moral and physical support. Now, if it didn't have that effect any longer—why, all right. I gave him a few inches leeway. It didn't make any difference to me. Lead travelling half a foot wouldn't lose much of its efficiency.

We went on again, the doctor bending—with me close on his trail. We turned the corner of the house and I saw the splash of light. We were nearing a window of which the shade was half up. Rather venturesome that. These lads felt safe in their retreat, or— And I rubbed my chin—the light in the window was not the only light at that minute. There was a little light slipping through the darkness of my mind. I nodded. We were going to get action, I thought.

So we swung towards the lighted window three feet above the ground—he crouching double again, those lean, long arms—the white fingers at the end of them standing out—swinging back and forth. He paused as he reached the window, and turned to me.

'They'll be in there. You can look in if you wish.'

And I was almost startled by the simplicity of the suggestion. While I looked in that window I would stand directly in the splash of light. Of course I couldn't be seen by those inside, but what about someone outside? If I could have been sure that my visit wasn't expected it would be all right. And really, even though the doctor was a charming chap, you could not expect me to put my entire trust in him.

'You look in, and tell me what's going on,' I said, half sarcastically. And I'll admit that I was surprised when he did stretch up and stand plumb in the light. Nothing happened to him either. But I did notice one thing. He had removed his slouch hat before he looked through the window. Just a habit, that? Maybe—then again, maybe not.

'They are there—both of them—and the girl. Now's your chance. We won't have to enter by the cellar. Come—look.' And he was as excited and as interested as a child.

I didn't say anything. Perhaps, after all, the doctor was on the up and up with me. But I took off my hat there in the darkness and, reaching suddenly out, I placed it on the doctor's head.

The hat had hardly landed; my hand was little more than out of the light; the white face of the doctor had no more than half turned in surprise, doubt, and then fear—when it happened. There was the roar of a gun, a choked scream, a hole in a white face—and the doctor pitched forward on his face. The trap had been sprung—and whether it was successful or not depended entirely upon the point of view you take.

Of course the thing was simple enough. A lad hid in the darkness and watched the lighted window. He was not to fire at a bare head, but was to shoot at the first covered one. My little experiment with the hat looked to him as if the heads had changed. He had made a mistake, of course—but life is full of mistakes; and here he was, coming to pay for his. Yep—he was dashing across the darkness towards the lighted window and the figure beneath it. He thought he had hit me. How sweet and simple of him! But then, I have often contended that crooks are like children.

'All right—all right,' he was calling as he came. Certainly he had the confidence of youth. And as he reached the window it opened, and I recognised the swarthy-faced lad, Ferganses; and I plainly saw the big automatic he held in his right hand.

'You got him, eh, Farro?' And there was something in his voice which was not entirely congratulatory. Farro recognised it, but too late. He was in the light of the window and I could just make out his face. Farro never had the chance to lift the gun in his hand—for Ferganses, in the window, fired at once. Without a cry Farro sank down on top of the doctor.

'It is done, eh, doctor?' Ferganses leaned from the window, his blinking eyes trying to get a good picture of me in the darkness. 'But come,' he went on, taking me for the doctor, 'this Williams is dead—this Farro will no longer want a share. We must burn the money out of the girl, for she is obstinate. Come!'

'Come!' was right. He was hanging half out of the window, with the gun dangling in his hand. And I came. I stepped forward and swung my gun through the air. There was a dull thud, and his chin pounded down on the window-sill. He just sprawled there until I dragged him out and dropped him to the grass.

Maybe I should have shot him and been done with it. But I didn't. It wasn't big-heartedness, nor even a hesitancy about taking a human life. I just thought of my own interest. It was better that he should live. There was a mess there beneath the window that couldn't be hidden from a police investigation. They'd need a victim and they might as well have Ferganses. The authorities would identify the doctor, question the girl, and drag me into it anyway. For once I'd face an investigation as innocent as a new-born babe.

But the girl. I found her all right, in the room above, where I had seen the flashlight. Horribly frightened, of course, yet physically all right but for the stiffness from her bound limbs. And—well, what more would you want, unless to have me go out and walk on Ferganses' face?—which little action I had already done when I climbed in the window. After all, Bernie hadn't gotten such bad service.

ARSON PLUS

Dashiell Hammett

Despite his importance as the first hardboiled dick, Race Williams'
fame has been somewhat overshadowed through the passing years by
two other pioneer sleuths, the anonymous Continental Op and Sam
Spade, both created by Dashiell Hammett. Although Hammett, like
Carroll John Daly, favoured a swift, terse style of storytelling, he put
a great deal more effort into the characterisation of his protagonists,
as well as creating stories that were rather more realistic. The first of
his private eyes, the Continental Op, was also something of a contrast
to Race Williams: middle-aged, heavily built, tough and sardonic, he
used a gun but was just as willing to wade into a criminal with his
bare hands if the need arose. He worked for the Continental Detective
Agency in San Francisco and in a long career proved himself loyal,
dedicated and totally incorruptible. Although, like Williams, the Op
helped many women in trouble, in stark contrast to his predecessor he
always co-operated with the police and solved most of his cases by
painstaking enquiry and meticulous attention to detail. He was not one
to boast of his abilities, and recounted all his cases in a detached style
that made his readers feel they were in the company of a complete
professional. He, too, made his first appearance in the pages of Black
Mask, *less than five months after Williams, in the story 'Arson Plus'*
which carried the by-line of 'Peter Collinson'. Although some readers
might have sensed that here was an important new character, few could
have had any idea just how *important—and even less what stature the*
pseudonymous author would later enjoy in crime fiction.

'Peter Collinson' was actually a curious name for Samuel Dashiell
Hammett (1894–1961) to have chosen. It derived from an underworld
expression, 'Peter Collins', used to refer to a nobody, thereby making
the author 'nobody's son'. Notwithstanding this, there was no denying
the authentic feel of his landmark story about the Continental Op, or
those that followed in the long-running series, due in considerable

measure to the fact that Hammett had himself been a private detective. Born in Maryland, he had been a high school drop-out at 13 who finally found a job with the famous Pinkerton Detective Agency in Baltimore. Eight years later, after being assigned to cases in a number of cities— foremost among them San Francisco—as well as being involved with the gangster Nick Arnstein and the infamous Fatty Arbuckle rape case, Hammett 'turned sour on being a detective', to use his own words, and decided instead to try his hand at writing for the pulps. It was natural enough for him to draw on his wealth of experience with Pinkerton's to make his mark on crime fiction, but it was with the creation of another detective, Sam Spade, who made his bow in The Maltese Falcon *(1930), that he presented the genre with a character many believe to be the most famous detective of the twentieth century. Here, however, is the story that began the Hammett—and Continental Op—legend more than seventy years ago . . .*

*   *   *

Jim Tarr picked up the cigar I rolled across his desk, looked at the band, bit off an end, and reached for a match.

'Three for a buck,' he said. 'You must want me to break a *couple* of laws for you this time.'

I had been doing business with this fat sheriff of Sacramento County for four or five years—ever since I came to the Continental Detective Agency's San Francisco office—and I had never known him to miss an opening for a sour crack; but it didn't mean anything.

'Wrong both times,' I told him. 'I get them for two bits each, and I'm here to do you a favour instead of asking for one. The company that insured Thornburgh's house thinks somebody touched it off.'

'That's right enough, according to the fire department. They tell me the lower part of the house was soaked with gasoline, but the Lord knows how they could tell—there wasn't a stick left standing. I've got McClump working on it, but he hasn't found anything to get excited about yet.'

'What's the layout? All I know is that there was a fire.'

Tarr leaned back in his chair, turned his red face to the ceiling, and bellowed:

'Hey, Mac!'

The pearl push-buttons on his desk are ornaments so far as he is concerned. Deputy sheriffs McHale, McClump and Macklin came to the door together—MacNab apparently wasn't within hearing.

'What's the idea?' the sheriff demanded of McClump. 'Are you carrying a bodyguard around with you?'

The two other deputies, thus informed as to whom 'Mac' referred this time, went back to their cribbage game.

'We got a city slicker here to catch our firebug for us,' Tarr told his deputy. 'But we got to tell him what it's all about first.'

McClump and I had worked together on an express robbery several months before. He's a rangy, tow-headed youngster of twenty-five or six, with all the nerve in the world—and most of the laziness.

'Ain't the Lord good to us?'

He had himself draped across a chair by now—always his first objective when he comes into a room.

'Well, here's how she stands: this fellow Thornburgh's house was a couple miles out of town, on the old county road—and old frame house. About midnight, night before last, Jeff Pringle—the nearest neighbour, a half-mile or so to the east—saw a glare in the sky from over that way, and phoned in the alarm; but by the time the fire wagons got there, there wasn't enough of the house left to bother about. Pringle was the first of the neighbours to get to the house, and the roof had already fallen in then.

'Nobody saw anything suspicious—no strangers hanging around or nothing. Thornburgh's help just managed to save themselves, and that was all. They don't know much about what happened—too scared, I reckon. But they did see Thornburgh at his window just before the fire got him. A fellow here in town—name of Henderson—saw that part of it too. He was driving home from Wayton, and got to the house just before the roof caved in.

'The fire department people say they found signs of gasoline. The Coonses, Thornburgh's help, say they didn't have no gas on the place. So there you are.'

'Thornburgh have any relatives?'

'Yeah. A niece in San Francisco—a Mrs Evelyn Trowbridge. She was up yesterday, but there wasn't nothing she could do, and she couldn't tell us nothing much, so she went home.'

'Where are the servants now?'

'Here in town. Staying at a hotel on I Street. I told 'em to stick around for a few days.'

'Thornburgh own the house?'

'Uh-huh. Bought it from Newning & Weed a couple months ago.'

'You got anything to do this morning?'

'Nothing but this.'

'Good. Let's get out and dig around.'

We found the Coonses in their room at the hotel on I Street. Mr Coons was a small-boned, plump man with the smooth, meaningless face, and the suavity of the typical male house-servant.

His wife was a tall, stringy woman, perhaps five years older than her husband—say, forty—with a mouth and chin that seemed shaped for gossiping. But he did all the talking, while she nodded her agreement to every second or third word.

'We went to work for Mr Thornburgh on the fifteenth of June, I think,' he said, in reply to my first question. 'We came to Sacramento around the first of the month, and put in applications at the Allis Employment Bureau. A couple of weeks later they sent us out to see Mr Thornburgh, and he took us on.'

'Where were you before you came here?'

'In Seattle, sir, with a Mrs Comerford; but the climate there didn't agree with my wife—she has bronchial trouble—so we decided to come to California. We most likely would have stayed in Seattle, though, if Mrs Comerford hadn't given up her house.'

'What do you know about Thornburgh?'

'Very little, sir. He wasn't a talkative gentleman. He hadn't any business that I know of. I think he was a retired seafaring man. He never said he was, but he had that manner and look. He never went out or had anybody in to see him, except his niece once, and he didn't write or get any mail. He had a room next to his bedroom fixed up as a sort of workshop. He spent most of his time in there. I always thought he was working on some kind of invention, but he kept the door locked, and wouldn't let us go near it.'

'Haven't you any idea at all what it was?'

'No, sir. We never heard any hammering or noises from it, and never smelled anything either. And none of his clothes were ever the least bit soiled, even when they were ready to go out to the laundry. They would have been if he had been working on anything like machinery.'

'Was he an old man?'

'He couldn't have been over fifty, sir. He was very erect, and his hair and beard were thick, with no grey hairs.'

'Ever have any trouble with him?'

'Oh, no, sir! He was, if I may say it, a very peculiar gentleman in a way; and he didn't care about anything except having his meals fixed right, having his clothes taken care of—he was very particular about them—and not being disturbed. Except early in the morning and at night, we'd hardly see him all day.'

'Now about the fire. Tell us the whole thing—everything you remember.'

'Well, sir, my wife and I had gone to bed about ten o'clock, our regular time, and had gone to sleep. Our room was on the second floor, in the rear. Some time later—I never did exactly know what time it was—I woke up, coughing. The room was all full of smoke, and my wife was sort of strangling. I jumped up, and dragged her down the back stairs and out the back door, not thinking of anything but getting her out of there.

'When I had her safe in the yard, I thought of Mr Thornburgh, and tried to get back in the house; but the whole first floor was just flames. I ran around front then, to see if he had got out, but didn't see anything of him. The whole yard was as light as day by then. Then I heard him scream—a horrible scream, sir—I can hear it yet! And I looked up at his window—that was the front second-storey room—and saw him there, trying to get out the window. But all the woodwork was burning, and he screamed again and fell back, and right after that the roof over his room fell in.

'There wasn't a ladder or anything that I could have put up to the window for him—there wasn't anything I could have done.

'In the meantime, a gentleman had left his automobile in the road, and come up to where I was standing; but there wasn't anything we could do—the house was burning everywhere and falling in here and there. So we went back to where I had left my wife, and carried her farther away from the fire, and brought her to—she had fainted. And that's all I know about it, sir.'

'Hear any noises earlier that night? Or see anybody hanging around?'

'No, sir.'

'Have any gasoline around the place?'

'No, sir. Mr Thornburgh didn't have a car.'

'No gasoline for cleaning?'

'No, sir, none at all, unless Mr Thornburgh had it in his workshop. When his clothes needed cleaning, I took them to town, and all his laundry was taken by the grocer's man, when he brought our provisions.'

'Don't know anything that might have some bearing on the fire?'

'No, sir. I was surprised when I heard that somebody had set the house afire. I could hardly believe it. I don't know why anybody should want to do that . . .'

'What do you think of them?' I asked McClump, as we left the hotel.

'They might pad the bills, or even go South with some of the silver, but they don't figure as killers in my mind.'

That was my opinion, too; but they were the only persons known to have been there when the fire started except the man who had died. We went around to the Allis Employment Bureau and talked to the manager.

He told us that the Coonses had come into his office on June second, looking for work; and had given Mrs Edward Comerford, 45 Woodmansee Terrace, Seattle, Washington, as reference. In reply to a letter—he always checked up the references of servants—Mrs Comerford had written that the Coonses had been in her employ for a number of years, and had been 'extremely satisfactory in every respect.' On June thirteenth, Thornburgh had telephoned the bureau, asking that a man and his wife be sent out to keep house for him, and Allis sent out two couples he had listed. Neither couple had been employed by Thornburgh, though Allis considered them more desirable than the Coonses, who were finally hired by Thornburgh.

All that would certainly seem to indicate that the Coonses hadn't deliberately manoeuvred themselves into the place, unless they were the luckiest people in the world—and a detective can't afford to believe in luck or coincidence, unless he has unquestionable proof of it.

At the office of the real-estate agents, through whom Thornburgh had bought the house—Newning & Weed—we were told that Thornburgh had come in on the eleventh of June, and had said that he had been told that the house was for sale, had looked it over, and wanted to know the price. The deal had been closed the next morning, and he had paid for the house with a cheque for $14,500 on the Seamen's Bank of San Francisco. The house was already furnished.

After luncheon, McClump and I called on Howard Henderson—the man who had seen the fire while driving home from Wayton. He had an office in the Empire Building, with his name and the title *Northern California Agent for Krispy Korn Krumbs* on the door. He was a big, careless-looking man of forty-five or so, with the professionally jovial smile that belongs to the travelling salesman.

He had been in Wayton on business the day of the fire, he said, and had stayed there until rather late, going to dinner and afterwards playing pool with a grocer named Hammersmith—one of his customers. He had left Wayton in his machine, at about ten-thirty, and set out for Sacramento. At Tavender he had stopped at the garage for oil and gas, and to have one of his tyres blown up.

Just as he was about to leave the garage, the garage man had called his attention to a red glare in the sky, and had told him that it was probably from a fire somewhere along the old county road that paralleled the State Road into Sacramento; so Henderson had taken the county road, and had arrived at the burning house just in time to see Thornburgh try to fight his way through the flames.

It was too late to make any attempt to put out the fire, and the man upstairs was beyond saving by then—undoubtedly dead even before the roof collapsed; so Henderson had helped Coons revive his wife, and stayed there watching the fire until it had burned itself out. He had seen no one on that county road while driving to the fire . . .

'What do you know about Henderson?' I asked McClump, when we were on the street.

'Came here, from somewhere in the East, I think, early in the summer to open that breakfast cereal agency. Lives at the Garden Hotel. Where do we go next?'

'We get a car, and take a look at what's left of the Thornburgh house.'

An enterprising incendiary couldn't have found a lovelier spot in which to turn himself loose, if he looked the whole county over. Tree-topped hills hid it from the rest of the world, on three sides; while away from the fourth, an uninhabited plain rolled down to the river. The county road that passed the front gate was shunned by automobiles, so McClump said, in favour of the State Highway to the north.

Where the house had been was now a mound of blackened ruins. We poked around in the ashes for a few minutes—not that we expected to find anything, but because it's the nature of man to poke around in ruins.

A garage in the rear, whose interior gave no evidence of recent occupation, had a badly scorched roof and front, but was otherwise undamaged. A shed behind it, sheltering an axe, a shovel, and various odds and ends of gardening tools, had escaped the fire altogether. The lawn in front of the house, and the garden behind the shed—about an acre in all—had been pretty thoroughly cut and trampled by wagon wheels, and the feet of the firemen and the spectators.

Having ruined our shoe-shines, McClump and I got back in our car and swung off in a circle around the place, calling at all the houses within a mile radius, and getting little besides jolts for our trouble.

The nearest house was that of Pringle, the man who had turned in the alarm; but he not only knew nothing about the dead man, he said he had never even seen him. In fact, only one of the neighbours had ever seen him: a Mrs Jabine, who lived about a mile to the south.

She had taken care of the key to the house while it was vacant; and a day or two before he bought it, Thornburgh had come to her house, enquiring about the vacant one. She had gone over there with him and shown him through it, and he had told her that he intended buying it, if the price, of which neither of them knew anything, wasn't too high.

He had been alone, except for the chauffeur of the hired car in which he had come from Sacramento, and, save that he had no family, he had told her nothing about himself.

Hearing that he had moved in, she went over to call on him several days later—'just a neighbourly visit'—but had been told by Mrs Coons that he was not at home. Most of the neighbours had talked to the Coonses, and had got the impression that Thornburgh did not care for visitors, so they had let him alone. The Coonses were described as 'pleasant enough to talk to when you meet them', but reflecting their employer's desire not to make friends.

McClump summarised what the afternoon had taught us as we pointed our car towards Tavender: 'Any of these folks could have touched off the place, but we got nothing to show that any of 'em even knew Thornburgh, let alone had a bone to pick with him.'

Tavender turned out to be a crossroads settlement of a general store and post office, a garage, a church, and six dwellings, about two miles from Thornburgh's place. McClump knew the storekeeper and postmaster, a scrawny little man named Philo, who stuttered moistly.

'I n-n-never s-saw Th-thornburgh,' he said, 'and I n-n-never had any m-mail for him. C-coons'—it sounded like one of these things butterflies come out of—'used to c-come in once a week t-to order groceries—they d-didn't have a phone. He used to walk in, and I'd s-send the stuff over in my c-c-car. Th-then I'd s-see him once in a while, waiting f-for the stage to S-s-sacramento.'

'Who drove the stuff out to Thornburgh's?'

'M-m-my b-boy. Want to t-talk to him?'

The boy was a juvenile edition of the old man, but without the stutter.

He had never seen Thornburgh on any of his visits, but his business had taken him only as far as the kitchen. He hadn't noticed anything peculiar about the place.

'Who's the night man at the garage?' I asked him.

'Billy Luce. I think you can catch him there now. I saw him go in a few minutes ago.'

We crossed the road and found Luce.

'Night before last—the night of the fire down the road—was there a man here talking to you when you first saw it?'

He turned his eyes upward in that vacant stare which people use to aid their memory.

'Yes, I remember now! He was going to town, and I told him that if he took the county road instead of the State Road he'd see the fire on his way in.'

'What kind of looking man was he?'

'Middle-aged—a big man, but sort of slouchy. I think he had on a brown suit, baggy and wrinkled.'

'Medium complexion?'

'Yes.'

'Smile when he talked?'

'Yes, a pleasant sort of fellow.'

'Brown hair?'

'Yeah, but have a heart!' Luce laughed. 'I didn't put him under a magnifying glass.'

From Tavender we drove over to Wayton. Luce's description had fit Henderson all right, but while we were at it, we thought we might as well check up to make sure that he had been coming from Wayton.

We spent exactly twenty-five minutes in Wayton; ten of them finding Hammersmith, the grocer with whom Henderson had said he dined and played pool; five minutes finding the proprietor of the pool room; and ten verifying Henderson's story . . .

'What do you think of it now, Mac?' I asked, as we rolled back towards Sacramento.

Mac's too lazy to express an opinion, or even form one, unless he's driven to it; but that doesn't mean they aren't worth listening to.

'There ain't a hell of a lot to think,' he said cheerfully. 'Henderson is out of it, if he ever was in it. There's nothing to show that anybody but the Coonses and Thornburgh were there when the fire started—but there may have been a regiment there. Them Coonses ain't too honest-looking, maybe, but they ain't killers, or I miss my guess. But the fact remains that they're the only bet we got so far. Maybe we ought to try to get a line on them.'

'All right,' I agreed. 'Soon as we get back to town, I'll get a wire off to our Seattle office asking them to interview Mrs Comerford, and see what she can tell about them. Then I'm going to catch a train for San Francisco and see Thornburgh's niece in the morning.'

Next morning, at the address McClump had given me—a rather elaborate apartment building on California Street—I had to wait three-quarters of an hour for Mrs Evelyn Trowbridge to dress. If I had been younger, or a social caller, I suppose I'd have felt amply rewarded when she finally came in—a tall, slender woman of less than thirty; in some sort of clinging black affair; with a lot of black hair over a very white face, strikingly set off by a small red mouth and big hazel eyes that looked black until you got close to them.

But I was a busy, middle-aged detective, who was fuming over having his time wasted; and I was a lot more interested in finding the bird who struck the match than I was in feminine beauty. However, I smothered my grouch, apologised for disturbing her at such an early hour, and got down to business.

'I want you to tell me all you know about your uncle—his family, friends, enemies, business connections—everything.'

I had scribbled on the back of the card I had sent in to her what my business was.

'He hadn't any family,' she said; 'unless I might be it. He was my mother's brother, and I am the only one of that family now living.'

'Where was he born?'

'Here in San Francisco. I don't know the date, but he was about fifty years old, I think—three years older than my mother.'

'What was his business?'

'He went to sea when he was a boy, and, so far as I know, always followed it until a few months ago.'

'Captain?'

'I don't know. Sometimes I wouldn't see or hear from him for several years, and he never talked about what he was doing; though he would mention some of the places he had visited—Rio de Janeiro, Madagascar, Tobago, Christiania. Then, about three months ago—some time in May—he came here and told me that he was through with wandering; that he was going to take a house in some quiet place where he could work undisturbed on an invention in which he was interested.

'He lived at the Francisco Hotel while he was in San Francisco. After a couple of weeks he suddenly disappeared. And then, about a month ago, I received a telegram from him, asking me to come to see him at his house near Sacramento. I went up the very next day, and I thought that he was acting queerly—he seemed very excited over something. He gave me a will that he had just drawn up and some life insurance policies in which I was beneficiary.

'Immediately after that he insisted that I return home, and hinted rather plainly that he did not wish me to either visit him again or write until I heard from him. I thought all that rather peculiar, as he had always seemed fond of me. I never saw him again.'

'What was this invention he was working on?'

'I really don't know. I asked him once, but he became so excited—even suspicious—that I changed the subject, and never mentioned it again.'

'Are you sure that he really did follow the sea all those years?'

'No, I am not. I just took it for granted; but he may have been doing something altogether different.'

'Was he ever married?'

'Not that I know of.'

'Know any of his friends or enemies?'

'No, none.'

'Remember anybody's name that he ever mentioned?'

'No.'

'I don't want you to think this next question insulting, though I admit it is. But it has to be asked. Where were you on the night of the fire?'

'At home; I had some friends here to dinner, and they stayed until about midnight. Mr and Mrs Walker Kellogg, Mrs John Dupree, and a Mr Killmer, who is a lawyer. I can give you their addresses, or you can get them from the phone book, if you want to question them.'

From Mrs Trowbridge's apartment I went to the Francisco Hotel. Thornburgh had been registered there from May tenth to June thirteenth, and hadn't attracted much attention. He had been a tall, broad-shouldered, erect man of about fifty, with rather long brown hair brushed straight back; a short, pointed, brown beard, and healthy, ruddy complexion—grave, quiet, punctilious in dress and manner; his hours had been regular and he had had no visitors that any of the hotel employees remembered.

At the Seamen's Bank—upon which Thornburgh's cheque, in payment of the house, had been drawn—I was told that he had opened an account there on May fifteenth, having been introduced by W. W. Jeffers & Sons, local stock brokers. A balance of a little more than four hundred dollars remained to his credit. The cancelled cheques on hand were all to the order of various life insurance companies; and for amounts that, if they represented premiums, testified to rather large policies. I jotted down the names of the life insurance companies, and then went to the office of W. W. Jeffers & Sons.

Thornburgh had come in, I was told, on the tenth of May with $15,000 worth of bonds that he wanted sold. During one of his conversations with Jeffers he had asked the broker to recommend a bank, and Jeffers had given him a letter to the Seamen's Bank.

That was all Jeffers knew about him. He gave me the numbers of the bonds, but tracing bonds isn't always the easiest thing in the world.

The reply to my Seattle telegram was waiting for me at the Continental Detective Agency when I arrived.

MRS EDWARD COMERFORD RENTED APARTMENT AT ADDRESS YOU GIVE ON MAY TWENTY-FIVE. GAVE IT UP JUNE SIX. TRUNKS TO SAN FRANCISCO SAME DAY. CHECK NUMBERS GN FOUR FIVE TWO FIVE EIGHT SEVEN AND EIGHT AND NINE

Tracing baggage is no trick at all, if you have the dates and check numbers to start with—as many a bird who is wearing somewhat similar numbers on his chest and back, because he overlooked that detail when making his getaway, can tell you—and twenty-five minutes in a baggage-room at the ferry and half an hour in the office of a transfer company gave me my answer.

The trunks had been delivered to Mrs Evelyn Trowbridge's apartment!

I got Jim Tarr on the phone.

'Good shooting!' he said, forgetting for once to indulge his wit. 'We'll grab the Coonses here and Mrs Trowbridge there, and that's the end of another mystery.'

'Wait a minute!' I cautioned him. 'It's not all straightened out yet—there's still a few kinks in the plot.'

'It's straight enough for me. I'm satisfied.'

'You're the boss, but I think you're being a little hasty. I'm going up to talk with the niece again. Give me a little time before you phone the police here to make the pinch. I'll hold her until they get there.'

*

Evelyn Trowbridge let me in this time, instead of the maid who had opened the door for me in the morning, and she led me to the same room in which we had had our first talk. I let her pick out a seat, and then I selected one that was closer to either door than hers was.

On the way up I had planned a lot of innocent-sounding questions that would get her all snarled up; but after taking a good look at this woman sitting in front of me, leaning comfortably back in her chair, coolly waiting for me to speak my piece, I discarded the trick stuff and came out cold-turkey.

'Ever use the name Mrs Edward Comerford?'

'Oh, yes.' As casual as a nod on the street.

'When?'

'Often. You see, I happen to have been married not so long ago to Mr Edward Comerford. So it's not really strange that I should have used the name.'

'Use it in Seattle recently?'

'I would suggest,' she said sweetly, 'that if you are leading up to the references I gave Coons and his wife, you might save time by coming right to it?'

'That's fair enough,' I said. 'Let's do that.'

There wasn't a tone or shading, in voice, manner, or expression, to indicate that she was talking about anything half so serious or important to her as a possibility of being charged with murder. She might have been talking about the weather, or a book that hadn't interested her particularly.

'During the time that Mr Comerford and I were married, we lived in Seattle, where he still lives. After the divorce, I left Seattle and resumed my maiden name. And the Coonses *were* in our employ, as you might learn if you care to look it up. You'll find my husband—or former husband—at the Chelsea apartments.

'Last summer, or late spring, I decided to return to Seattle. The truth of it is—I suppose all my personal affairs will be aired anyhow—that I thought perhaps Edward and I might patch up our differences; so I went back and took an apartment on Woodmansee Terrace. As I was known in Seattle as Mrs Edward Comerford, and as I thought my using his name might influence him a little, I used it while I was there.

'Also I telephoned the Coonses to make tentative arrangements in case Edward and I should open our house again; but Coons told me that they were going to California, and so I gladly gave them an excellent recommendation when, some days later, I received a letter of enquiry from an employment bureau in Sacramento. After I had been in Seattle for about two weeks, I changed my mind about the reconciliation— Edward's interest, I learned, was all centred elsewhere; so I returned to San Francisco—'

'Very nice! But—'

'If you will permit me to finish,' she interrupted. 'When I went to see my uncle in response to his telegram, I was surprised to find the Coonses in his house. Knowing my uncle's peculiarities, and finding them now increased, and remembering his extreme secretiveness about his mysterious invention, I cautioned the Coonses not to tell him that they had been in my employ.

'He certainly would have discharged them, and just as certainly would have quarrelled with me—he would have thought that I was having him spied on. Then, when Coons telephoned me after the fire, I knew that to admit that the Coonses had been formerly in my employ would, in view of the fact that I was my uncle's only heir, cast suspicion on all three of us. So we foolishly agreed to say nothing about it and carry on the deception.'

That didn't sound all wrong—but it didn't sound all right. I wished Tarr had taken it easier and let us get a better line on these people, before having them thrown in the coop.

'The coincidence of the Coonses stumbling into my uncle's house is, I fancy, too much for your detecting instincts,' she went on, as I didn't say anything. 'Am I to consider myself under arrest?'

I'm beginning to like this girl; she's a nice, cool piece of work.

'Not yet,' I told her. 'But I'm afraid it's going to happen pretty soon.'

She smiled a little mocking smile at that, and another when the doorbell rang.

It was O'Hara from police headquarters. We turned the apartment upside down and inside out, but didn't find anything of importance except the will she had told me about, dated July eighth, and her uncle's life insurance policies. They were all dated between May fifteenth and June tenth, and added up to a little more than $200,000.

I spent an hour grilling the maid after O'Hara had taken Evelyn Trowbridge away, but she didn't know any more than I did. However, between her, the janitor, the manager of the apartments, and the names Mrs Trowbridge had given me, I learned that she had really been entertaining friends on the night of the fire—until after eleven o'clock, anyway—and that was late enough.

Half an hour later I was riding the Short Line back to Sacramento.

I was getting to be one of the line's best customers, and my anatomy was on bouncing terms with every bump in the road!

Between bumps I tried to fit the pieces of this Thornburgh puzzle together. The niece and the Coonses fitted in somewhere, but not just where we had them. We had been working on the job sort of lopsided, but it was the best we could do with it. In the beginning we had turned to the Coonses and Evelyn Trowbridge because there was no other direction to go; and now we had something on them—but a good lawyer could make hash out of it.

The Coonses were in the county jail when I got to Sacramento. After some questioning they had admitted their connection with the niece, and had come through with stories that matched hers in every detail.

Tarr, McClump and I sat around the sheriff's desk and argued.

'Those yarns are pipe dreams,' the sheriff said. 'We got all three of 'em cold, and there's nothing else to it. They're as good as convicted.'

McClump grinned derisively at his superior, and then turned to me.

'Go on, you tell him about the holes in his little case. He ain't your boss, and can't take it out on you later for being smarter than he is!'

Tarr glared from one of us to the other.

'Spill it, you wise guys!' he ordered.

'Our dope is,' I told him, figuring that McClump's view of it was the same as mine, 'that there's nothing to show that even Thornburgh knew he was going to buy that house before the tenth of June, and that the Coonses were in town looking for work on the second. And besides, it was only by luck that they got the jobs. The employment office sent two couples out there ahead of them.'

'We'll take a chance on letting the jury figure that out.'

'Yes? You'll also take a chance on them figuring out that Thornburgh, who seems to have been a nut, might have touched off the place himself! We've got something on these people, Jim, but not enough to go into court with them. How are you going to prove that when the Coonses were planted in Thornburgh's house—if you can even prove that they and the Trowbridge woman knew he was going to load up with insurance policies?'

The sheriff spat disgustedly.

'You guys are the limit! You run around in circles, digging up the dope on these people until you get enough to hang 'em, and then you run around hunting for outs! What's the matter with you now?'

I answered him from halfway to the door—the pieces were beginning to fit together under my skull.

'Going to run some more circles—come on, Mac!'

McClump and I held a conference on the fly, and then I got a car from the nearest garage and headed for Tavender. We made time going out, and got there before the general store had closed for the night. The stuttering Philo separated himself from the two men with whom he had been talking, and followed me to the rear of the store.

'Do you keep an itemised list of the laundry you handle?'

'N-n-no; just the amounts.'

'Let's look at Thornburgh's.'

He produced a begrimed and rumpled account book, and we picked out the weekly items I wanted: $2.60, $3.10, $2.25, and so on.

'Got the last batch of laundry here?'

'Y-yes,' he said. 'It j-just c-c-came out from the city t-today.'

I tore open the bundle—some sheets, pillowcases, tablecloths, towels, napkins; some feminine clothing; some shirts, collars, underwear, and socks that were unmistakably Coons's. I thanked Philo while running back to the car.

Back in Sacramento again, McClump was waiting for me at the garage where I had hired the car.

'Registered at the hotel on June fifteenth, rented the office on the sixteenth. I think he's in the hotel now,' he greeted me.

We hurried around the block to the Garden Hotel.

'Mr Henderson went out a minute or two ago,' the night clerk told us. 'He seemed to be in a hurry.'

'Know where he keeps his car?'

'In the hotel garage around the corner.'

We were within ten feet of the garage, when Henderson's automobile shot out and turned up the street.

'Oh, Mr Henderson!' I cried, trying to keep my voice level.

He stepped on the gas and streaked away from us.

'Want him?' McClump asked; and at my nod he stopped a passing roadster by the simple expedient of stepping in front of it.

We climbed in, McClump flashed his star at the bewildered driver, and pointed out Henderson's dwindling tail-light. After he had persuaded himself that he wasn't being boarded by a couple of bandits, the commandeered driver did his best, and we picked up Henderson's tail-light after two or three turnings, and closed in on him—though his car was going at a good clip.

By the time we reached the outskirts of the city, we had crawled up to within safe shooting distance, and I sent a bullet over the fleeing man's head. Thus encouraged, he managed to get a little more speed out of his car; but we were definitely overhauling him now.

Just at the wrong minute Henderson decided to look over his shoulder at us—an unevenness in the road twisted his wheels—his machine swayed—skidded—went over on its side. Almost immediately, from the heart of the tangle, came a flash and a bullet moaned past my ear. Another. And then, while I was still hunting for something to shoot at in the pile of junk we were drawing down upon, McClump's ancient and battered revolver roared in my other ear.

Henderson was dead when we got to him—McClump's bullet had taken him over one eye.

McClump said over the body:

'I ain't an inquisitive sort of fellow, but I hope you don't mind telling me why I shot this lad.'

'Because he was—*Thornburgh*.'

He didn't say anything for about five minutes. Then: 'I reckon that's right. How'd you know it?'

We were sitting beside the wreckage now, waiting for the police that we had sent our commandeered chauffeur to phone for.

'He had to be,' I said, 'when you think it all over. Funny we didn't hit on it before! All that stuff we were told about Thornburgh had a fishy sound. Whiskers and an unknown profession, immaculate and working on a mysterious invention, very secretive and born in San Francisco—where the fire wiped out all the old records—just the sort of fake that could be cooked up easily.

'Now, consider Henderson. You had told me he came to Sacramento sometime early this summer—and the dates you got tonight show that he didn't come until *after* Thornburgh had bought his house. All right! Now compare Henderson with the descriptions we got of Thornburgh.

'Both are about the same size and age, and with the same colour hair. The differences are all things that can be manufactured—clothes, a little sunburn, and a month's growth of beard, along with a little acting, would do the trick. Tonight I went out to Tavender and took a look at the last batch of laundry—*and there wasn't any that didn't fit the Coonses!* And none of the bills all the way back were large enough for Thornburgh to have been as careful about his clothes as we were told he was.'

'It must be great to be a detective!' McClump grinned as the police ambulance came up and began disgorging policemen. 'I reckon somebody must have tipped Henderson off that I was asking about him this evening.' And then, regretfully: 'So we ain't going to hang them folks for murder after all.'

'No, but we oughtn't have any trouble convicting them of arson plus conspiracy to defraud, and anything else that the Prosecuting Attorney can think up.'

THE MAN WHO LIKED DOGS
Raymond Chandler

*Among the many authors inspired by Dashiell Hammett to write for the
pulps was Raymond Chandler, creator of another of the best-known
'hardboiled dicks', Philip Marlowe. Like his predecessors, Marlowe,
who was in his forties and described as tall, with grey eyes and 'a
jaw of stone', was tough, laconic and wisecracking—but also highly
intelligent (he had been college educated), introspective and a fearless
judge of character. Although he solved the cases brought to him by
(mostly) wealthy and (occasionally) corrupt clients, he was invariably
short of cash. Marlowe operated his one-man business in Los Angeles,
a city famed for its beauty but also its squalor, where he lived in a
run-down apartment and worked out of an equally shabby office. He
was a man driven by a sense of justice and co-operated with the police
as long as the officers were not corrupt. For such men, Marlowe had
nothing but contempt. Of his private eye, Chandler wrote, 'To me [he]
is the American mind; a heavy portion of rugged realism, a dash of
good hard vulgarity, a strong overtone of strident wit, an equally strong
undertone of pure sentimentalism, an ocean of slang, and an utterly
unexpected range of sensitivity.'*

*Philip Marlowe did not, however, spring fully formed into his
creator's mind. When Chandler first began writing hardboiled yarns in
1933, his sleuths bore a variety of different names—such as John
Dalmas (who featured in 'Mandarin's Jade' and 'Smart-Aleck Kill')—
or were tersely referred to as Carmody, Malvern and Mallory. Some,
in the tradition of his mentor's Continental Op, were nameless, merely
pushing a business card into the face or hand of a potential client
without so much as a word. However, after the acclaimed début of
Philip Marlowe in the novel* The Big Sleep *(1939), Chandler cannibal-
ised some of his earlier stories for subsequent books, or republished
the stories with the detective renamed Marlowe. Thanks to the huge
success of the novels that followed, including* Farewell, My Lovely

(1940), The Lady in the Lake *(1943) and* The Long Goodbye *(1953), as well as the numerous movies starring Dick Powell, Humphrey Bogart, Robert Mitchum and so on, Chandler's creation has deservedly come to be regarded as the epitome of the private eye in detective fiction.*

Raymond Chandler (1888–1959) was born in Chicago but educated in England, and worked as a journalist for several English magazines before returning to America. After being employed for a time as the Daily Express *correspondent in Los Angeles and then as an oil executive, he fell on hard times during the Depression and took up writing for the pulps. Fame did not come until the publication of* The Big Sleep, *but following this he was lured into screen-writing in Hollywood where he worked on a number of very successful movies; these included* Double Indemnity *(1944), for which he received an Oscar nomination. The illness of his wife caused Chandler to neglect his work in order to care for her, and after her death in 1954 he began drinking heavily and ruined his own health. His fame has, however, grown increasingly since his death and many critics consider his books works of literature rather than just crime fiction. 'The Man Who Liked Dogs' is one of his early stories, written for* Black Mask *in 1936, and features a nameless sleuth who is clearly a prototype of Marlowe. The story is also of particular interest because it was later altered, expanded and mixed with other elements to form the nucleus of perhaps the most famous of all the novels about the Californian private eye,* Farewell, My Lovely.

*   *   *

There was a brand-new aluminium-grey DeSoto sedan in front of the door. I walked around that and went up three white steps, through a glass door and up three more carpeted steps. I rang a bell on the wall.

Instantly a dozen dog voices began to shake the roof. While they bayed and howled and yapped I looked at a small alcove office with a rolltop desk and a waiting-room with leather chairs and three diplomas on the wall, at a table scattered with copies of the *Dog Fancier's Gazette.*

Somebody quieted the dogs out back, then an inner door opened and a small pretty-faced man in a tan smock came in on rubber soles, with a solicitous smile under a pencil-line moustache. He looked around and under me, didn't see a dog. His smile got more casual.

He said, 'I'd like to break them of that, but I can't. Every time they hear a buzzer they start up. They get bored and they know the buzzer means visitors.'

I said, 'Yeah,' and gave him my card. He read it, turned it over and looked at the back, turned it back and read the front again.

'A private detective,' he said softly, licking his moist lips. 'Well— I'm Sharp. What can I do for you?'

'I'm looking for a stolen dog.'

His eyes flicked at me. His soft little mouth tightened. Very slowly his whole face flushed.

I said, 'I'm not suggesting *you* stole the dog. Almost anybody could plant an animal in a place like this and you wouldn't think about that chance they didn't own it, would you?'

'One just doesn't like the idea,' he said stiffly. 'What kind of dog?'

'Police dog.'

He scuffed a toe on the thin carpet, looked at a corner of the ceiling. The flush went off his face, leaving it with a sort of shiny whiteness. After a long moment he said, 'I have only one police dog here, and I know the people he belongs to. So I'm afraid—'

'Then you won't mind my looking at him?' I cut in, and started towards the inner door.

Sharp didn't move. He scuffed some more. 'I'm not sure that's convenient,' he said softly. 'Perhaps later in the day.'

'Now would be better for me,' I said, and reached for the knob.

He scuttled across the waiting-room to his little rolltop desk. His small hand went around the telephone there.

'I'll—I'll just call the police if you want to get tough,' he said hurriedly.

'Ask for Chief Fulwider. I just came from his office.'

Sharp took his hand away from the phone. I grinned at him and rolled a cigarette around in my fingers.

'Come on,' I said. 'Shake the hair out of your eyes and let's go. Be nice and maybe I'll tell you the story.'

He chewed both his lips in turn, stared at the brown blotter on his desk, fiddled with a corner of it, stood up and crossed the room, opened the door in front of me and we went along a narrow grey hallway. We went through a door farther along, into a bare room with a concrete floor, a gas heater in the corner with a bowl of water beside it, and all along one wall two tiers of stalls with heavy wire mesh doors.

Dogs and cats stared at us silently, expectantly, behind the mesh. A tiny chihuahua snuffled under a big red Persian with a wide sheepskin collar around its neck. There was a sour-faced Scottie and a mutt with all the skin off one leg and a silky-grey Angora and a Sealyham and two more mutts and a razor-sharp fox terrier with a barrel snout and just the right droop to the last two inches of it.

Their noses were wet and their eyes were bright and they wanted to know whose visitor I was.

I looked them over. 'These are toys,' I growled. 'I'm talking police dog. Grey and black, no brown. A male. Nine years old. Swell points all around except that his tail is too short. Do I bore you?'

He stared at me, made an unhappy gesture. 'Yes, but—' he mumbled. 'Well, this way.'

We went back out of the room. The animals looked disappointed, especially the chihuahua, which tried to climb through the wire mesh and almost made it. We went back out of a rear door into a cement yard with two garages fronting on it. One of them was empty. The other, with its door open a foot, was a box of gloom at the back of which a big dog clanked a chain and put his jaw down flat on the old comforter that was his bed.

'Be careful,' Sharp said. 'He's pretty savage at times. I had him inside, but he scared the others.'

I went into the garage. The dog growled. I went towards him and he hit the end of his chain with a bang. I said, 'Hullo there, Voss. Shake hands.'

He put his head back down on the comforter. His eyes came forward halfway. He was very still. His eyes were wolfish, black-rimmed. Then the curved, too-short tail began to thump the floor slowly.

I said, 'Shake hands, boy,' and put mine out. In the doorway behind me the little vet was telling me to be careful. The dog came up slowly on his big rough paws, swung his ears back to normal and lifted his left paw. I shook it.

The little vet complained, 'This is a great surprise to me—'

'Yeah, it would be,' I said.

I patted the dog's head and went back out of the garage.

We went into the house, into the waiting-room. I pushed magazines out of the way and sat on a corner of the table, looked the pretty little man over.

'OK,' I said. 'Give. What's the name of his folks and where do they live?'

He thought it over sullenly. 'Their name is Voss. They've moved east and they are to send for the dog when they're settled.'

'Cute at that,' I said. 'The dog's named Voss after a German war flier. The folks are named after the dog.'

'You think I'm lying,' the little man said hotly.

'Uh-uh. You scare too easy for a crook. I think somebody wanted to ditch the dog. Here's my story. A girl named Isobel Snare disappeared from her home in San Angelo two weeks ago. She lives with her great-aunt, a nice old lady in grey silk who isn't anybody's fool. The girl had been stepping out with some pretty shady company in the night spots and gambling joints. So the old lady smelled a scandal and didn't go to the law. She didn't get anywhere until a girlfriend of the Snare girl happened to see the dog in your joint. She told the aunt. The aunt hired me—because when the niece drove off in her roadster and didn't come back she had the dog with her.'

I mashed out my cigarette on my heel and lit another. Sharp's little face was as white as dough. Perspiration twinkled in his cute little moustache.

I added gently, 'It's not a police job yet. I was kidding you about Chief Fulwider.'

'What—what do you want me to do?' the little man stammered.

'Think you'll hear anything more about the dog?'

'Yes,' he said quickly. 'The man seemed very fond of him. A genuine dog lover. The dog was gentle with him.'

'Then you'll hear from him,' I said. 'When you do I want to know. What's the guy look like?'

'He was tall and thin with very sharp black eyes. His wife is tall and thin like him. Well-dressed, quiet people.'

'The Snare girl is a little runt,' I said. 'What made it so hush-hush?'

He stared at his foot and didn't say anything.

'OK,' I said. 'Business is business. Play ball with me and you won't get any adverse publicity. Is it a deal?' I held my hand out.

'I'll play with you,' he said softly, and put a moist fishy paw in mine. I shook it carefully, so as not to bend it.

I told him where I was staying and went back out to the sunny street and walked a block down to where I had left my Chrysler. I got into it and poked it forward from around the corner, far enough so that I could see the DeSoto and the front of Sharp's place.

I sat like that for half an hour. Then Sharp came out of his place and got into the DeSoto. He drove it off around the corner and swung into the alley that ran behind his yard.

Then the DeSoto backed out of the alley. A big police dog with a muzzle on his head was chained in the back of the sedan. I could just see his head straining at the chain.

I trailed the DeSoto.

Carolina Street was away off at the edge of the little beach city. There were just two houses in the last block, so I hid behind the first, which was on the corner, with a weedy grass plot and a high dusty red and yellow lantana fighting with a honeysuckle vine against the front wall.

Beyond that was a ramshackle mud-coloured bungalow with a wire fence. The DeSoto stopped in front of it.

Its door slammed open and Sharp dragged the muzzled dog out of the back and fought him through a gate and up the walk.

I put my stomach down in the weeds and sighted the bungalow and waited. Boomingly on the afternoon air came the deep-toned woof-woofing of the police dog.

Nothing happened for about fifteen minutes except that the dog kept right on barking. Then the barking suddenly got harder and harsher. Then somebody shouted. Then a man screamed.

I picked myself up and sprinted. As I got near the house I heard the low, furious growling of the dog worrying something, and behind it the staccato rattle of a woman's voice, in anger more than in fear.

I went through the gate and thumped up wooden steps to a sagging porch. I banged on the door.

The growling was still going on inside, but the scolding voice had stopped. Nobody came to the door. I tried the knob, opened the door, and went in. There was a heavy smell of chloroform.

In the middle of the floor, on a twisted rug, Sharp lay spread-eagled on his back, with blood pumping out of the side of his neck. The blood had made a thick glossy pool around his head. The dog leaned away from it, crouched on his forelegs, his ears flat to his head, fragments of a torn muzzle hanging about his neck. His throat bristled and the hair on his spine stood up and there was a low pulsing growl deep in his throat.

Behind the dog a cupboard door was smashed back against the wall and on the floor of the cupboard a big wad of cottonwool sent sickening waves of chloroform out on the air.

A dark handsome woman in a print house dress held a big automatic pointed at the dog and didn't fire it.

She threw a quick glance at me over her shoulder, started to turn.

The dog watched her, with narrow, black-rimmed eyes. I took my Luger out and held it down at my side.

Something creaked and a tall black-eyed man in faded blue overalls and a blue work-shirt came through the swing door at the back with a sawn-off double-barrel shotgun in his hands. He pointed it at me.

'Hey, you! Drop that gat!' he said angrily.

I moved my jaw with the idea of saying something. The man's finger tightened on the front trigger. My gun went off—without my having much to do with it. The slug hit the stock of the shotgun, knocked it clean out of the man's hands. It pounded on the floor and the dog jumped sideways about seven feet and crouched again.

With an utterly incredulous look on his face the man put his hands up in the air.

I couldn't lose. I said, 'Down yours too, lady.'

She worked her tongue along her lips and lowered the automatic to her side and walked away from the body on the floor.

The man said, 'Hell, don't shoot him. I can handle him.'

I blinked, then I got the idea. He had been afraid I was going to shoot the dog. He hadn't been worrying about himself.

I lowered the Luger a little. 'What happened?'

'That—tried to chloroform—*him*, a fighting dog!'

I said, 'Yeah. If you've got a phone, you'd better call an ambulance. Sharp won't last long with that tear in his neck.'

The woman went along the wall to a window seat full of crumpled newspapers, reached down for a phone at one end of it. I looked down at the little vet. His face was the whitest face I had ever seen.

'Never mind the ambulance,' I told the woman. 'Just call Police Headquarters.'

The man in the overalls put his hands down and dropped on one knee, began to pat the floor and talk soothingly to the dog.

'Steady, old-timer. Steady. We're all friends now—all friends. Steady, Voss.'

The dog growled and swung his hind end a little. The man kept on talking to him. The dog stopped growling and the hackles on his back went down. The man in overalls kept on crooning to him.

The woman on the window seat put the phone aside and said, 'On the way. Think you can handle it, Jerry?'

'Sure,' the man said, without taking his eyes off the dog.

The dog let his belly touch the floor now and opened his mouth and let his tongue hang out. The tongue dripped saliva, pink saliva with blood mixed in it. The hair at the side of the dog's mouth was stained with blood.

The man called Jerry said, 'Hey, Voss. Hey, Voss old kid. You're fine now. You're fine.'

The dog panted, didn't move. The man straightened up and went close to him, pulled one of the dog's ears. The dog turned his head sideways and let his ear be pulled. The man stroked his head, unbuckled the chewed muzzle and got it off.

He stood up with the end of the broken chain and the dog came up on his feet obediently, went out through the swing door into the back part of the house, at the man's side.

I moved a little, out of line with the swing door. Jerry might have more shotguns. There was something about Jerry's face that worried me. As if I had seen him before, but not very lately, or in a newspaper.

I looked at the woman. She was a handsome brunette in her early thirties. Her print house dress didn't seem to belong with her finely arched eyebrows and her long soft hands.

'How did it happen?' I asked casually, as if it didn't matter very much.

Her voice snapped at me, as if she was aching to turn it loose. 'We've been in the house about a week. Rented it furnished. I was in the kitchen, Jerry in the yard. The car stopped out front and the little guy marched in just as if he lived here. The door didn't happen to be locked, I guess. I opened the swing door a crack and saw him pushing the dog into the cupboard. Then I smelled the chloroform. Then things began to happen all at once and I went for a gun and called Jerry.'

'It was all over then?' I said. 'He had Sharp chewed up on the floor?'

'Yes—if Sharp is his name.'

'You and Jerry didn't know him?'

'Never saw him before. Or the dog. But Jerry loves dogs.'

'Better change a little of that,' I said. 'Jerry knew the dog's name. Voss.'

Her eyes got tight and her mouth got stubborn. 'I think you must be mistaken,' she said in a sultry voice.

'Who's Jerry?' I asked. 'I've seen him somewhere. Where'd he get the sawn-off? You going to let the cops see that?'

She bit her lip, then stood up suddenly, went towards the fallen shotgun. I let her pick it up, saw she kept her hand away from the triggers. She went back to the window seat and pushed it under the pile of newspapers.

She faced me. 'OK, what's the pay-off?' she asked grimly.

I said slowly, 'The dog is stolen. His owner, a girl, happens to be missing. I'm hired to find her. The people Sharp said he got the dog from sounded like you and Jerry. Their name was Voss. They moved east. Ever hear of a lady called Isobel Snare?'

The woman said, 'No,' tonelessly, and stared at the end of my chin.

The man in overalls came back through the swing door wiping his face on the sleeve of his blue work-shirt. He didn't have any fresh guns with him. He looked me over without much concern.

Tyres squealed, taking a distant corner.

'Aw, loosen up,' I said quickly. 'Sharp was scared. He brought the dog back to where he got him. He must have thought the house was empty. The chloroform idea wasn't so good, but the little guy was all rattled.'

They didn't make a sound, either of them. They just stared at me.

'OK,' I said, and stepped over to the corner of the room. 'I think you're on the lam. If whoever's coming isn't law, I'll start shooting. Don't ever think I won't.'

The woman said very calmly, 'Suit yourself.'

Then a car rushed along the block and ground to a harsh stop before the house. Two big bruisers in plain-clothes tumbled out and slammed through the gate, up the steps.

The door swung wide and the two dicks charged in with drawn guns.

They stopped dead, stared at what lay on the floor. Their guns jerked at Jerry and me. The one who covered me was a big red-faced man in a baggy grey suit.

'Reach—and reach empty!' he yelled in a large tough voice.

I reached, but held on to my Luger. 'Easy,' I said. 'A dog killed him, not a gun. I'm a private dick. I'm on a case here.'

'Yeah?' He closed in on me heavily, bored his gun into my stomach. 'Maybe so, bud. We'll know all that later on.'

He reached up and jerked my gun loose from my hand, sniffed at it, leaning his gun into me.

'Fired, huh? Sweet! Turn around.'

'Listen—'

'Turn around, bud.'

I turned slowly. Even as I turned he was dropping his gun into a side-pocket and reaching for his hip.

That should have warned me, but it didn't. I may have heard the swish of the blackjack. Certainly I must have felt it. There was a sudden pool of darkness at my feet. I dived into it.

When I came to the room was full of smoke. The smoke hung in the air, in thin lines straight up and down, like a bead curtain. I had never seen the room before.

I lay a little while thinking, then I opened my mouth and yelled, 'Fire!' at the top of my lungs.

Then I fell back on the bed and started laughing. I didn't like the sound I made laughing. It had a goofy ring, even to me.

Steps ran along somewhere and a key turned in the door and the door opened. A man in a short white coat looked in at me, hard-eyed. I turned my head a little and said, 'Don't count that one, Jack. It slipped out.'

He scowled sharply. He had a hard small face, beady eyes. I didn't know him.

'Maybe you want some more strait-jacket,' he sneered.

'I'm fine, Jack,' I said. 'Just fine. I'm going to have me a short nap now.'

'Better be just that,' he snarled.

The door shut, the key turned, the steps went away.

I lay still and looked at the smoke. I knew now that there wasn't any smoke there really. It must have been night because a porcelain bowl hanging from the ceiling on three chains had light behind it.

I took hold of the corner of the rough sheet and wiped the sweat off my face. I sat up, put my feet down on the floor. They were bare. I was wearing canton flannel pyjamas. There was no feeling in my feet when I put them down. After a while they began to tingle and then got full of pins and needles.

Then I could feel the floor. I took hold of the side of the bed and stood up and walked.

A voice that was probably my own was saying to me, 'You have the DTs . . . you have the DTs . . . you have the DTs . . .'

I saw a bottle of whisky on a small white table between the two windows. I started towards it. It was a Johnny Walker bottle, half full. I got it up, took a long drink from the neck. I put the bottle down again.

The whisky had a funny taste. While I was realising that it had a funny taste I saw a washbowl in the corner. I just made it to the washbowl before I vomited.

I got back to the bed and lay there. The vomiting had made me very weak, but the room seemed a little more real, a little less fantastic. I could see bars on the two windows, a heavy wooden chair, no other furniture but the white table with the doped whisky on it. There was a cupboard door, shut, probably locked.

The bed was a hospital bed and there were two leather straps attached to the sides, about where a man's wrists would be. I knew I was in some kind of a prison ward.

My left arm suddenly began to feel sore. I rolled up the loose sleeve, looked at half a dozen pin-pricks on the upper arm, and a black and blue circle around each one.

I had been shot so full of dope to keep me quiet that I was having the French fits coming out of it. That accounted for the smoke. The doped whisky was probably part of somebody else's cure.

I got up again and walked, kept on walking. After a while I drank a little water from the tap, kept it down, drank more. Half an hour or more of that and I was ready to talk to somebody.

The closet door was locked and the chair was too heavy for me. I stripped the bed, slid the mattress to one side. There was a mesh spring underneath, fastened at the top and bottom by heavy coil springs about nine inches long. It took me half an hour and much misery to work one of these loose.

I rested a little and drank a little more cold water and went over to the hinge side of the door.

I yelled 'Fire!' at the top of my voice, several times.

I waited, but not long. Steps ran along the hallway outside. The key jabbed into the door, the lock clicked. The hard-eyed little man in the short white coat dodged in furiously, his eyes on the bed.

I laid the coil spring on the angle of his jaw, then on the back of his head as he went down. I got him by the throat. He struggled a good deal. I used a knee on his face. It hurt my knee.

He didn't say how his face felt. I got a blackjack out of his right hip pocket and reversed the key in the door and locked it from the inside. There were other keys on the ring. One of them unlocked my closet. I looked in at my clothes.

I put them on slowly, with fumbling fingers. I yawned a great deal. The man on the floor didn't move.

I locked him in and left him.

From a wide silent hallway, with a parquetry floor and a narrow carpet down its middle, flat white oak banisters swept down in long curves to the entrance hall. There were closed doors, big, heavy, old-fashioned. No sound behind them. I went down the carpet runner, walking on the balls of my feet.

There were stained glass inner doors to a vestibule from which the front door opened. A telephone rang as I got that far. A man's voice answered it, from behind a half-open door through which light came out into the dim hall.

I went back, sneaked a glance, saw a man at a desk, talking into the phone. I waited until he hung up. Then I went in.

He had a pale, bony, high-crowned head, across which a thin wave of brown hair curled and was plastered to his skull. He had a long, pale, joyless face. His eyes jumped at me. His hand jumped towards a button on his desk.

I grinned, growled at him, 'Don't. I'm a desperate man, warden.' I showed him the blackjack.

His smile was as stiff as a frozen fish. His long pale hands made gestures like sick butterflies over the top of his desk. One of them began to drift towards a side drawer of the desk.

He worked his tongue loose. 'You've been a very sick man, sir. A very sick man. I wouldn't advise—'

I flicked the blackjack at his wandering hand. It drew into itself like a slug on a hot stone. I said, 'Not sick, warden, just doped within an inch of my reason. Out is what I want, and some clean whisky. Give.'

He made vague motions with his fingers. 'I'm Doctor Sundstrand,' he said. 'This is a private hospital—not a jail.'

'Whisky,' I croaked. 'I get all the rest. Private funny house. A lovely racket. Whisky.'

'In the medicine cabinet,' he said with a drifting, spent breath.

'Put your hands behind your head.'

'I'm afraid you'll regret this.' He put his hands behind his head.

I got to the far side of the desk, opened the drawer his hand had wanted to reach, took an automatic out of it. I put the blackjack away, went back round the desk to the medicine cabinet on the wall. There was a pint bottle of bond bourbon in it, three glasses. I took two of them.

I poured two drinks. 'You first, warden.'

'I—I don't drink. I'm a total abstainer,' he muttered, his hands still behind his head.

I took the blackjack out again. He put a hand down quickly, gulped from one of the glasses. I watched him. It didn't seem to hurt him. I smelled my dose, then put it down my throat. It worked, and I had another, then slipped the bottle into my coat pocket.

'OK,' I said. 'Who put me in here? Shake it up. I'm in a hurry.'

He hunched his shoulders down in the chair. He looked sick. 'A man named Galbraith signed as complaining witness. Strictly legal, I assure you. He is a police officer.'

I said, 'Since when can a cop sign as complaining witness on a psycho case?'

He didn't say anything.

'Who gave me the dope in the first place?'

'I wouldn't know that. I presume it has been going on a long time.'

I felt my chin. 'All of two days,' I said. 'They ought to have shot me. Less kick-back in the long run. So long, warden.'

As I went out he still had his hands behind his head.

Chief of Police Fulwider was a hammered-down, fattish heavyweight, with restless eyes and that shade of red hair that is almost pink. It was cut very short and his pink scalp glistened among the pink hairs. He wore a fawn-coloured flannel suit with patch pockets and lapped seams, cut as every tailor can't cut flannel.

He shook hands with me and turned his chair sideways and crossed his legs. That showed me French lisle socks at three or four dollars a pair, and hand-made English walnut brogues at fifteen to eighteen, Depression prices.

I figured that probably his wife had money.

'Ah,' he said, chasing my card over the glass top of his desk, 'down here on a job?'

'A little trouble,' I said. 'You can straighten it out, if you will.'

He stuck his chest out, waved a pink hand and lowered his voice a couple of notches.

'Trouble,' he said, 'is something our little town don't have a lot of. Our little city is small, but very, very clean. I look out of my west window and I see the Pacific Ocean. Nothing cleaner than that. On the north Arguello Boulevard and the foothills. On the east the finest little business section you would want to see and beyond it a paradise of well-kept homes and gardens. On the south—if I had a south window, which I don't have—I would see the finest little yacht harbour in the world, for a small yacht harbour.'

'I brought my trouble with me,' I said. 'That is, some of it. The rest went on ahead. A girl named Isobel Snare ran off from home in the big city and her dog was seen here. I found the dog, but the people who had the dog went to a lot of trouble to sew me up.'

'Is that so?' the Chief asked absently. His eyebrows crawled around on his forehead. I wasn't sure whether I was kidding him or he was kidding me. He had a right-looking bottle and two pony glasses on the desk, and a handful of cardamom seeds.

We had a drink and he cracked three or four of the cardamom seeds and we chewed them and looked at one another.

'Just tell me about it,' he said then. 'I can take it now.'

'Did you ever hear of a guy called Farmer Saint?'

'*Did* I?' He banged his desk and the cardamom seeds jumped. 'Why, there's a thousand reward on that bimbo. A bank stick-up, ain't he?'

I nodded, trying to look behind his eyes without seeming to. 'He and his sister work together. Diana is her name. They dress up like country folks and smack down small town banks, state banks. That's why he's called Farmer Saint. There's a grand on the sister too.'

'I would certainly like to put the sleeves on that pair,' the Chief said firmly.

'Then why the hell didn't you?' I asked him.

He didn't quite hit the ceiling, but he opened his mouth so wide I was afraid his lower jaw was going to fall in his lap. His eyes stuck out like peeled eggs. He shut his mouth with all the deliberation of a steam-shovel. It was a great act, if it was an act.

'Say that again,' he whispered.

I opened a folded newspaper I had with me and pointed to a column.

'Look at this Sharp killing. Your local paper didn't do so good on it. It says some unknown rang the department and the boys ran out and found a dead man in an empty house. That's a lot of noodles. I was there. Farmer Saint and his sister were there. Your cops were there when we were there.'

'Treachery!' he shouted suddenly. 'Traitors in the department.' His face was now as grey as arsenic flypaper. He poured two more drinks, with a shaking hand. It was my turn to crack the cardamom seeds.

He put his drink down in one piece and lunged for a mahogany call box on his desk. I caught the name Galbraith.

We didn't wait very long, but long enough for the Chief to have two more drinks. His face got a better colour.

Then the door opened and the big red-faced dick who had sapped me loafed through it, with a bulldog pipe clamped in his teeth and his hands in his pockets. He shouldered the door shut, leaned against it casually.

I said, 'Hullo, Sarge.'

He looked at me as if he would like to kick me in the face and not have to hurry about it.

'Badge!' the fat Chief yelled. 'Badge! Put it on the desk. You're fired!'

Galbraith went over to the desk slowly and put an elbow down on it, put his face about a foot from the Chief's nose.

'What was that crack?' he asked thickly.

'You had Farmer Saint under your hand and let him go,' the Chief yelled. 'You and that saphead Duncan. You let him stick a shotgun in your belly and get away. You're through. Fired. You ain't got no more job than a canned oyster. Gimme your badge!'

'Who the hell is Farmer Saint?' Galbraith asked, unimpressed, and blew pipe smoke in the Chief's face.

'He don't know,' the Chief whined at me. 'He don't know. That's the kind of material I got to work with.'

'What do you mean, work?' Galbraith enquired loosely.

The fat Chief jumped as though a bee had stung the end of his nose. Then he doubled a meaty fist and hit Galbraith's jaw with what looked like a lot of power. Galbraith's head moved about half an inch.

'Don't do that,' he said. 'You'll bust a gut and then where would the department be?'

Fulwider looked at me, to see how the show was going over. I had my mouth open and a blank expression on my face, like a farm boy at a Latin lesson.

Galbraith stuck a thick leg over a corner of the desk and knocked his pipe out, reached for the whisky and poured himself a drink in the Chief's glass. He wiped his lips, grinned. When he grinned he opened his mouth wide, and he had a mouth a dentist could have got both hands in, up to the elbows.

He said calmly to me, 'When me and Dunc crash the joint you was cold on the floor and the lanky guy was over you with a sap. The broad was on a window seat, with a lot of newspapers around her. OK. The lanky guy starts to tell us some yarn when a dog begins to howl out back and we look that way and the broad slips a sawn-off 12-gauge out of the newspapers and shows it to us. Well, what could we do except be nice? She couldn't have missed and we could. So the guy gets more guns out of his pants and they tie knots around us and stick us in a cupboard that has enough chloroform in it to make us quiet, without the ropes. After a while we hear 'em leave, in two cars. When we get loose the stiff has the place to hisself. So we fudge it a bit for the papers. We don't get no new line yet. How's it tie to yours?'

'Not bad,' I told him. 'As I remember the woman phoned for some law herself. But I could be mistaken. The rest of it ties in with me being sapped on the floor and not knowing anything about it.'

Galbraith gave me a nasty look. The Chief looked at his thumb.

'When I came to,' I said, 'I was in a private dope cure. Run by a man named Sundstrand. I was shot so full of dope myself I could have been Rockefeller's pet dime trying to spin myself.'

'That Sundstrand,' Galbraith said heavily. 'That guy's been a flea in our pants for a long time. Should we go out and push him in the face, Chief?'

The Chief looked at the whisky bottle. He said carefully, 'There's a grand each on this Saint and his sister. If we gather them in, how do we cut it?'

'You cut me out,' I said. 'I'm on a straight salary and expenses.'

Galbraith grinned. He teetered on his heels, grinning with thick amiability.

'Okydoke. We picked up your car. We'll use that to go in—just you and me.'

'Maybe you ought to have more help, Gal,' the Chief said doubtfully.

'Uh-uh. Just me and him's plenty. He's a tough baby, or he wouldn't be walkin' around.'

'Well, all right,' the Chief said brightly. 'And we'll just have a little drink on it.'

But he was still rattled. He forgot the cardamom seeds.

It was a cheerful spot by daylight. Tea-rose begonias made a solid mass under the front windows and pansies were a round carpet about the base of an acacia. A scarlet climbing rose covered a trellis to one side of the house, and a bronze-green humming-bird was prodding delicately in a mass of sweet peas that grew up the garage wall.

It looked like the home of a well-fixed elderly couple who had come to the ocean to get as much sun as possible in their old age.

Galbraith spat on my running-board and shook his pipe out and tickled the gate open, stamped up the path and flattened his thumb against a neat copper bell.

We waited. A grille opened in the door and a long sallow face looked out at us under a starched nurse's cap.

'Open up. It's the law,' the big cop growled.

A chain rattled and a bolt slid back. The door opened. The nurse was a six-footer with long arms and big hands, an ideal torturer's assistant. Something happened to her face and I saw she was smiling.

'Why, it's Mister Galbraith,' she chirped, in a voice that was high-pitched and throaty at the same time. 'Did you want to see Doctor?'

'Yeah, and sudden,' Galbraith growled, pushing past her.

The door of the office was shut. Galbraith kicked it open, with me at his heels and the big nurse chirping at mine.

Doctor Sundstrand, the total abstainer, was having a morning bracer out of a fresh whisky bottle. His bony mask of a face seemed to have a lot of lines in it that hadn't been there the night before.

He took his hand off the bottle hurriedly and gave us his frozen fish smile. He said fussily, 'What's this? What's this? I thought I gave orders—'

'Aw, pull your belly in,' Galbraith said, and yanked a chair near the desk. 'Dangle, sister.'

The nurse chirped something more and went back through the door. The door was shut. Doctor Sundstrand worked his eyes up and down my face and looked unhappy.

Galbraith put both his elbows on the desk and took hold of his bulging jowls with his fists. He stared fixedly, venomously, at the squirming doctor. After what seemed a very long time he said, almost softly, 'Where's Farmer Saint?'

The doctor's eyes popped wide. His greenish eyes began to look bilious.

'Don't stall!' Galbraith roared. 'We know all about your private hospital racket, the crook hideout you're runnin', the dope and women on the side. You made one slip too many when you hung a snatch on this shamus from the big town. Come on, where is Saint? And where's that girl?'

I remembered, quite casually, that I had not said anything about Isobel Snare in front of Galbraith—if that was the girl he meant.

Doctor Sundstrand's hand flopped about on his desk. Sheer astonishment seemed to be adding a final touch of paralysis to his uneasiness.

'Where are they?' Galbraith yelled again.

The door opened and the big nurse fussed in again. 'Now,

Mister Galbraith, the patients. Please remember the patients, Mister Galbraith.'

'Go climb up your thumb,' Galbraith told her, over his shoulder.

She hovered by the door. Sundstrand found his voice at last. It was a mere wisp of a voice. It said wearily, 'As if you didn't know.'

Then his darting hand swept into his smock, and out again, with a gun glistening in it. Galbraith threw himself sideways, clean out of the chair. The doctor shot at him twice, missed twice. My hand touched a gun, but didn't draw it. Galbraith laughed on the floor and his big right hand snatched at his armpit, came up with a Luger. It looked like my Luger. It went off, just once.

Nothing changed in the doctor's long face. I didn't see where the bullet hit him. His head came down and hit the desk and his gun made a thud on the floor. He lay with his face on the desk, motionless.

Galbraith pointed his gun at me, and got up off the floor. I looked at the gun again. I was sure it was my gun.

'That's a swell way to get information,' I said aimlessly. 'I suppose this whole scene was framed just to put the chill on Doc.'

'He shot first, didn't he?'

'Yeah,' I said thinly. 'He shot first.'

The nurse was sidling along the wall towards me. No sound had come from her since Sundstrand pulled his act. She was almost at my side. Suddenly, much too late, I saw the flash of knuckles on her good right hand, and hair on the back of the hand.

I dodged, but not enough. A crunching blow seemed to split my head wide open. I brought up against the wall, my knees full of water. Galbraith leered at me.

'Not so very smart,' I said. 'You're still holding my Luger. That sort of spoils the plant, doesn't it?'

'I see you get the idea, shamus.'

The chirpy-voiced nurse said, in a blank pause, 'Jeeze, the guy's got a jaw like an elephant's foot. Damn' if I didn't split a knuck on him. Should I try one more swing?'

'What for? He didn't go for his gat, and he's too tough for you, baby. Lead is his meat.'

I said, 'You ought to shave baby twice a day on this job.'

The nurse grinned, pushed the starched cap and the stringy blonde wig askew on a bullet head. She—or more properly he—reached a gun from under the nurse's white uniform.

Galbraith said, 'It was self-defence, see? You tangled with the doctor, but he shot first. Be nice and me and Dunc will try to remember it that way.'

I rubbed my jaw with my left hand. 'Listen, Sarge. I can take a joke as well as the next fellow. You sapped me in that house on Carolina Street and didn't tell about it. Neither did I. I figured you had reasons and you'd let me in on them at the right time. Maybe I can guess what the reasons are. I think you know where Saint is, or can find out. Saint knows where the Snare girl is because he had her dog. Let's put a little more into this deal, something for both of us.'

'We've got ours, sap. I promised the doctor I'd bring you back and let him play with you. I put Dunc in here in the nurse's rig to handle you for him. But *he* was the one we really wanted to handle.'

'All right,' I said. 'What do I get out of it?'

'Maybe a little more living.'

I said, 'Yeah. Don't think I'm kidding you—but look at that little window in the wall behind you.'

Galbraith didn't move, didn't take his eyes off me. A thick sneer curved his lips.

Duncan, the female impersonator, looked—and yelled.

A small, square, tinted glass window high up in the corner of the back wall had swung open quite silently. I was looking at it, past Galbraith's ear, straight at the black snout of a tommy-gun, on the sill, at the two hard black eyes behind the gun.

A voice I had last heard soothing a dog said, 'How's to drop the rod, sister? And you at the desk—grab a cloud.'

The big cop's mouth sucked for air. Then his whole face tightened and he jerked around and the Luger gave one hard, sharp cough.

I dropped to the floor as the tommy-gun cut loose in a short burst. Galbraith crumpled beside the desk, fell on his back with his legs twisted. Blood came out of his nose and mouth.

The cop in nurse's uniform turned as white as the starched cap. His gun bounced. His hands tried to claw at the ceiling.

There was a queer, stunned silence.

A door opened and shut distinctly and running steps came along the hall. The door of our room was pushed wide. Diana Saint came in with a brace of automatics in her hands.

I got up off the floor, keeping my hands in sight. She tossed her voice calmly at the window, without looking towards it.

'OK, Jerry. I can hold them.'

Saint's head and shoulders and his submachine-gun went away from the frame of the window, leaving blue sky and the thin, distinct branches of a tall tree.

In the room we were five statues, two fallen.

Somebody had to move. The situation called for two more killings. From Saint's angle I couldn't see it any other way. There had to be a clean-up.

The gag hadn't worked when it wasn't a gag. I tried it again when it was. I looked past the woman's shoulder, kicked a hard grin on to my face, said hoarsely, 'Hullo, Mike. Just in time.'

It didn't fool her, of course, but it made her mad. She stiffened her body and snapped a shot at me from the right-hand gun. It was a big gun for a woman and it jumped. The other gun jumped with it. I didn't see where the shot went.

I wasn't too nice about knocking the guns out of her hands. I kicked the door shut, reached up and yanked the key around, then scrambled back from a high-heeled shoe that was doing its best to smash my nose for me.

Duncan dived for his gun on the floor.

'Watch that little window, if you want to live,' I snarled at him.

Then I was behind the desk, dragging the phone away from Doctor Sundstrand's dead body, dragging it as far from the line of the door as the cord would let me. I lay down on the floor with it and started to dial, on my stomach.

Diana's eyes came alive on the phone. She screeched: 'They've got me, Jerry! They've got me!'

The machine-gun began to tear the door apart as I bawled into the ear of a bored desk sergeant.

Pieces of plaster and wood flew like fists at an Irish wedding. Slugs jerked the body of Doctor Sundstrand as though a chill was shaking him back to life. I grabbed Diana's guns and started in on the door for our side. Through a wide crack I could see cloth. I shot at that.

I couldn't see what Duncan was doing. Then I knew. A shot that couldn't have come through the door smacked Diana Saint square on the end of her chin.

She went down again, stayed down.

Another shot that didn't come through the door lifted my hat. I rolled and yelled at Duncan. His gun moved in a stiff arc, following me. His mouth was an animal snarl.

I yelled again.

Four round patches of red appeared in a diagonal line across the nurse's uniform, chest high. They spread even in the short time it took Duncan to fall.

There was a siren somewhere. It was my siren, coming my way, getting louder. Saint had to go. I heard his step running away down the hall. A door slammed. A car started out back in an alley.

I crawled over to the woman and looked at blood on her face and hair and soft soggy places on the front of her coat. I touched her face. She opened her eyes slowly, as if the lids were very heavy.

'Jerry—' she whispered.

'Dead,' I lied grimly. 'Where's Isobel Snare, Diana?'

The eyes closed. Tears glistened, the tears of the dying.

'Where's Isobel, Diana?' I pleaded. 'Be regular and tell me. I'm no cop. I'm her friend. Tell me, Diana.'

I put tenderness and wistfulness into it, everything I had.

The eyes half opened. The whisper came again: 'Jerry—' The lips moved once more, breathed a word that sounded like 'Monty.'

That was all. She died.

I stood up slowly and listened to the sirens.

It was getting late and lights were going on here and there in a tall office building across the street. I had been in Fulwider's office all the afternoon. I had told my story twenty times. It was all true—what I told.

The fat Chief was sweaty and suspicious. His coat was off and his armpits were black and his short red hair curled as if it had been singed. Not knowing how much or little I knew he didn't dare lead me. All he could do was yell at me and whine at me by turns, and try to get me drunk in between.

I was getting drunk and liking it.

He took hold of his jaw and cranked it. 'Damn funny,' he sneered. 'Four dead ones on the floor and you not even nicked.'

'I was the only one,' I said, 'that lay down on the floor while still healthy.'

He took hold of his right ear and worried that. 'You been here three days,' he howled. 'In them three days we got more crime than in three years before you come. It ain't human.'

'You can't blame me, Chief,' I grumbled. 'I came down here to look for a girl. I'm still looking for her. I didn't tell Saint and his sister to hide out in your town. I didn't shoot Doc Sundstrand before anything could be got out of him. I still haven't any idea why the phoney nurse was planted there.'

'Nor me,' Fulwider yelled. 'But it's my job that's shot full of holes. For all the chance I got to get out of this I might as well go fishin' right now.'

I took another drink, hiccupped cheerfully. 'Don't say that, Chief,' I pleaded. 'You cleaned the town up once and you can do it again.'

He took a turn around the office and tried to punch a hole in the end wall, then slammed himself back in his chair.

'I'll make a deal with you,' he growled. 'You run on back to San Angelo and I'll forget it was your gun croaked Sundstrand.'

'That's not a nice thing to say to a man that's trying to earn his living, Chief. You know how it happened to be my gun.'

His face looked grey again, for a moment. He measured me for a coffin. Then the mood passed and he smacked his desk, said heartily, 'You're right. I couldn't do that, could I? You still got to find that girl, ain't you? OK, you run on back to the hotel and get some rest. I'll work on it tonight and see you in the a.m.'

I took another short drink, which was all there was left in the bottle. I felt fine. I shook hands with him twice and staggered out of his office.

I went on down the sidestreets to the ocean front, walked along the wide cement walk towards the two amusement piers.

It was getting dusk now. Lights on the piers came out. Mast-head lights were lit on the small yachts riding at anchor behind the yacht harbour breakwater. In a white barbecue stand a man tickled wienies with a long fork and droned, 'Get hungry, folks. Nice hot doggies here. Get hungry, folks.'

I lit a cigarette and stood there looking out to sea. Very suddenly, far out, lights shone from a big ship. I watched them, but they didn't move.

I went over to the hot dog man.

'Anchored?' I asked him, pointing.

He looked around the end of his booth, wrinkled his nose with contempt.

'Hell, that's the gambling boat. The Cruise to Nowhere, they call the act, because it don't go no place. Yes, sir, that's the good ship *Montecito*. How about a nice warm doggie?'

I put a quarter on his counter. 'Have one yourself,' I said softly.

I had no gun. I went on back to the hotel to get my spare.

The dying Diana Saint had said 'Monty'.

Perhaps she just hadn't lived long enough to say 'Montecito'.

I was tailed from the hotel, but not very far. Of course the clean little city didn't have enough crime for the dicks to be very good shadows . . .

It was a long ride for forty cents. The water taxi, an old speedboat without trimmings, slid through the anchored yachts and rounded the breakwater. The swell hit us. All the company I had besides the tough-looking citizen at the wheel was two spooning couples who began to peck at each other's faces as soon as the darkness folded down.

The portholes of the *Montecito* got large and the taxi swept out in a wide turn, tipped to an angle of forty-five degrees, and careened neatly to the side of a brightly-lit stage.

A sloe-eyed boy in a tight blue mess jacket and a gangster mouth handed the girls out, swept their escorts with a keen glance, sent them on up. The look he gave me told me something about him. The way he bumped into my gun holster told me more.

'Nix,' he said softly. 'Nix.'

He jerked his chin at the taxi man. The taxi man dropped a short noose over a bitt, turned his wheel a little and climbed on the stage. He got behind me.

'Nix,' the one in the mess jacket purred. 'No gats on this boat, mister. Sorry.'

'Part of my clothes,' I told him. 'I'm a private dick. I'll check it.'

The taxi man hooked a wrist through my right arm. I shrugged.

'Back in the boat,' the taxi man growled behind me. 'I owe you forty cents, mister. Come on.'

I got back into the boat.

Mess jacket's sleek, silent smile was the last thing I saw as the taxi cast off and hit the swell on the way back. I hated to leave that smile.

The way back seemed longer. I didn't speak to the taxi man and he didn't speak to me. As I got out on to the float at the pier he sneered at my back, 'Some other night when we ain't so busy, shamus.'

Half a dozen customers waiting to go out stared at me. I went past them, past the door of the waiting-room on the float, towards the steps at the landward end.

A big red-headed roughneck in dirty sneakers and tarry pants and a torn blue jersey straightened from the railing and bumped into me casually. I stopped, got set. He said softly, ''Smatter, dick? No soap on the hell ship?'

'Do I have to tell you?'

'I'm a guy that can listen.'

'Who are you?'

'Just call me Red.'

'Out of the way, Red. I'm busy.'

He smiled sadly, touched my left side. 'The gat's kind of bulgy under the light suit,' he said. 'Want to get on board? It can be done, if you got a reason.'

'How much is the reason?' I asked him.

'Fifty bucks. Ten more if you bleed in my boat.'

I started away. 'Twenty-five,' he said quickly. 'Maybe you come back with friends, huh?'

I went four steps away from him before I half turned, said, 'Sold,' and went on.

At the foot of the bright amusement pier there was a flaring Tango Parlour, jammed full even at that still early hour. I went into it, leaned against a wall.

A large blueness took form beside me and I smelled tar. A soft, deep, sad voice said, 'Need help out there?'

'I'm looking for a girl, but I'll look alone. What's your racket?' I didn't look at him.

'A dollar here, a dollar there. I like to eat. I was on the cops but they bounced me.'

I liked his telling me that. 'You must have been levelling,' I said, and watched the house player slip his card across with his thumb over the wrong number, watched the counter man get his own thumb in the same spot and hold the card up.

I could feel Red's grin. 'I see you been around our little city.'

I got my wallet out and slipped a twenty and a five from it, passed them over in a wad. They went into a tarry pocket.

Red said, 'Thanks,' softly and walked away. I gave him a small start and went after him. He was easy to follow by his size, even in a crowd.

We went past the yacht harbour and the second amusement pier and beyond that the lights got fewer and the crowd thinned to nothing. A short black pier stuck out into the water with boats moored all along it.

He stopped almost at the end of it, at the head of a wooden ladder.

'I'll bring her down to here,' he said.

'Listen,' I said urgently. 'I have to phone a man. I forgot.'

'Can do. Come on.'

He led the way farther along the pier, knelt, rattled keys on a chain, and opened a padlock. He lifted a small trap and took a phone out, listened to it.

'Still working,' he said with a grin in his voice. 'Must belong to some crooks. Don't forget to snap the lock back on.'

He slipped away silently into the darkness. I listened to water slapping the piles of the pier, the occasional whir of a seagull in the gloom. Then far off a motor roared and kept on roaring.

I dialled a number, asked for Chief Fulwider. He had gone home. I dialled another number, got a woman, asked her for the Chief, said I was headquarters.

I waited again. Then I heard the fat Chief's voice. It sounded full of baked potato.

'Yeah? Can't a guy even eat? Who is it?'

'Me, Chief. Saint is on the *Montecito*. Too bad that's over your line.'

He began to yell like a wild man. I hung up in his face, put the phone back in its zinc-lined cubbyhole and snapped the padlock. I went down the ladder to Red.

There were no floodlights on the seaward side of the ship.

Red cut his motor to half of nothing and curved in under the overhang of the stern, sidled up to the greasy plates as coyly as a clubman in a hotel lobby.

Double iron doors loomed high over us, forward a little from the slimy links of a chain cable. The speedboat scuffed the *Montecito*'s ancient plates and the sea-water slapped loosely at the bottom of the speedboat under our feet. The shadow of the big ex-cop rose over me. A coiled rope flicked against the dark, caught on something, and fell back into the boat. Red pulled it tight, made a turn around something on the engine cowling.

I took the wheel and held the nose of the speedboat against the slippery hull, and Red reached for an iron ladder flat to the side of the ship, hauled himself up into the darkness.

After a while something creaked up above and feeble yellow light trickled out into the foggy air. The outline of a heavy door showed, and Red's crouched head against the light.

I went up the ladder after him. It was hard work. It landed me panting in a sour, littered hold full of cases and barrels. Rats skittered out of sight in the dark corners. The big man put his lips to my ear: 'From here we got an easy way to the boiler-room catwalk. From the boiler-room I'll show you a ventilator with no grating in it. Goes to the boat deck. Then it's all yours. Will you come back fast?'

'I ought to make a good splash from the boat deck.' I fished more bills out of my wallet, pushed them at him. 'Here.'

He shook his red head.

'Uh-huh. That's for the trip back.'

'I'm buying it now,' I said. 'Even if I don't use it. Take the dough before I bust out crying.'

'Well—thanks, pal. You're a right guy.'

We went among the cases and barrels. The yellow light came from a passage beyond, and we went along the passage to a narrow iron door. That led to the catwalk. We sneaked along it, down an oily steel ladder, heard the slow hiss of oil-burners and went among mountains of iron towards the sound.

Around a corner we looked at a short, dirty Italian in a purple silk shirt who sat in a wired-together office chair, under a naked bulb, and read the paper with the aid of steel-rimmed spectacles and a black forefinger.

Red said gently, 'Hi, Shorty. How's all the little bambinos?'

The Italian opened his mouth and Red hit him. We put him down on the floor and tore his purple shirt into shreds for ties and a gag.

'You ain't supposed to hit a guy with glasses on,' Red said. 'But the idea is you make a hell of a racket goin' up a ventilator—to a guy down here. Upstairs they won't hear nothing.'

I said that was the way I would like it, and we left the Italian bound up on the floor and found the ventilator that had no grating in it. I shook hands with Red, said I hoped to see him again, and started up the ladder inside the ventilator.

It was cold and black and the foggy air rushed down it and the way up seemed a long way. After three minutes that felt like an hour I reached the top and poked my head out cautiously.

I listened, but didn't hear any police-boat sirens. I got out of the ventilator, lowered myself to the deck.

Whispering came from a necking couple huddled under a boat. They didn't pay any attention to me. I went along the deck past the closed doors of three or four cabins. There was a little light behind the shutters of two of them. I listened, didn't hear anything but the merry-making of the customers down below on the main deck.

I dropped into a dark shadow, took a lungful of air and let it out in a howl—the snarling howl of a grey timber wolf, lonely and hungry and far from home, and mean enough for seven kinds of trouble.

The deep-toned woof-woofing of a police dog answered me.

I straightened and unshipped my gun and ran towards the barking. The noise came from a cabin on the other side of the deck.

I put an ear to the door, listened to a man's voice soothing the dog. The dog stopped barking and growled once or twice, then was silent. A key turned in the door I was touching.

I dropped away from it, down on one knee. The door opened a foot and a sleek head came forward past its edge. Light from a hooded deck lamp made a shine on the black hair.

I stood up and slammed the head with my gun barrel. The man fell softly out of the doorway into my arms. I dragged him back into the cabin, pushed him down on a made-up berth.

I shut the door again, locked it. A small, wide-eyed girl crouched on the other berth.

I said, 'Hullo, Miss Snare. I've had a lot of trouble finding you. Want to go home?'

Farmer Saint rolled over and sat up, holding his head. Then he was very still, staring at me with his sharp black eyes. His mouth had a strained smile, almost good-humoured.

I ranged the cabin with a glance, didn't see where the dog was, but saw an inner door behind which he could be. I looked at the girl again.

She was not much to look at, like most of the people that make most of the trouble. She was crouched on the berth with her knees drawn up and hair falling over one eye. She wore a knitted dress and golf socks and sports shoes with wide tongues that fell down over the instep. Her knees were bare and bony under the hem of the dress. She looked like a schoolgirl.

I went over Saint for a gun, didn't find one. He grinned at me.

The girl lifted her hand and threw her hair back. She looked at me as if I was a couple of blocks away. Then her breath caught and she began to cry.

'We're married,' Saint said softly. 'She thinks you're set to blow holes in me. That was a smart trick with the wolf howl.'

I didn't say anything. I listened. No noises outside.

'How'd you know where to come?' Saint asked.

'Diana told me—before she died,' I said brutally.

His eyes looked hurt.

'I don't believe it, shamus.'

'You ran out and left her in the ditch. What would you expect?'

'I figured the cops wouldn't bump a woman and I could make some kind of a deal on the outside. Who got her?'

'One of Fulwider's cops. You got him.'

His head jerked back and a wild look came over his face, then went away. He smiled sideways at the weeping girl.

'Hullo, sugar. I'll get you clear.' He looked back at me. 'Suppose I come in without a scrap. Is there a way for her to get loose?'

'You got her into it,' I said. 'You can't get her out. That's part of the pay-off.'

He nodded slowly, looked down at the floor between his feet. The girl stopped crying long enough to mop at her cheeks, then started in again.

'Fulwider know I'm here?' Saint asked me slowly.

'Yeah.'

He shrugged. 'That's OK from your end. Sure. Only I'll never get to talk, if Fulwider pinches me. If I could get to talk to a DA I could maybe convince him *she's* not hep to my stuff.'

'You could have thought of that, too,' I said heavily. 'You didn't have to go back to Sundstrand's and cut loose with your stutter-gun.'

He threw his head back and laughed. 'No? Suppose you paid a guy ten grand for protection and he crossed you up by grabbing your wife and sticking her in a crooked dope hospital and telling you to run along far away and be good, or the tide would wash her up on the beach? What would you do—smile, or trot over with some heavy iron to talk to the guy?'

'She wasn't there then,' I said. 'You were just kill-screwy. And if you hadn't hung on to that dog until he killed a man, the protection wouldn't have been scared into selling you out.'

'I like dogs,' Saint said quietly. 'I'm a nice guy when I'm not workin', but I can get shoved around just so much.'

I listened. Still no noises on deck outside.

'Listen,' I said quickly. 'If you want to play ball with me, I've got a boat at the back door and I'll try to get the girl home before they want her. What happens to you is past me.'

The girl said suddenly, in a shrill, little-girl voice, 'I don't want to go home! I won't go home!'

'A year from now you'll thank me,' I snapped at her.

'He's right, sugar,' Saint said. 'Better beat it with him.'

'I won't,' the girl shrilled angrily. 'I just won't. That's all.'

Out of the silence on the deck something hard slammed the outside of the door. A grim voice shouted, 'Open up! It's the law!'

I backed swiftly to the door, keeping my eyes on Saint. I spoke back over my shoulder.

'Fulwider there?'

'Yeah,' the Chief's fat voice growled.

'Listen, Chief. Saint's in here and he's ready to surrender. There's a girl here with him, the one I told you about. So come in easy, will you?'

'Right,' the Chief said. 'Open the door.'

I twisted the key, jumped across the cabin and put my back against the inner partition, beside the door behind which the dog was moving around now, growling a little.

The outer door whipped open. Two men I hadn't seen before charged in with drawn guns. The fat Chief was behind them. Briefly, before he shut the door, I caught a glimpse of ship's uniforms.

The two dicks jumped on Saint, slammed him around, put cuffs on him. Then they stepped back beside the Chief. Saint grinned at them, with blood trickling down his lower lip.

Fulwider looked at me reprovingly and moved a cigar around in his mouth. Nobody seemed to take any interest in the girl.

One of the dicks said roughly, 'Put the heater away, shamus.'

'Try and make me,' I told him.

He started forward, but the Chief waved him back. The other dick watched Saint, looked at nothing else.

'How'd you find him then?' Fulwider wanted to know.

'Not by taking his money to hide him out,' I said.

Nothing changed in Fulwider's face. His voice became almost lazy.

'Oh, oh, you've been peekin',' he said very gently.

I said disgustedly, 'Just what kind of a sap did you and your gang take me for? Your clean little town stinks. It's the well-known whited sepulchre. A crook sanctuary where the hot rods can lie low—if they pay off nice and don't pull any local capers—and where they can jump off for Mexico in a fast boat, if the finger waves towards them.'

The Chief said very carefully, 'Any more?'

'Yeah,' I shouted. 'I've saved it for you too damn long. *You* had me doped until I was half goofy and stuck me in a private jail. When that didn't hold me *you* worked a plant up with Galbraith and Duncan to have my gun kill Sundstrand, your helper, and then have me killed resisting some arrest. Saint spoilt that party for you and saved my life. Not intending to, perhaps, but he did it. *You* knew all along where the little Snare girl was. She was Saint's wife and you were holding her yourself to make him stay in line. Hell, why do you suppose I tipped you he was out here? That was something you *didn't* know!'

The dick who had tried to make me put up my gun said, 'Now, Chief. We better make it fast. The Feds—'

Fulwider's jaw shook. His face was grey and his eyes were far back in his head. The cigar twitched in his fat mouth. 'Wait a minute,' he said thickly. Then to me: 'Well—why did you tip me?'

'To get you where you're no more law than Billy the Kid,' I said, 'and see if you have the guts to go through with murder on the high seas.'

Saint laughed. He shot a low, snarling whistle between his teeth. A tearing animal growl answered him. The door beside me crashed open as though a mule had kicked it. The big police dog came through the opening in a looping spring that carried him clear across the cabin. The grey body twisted mid-air. A gun banged harmlessly.

'Eat 'em up, Voss!' Saint yelled. 'Eat 'em alive, boy!'

The cabin filled with gunfire. The snarling of the dog blended with a thick, choked scream. Fulwider and one of the dicks were down on the floor and the dog was at Fulwider's throat.

The girl screamed and plunged her face into a pillow. Saint slid softly down from the bunk and lay on the floor with blood running slowly down his neck.

The dick who hadn't gone down jumped to one side, almost fell headlong on the girl's berth, then caught his balance and pumped bullets into the dog's long grey body—wildly, without pretence of aim.

The dick on the floor pushed at the dog. The dog almost bit his hand off. The man yelled. Feet pounded on the deck. Yelling outside. Something was running down my face that tickled. My head felt funny, but I didn't know what had hit me.

I got the dog off Fulwider and I saw where a stray bullet had drilled the Chief's forehead between the eyes, with the delicate exactness of pure chance.

The standing dick's gun hammer clicked on a discharged shell. He cursed, started to reload frantically.

I touched the blood on my face and looked at it. It seemed very black. The light in the cabin seemed to be failing.

Then all the lights went out very slowly, as in a theatre just as the curtain goes up. Just as it got quite dark my head hurt me, but I didn't know then that a bullet had creased my skull.

I woke up two days later in the hospital. I was there three weeks. Saint didn't live long enough to hang, but he lived long enough to tell his story. He must have told it well, because they let Mrs Jerry (Farmer) Saint and her dog go home to her aunt. I never saw her again.

There were a lot of new faces around the City Hall, I heard. One of them was a big red-headed detective sergeant who said he owed me twenty-five dollars but had had to use it to buy a new suit when he got his job back. He said he would pay me out of his first cheque. I said I would try to wait.

DEAD MAN'S HEAD

Robert Leslie Bellem

Los Angeles was the locale for another highly popular hardboiled dick, Dan Turner, known as the Hollywood Detective. Set against the back-drop of the film studios, his cases in the main involved people in the business, ranging from movie moguls to pretty young starlets who got mixed up in every kind of crime from theft to blackmail and even murder. All Dan's stories were told in the first person, showing him to be a flippant, tough man of action, irresistible to women, although he treated them all with the same kind of casual brutality he dished out to anyone who crossed or threatened him. The Hollywood Detective made his debut in the June 1934 issue of Spicy Detective Stories, *a pulp with even more lurid and suggestive covers than its contemporaries. The text of Dan's slam-bang adventures was illustrated with pictures of beautiful girls constantly wrestling to keep on their flimsy clothing, and as a result the stories became so popular that at their peak they were featured in no less than three pulps as well as a monthly,* Dan Turner, Hollywood Detective, *solely dedicated to his particular brand of showbiz sex and violence. No other private eye enjoyed quite such fame.*

The racy dialogue and titillation of the Dan Turner stories attracted a number of unexpected admirers, including the famous humorist S. J. Perelman, who wrote an article about the sleuth in the New Yorker *in which he described him as 'the apotheosis of all private eyes—out of Ma Baker by Dashiell Hammett's Sam Spade'. Perelman, who later wrote a wonderful spoof on the whole hardboiled genre entitled 'Fare-well, My Lovely Appetizer', featuring a detective called Mike Noonan, was not one of those who complained about the stories under the mistaken impression that they were intended to be taken seriously. He shared the more commonplace view as expressed by the pulp historian Stephen Mertz when writing the epitaph to the Dan Turner saga in the summer of 1950. 'The whole series,' he wrote, 'provided Bellem with an ongoing vehicle for constantly twisting fresh, irreverent, funny angles out of the Hammett/Chandler tradition.'*

Robert Leslie Bellem (1894–1968) in all probability knew Los Angeles even better than Raymond Chandler, having lived there since the early 1920s, working as a newspaper reporter, radio announcer and occasional film extra. Thanks to this inside knowledge, and the fact that he kept his descriptions of places to the minimum in favour of rapid-fire action, the authenticity of the milieu he describes is never in doubt. Like so many of the pulp writers, Bellem was enormously productive, often writing all the stories in Dan Turner, Hollywood Detective *under various pen-names, as well as finding time to contribute to other crime and mystery magazines. After the demise of the pulps, he turned naturally to scriptwriting for TV and wrote for a number of shows including* Dick Tracy, 77 Sunset Strip *and* Superman. *(By coincidence, at the time of writing, plans have been announced in Los Angeles by Fries Distribution Co. to film a Dan Turner series for TV.) Today, the Hollywood Detective's fame may be somewhat less than that of his contemporaries, but his importance to the genre has been acknowledged by several authorities, including pulp historian Ron Goulart who referred to him in 1988 as 'a blownup version of Race Williams and anticipation of Spillane's Mike Hammer'. The horrifying opening scene in the case of the 'Dead Man's Head', from* Spicy Detective Stories *of August 1935, is something of an anticipation, too—in particular, of one of the most gruesome moments in that classic movie about Thirties crime,* The Godfather Part II.

*   *   *

I opened the package and a human head rolled out into my lap. A man's head—with a bullet-hole between the eyes.

It was late at night, in my apartment. I'd been to see Chaplin's latest picture at the Chinese, and when I got home I found a bundle wrapped in brown paper outside the door of my flat. I picked it up and carried it in.

There weren't any postage stamps on it; no express-tags, either. Evidently someone had delivered it personally. Printed across the front was: 'For Dan Turner, private detective'. That was all. No sender's name; no return address.

I cut the strings and unwrapped the bundle. And that's when the severed head rolled spang into my lap.

It startled hell out of me. I said: 'What the hell!' and jumped to my feet. The head hit the floor with a gruesome bounce. It rolled halfway across my living-room rug. Then it came to rest, face upward. A damned nasty sight.

For a minute I was shaky as hell. I reached for a bottle of Vat 69 and tilted it down my throat. That made me feel a little better, but not much. I walked over and picked up the severed head.

There wasn't any blood around the bullet-wound in its forehead. None at the neck, either. That had all been washed away, nice and clean. I took one good gander at the white, cold features; and I recognised the face right away.

It was the head of Skinny Arkle. Maybe you remember him. He was a big-shot screen comedian back in the silent days. Skinny Arkle had been even funnier than his name. He'd been tops in the old pie-throwing class, and the way he used to pop his false teeth out of his mouth and fold up his face kept the whole country in stitches. But at the height of his popularity, Skinny Arkle had got himself in a hell of a jam.

He'd gone on a binge in San Diego with an obscure extra dame named Nancy Norward. He and the Norward girl had got plastered together—and the dame kicked the bucket. They'd tried to pin her death on Skinny Arkle, but a jury finally decided she'd cashed in from acute alcoholism coupled with gizzard trouble or something. Anyhow, they turned Skinny loose.

Just the same, the scandal had cooked Skinny Arkle's goose in the movies. All the studios blacklisted him; the stink had given Hollywood too much of a black eye, so Skinny had to take the rap—be the goat.

He'd faded out of pictures; hadn't appeared in a single film since the mess. For a while he went back to his native Jugoslavia; then he returned to Hollywood and married a cute kid named Kitty Calvert—a wren with red hair and a shape like seven million bucks. She was an Alta-mount semi-star, and she dragged down enough cookies in her weekly pay-envelope to keep herself and Skinny well fixed. For that matter, it was rumoured that Skinny himself had salted away a nice stack of geetus from the days when he was in the big dough.

Well, that was Skinny Arkle's history as I remembered it. And now, here was his decapitated head grinning at me from my living-room floor—with a bullet-hole in its brain.

I picked up the head and put it on my library table. Then I grabbed for my phone. I dialled the home number of my friend, Dave Donaldson of the homicide squad. When he answered, I said: 'This is Dan Turner. Listen, Dave—something screwy has happened.' I told him.

Dave said: 'For God's sake! Say—you're not drunk, are you? You haven't got pink elephants, have you?'

'Hell, no. This is on the level,' I told him.

He said: 'Cripes! Meet me down at headquarters in fifteen minutes. Bring that head with you!'

I said: 'Okay,' and hung up. Then all of a sudden I thought I heard a sound outside my door.

I was nervous anyhow. I had the jitters. I dragged out the .32 automatic I always carry in a shoulder-holster, and I dived for the door.

There was a tall, statuesque blonde bimbo standing outside my door for some while. She looked scared as hell when I popped out at her. She said: 'Oh-h-h—!' in a sort of muffled gasp.

I said: 'Who the hell are you? What do you want?'

'I—I'm looking for Dan Turner,' she answered me.

I looked her over. She seemed worried, all right. But she was gorgeous, too—in a flashy sort of way. Her blonde head came above my shoulder, and I'm over six-feet-two. At a guess, I'd say she was close to thirty—but she wore a damned good make-up that made her look younger. And her figure was something to remember.

She wasn't skinny, like a lot of tall dames. She wasn't too hefty, either. Just well-proportioned for her size. Sleek and slinky! Every lithe contour, every curve exactly right.

I said: 'Well, kiddo, I'm sorry you're worried, but I haven't got time to talk to you now. See me at my office tomorrow.'

She said: 'No! You've got to listen to me right now, Mr Turner! You must!'

I thought of my date with Donaldson at headquarters in fifteen minutes. I said: 'Sorry, sister. You'll have to excuse me.'

'You—you mean you won't listen to me?'

'Sure I'll listen to you. Tomorrow.'

Her eyes got sort of wild-looking. She said: 'I'll *make* you listen!' And before I could stop her she rumpled up her yellow hair and ripped at the front of her dress. She said: 'I'll scream and tell people you attacked me!'

'Hell!' I said. 'If it's that important, go ahead and spill your story. But cover yourself up or maybe you'll have something to scream about.'

I reached over and pulled her frock together. My fingers were tingling at the near contact.

The girl said: 'I—I'm Constance Calvert. I'm Kitty Calvert's sister. Kitty Calvert, the Altamount star. She's Skinny Arkle's wife.'

I stiffened. 'Yeah?'

'Yes. And I'm worried for Kitty. Afraid for her. Skinny Arkle and she have had a terrible row. Skinny left after the fight. That was three days ago. He left, threatening to come back and m-murder Kitty. We haven't seen him since, but I'm frightened. I want you to find him—'

I grabbed her by the arm and said: 'Come on in my apartment. I want to show you something. You won't have to worry about Skinny Arkle any more.'

I pulled her into my living-room. She saw Skinny Arkle's severed head on my table. She went white. 'Oh, my God!' she choked. And then damn' if she didn't faint!

She fell sprawling on the floor, and the torn front of her dress gaped open. White skin peeped from the ripped frock.

I said: 'What the hell—!' and leaned over her, lifted her up. I carried her into the next room, put her on the divan. She was dead to the world. I didn't know how long it would take me to bring her round—but I didn't have time, just then. I had to scram down to headquarters to keep my date with Donaldson.

On the other hand it struck me that this blonde baby, Constance Calvert, might be a key to the whole business.

It was stretching the long leg of coincidence to think she had just accidentally come to me the same night I'd received Arkle's decapitated noggin. She was mixed up in the deal some way. Maybe she was the one who'd brought that package and left it at my door!

Well, I couldn't take her down to headquarters with me. Not when she was unconscious. But I didn't want her to get away. So I used a trick I'd pulled many a time before.

I stripped the dress off her limp form, and took her shoes and chiffon stockings off while I was at it. The whole business got me hot under the collar. But I stuck to my job and pretty soon I had her down to black lace underthings.

She was a hell of a sweet number. Her skin was as smooth and warm as new cream, and she had what it takes to drive a man utsnay. But I didn't have time to be driven utsnay, so I covered her with a blanket and left her.

I carried her duds out with me. I picked up Skinny's head, wrapped it in the brown paper, and went down to my jalopy. Then I drove to beat hell.

Dave Donaldson was waiting outside headquarters. We went into his office and I showed him the head. He said: 'For Cripes' sake! It's Arkle, all right. Now, who in hell—?'

I said: 'Wait a minute. Don't pop off with a lot of screwy questions. Don't ask me why this damned thing was delivered to my apartment. That's one goofy thing I don't pretend to understand. But I've got a theory about Skinny Arkle's death.'

Donaldson said: 'A theory?'

'Yes. Now listen. Arkle was married to a girl named Kitty Calvert. Kitty has a sister, Constance Calvert. Well, just as I was starting downtown to meet you, Constance came to my door. She's a tall, blonde bimbo with plenty of sex-appeal.'

'The hell with that,' Donaldson grunted. 'What did she want?'

'She claimed she was scared for her sister,' I said. 'She said Kitty and Skinny Arkle had a hell of a row three days ago. Skinny threatened Kitty's life. Then he took it on the lam and hasn't been seen since.'

'So what?' Donaldson rasped.

'So this. Maybe Constance Calvert's story was a frame-up. Maybe her sister did have a fight with Skinny; and maybe Kitty shot the poor devil. Then maybe Kitty sent her sister to see me.'

'What for?'

I said: 'To cover the murder. To make it look as if they didn't know where Skinny had gone to.'

Donaldson said: 'Where is Kitty Calvert's sister now?'

'In my apartment. She won't get away.'

He said: 'Wait till I turn this head over to the medical examiner. Then we'll go see Kitty.'

He was gone about two minutes. Then we went out and piled into my jalopy. I drove—and I didn't spare the speedometer. Pretty soon we parked outside the Arkle home in Westwood.

I noticed another machine standing at the kerb a couple of doors away. It was a big, shiny maroon Cad, and somehow I thought I recognised it. But I couldn't be sure, and there was no point in checking it up just then. Donaldson and I went up to the porch of the Arkle house and rang the bell.

A cute little Chink maid opened up. I said: 'We want to see Mrs Arkle, please.'

The Chink maid spoke perfect English. American-born, probably. She said: 'Miss Kitty Calvert has retired, sir. You'll have to come in the morning.'

Dave Donaldson shoved me aside and flashed his badge. 'We'll see her now!' he growled.

The maid widened her slanted eyes. 'But—there's someone with—' she started to say. Then she stopped and blushed a little.

I said: 'Somebody with her, eh? A man?'

'I—don't know anything about it, sir,' the Chink dame said. I could tell she was lying. Her left hand sort of fluttered towards her heart, covering her breast through her uniform.

Donaldson didn't waste any more time. He pushed the Oriental girl aside and said: 'Come on, Turner.' He ran up the stairs. I followed him. And then, just as we reached the second floor, I heard a shot.

I said: 'What the hell—!' and made a dive for a closed door. The shot had sounded from within the room beyond that door. I jammed into it with my shoulder, burst it open. I had my .32 automatic in my fist. I leaped into the room, with Donaldson at my heels.

The room was all done in pink, with a pink-shaded lamp glowing in one corner. I sniffed the scent of expensive perfume. But I smelled something else, too. It was the acrid odour of powder-smoke.

In one second I caught the whole scene. There on the bed lay an almost nude woman—a girl. A girl with red hair and the prettiest figure I ever saw; the prettiest legs. An absolute knockout. It was Kitty Calvert—Skinny Arkle's wife.

She was as dead as a smoked fish.

There was a bullet-hole in her breast, right over the heart. She'd been shot plumb centre. And where she was shot there was a round red hole, with blood seeping out of it.

Directly beyond the bed I saw a man standing. He had his coat and vest off, and he looked white as hell. And he had a roscoe in his mitt.

I recognised him. He was Billy Sanston—a big-shot director for Alta-mount Studios. In fact, he directed all Kitty Calvert's productions. And now I knew where I'd seen that maroon Cad before—the one that was parked downstairs. It was Sanston's own Cad. I'd seen him driving it many a time.

Donaldson said: 'You murdering rat!' and took aim at Sanston. 'Drop that gun, you louse!'

Sanston dropped the gun. It hit the floor. He said: 'Good God—you don't think I—?'

Donaldson said: 'I don't think anything. If you've got anything to say, save it for your lawyer. Stick out your fins for the nippers.'

The movie director staggered a little. 'But—but you can't arrest me for something I didn't do! My God, I'll be ruined! My wife will divorce me—I'll lose my job—'

'You should have thought of that before. You been playing around with Kitty Calvert, haven't you?'

Sanston flushed. 'Y-yes, but I didn't kill her; I swear I didn't! I was here with her tonight. I admit that. I—I just went into the next room for a minute. Then I heard a shot. I ran in here and saw Kitty on the bed. She was dead; the gun was beside her. I—I picked it up, and then you men broke in. She—she must have shot herself—'

'Nuts!' Donaldson growled. 'Come on—or shall I sock you on the dome with the soft end of my roscoe?'

Sanston swayed towards us, holding out his hands for the bracelets. Then he pulled an unexpected stunt. With his left he smashed Dave Donaldson's service .38 aside. Then he planted a haymaker on Donaldson's jaw. Dave went down.

I leaped at Sanston, but he got away from me. He scooped up the gat he had dropped. I drew a bead on him, pulled my trigger. But like a damn' fool I'd forgotten to unlatch the safety on my automatic. When I squeezed the trigger, nothing happened.

And by that time, Billy Sanston was out of the room and pelting hell-for-leather down the stairs.

I hurled myself after him. Behind me I heard Donaldson getting on his feet. Dave was cursing and staggering along in my trail. I hit the stairs, started down. But Sanston had a good start. Before I was halfway down, I heard the front door slam shut. It slammed so hard that the glass shattered. I knew damned well that Sanston was out of the house.

I yelled: 'You lousy rat!' and took the last five steps in one flying jump. I jerked open the front door, raced outside. I saw Sanston in his maroon Cad—at the wheel. Then two shots roared in the night.

I ducked, thinking Sanston was firing at me. But I didn't hear any slugs whistling past my ears. Then I noticed something queer. Sanston wasn't trying to step on his starter, get his car under way. He was sort of slumped over his wheel.

Dave Donaldson caught up with me. We both jumped for the maroon Cad, yanked its front door open. I said: 'What the hell!'

Sanston was bleeding at the mouth—great, crimson gushes of blood spewing out of him. He coughed once. A nasty sound, the bloody cough of a dying man. Then he shuddered, stiffened and went limp.

Donaldson looked at the gun in Sanston's relaxed hand where it rested on the upholstered seat. The gun which Sanston had carried with him out of Kitty Calvert's boudoir. A trickle of smoke curled up from the gat's muzzle. Donaldson said:'God! He shot himself!'

I said: 'Yeah. Maybe.'

'What do you mean, maybe?'

I said: 'Well, maybe he didn't commit suicide. Maybe he was murdered.'

Donaldson looked at me. 'Are you bug-house?'

'No. I don't think so. I'm just trying to figure a couple of things out. Listen—suppose Sanston told us the truth a minute ago. Suppose he was in Kitty's house, making whoopee with her. And suppose he left her for a minute to get a drink of water or see a dog about a man. And suppose while he was gone, Kitty was shot?'

'You mean maybe she really killed herself and he walked in and picked up the roscoe where she'd dropped it?'

I said: 'Don't be dense, Dave. You didn't see any powder-burns on Kitty Calvert, did you?'

'No. Come to think of it, I didn't.'

'Well, then, she didn't shoot herself.'

Donaldson said: 'Well, hell! It was Sanston that killed her. Now he's bumped himself off because he realised he was caught red-handed.'

I said: 'Not so fast. You heard Sanston say something about his wife? He didn't want to be arrested, because his wife would divorce him and the scandal would make him lose his movie job?'

Dave narrowed his eyes. 'By God! You think it was Sanston's wife—?'

I pointed towards the side of Kitty Calvert's house. I said: 'Take a look. There's a ladder up against the house. It's right up against Kitty's boudoir window.'

Donaldson said: 'I get it! Mrs Sanston followed her hubby here, saw him with Kitty Calvert, and shot Kitty. But she didn't have a chance to shoot her husband too, because he was out of the room a minute, and when he came back we busted in. So she laid for him out here by his car. Huh?'

'At least that's a theory,' I said. 'It matches with the ladder against the window.'

Dave said: 'Then we've got to get Mrs Sanston, by God! Maybe she's still around here somewhere. Come on—let's start searching!'

Even as he spoke, I heard the sound of a motor roaring from somewhere around the next corner. I said: 'If it was Mrs Sanston, she's making her getaway right now. She'll probably go home to establish an alibi for herself.'

'Alibi, hell!' Dave Donaldson roared. 'I'll catch her! I'll put the collar on her and sweat the truth out of her!'

I said: 'Go ahead. Use my jalopy. I'll go back in the house and phone headquarters to come and take the two corpses away.'

So Dave got into my coupé and got going.

I went back into the house. I picked up the phone, notified headquarters what had happened. When I hung up, I thought I heard somebody tiptoeing in the back of the place. Funny thing about people trying to sneak around without making any noise. You'll notice it quicker than you'll notice ordinary footsteps.

I made a flying dive for the dining-room where I'd heard the sound. Then I saw the Chink maid. She was trying to get out through a French window.

I jumped for her, grabbed her. She was trying to stuff something down the neck of her dress. I got my fingers into the vee of her uniform and yanked. The material tore. I ripped at the bosom of her dress until something fluttered to the floor. I grabbed it. It was an oblong of yellow paper.

The Chink girl tried to grab it from me. I slapped her across the face, pinioned her slim wrists with one hand. Then I looked at the slip of yellow paper. It was a cheque. It was made out to Miss Violet Chang, and it was signed: 'Rodney Arkle.' That had been Skinny Arkle's real name. The cheque was for five hundred smacks.

I said: 'Where the hell did you get this?'

'Mr Arkle g-gave it to me two or three d-days ago,' she whimpered. She looked scared as hell.

I said: 'What for?'

She closed up like a clam. Her red lips got tight. I knew I'd have to pull the caveman stuff on her to find out anything. So I grabbed her shoulders, shook her until her teeth rattled.

I said: 'Now look, Miss Violet Chang. If you don't want to get mauled groggy, you'll talk. How would you like a good punch in the jaw?'

'No—no—! Don't hit me!'

'Okay, then. Answer me. Why were you trying to sneak out that window?'

She said: 'Be-because I'm afraid! I don't want to get mixed up in this case.'

I ran my fingers over her shoulder, pretended I was about to pinch hell out of her. I'll admit I got something of a kick out of touching her. But I didn't let on. I said: 'Why are you afraid to get mixed up in the case?'

All of a sudden the slant-eyed cutie pressed herself up against me, put her arms around my neck. She said: 'Please, Mr Detective—I'll do anything you ask if you'll keep me out of this! I—I have a brother who was smuggled into this country illegally. If I'm dragged into this shooting, the police will question me, look into my family. They might find out about my brother and deport him—'

She fitted against me like tissue paper. Warm, soft curves were touching my chest, and she was offering me her lips—

Well, after all, I'm human. So I leaned down and kissed her . . . felt her lips part against my mouth. My blood was racing, way out of control . . .

It was some time later when I said: 'Okay, baby. Now that you know I'm your friend, maybe you'll answer a couple of questions, huh?'

'Such as what?' she asked me.

I said: 'Well, for one thing, how long had Billy Sanston been intimate with your mistress, Kitty Calvert? How long had he been coming to visit her?'

'A—a long time. Almost a year. N-now let me go, please—!'

'Not yet. Tell me something else. Did Kitty know Billy's wife?'

'Y-yes. Just slightly. They weren't good friends. Sometimes I got the impression that Mrs Sanston suspected her husband of being in love with Miss Calvert. Of course I wasn't sure. Now please let me get away—before the police come!'

Outside, in the distance, I heard sirens moaning. I said: 'Sure, kiddo.

Put on a coat to cover yourself. Then scram out the window.'

She got a coat and I held it for her. I fumbled the job, killing time. Then finally I helped her out through the French window in the dining-room, just as the headquarters men rang the front door-bell.

I raced for the hall, yelled through the broken glass in the door. I said: 'Quick—around the side! A Chink dame on the lam! Grab her!'

Those coppers moved fast. I heard them running round the side of the house. That was what I wanted.

For a minute I was alone. I set fire to a gasper and went upstairs. I didn't know what I was going to look for, but I figured maybe I might find something. I had three murders on my mind: Skinny Arkle's, his wife's, and Billy Sanston's. I was convinced they were all murders; and I had a hunch they were linked together some way or other.

First I squinted around the boudoir where Kitty Calvert's corpse was. Then I walked into the next bedroom. It had been Skinny Arkle's room. I saw a desk-drawer open.

I saw an old book of faded press-clippings from the days when Skinny had been a big-shot comedian. There were pictures of him in costume and in everyday dress. There was even a picture of Skinny as a kid with his family, back in Jugoslavia. It showed his mother, father, grand-parents, a brother exactly the same age, two older sisters, and a couple of uncles and aunts. But I didn't take the scrap-book. It was too big, too bulky.

Then I found an empty book of cheque-stubs. I looked at the last three stubs. One showed that cheque for five yards drawn to the Chink maid, Violet Chang. The second said: 'Pasadena Hospital, $250.00, in full.' The third was to cash—for fifty grand!

Before I could look around any further, I heard a hell of a rumpus down below. The headquarters men had put the nab on the Chinese girl. I didn't want them to catch me going through Skinny Arkle's things, so I went downstairs on the run. I said: 'You guys better take that girl to the jug. I think she knows something. And how about lending me a car for a while? Dave Donaldson took my hack.'

One of the dicks said: 'All right. Use the red roadster, Mr Turner. Run it back to headquarters when you get through with it.'

I went out, got into the red roadster. I drove back to my apartment. Just as I parked outside my building, I saw somebody in the entrance. Somebody in a suit that looked familiar.

It was one of my own suits!

I said: 'What the hell!' and jumped for the guy. I grabbed him. Only it wasn't a him; it was a her. It was the blonde bimbo, Constance Calvert.

She fought at me. She said: 'Damn you! Let me go!'

'Like hell!' I told her. 'How long have you been out of my place?'

'I—I just got out. I found a suit of yours and put it on. Why did you take my clothes?'

Before I could answer her, I heard brakes squeaking. I turned. There was Dave Donaldson driving up in my jalopy. He jumped out, saw me holding the blonde dame. He said: 'What—?'

'Put the nippers on this girl, Dave,' I told him. 'She's hard to hold.'

Dave slipped the cuffs on her. Then he said: 'Turner, I've got news!'

I said: 'What kind of news?'

'Well, in the first place,' Donaldson growled disgustedly, 'Mrs Sanston had a perfect alibi. She's been playing bridge with friends all evening. Hasn't been outdoors. That eliminates her as a suspect. But down at headquarters I found out something damned interesting. Billy Sanston had been married before. His first wife's name was Nancy Norward. Ever hear of her?'

I said: 'Good God! Nancy Norward was the girl who died down in San Diego on a party with Skinny Arkle.'

Dave said: 'Yeah. Now do you see the set-up? Sanston must have nursed a grudge against Arkle all these years. To get even he played around with Kitty Calvert, Arkle's wife. Then, finally, he bumped Arkle off and decapitated the body. Maybe Kitty found out about it, so he had to kill her too. Then when we busted in on him in Kitty's boudoir he committed suicide. There was no other way out.'

I said: 'Dave, maybe you're right. It all checks up pretty well. Except one thing. Why was Arkle's severed head sent to me?'

'I don't know that,' Donaldson grunted. 'And there's one other goofy point, too. The medical examiner's report says that the bullet was fired into Arkle's noggin *after he was dead*! The condition of the tissues, or something. Look—here's the report.'

He handed me a sheet of paper. I let him hang onto Constance while I took the paper to a street-light. It was the usual formal report of the medical examiner—the description of the bullet-wound, condition of the flesh, colour of the hair and eyes, so many fillings in the teeth, and the way the head had evidently been sliced from the body itself. I read it over once. And then, suddenly, I had the answer.

I jumped back towards Donaldson. I said: 'Quick! Get in my hack! We'll take this dame with us. And we've got to move fast!'

Dave said: 'Where the hell are we headed?'

'Pasadena!' I told him. 'The Pasadena Hospital!'

It took us just thirty minutes to make the trip, and I thumbed my nose at a dozen stop-signs on the way. I jerked all the tread off my tyres skidding to a stop outside the Pasadena Hospital, and I grabbed Donaldson's arm. 'Come on!' I yelled.

'What about this dame?' He pointed to Constance Calvert.

'Leave her here in my hack. She's handcuffed.' I shoved Donaldson into the hospital and we went up to the desk.

There was an elderly woman on duty. I said: 'I want to see a record of the deaths in this place during the past three days.' Dave Donaldson flashed his badge for authority.

The woman dug into her records, handed me four or five cards. I found the one I wanted. It said: 'Rodney Arkellmeister. Age 48. Male. White. Entered hospital in dying condition. Pneumonia. Unable to talk. Died two days later . . .' Then it gave the date of death and all that stuff.

I whirled on Donaldson. 'Get it?' I said. 'Rodney Arkellmeister! That was Skinny Arkle's real name before he came to America from Jugoslavia.'

Dave said: 'You mean Skinny died a natural death? Then who the hell cut off his head and put a bullet in it? Who sent the head to you?'

Before I could answer him, I heard a scream from outside. A woman's scream. I said: 'What the hell—!' and jumped for the door. I saw a car parked behind my coupé. There was a guy leaning in my hack. He was choking Constance Calvert.

I said: 'Damn! He must have been lurking around my apartment-house! He heard me saying we were coming here! He followed us!' And I hurled myself at the guy.

He heard me. He turned. I saw a roscoe in his fist. It vomited flame. A slug zinged past my skull. I whipped out my own automatic, thumbed the safety, squeezed the trigger. I sent three slugs into the guy's guts.

Even before he fell I yelled out to Donaldson. I said: 'There's your killer. It's Skinny Arkle!'

Dave said: 'You're crazy! How can a headless corpse get up and walk around—?'

By that time I was kneeling over the fallen man. I turned him over.

It was Skinny Arkle, all right. I'd have known his face anywhere. Especially after seeing the decapitated head drop in my lap earlier that night, in my apartment.

Donaldson stared. He said: 'Good God!'

I reached down, shoved my fingers in Skinny Arkle's mouth. I twisted—and pulled out his false teeth. I said: 'Well, that proves it, Skinny.'

Arkle glared up at me. His eyes were beginning to glaze. He said: 'Damn you—!'

I said: 'I see the whole thing now. You were the murderer, Arkle. You knew your wife, Kitty Calvert, was intimate with her director, Billy Sanston. You got proof of your suspicions from your wife's Chink maid, Violet Chang. You gave her your cheque for five hundred clams for telling you the low-down.'

Skinny Arkle gurgled in his throat and vomited a little blood from his punctured guts.

I said: 'By sheer luck, your brother had just come to visit you from Jugoslavia. *Your twin brother!* You and he were identical twins; looked exactly alike. I saw a picture of you two in your scrap-book a while ago.

'It showed you and your twin as kids back in the old country. You looked alike even in those days.'

Dave Donaldson said: 'I'll be damned!'

I went on talking to Skinny Arkle. 'When your brother got to Hollywood, he was already stricken with pneumonia. You knew he was going to die. You saw a swell chance to murder your chiselling wife and her lover without being suspected of the crime. So you had your brother brought here to Pasadena—to a hospital. He died here. You arranged his burial somewhere—then you exhumed his corpse and cut its head off, put a bullet in it as a blind. That was the head you sent to me!'

Arkle said: 'Ar-r-r-gh—!'

'You sent your twin brother's severed head to me, knowing I'd call the cops and notify them you'd been murdered. Then, tonight, you put a ladder outside your wife's boudoir and climbed up. You shot her and threw the gun on the bed alongside her, to make it look like suicide. Maybe you'd have shot Billy Sanston at the same time, but he'd gone into the next room.

'Then when Donaldson and I broke in, you saw that Sanston would be accused of murdering Kitty Calvert—and probably convicted. So you sneaked down the ladder, satisfied. But a moment later, Billy Sanston escaped. So you shot him with a second gun you had on you. You shot him as he got into his Cad. That made it look as if Sanston, too, was a suicide.'

Donaldson stared at me. 'How the hell did you guess?'

I said: 'I knew, the minute you showed me the medical examiner's report of that severed head. It mentioned several fillings in the teeth. And I knew that the real Skinny Arkle *had false teeth*! He used to take them out and fold up his face, in the movies! Then I remembered that cheque-stub I'd seen in Arkle's book—a cheque made out to the Pasadena Hospital. I realised the truth. Arkle had done the killings, and now he'd probably try to escape by going back to Jugoslavia on his dead brother's passport.'

Dave Donaldson leaned over Skinny Arkle, felt in his pockets. He brought out a passport and a steamship ticket. That cinched the thing.

Skinny Arkle's eyes fluttered. He mumbled: 'Well—Turner . . . they won't—hang me . . . you took . . . care of that . . . damn you . . .' A spew of crimson gushed out of his kisser, and he folded up. And that was the end of Skinny Arkle.

Then I remembered Constance Calvert. She was slumped over in my jalopy. Arkle must have followed us; and maybe she'd spotted him. Anyhow, he'd tried to murder her quietly; probably figured on bumping Donaldson and me, too, when we came out of the hospital. He must have known the jig was up. But I wasn't thinking about Skinny Arkle any more. I was thinking of the blonde Calvert wren.

She'd been choked unconscious; but she wasn't seriously hurt. I turned to Dave Donaldson. I said: 'Dave, you stay here and notify the Pasadena police—have them take Skinny's carcass away.'

Dave said: 'Where are you going?'

I said: 'Well, I left this girl's clothes in my apartment earlier tonight. So now I'm going to take her back to get 'em.'

'Hell!' Donaldson growled. 'I'll bet you won't hurry about it.'

I said: 'You flatter me, Dave.' But it turned out that he was right, at that!

THE SINGING PIGEON

Ross Macdonald

Lew Archer is an ex-policeman from Long Beach, California, who was fired because he could not stomach the corrupt police administration he was forced to work for and instead became a private eye—the most famous of his ilk in fiction during the Sixties and Seventies. Described as a private man who operates most effectively in the shadows, he is still a 'not unwilling catalyst for trouble'. He works from a small, bleak office, although this is surprisingly full of books (which he reads avidly when not working on a case), and the walls are hung with good modern paintings (his favourites are by the Japanese artist Kuniyoshi). Archer is unlike many of the other hardboiled dicks in that he does not indulge in promiscuous sex and has a real affinity with young people. He is also unique among his breed in being a vocal campaigner on behalf of a better environment. Immortalised on the screen by Paul Newman in The Moving Target *(1966), in which he was inexplicably renamed Harper, and* The Drowning Pool *(1975), Archer has also featured in eighteen novels and a 1975 TV series starring Brian Keith.*

The cop turned private eye was created by Ross Macdonald (1915–1983), the pseudonym of Kenneth Miller whom several critics have described as the heir to Dashiell Hammett and Raymond Chandler. Although Miller was born in California, he grew up in Canada with his mother who had separated from her husband. For a time he travelled in Europe and was then a teacher before meeting and marrying another writer, Margaret Strum, who introduced him to crime fiction. Although his early short stories and novels were popular, it was with the advent of Lew Archer that he became a household name. Anthony Boucher, the New York Times *book reviewer who was among the first to spot the significance of Macdonald's work, said that he was actually a better writer than either Hammett or Chandler and that his fiction had been responsible for developing the hardboiled private eye novel into a medium where there were 'people with enough feeling to be hurt and enough complexity to do wrong'. Although Macdonald admitted to reading the hardboiled stories of many of his contemporaries, he claimed there was more of himself in the private eye than any outside influence. 'The Singing Pigeon', written in 1953, finds an exhausted Archer trying to get some rest in a motel after a fruitless chase to the Mexican border—and instead being plunged into the hunt for the killer of a man whose body is discovered in a car on a nearby beach.*

*   *   *

It was Friday night. I was tooling home from the Mexican border in a light blue convertible and a dark blue mood. I had followed a man from Fresno to San Diego and lost him in the maze of streets in Old Town. When I picked up his trail again, it was cold. He had crossed the border, and my instructions went no further than the United States.

Halfway home, just above Emerald Bay, I overtook the worst driver in the world. He was driving a black fishtail Cadillac as if he was tacking a sailboat. The heavy car wove back and forth across the freeway, using two of its four lanes, and sometimes three. It was late, and I was in a hurry to get some sleep. I started to pass it on the right, at a time when it was riding the double line. The Cadillac drifted towards me like an unguided missile, and forced me off the road in a screeching skid.

I speeded up to pass on the left. Simultaneously, the driver of the Cadillac accelerated. My acceleration couldn't match his. We raced neck and neck down the middle of the road. I wondered if he was drunk or crazy or afraid of me. Then the freeway ended. I was doing eighty on the wrong side of a two-lane highway, and a truck came over a rise ahead like a blazing double comet. I floorboarded the gas pedal and cut over sharply to the right, threatening the Cadillac's fenders and its driver's life. In the approaching headlights, his face was as blank and white as a piece of paper, with charred black holes for eyes. His shoulders were naked.

At the last possible second he slowed enough to let me get by. The truck went off into the shoulder, honking angrily. I braked gradually, hoping to force the Cadillac to stop. It looped past me in an insane arc, tyres skittering, and was sucked away into darkness.

When I finally came to a full stop, I had to pry my fingers off the wheel. My knees were remote and watery. After smoking part of a cigarette, I U-turned and drove very cautiously back to Emerald Bay. I was long past the hot-rod age, and I needed rest.

The first motel I came to, the Siesta, was decorated with a vacancy sign and a neon Mexican sleeping luminously under a sombrero. Envying him, I parked on the gravel apron in front of the motel office. There was a light inside. The glass-panelled door was standing open, and I went in. The little room was pleasantly furnished with rattan and chintz. I jangled the bell on the desk a few times. No one appeared, so I sat down to wait and lit a cigarette. An electric clock on the wall said a quarter to one.

I must have dozed for a few minutes. A dream rushed by the threshold of my consciousness, making a gentle noise. Death was in the dream. He drove a black Cadillac loaded with flowers. When I woke up, the cigarette was starting to burn my fingers. A thin man in a grey flannel shirt was standing over me with a doubtful look on his face.

He was big-nosed and small-chinned, and he wasn't as young as he gave the impression of being. His teeth were bad, the sandy hair was thinning and receding. He was the typical old youth who scrounged and wheedled his living around motor courts and restaurants and hotels, and hung on desperately to the frayed edge of other people's lives.

'What do you want?' he said. 'Who are you? What do you want?' His voice was reedy and changeable like an adolescent's.

'A room.'

'Is that all you want?'

From where I sat, it sounded like an accusation. I let it pass. 'What else is there? Circassian dancing girls? Free popcorn?'

He tried to smile without showing his bad teeth. The smile was a dismal failure, like my joke. 'I'm sorry, sir,' he said. 'You woke me up. I never make much sense right after I just wake up.'

'Have a nightmare?'

His vague eyes expanded like blue bubblegum bubbles. 'Why did you ask me that?'

'Because I just had one. But skip it. Do you have a vacancy or don't you?'

'Yessir. Sorry, sir.' He swallowed whatever bitter taste he had in his mouth, and assumed an impersonal, obsequious manner. 'You got any luggage, sir?'

'No luggage.'

Moving silently in tennis sneakers like a frail ghost of the boy he once had been, he went behind the counter, and took my name, address, licence number, and five dollars. In return, he gave me a key numbered fourteen and told me where to use it. Apparently he despaired of a tip.

Room fourteen was like any other middle-class motel room touched with the California-Spanish mania. Artificially roughened plaster painted adobe colour, poinsettia-red curtains, imitation parchment lampshade on a twisted black iron stand. A Rivera reproduction of a sleeping Mexican hung on the wall over the bed. I succumbed to its suggestion right away, and dreamed about Circassian dancing girls.

Along towards morning one of them got frightened, through no fault of mine, and began to scream her little Circassian lungs out. I sat up in bed, making soothing noises, and woke up. It was nearly nine by my wristwatch. The screaming ceased and began again, spoiling the morning like a fire siren outside the window. I pulled on my trousers over the underwear I'd been sleeping in, and went outside.

A young woman was standing on the walk outside the next room. She had a key in one hand and a handful of blood in the other. She wore a wide multi-coloured skirt and a low-cut gypsy sort of blouse. The blouse was distended and her mouth was open, and she was yelling her head off. It was a fine dark head, but I hated her for spoiling my morning sleep.

I took her by the shoulders and said, 'Stop it.'

The screaming stopped. She looked down sleepily at the blood on her hand. It was as thick as axle grease, and almost as dark in colour.

'Where did you get that?'

'I slipped and fell in it. I didn't see it.'

Dropping the key on the walk, she pulled her skirt to one side with her clean hand. Her legs were bare and brown. Her skirt was stained at the back with the same thick fluid.

'Where? In this room?'

She faltered, 'Yes.'

Doors were opening up and down the drive. Half-a-dozen people began to converge on us. A dark-faced man about four-and-a-half feet high came scampering from the office, his little pointed shoes dancing in the gravel.

'Come inside and show me,' I said to the girl.

'I can't. I won't.' Her eyes were very heavy, and surrounded by the bluish pallor of shock.

The little man slid to a stop between us, reached up and gripped the upper part of her arm. 'What is the matter, Ella? Are you crazy, disturbing the guests?'

She said, 'Blood,' and leaned against me with her eyes closed.

His sharp black glance probed the situation. He turned to the other guests, who had formed a murmurous semicircle around us.

'It is perfectly hokay. Do not be concerned, ladies and gentlemen. My daughter cut herself a little bit. It is perfectly all right.'

Circling her waist with one long hairy arm, he hustled her through the open door and slammed it behind him. I caught it on my foot and followed them in.

The room was a duplicate of mine, including the reproduction over the unmade bed, but everything was reversed as in a mirror image. The girl took a few weak steps by herself and sat on the edge of the bed. Then she noticed the blood spots on the sheets. She stood up quickly. Her mouth opened rimmed with white teeth.

'Don't do it,' I said. 'We know you have a very fine pair of lungs.'

The little man turned on me. 'Who do you think you are?'

'The name is Archer. I have the next room.'

'Get out of this one, please.'

'I don't think I will.'

He lowered his greased black head as if he was going to butt me. Under his sharkskin jacket, a hunch protruded from his back like a displaced elbow. He seemed to reconsider the butting gambit, and decided in favour of diplomacy:

'You are jumping to conclusions, mister. It is not so serious as it looks. We had a little accident here last night.'

'Sure, your daughter cut herself. She heals remarkably fast.'

'Nothing like that.' He fluttered one long hand. 'I said to the people outside the first thing that came to my mind. Actually, it was a little scuffle. One of the guests suffered a nosebleed.'

The girl moved like a sleepwalker to the bathroom door and switched on the light. There was a pool of blood coagulating on the black and white chequerboard linoleum, streaked where she had slipped and fallen in it.

'Some nosebleed,' I said to the little man. 'Do you run this joint?'

'I am the proprietor of the Siesta motor hotel, yes. My name is Salanda. The gentleman is susceptible to nosebleed. He told me so himself.'

'Where is he now?'

'He checked out early this morning.'

'In good health?'

'Certainly in good health.'

I looked around the room. Apart from the unmade bed with the brown spots on the sheets, it contained no signs of occupancy. Someone had spilled a pint of blood and vanished.

The little man opened the door wide and invited me with a sweep of his arm to leave. 'If you will excuse me, sir, I wish to have this cleaned up as quickly as possible. Ella, will you tell Lorraine to get to work on it right away pronto? Then maybe you better lie down for a little while.'

'I'm all right now, Father. Don't worry about me.'

When I checked out a few minutes later, she was sitting behind the desk in the front office, looking pale but composed. I dropped my key on the desk in front of her.

'Feeling better, Ella?'

'Oh. I didn't recognise you with all your clothes on.'

'That's a good line. May I use it?'

She lowered her eyes and blushed. 'You're making fun of me. I know I acted foolishly this morning.'

'I'm not so sure. What do *you* think happened in thirteen last night?'

'My father told you, didn't he?'

'He gave me a version, two of them in fact. I doubt that they're the final shooting script.'

Her hand went to the central hollow in the gypsy blouse. Her arms and shoulders were slender and brown, the tips of her fingers carmine. 'Shooting?'

'A cinema term,' I said. 'But there might have been a real shooting at that. Don't you think so?'

Her front teeth pinched her lower lip. She looked like somebody's pet rabbit. I restrained an impulse to pat her sleek brown head.

'That's ridiculous. This is a respectable motel. Anyway, Father asked me not to discuss it with anybody.'

'Why would he do that?'

'He loves this place, that's why. He doesn't want any scandal made out of nothing. If we lost our good reputation here, it would break my father's heart.'

'He doesn't strike me as the sentimental type.'

She stood up, smoothing her skirt. I saw that she'd changed it. 'You leave him alone. He's a dear little man. I don't know what you think you're doing, trying to stir up trouble where there isn't any.'

I backed away from her righteous indignation—female indignation is always righteous—and went out to my car. The early spring sun was dazzling. Beyond the freeway and the drifted sugary dunes, the bay was Prussian blue. The road cut inland across the base of the peninsula and returned to the sea a few miles north of the town. Here a wide blacktop parking space shelved off to the left of the highway, overlooking the white beach and whiter breakers. Signs at each end of the turnout stated that this was County Park, No Beach Fires.

The beach and the blacktop expanse above it were deserted except for a single car, which looked very lonely. It was a long black Cadillac nosed into the cable fence at the edge of the beach. I braked and turned off the highway and got out. The man in the driver's seat of the Cadillac didn't turn his head as I approached him. His chin was propped on the steering wheel, and he was gazing out across the endless blue sea.

I opened the door and looked into his face. It was paper white. The dark brown eyes were sightless. The body was unclothed except for the thick fur matted on the chest, and a clumsy bandage tied around the waist. The bandage was composed of several bloodstained towels, held in place by a knotted piece of nylon fabric whose nature I didn't recognise immediately. Examining it more closely, I saw that it was a woman's slip. The left breast of the garment was embroidered in purple with a heart, containing the name 'Fern', in slanting script. I wondered who Fern was.

The man who was wearing her purple heart had dark curly hair, heavy black eyebrows, a heavy chin sprouting black beard. He was rough-looking in spite of his anaemia and the lipstick smudged on his mouth.

There was no registration on the steering-post, and nothing in the glove compartment but a half-empty box of shells for a .38 automatic. The ignition was still turned on. So were the dash and headlights, but they were dim. The gas gauge registered empty. Curlyhead must have pulled off the highway soon after he passed me, and driven all the rest of the night in one place.

I untied the slip, which didn't look as if it would take fingerprints, and went over it for a label. It had one: Gretchen, Palm Springs. It occurred to me that it was Saturday morning and that I'd gone all winter without a weekend in the desert. I retied the slip the way I'd found it, and drove back to the Siesta Motel.

Ella's welcome was a few degrees colder than absolute zero. 'Well!' She glared down her pretty rabbit nose at me. 'I thought we were rid of you.'

'So did I. But I just couldn't tear myself away.'

She gave me a peculiar look, neither hard nor soft, but mixed. Her hand went to her hair, then reached for a registration card. 'I suppose if you want to rent a room, I can't stop you. Only please don't imagine you're making an impression on me. You leave me cold, mister.'

'Archer,' I said. 'Lew Archer. Don't bother with the card. I came back to use your phone.'

'Aren't there any other phones?' She pushed the telephone across the desk. 'I guess it's all right, long as it isn't a toll call.'

'I'm calling the Highway Patrol. Do you know their local number?'

'I don't remember.' She handed me the telephone directory.

'There's been an accident,' I said as I dialled.

'A highway accident? Where did it happen?'

'Right here, sister. Right here in room thirteen.'

But I didn't tell that to the Highway Patrol. I told them I had found a dead man in a car on the parking lot above the county beach. The girl listened with widening eyes and nostrils. Before I finished she rose in a flurry and left the office by the rear door.

She came back with the proprietor. His eyes were black and bright like nailheads in leather, and the scampering dance of his feet was almost frenzied. 'What is this?'

'I came across a dead man up the road a piece.'

'So why do you come back here to telephone?' His head was in butting position, his hands outspread and gripping the corners of the desk. 'Has it got anything to do with us?'

'He's wearing a couple of your towels.'

'What?'

'And he was bleeding heavily before he died. I think somebody shot him in the stomach. Maybe you did.'

'You're loco,' he said, but not very emphatically. 'Crazy accusations like that, they will get you into trouble. What is your business?'

'I'm a private detective.'

'You followed him here, is that it? You were going to arrest him, so he shot himself?'

'Wrong on both counts,' I said. 'I came here to sleep. And they don't shoot themselves in the stomach. It's too uncertain, and slow. No suicide wants to die of peritonitis.'

'So what are you doing now, trying to make scandal for my business?'

'If your business includes trying to cover for murder.'

'He shot himself,' the little man insisted.

'How do you know?'

'Donny. I spoke to him just now.'

'And how does Donny know?'

'The man told him.'

'Is Donny your night keyboy?'

'He was. I think I will fire him, for stupidity. He didn't even tell me about this mess. I had to find it out for myself. The hard way.'

'Donny means well,' the girl said at his shoulder. 'I'm sure he didn't realise what happened.'

'Who does?' I said. 'I want to talk to Donny. But first let's have a look at the register.'

He took a pile of cards from a drawer and riffled through them. His large hands, hairy-backed, were calm and expert, like animals that lived a serene life of their own, independent of their emotional owner. They dealt me one of the cards across the desk. It was inscribed in block capitals: Richard Rowe, Detroit, Mich.

I said: 'There was a woman with him.'

'Impossible.'

'Or he was a transvestite.'

He surveyed me blankly, thinking of something else. 'The HP, did you tell them to come here? They know it happened here?'

'Not yet. But they'll find your towels. He used them for a bandage.'

'I see. Yes. Of course.' He struck himself with a clenched fist on the temple. It made a noise like someone maltreating a pumpkin. 'You are a private detective, you say. Now if you informed the police that you were on the trail of a fugitive, a fugitive from justice. He shot himself rather than face arrest. For five hundred dollars?'

'I'm not that private,' I said. 'I have some public responsibility. Besides, the cops would do a little checking and catch me out.'

'Not necessarily. He *was* a fugitive from justice, you know.'

'I hear you telling me.'

'Give me a little time, and I can even present you with his record.'

The girl was leaning back away from her father, her eyes starred with broken illusions. 'Daddy,' she said weakly.

He didn't hear her. All of his bright black attention was fixed on me. 'Seven hundred dollars?'

'No sale. The higher you raise it, the guiltier you look. Were you here last night?'

'You are being absurd,' he said. 'I spent the entire evening with my wife. We drove up to Los Angeles to attend the ballet.' By way of supporting evidence, he hummed a couple of bars from Tchaikovsky. 'We didn't arrive back here in Emerald Bay until nearly two o'clock.'

'Alibis can be fixed.'

'By criminals, yes,' he said. 'I'm not a criminal.'

The girl put a hand on his shoulder. He cringed away, his face creased by monkey fury, but his face was hidden from her.

'Daddy,' she said. 'Was he murdered, do you think?'

'How do I know?' His voice was wild and high, as if she had touched the spring of his emotion. 'I wasn't here. I only know what Donny told me.'

The girl was examining me with narrowed eyes, as if I was a new kind of animal she had discovered and was trying to think of a use for.

'This gentleman is a detective,' she said, 'or claims to be.'

I pulled out my photostat and slapped it down on the desk. The little man picked it up and looked from it to my face. 'Will you go to work for me?'

'Doing what, telling little white lies?'

The girl answered for him: 'See what you can find out about this— this death. On my word of honour, Father had nothing to do with it.'

I made a snap decision, the kind you live to regret. 'All right. I'll take a fifty-dollar advance. Which is a good deal less than five hundred. My first advice to you is to tell the police everything you know. Provided that you're innocent.'

'You insult me,' he said.

But he flicked a fifty-dollar bill from the cash drawer and pressed it into my hand fervently, like a love token. I had a queasy feeling that I had been conned into taking his money, not much of it but enough. The feeling deepened when he still refused to talk. I had to use all the arts of persuasion even to get Donny's address out of him.

The keyboy lived in a shack on the edge of a desolate stretch of dunes. I guessed that it had once been somebody's beach house, before sand had drifted like unthawing snow in the angles of the walls and winter storms had broken the tiles and cracked the concrete foundations. Huge chunks of concrete were piled haphazardly on what had been a terrace overlooking the sea.

On one of the tilted slabs, Donny was stretched like a long albino lizard in the sun. The onshore wind carried the sound of my motor to his ears. He sat up blinking, recognised me when I stopped the car, and ran into the house.

I descended flagstone steps and knocked on the warped door. 'Open up, Donny.'

'Go away,' he answered huskily. His eyes gleamed like a snail through a crack in the wood.

'I'm working for Mr Salanda. He wants us to have a talk.'

'You both can go and take a running jump.'

'Open it or I'll break it down.'

I waited for a while. He shot back the bolt. The door creaked reluctantly open. He leaned against the doorpost, searching my face with his eyes, his hairless body shivering from an internal chill. I pushed past him, through a kitchenette that was indescribably filthy, littered with the remnants of old meals, and gaseous with their odours. He followed me silently on bare soles into a larger room whose sprung floorboards undulated under my feet. The picture window had been broken and patched with cardboard. The stone fireplace was choked with garbage. The only furniture was an army cot in one corner where Donny apparently slept.

'Nice homey place you have here. It has that lived-in quality.'

He seemed to take it as a compliment, and I wondered if I was dealing with a moron. 'It suits me. I never was much of a one for fancy quarters. I like it here, where I can hear the ocean at night.'

'What else do you hear at night, Donny?'

He missed the point of the question, or pretended to. 'All different things. Big trucks going past on the highway. I like to hear those night sounds. Now I guess I can't go on living here. Mr Salanda owns it, he lets me live here for nothing. Now he'll be kicking me out of here, I guess.'

'On account of what happened last night?'

'Uh-huh.' He subsided onto the cot, his doleful head supported by his hands.

I stood over him. 'Just what did happen last night, Donny?'

'A bad thing,' he said. 'This fella checked in about ten o'clock—'

'The man with the dark curly hair?'

'That's the one. He checked in about ten, and I gave him room thirteen. Around about midnight I thought I heard a gun go off from there. It took me a little while to get my nerve up, then I went back to see what was going on. This fella came out of the room, without no clothes on. Just some kind of bandage around his waist. He looked like some kind of crazy Indian or something. He had a gun in his hand, and he was staggering, and I could see that he was bleeding some. He come right up to me and pushed the gun in my gut and told me to keep my trap shut. He said I wasn't to tell anybody I saw him, now or later. He said if I opened my mouth about it to anybody, that he would come back and kill me. But now he's dead, isn't he?'

'He's dead.'

I could smell the fear on Donny: there's an unexplained trace of canine in my chromosomes. The hairs were prickling on the back of my neck, and I wondered if Donny's fear was of the past or for the future. The pimples stood out in bas-relief against his pale lugubrious face.

'I think he was murdered, Donny. You're lying, aren't you?'

'Me lying?' But his reaction was slow and feeble.

'The dead man didn't check in alone. He had a woman with him.'

'What woman?' he said in elaborate surprise.

'You tell me. Her name was Fern. I think she did the shooting, and you caught her red-handed. The wounded man got out of the room and into his car and away. The woman stayed behind to talk to you. She probably paid you to dispose of his clothes and fake a new registration card for the room. But you both overlooked the blood on the floor of the bathroom. Am I right?'

'You couldn't be wronger, mister. Are you a cop?'

'A private detective. You're in deep trouble, Donny. You'd better talk yourself out of it if you can, before the cops start on you.'

'I didn't do anything.' His voice broke like a boy's. It went strangely with the glints of grey in his hair.

'Faking the register is a serious rap, even if they don't hang accessory to murder on you.'

He began to expostulate in formless sentences that ran together. At the same time his hand was moving across the dirty grey blanket. It burrowed under the pillow and came out holding a crumpled card. He tried to stuff it into his mouth and chew it. I tore it away from between his discoloured teeth.

It was a registration card from the motel, signed in a boyish scrawl: Mr and Mrs Richard Rowe, Detroit, Mich.

Donny was trembling violently. Below his cheap cotton shorts, his bony knees vibrated like tuning forks. 'It wasn't my fault,' he cried. 'She held a gun on me.'

'What did you do with the man's clothes?'

'Nothing. She didn't even let me into the room. She bundled them up and took them away herself.'

'Where did she go?'

'Down the highway towards town. She walked away on the shoulder of the road and that was the last I saw of her.'

'How much did she pay you, Donny?'

'Nothing, not a cent. I already told you, she held a gun on me.'

'And you were so scared you kept quiet until this morning?'

'That's right. I was scared. Who wouldn't be scared?'

'She's gone now,' I said. 'You can give me a description of her.'

'Yeah.' He made a visible effort to pull his vague thoughts together. One of his eyes was a little off centre, lending his face a stunned, amorphous appearance. 'She was a big tall dame with blondey hair.'

'Dyed?'

'I guess so, I dunno. She wore it in a braid like, on top of her head. She was kind of fat, built like a lady wrestler, great big watermelons on her. Big legs.'

'How was she dressed?'

'I didn't hardly notice, I was so scared. I think she had some kind of purple coat on, with black fur around the neck. Plenty of rings on her fingers and stuff.'

'How old?'

'Pretty old, I'd say. Older than me, and I'm going on thirty-nine.'

'And she did the shooting?'

'I guess so. She told me to say if anybody asked me, I was to say that Mr Rowe shot himself.'

'You're very suggestible, aren't you, Donny? It's a dangerous way to be, with people pushing each other around the way they do.'

'I didn't get that, mister. Come again.' He batted his pale blue eyes at me, smiling expectantly.

'Skip it,' I said and left him.

A few hundred yards up the highway I passed an HP car with two uniformed men in the front seat looking grim. Donny was in for it now. I pushed him out of my mind and drove across country to Palm Springs.

Palm Springs is still a one-horse town, but the horse is a Palomino with silver trappings. Most of the girls were Palomino, too. The main street was a cross-section of Hollywood and Vine transported across the desert by some unnatural force and disguised in western costumes which fooled nobody. Not even me.

I found Gretchen's lingerie shop in an expensive-looking arcade built around an imitation flagstone patio. In the patio's centre a little fountain gurgled pleasantly, flinging small lariats of spray against the heat. It was late in March, and the season was ending. Most of the shops, including the one I entered, were deserted except for the hired help.

It was a small cool shop, faintly perfumed by a legion of vanished dolls. Stockings and robes and other garments were coiled on the glass counters or hung like brilliant tree-snakes on display stands along the narrow walls. A henna-headed woman emerged from rustling recesses at the rear and came tripping towards me on her toes.

'You are looking for a gift, sir?' she cried with a wilted kind of gaiety. Behind her painted mask, she was tired and ageing and it was Saturday afternoon and the lucky ones were dunking themselves in kidney-shaped swimming pools behind walls she couldn't climb.

'Not exactly. In fact, not at all. A peculiar thing happened to me last night. I'd like to tell you about it, but it's kind of complicated.'

She looked me over quizzically and decided that I worked for a living, too. The phoney smile faded away. Another smile took its place, which I liked better. 'You look as if you had a fairly rough night. And you could do with a shave.'

'I met a girl,' I said. 'Actually she was a mature woman, a statuesque blonde to be exact. I picked her up on the beach at Laguna, if you want me to be brutally frank.'

'I couldn't bear it if you weren't. What kind of a pitch is this, brother?'

'Wait. You're spoiling my story. Something clicked when we met, in that sunset light, on the edge of the warm summer sea.'

'It's always bloody cold when I go in.'

'It wasn't last night. We swam in the moonlight and had a gay time and all. Then she went away. I didn't realise until she was gone that I didn't know her telephone number, or even her last name.'

'Married woman, eh? What do you think I am, a lonely hearts club?' Still, she was interested, though she probably didn't believe me. 'She mentioned me, is that it? What was her first name?'

'Fern.'

'Unusual name. You say she was a big blonde?'

'Magnificently proportioned,' I said. 'If I had a classical education I'd call her Junoesque.'

'You're kidding me, aren't you?'

'A little.'

'I thought so. Personally I don't mind a little kidding. What did she say about me?'

'Nothing but good. As a matter of fact, I was complimenting her on her—er—garments.'

'I see.' She was long past blushing. 'We had a customer last fall some time, by the name of Fern. Fern Dee. She had some kind of a job at the Joshua Club, I think. But she doesn't fit the description at all. This one was a brunette, a middle-sized brunette, quite young. I remember the name Fern because she wanted it embroidered on all the things she bought. A corny idea if you ask me, but that was her girlish desire and who am I to argue with girlish desires?'

'Is she still in town?'

'I haven't seen her lately, not for months. But it couldn't be the woman you're looking for. Or could it?'

'How long ago was she in here?'

She pondered. 'Early last fall, around the start of the season. She only came in that once, and made a big purchase, stockings and night-wear and underthings. The works. I remember thinking at the time, here was a girlie who suddenly hit the chips but heavily.'

'She might have put on weight since then, and dyed her hair. Strange things can happen to the female form.'

'You're telling me,' she said. 'How old was—your friend?'

'About forty, I'd say, give or take a little.'

'It couldn't be the same one then. The girl I'm talking about was twenty-five at the outside, and I don't make mistakes about women's ages. I've seen too many of them in all stages, from Quentin quail to hags, and I certainly do mean hags.'

'I bet you have.'

She studied me with eyes shadowed by mascara and experience. 'You a policeman?'

'I have been.'

'You want to tell mother what it's all about?'

'Another time. Where's the Joshua Club?'

'It won't be open yet.'

'I'll try it anyway.'

She shrugged her shoulders and gave me directions. I thanked her.

It occupied a plain-faced one-storey building half a block off the main street. The padded leather door swung inward when I pushed it. I passed through a lobby with a retractable roof, which contained a jungle growth of banana trees. The big main room was decorated with tinted desert photomurals. Behind a rattan bar with a fishnet canopy, a white-coated Caribbean type was drying shot-glasses with a dirty towel. His face looked uncommunicative.

On the orchestra dais beyond the piled chairs in the dining area, a young man in shirt-sleeves was playing bop piano. His fingers shadowed the tune, ran circles around it, played leap-frog with it, and managed never to hit it on the nose. I stood beside him for a while and listened to him work. He looked up finally, still strumming with his left hand in the bass. He had soft-centred eyes and frozen-looking nostrils and a whistling mouth.

'Nice piano,' I said.

'I think so.'

'Fifty-second Street?'

'It's the street with the beat and I'm not effete.' His left hand struck the same chord three times and dropped away from the keys. 'Looking for somebody, friend?'

'Fern Dee. She asked me to drop by some time.'

'Too bad. Another wasted trip. She left here end of last year, the dear. She wasn't a bad little nightingale but she was no pro, Joe, you know? She had it but she couldn't project it. When she warbled the evening died, no matter how hard she tried, I don't wanna be snide.'

'Where did she lam, Sam, or don't you give a damn?'

He smiled like a corpse in a deft mortician's hands. 'I heard the boss retired her to private life. Took her home to live with him. That is what I heard. But I don't mix with the big boy socially, so I couldn't say for sure that she's impure. Is it anything to you?'

'Something, but she's over twenty-one.'

'Not more than a couple of years over twenty-one.' His eyes darkened, and his thin mouth twisted sideways angrily. 'I hate to see it happen to a pretty little twist like Fern. Not that I yearn—'

I broke in on his nonsense rhymes: 'Who's the big boss you mentioned, the one Fern went to live with?'

'Angel. Who else?'

'What heaven does he inhabit?'

'You must be new in these parts—' His eyes swivelled and focused on something over my shoulder. His mouth opened and closed.

A grating tenor said behind me: 'Got a question you want answered, bud?'

The pianist went back to the piano as if the ugly tenor had wiped me out, annulled my very existence. I turned to its source. He was standing in a narrow doorway behind the drums, a man in his thirties with thick black curly hair and a heavy jaw blue-shadowed by closely shaven beard. He was almost the living image of the dead man in the Cadillac. The likeness gave me a jolt. The heavy black gun in his hand gave me another.

He came around the drums and approached me, bull-shouldered in a fuzzy tweed jacket, holding the gun in front of him like a dangerous gift. The pianist was doing wry things in quickened tempo with the dead march from *Saul*. A wit.

The dead man's almost-double waved his cruel chin and the crueller gun in unison. 'Come inside, unless you're a government man. If you are, I'll have a look at your credentials.'

'I'm a freelance.'

'Inside then.'

The muzzle of the automatic came into my solar plexus like a pointing iron finger. Obeying its injunction, I made my way between empty music stands and through the narrow door behind the drums. The iron finger, probing my back, directed me down a lightless corridor to a small square office containing a metal desk, a safe, a filing cabinet. It was windowless, lit by fluorescent tubes in the ceiling. Under their pitiless glare, the face above the gun looked more than ever like the dead man's face. I wondered if I had been mistaken about his deadness, or if the desert heat had addled my brain.

'I'm the manager here,' he said, standing so close that I could smell the piney stuff he used on his crisp dark hair. 'You got anything to ask about the members of the staff, you ask me.'

'Will I get an answer?'

'Try me, bud.'

'The name is Archer,' I said. 'I'm a private detective.'

'Working for who?'

'You wouldn't be interested.'

'I am, though, very much interested.' The gun hopped forward like a toad into my stomach again, with the weight of his shoulder behind it. 'Working for who did you say?'

I swallowed anger and nausea, estimating my chances of knocking the gun to one side and taking him bare-handed. The chances seemed pretty slim. He was heavier than I was, and he held the automatic as if it had grown out of the end of his arm. You've seen too many movies, I told myself. I told him: 'A motel owner on the coast. A man was shot in one of his rooms last night. I happened to check in there a few minutes later. The old boy hired me to look into the shooting.'

'Who was it got himself ventilated?'

'He could be your brother,' I said. 'Do you have a brother?'

He lost his colour. The centre of his attention shifted from the gun to my face. The gun nodded. I knocked it up and sideways with a hard left uppercut. Its discharge burned the side of my face and drilled a hole in the wall. My right sank into his neck. The gun thumped the cork floor.

He went down but not out, his spread hand scrabbling for the gun, then closing on it. I stamped his wrist. He grunted but wouldn't let go of it. I threw a rabbit punch at the short hairs on the back of his neck. He took it and came up under it with the gun, shaking his head from side to side like a bull.

'Up with the hands now,' he murmured. He was one of those men whose voices went soft and mild when they were in killing mood. He had the glassy impervious eyes of a killer. 'Is Bart dead?'

'Very dead. He was shot in the belly.'

'Who shot him?'

'That's the question.'

'Who shot him?' he said in a quiet white-faced rage. The single eye of the gun stared emptily at my midriff. 'It could happen to you, bud, here and now.'

'A woman was with him. She took a quick powder after it happened.'

'I heard you say a name to Alfie piano-player. Was it Fern?'

'It could have been.'

'What do you mean, it could have been?'

'She was there in the room apparently. If you can give me a description of her?'

His hard brown eyes looked past me. 'I can do better than that. There's a picture of her on the wall behind you. Take a look at it. Keep those hands up high.'

I shifted my feet and turned uneasily. The wall was blank. I heard him draw a breath and move, and I tried to evade his blow. No use. It caught the back of my head. I pitched forward against the blank wall and slid down it into three dimensions of blankness.

The blankness coagulated into coloured shapes. The shapes were half human and half beast and they dissolved and reformed, dancing through the eaves of my mind to dream a mixture of both jive and nightmare music. A dead man with a furred breast climbed out of a hole and doubled and quadrupled. I ran away from them through a twisting tunnel which led to an echo chamber. Under the roaring surge of the nightmare music, a rasping tenor was saying:

'I figure it like this. Vario's tip was good. Bart found her in Acapulco, and he was bringing her back from there. She conned him into stopping off at this motel for the night. Bart always went for her.'

'I didn't know that,' a dry old voice put in. 'This is very interesting news about Bart and Fern. You should have told me before this. Then I would not have sent him for her and this would not have happened. Would it, Gino?'

My mind was still partly absent, wandering underground in the echoing caves. I couldn't recall the voices, or who they were talking about. I had barely sense enough to keep my eyes closed and go on listening. I was lying on my back on a hard surface. The voices were above me.

The tenor said: 'You can't blame Bartolomeo. She's the one, the dirty treacherous lying little bitch.'

'Calm yourself, Gino. I blame nobody. But more than ever now, we want her back, isn't that right?'

'I'll kill her,' he said softly, almost wistfully.

'Perhaps. It may not be necessary now. I dislike promiscuous killing—'

'Since when, Angel?'

'Don't interrupt, it's not polite. I learned to put first things first. Now what is the most important thing? Why did we want her back in the first place? I will tell you: to shut her mouth. The government heard she left me, they wanted her to testify about my income. We wanted to find her first and shut her mouth, isn't that right?'

'I know how to shut her mouth,' the younger man said very quietly.

'First we try a better way, my way. You learn when you're as old as I am there is a use for everything, and not to be wasteful. Not even wasteful with somebody else's blood. She shot your brother, right? So now we have something on her, strong enough to keep her mouth shut for good. She'd get off with second degree, with what she's got, but even that is five to ten in Tehachapi. I think all I need to do is tell her that. First we have to find her, eh?'

'I'll find her. Bart didn't have any trouble finding her.'

'With Vario's tip to help him, no. But I think I'll keep you here with me, Gino. You're too hot-blooded, you and your brother both. I want her alive. Then I can talk to her, and then we'll see.'

'You're going soft in your old age, Angel.'

'Am I?' There was a light slapping sound, of a blow on flesh. 'I have killed many men, for good reasons. So I think you will take that back.'

'I take it back.'

'And call me Mr Funk. If I am so old, you will treat my grey hairs with respect. Call me Mr Funk.'

'Mr Funk.'

'All right, your friend here, does he know where Fern is?'

'I don't think so.'

'Mr Funk.'

'Mr Funk.' Gino's voice was a whining snarl.

'I think he is coming to. His eyelids fluttered.'

The toe of a shoe prodded my side. Somebody slapped my face a number of times. I opened my eyes and sat up. The back of my head was throbbing like an engine fuelled by pain. Gino rose from a squatting position and stood over me.

'Stand up.'

I rose shakily to my feet. I was in a stone-walled room with a high beamed ceiling, sparsely furnished with stiff old black oak chairs and tables. The room and the furniture seemed to have been built for a race of giants.

The man behind Gino was small and old and weary. He might have been an unsuccessful grocer or a superannuated barkeep who had come to California for his health. Clearly his health was poor. Even in the stifling heat he looked pale and chilly, as if he had caught chronic death from one of his victims. He moved closer to me, his legs shuffling feebly in wrinkled blue trousers that bagged at the knees. His shrunken torso was swathed in a heavy blue turtleneck sweater. He had two days' beard on his chin, like moth-eaten grey plush.

'Gino informs me that you are investigating a shooting.' His accent was Middle-European and very faint, as if he had forgotten his origins. 'Where did this happen, exactly?'

'I don't think I'll tell you that. You can read it in the papers tomorrow night if you are interested.'

'I am not prepared to wait. I am impatient. Do you know where Fern is?'

'I wouldn't be here if I did.'

'But you know where she was last night.'

'I couldn't be sure.'

'Tell me anyway to the best of your knowledge.'

'I don't think I will.'

'He doesn't think he will,' the old man said to Gino.

'I think you better let me out of here. Kidnapping is a tough rap. You don't want to die in the pen.'

He smiled at me, with a tolerance more terrible than anger. His eyes were like thin stab-wounds filled with watery blood. Shuffling unhurriedly to the head of the mahogany table behind him, he pressed a spot in the rug with the toe of one felt slipper. Two men in blue serge suits entered the room and stepped towards me briskly. They belonged to the race of giants it had been built for.

Gino moved behind me and reached to pin my arms. I pivoted, landed one short punch, and took a very hard counter below the belt. Something behind me slammed my kidneys with the heft of a trailer truck bumper. I turned on weakening legs and caught a chin with my elbow. Gino's fist, or one of the beams from the ceiling, landed on my neck. My head rang like a gong. Under its clangour, Angel was saying pleasantly:

'Where was Fern last night?'

I didn't say.

The men in blue serge held me upright by the arms while Gino used my head as a punching bag. I rolled with his lefts and rights as well as I could but his timing improved and mine deteriorated. His face wavered and receded. At intervals Angel enquired politely if I was willing to assist him now. I asked myself confusedly in the hail of fists what I was holding out for or who I was protecting. Probably I was holding out for myself. It seemed important to me not to give in to violence. But my identity was dissolving and receding like the face in front of me.

I concentrated on hating Gino's face. That kept it clear and steady for a while: a stupid square-jawed face barred by a single black brow, two close-set brown eyes staring glassily. His fist continued to rock me like an air-hammer.

Finally Angel placed a clawed hand on his shoulder, and nodded to my handlers. They deposited me in the chair. It swung on an invisible wire from the ceiling in great circles. It swung out wide over the desert, across a bleak horizon, into darkness.

I came to cursing. Gino was standing over me again. There was an empty water-glass in his hand, and my face was dripping. Angel spoke up beside him, with a trace of irritation in his voice:

'You stand up good under punishment. Why go to all the trouble, though? I want a little information, that is all. My friend, my little girlfriend, ran away. I'm impatient to get her back.'

'You're going about it the wrong way.'

Gino leaned close, and laughed harshly. He shattered the glass on the arm of my chair, held the jagged base up to my eyes. Fear ran through me, cold and light in my veins. My eyes were my connection with everything. Blindness would be the end of me. I closed my eyes, shutting out the cruel edges of the broken thing in his hand.

'Nix, Gino,' the old man said. 'I have a better idea, as usual. There is heat on, remember.'

They retreated to the far side of the table and conferred there in low voices. The young man left the room. The old man came back to me. His storm troopers stood one on each side of me, looking down at him in ignorant awe.

'What is your name, young fellow?'

I told him. My mouth was puffed and lisping, tongue tangled in ropes of blood.

'I like a young fellow who can take it, Mr Archer. You say that you're a detective. You find people for a living, is that right?'

'I have a client,' I said.

'Now you have another. Whoever he is, I can buy and sell him, believe me. Fifty times over.' His thin blue hands scoured each other. They made a sound like two dry sticks rubbing together on a dead tree.

'Narcotics?' I said. 'Are you the wheel in the heroin racket? I've heard of you.'

His watery eyes veiled themselves like a bird's. 'Now don't ask foolish questions, or I will lose my respect for you entirely.'

'That would break my heart.'

'Then comfort yourself with this.' He brought an old-fashioned purse out of his hip pocket, abstracted a crumpled bill and smoothed it out on my knee. It was a five-hundred-dollar bill.

'This girl of mine you are going to find for me, she is young and foolish. I am old and foolish, to have trusted her. No matter. Find her for me and bring her back and I will give you another bill like this one. Take it.'

'Take it,' one of my guards repeated. 'Mr Funk said for you to take it.'

I took it. 'You're wasting your money. I don't even know what she looks like. I don't know anything about her.'

'Gino is bringing a picture. He came across her last fall at a recording studio in Hollywood where Alfie had a date. He gave her an audition and took her on at the club, more for her looks than for the talent she had. As a singer she flopped. But she is a pretty little thing, about five foot four, nice figure, dark brown hair, big hazel eyes. I found a use for her.' Lechery flickered briefly in his eyes and went out.

'You find a use for everything.'

'That is good economics. I often think if I wasn't what I am, I would make a good economist. Nothing would go to waste.' He paused, and dragged his dying old mind back to the subject:'She was here for a couple of months, then she ran out on me, silly girl. I heard last week that she was in Acapulco, and the federal Grand Jury was going to subpoena her. I have tax troubles, Mr Archer, all my life I have tax troubles. Unfortunately I let Fern help with my books a little bit. She could do me great harm. So I sent Bart to Mexico to bring her back. But I meant no harm to her. I still intend her no harm, even now. A little talk, a little realistic discussion with Fern, that is all that will be necessary. So even the shooting of my good friend Bart serves its purpose. Where did it happen, by the way?'

The question flicked out like a hook on the end of a long line.

'In San Diego,' I said, 'at a place near the airport: the Mission Motel.'

He smiled paternally. 'Now you are showing good sense.'

Gino came back with a silver-framed photograph in his hand. He handed it to Angel, who passed it on to me. It was a studio portrait, of the kind intended for publicity cheesecake. On a black velvet divan, against an artificial night sky, a young woman reclined in a gossamer robe that was split to show one bent leg. Shadows accented the lines of her body and the fine bones in her face. Under the heavy make-up which widened the mouth and darkened the half-closed eyes, I recognised Ella Salanda. The picture was signed in white, in the lower right-hand corner: 'To my Angel, with all my love, Fern.'

A sickness assailed me, worse than the sickness induced by Gino's fists. Angel breathed into my face: 'Fern Dee is a stage name. Her real name I never learned. She told me one time that if her family knew where she was they would die of shame.' He chuckled. 'She will not want them to know that she killed a man.'

I drew away from his charnel-house breath. My guards escorted me out. Gino started to follow, but Angel called him back.

'Don't wait to hear from me,' the old man said after me. 'I expect to hear from you.'

The building stood on a rise in the open desert. It was huge and turreted, like somebody's idea of a castle in Spain. The last rays of the sun washed its walls in purple light and cast long shadows across its barren acreage. It was surrounded by a ten-foot hurricane fence topped with three strands of barbed wire.

Palm Springs was a clutter of white stones in the distance, diamonded by an occasional light. The dull red sun was balanced like a glowing cigar-butt on the rim of the hills above the town. A man with a bulky shoulder harness under his brown suede windbreaker drove me towards it. The sun fell out of sight, and darkness gathered like an impalpable ash on the desert, like a column of blue-grey smoke towering into the sky.

The sky was blue-black and swarming with stars when I got back to Emerald Bay. A black Cadillac followed me out of Palm Springs. I lost it in the winding streets of Pasadena. So far as I could see, I had lost if for good.

The neon Mexican lay peaceful under the stars. A smaller sign at his feet asserted that there was No Vacancy. The lights in the long low stucco buildings behind him shone brightly. The office door was open behind a screen, throwing a barred rectangle of light on the gravel. I stepped into it, and froze.

Behind the registration desk in the office, a woman was avidly reading a magazine. Her shoulders and bosom were massive. Her hair was blonde, piled on her head in coroneted braids. There were rings on her fingers, a triple strand of cultured pearls around her thick white throat. She was the woman Donny had described to me.

I pulled the screen door open and said rudely: 'Who are you?'

She glanced up, twisting her mouth in a sour grimace. 'Well! I'll thank you to keep a civil tongue in your head.'

'Sorry. I thought I'd seen you before somewhere.'

'Well, you haven't.' She looked me over coldly. 'What happened to your face, anyway?'

'I had a little plastic surgery done. By an amateur surgeon.'

She clucked disapprovingly. 'If you're looking for a room, we're full up for the night. I don't believe I'd rent you a room even if we weren't. Look at your clothes.'

'Uh-huh. Where's Mr Salanda?'

'Is it any business of yours?'

'He wants to see me. I'm doing a job for him.'

'What kind of a job?'

I mimicked her: 'Is it any business of yours?' I was irritated. Under her mounds of flesh she had a personality as thin and hard and abrasive as a rasp.

'Watch who you're getting flip with, sonny boy.' She rose, and her shadow loomed immense across the back door of the room. The magazine fell closed on the desk: it was *Teen-age Confessions*. 'I am Mrs Salanda. Are you a handyman?'

'A sort of one,' I said. 'I'm a garbage collector in the moral field. You look as if you could use me.'

The crack went over her head. 'Well, you're wrong. And I don't think my husband hired you, either. This is a respectable motel.'

'Uh-huh. Are you Ella's mother?'

'I should say not. That little snip is no daughter of mine.'

'Her stepmother?'

'Mind your own business. You better get out of here. The police are keeping a close watch on this place tonight, if you're planning any tricks.'

'Where's Ella now?'

'I don't know and I don't care. She's probably gallivanting off around the countryside. It's all she's good for. One day at home in the last six months, that's a fine record for a young unmarried girl.' Her face was thick and bloated with anger against her step-daughter. She went on talking blindly, as if she had forgotten me entirely: 'I told her father he was an old fool to take her back. How does he know what she's been up to? I say let the ungrateful filly go and fend for herself.'

'Is that what you say, Mabel?' Salanda had softly opened the door behind her. He came forward into the room, doubly dwarfed by her blonde magnitude. 'I say if it wasn't for you, my dear, Ella wouldn't have been driven away from home in the first place.'

She turned on him in a blubbering rage. He drew himself up tall and reached to snap his fingers under her nose. 'Go back into the house. You are a disgrace to women, a disgrace to motherhood.'

'I'm not *her* mother, thank God.'

'Thank God,' he echoed, shaking his fist at her. She retreated like a schooner under full sail, menaced by a gunboat. The door closed on her. Salanda turned to me:

'I'm sorry, Mr Archer. I have difficulties with my wife, I am ashamed to say it. I was an imbecile to marry again. I gained a senseless hulk of flesh, and lost my daughter. Old imbecile!' he denounced himself, wagging his great head sadly. 'I married in hot blood. Sexual passion has always been my downfall. It runs in my family, this insane hunger for blondeness and stupidity and size.' He spread his arms in a wide and futile embrace on emptiness.

'Forget it.'

'If I could.' He came closer to examine my face. 'You are injured, Mr Archer. Your mouth is damaged. There is blood on your chin.'

'I was in a slight brawl.'

'On my account?'

'On my own. But I think it's time you levelled with me.'

'Levelled with you?'

'Told me the truth. You knew who was shot last night, and who shot him, and why.'

He touched my arm, with a quick, tentative grace. 'I have only one daughter, Mr Archer, only the one child. It was my duty to defend her, as best as I could.'

'Defend her from what?'

'From shame, from the police, from prison.' He flung one arm out, indicating the whole range of human disaster. 'I am a man of honour, Mr Archer. But private honour stands higher with me than public honour. The man was abducting my daughter. She brought him here in the hope of being rescued. Her last hope.'

'I think that's true. You should have told me this before.'

'I was alarmed, upset. I feared your intentions. Any minute the police were due to arrive.'

'But you had a right to shoot him. It wasn't even a crime. The crime was his.'

'I didn't know that then. The truth came out to me gradually. I feared that Ella was involved with him.' His flat black gaze sought my face and rested on it. 'However, I did not shoot him, Mr Archer. I was not even here at the time. I told you that this morning, and you may take my word for it.'

'Was Mrs Salanda here?'

'No sir, she was not. Why should you ask me that?'

'Donny described the woman who checked in with the dead man. The description fits your wife.'

'Donny was lying. I told him to give a false description of the woman. Apparently he was unequal to the task of inventing one.'

'Can you prove that she was with you?'

'Certainly I can. We had reserved seats at the theatre. Those who sat around us can testify that the seats were not empty. Mrs Salanda and I, we are not an inconspicuous couple.' He smiled wryly.

'Ella killed him then.'

He neither assented, nor denied it. 'I was hoping that you were on my side, my side and Ella's. Am I wrong?'

'I'll have to talk to her, before I know myself. Where is she?'

'I do not know, Mr Archer, sincerely I do not know. She went away this afternoon, after the policemen questioned her. They were suspicious, but we managed to soothe their suspicions. They did not know that she had just come home, from another life, and I did not tell them. Mabel wanted to tell them. I silenced her.' His white teeth clicked together.

'What about Donny?'

'They took him down to the station for questioning. He told them nothing damaging. Donny can appear very stupid when he wishes. He has the reputation of an idiot, but he is not so dumb. Donny has been with me for many years. He has a deep devotion for my daughter. I got him released tonight.'

'You should have taken my advice,' I said, 'taken the police into your confidence. Nothing would have happened to you. The dead man was a mobster, and what he was doing amounts to kidnapping. Your daughter was a witness against his boss.'

'She told me that. I am glad that it is true. Ella has not always told me the truth. She has been a hard girl to bring up, without a good mother to set her an example. Where has she been these last six months, Mr Archer?'

'Singing in a night club in Palm Springs. Her boss was a racketeer.'

'A racketeer?' His mouth and nose screwed up, as if he sniffed the odour of corruption.

'Where she was isn't important, compared with where she is now. The boss is still after her. He hired me to look for her.'

Salanda regarded me with fear and dislike, as if the odour originated in me. 'You let him hire you?'

'It was my best chance of getting out of his place alive. I'm not his boy, if that's what you mean.'

'You ask me to believe you?'

'I'm telling you. Ella is in danger. As a matter of fact, we all are.' I didn't tell him about the second black Cadillac. Gino would be driving it, wandering the night roads with a ready gun in his armpit and revenge corroding his heart.

'My daughter is aware of the danger,' he said. 'She warned me of it.'

'She must have told you where she was going.'

'No. But she may be at the beach house. The house where Donny lives. I will come with you.'

'You stay here. Keep your doors locked. If any strangers show and start prowling the place, call the police.'

He bolted the door behind me as I went out. Yellow traffic lights cast wan reflections on the asphalt. Streams of cars went by to the north, to the south. To the west, where the sea lay, a great black emptiness opened under the stars. The beach house sat on its white margin, a little over a mile from the motel.

For the second time that day, I knocked on the warped kitchen door. There was a light behind it, shining through the cracks. A shadow obscured the light.

'Who is it?' Donny said. Fear or some other emotion had filled his mouth with pebbles.

'You know me, Donny.'

The door groaned on its hinges. He gestured dumbly to me to come in, his face a white blur. When he turned his head, and the light from the living-room caught his face, I saw that grief was the emotion that marked it. His eyes were swollen as if he had been crying. More than ever he resembled a dilapidated boy whose growing pains had never paid off in manhood.

'Anybody with you?'

Sounds of movement in the living-room answered my question. I brushed him aside and went in. Ella Salanda was bent over an open suitcase on the camp cot. She straightened, her mouth thin, eyes wide and dark. The .38 automatic in her hand gleamed dully under the naked bulb suspended from the ceiling.

'I'm getting out of here,' she said, 'and you're not going to stop me.'

'I'm not sure I want to try. Where are you going, Fern?'

Donny spoke behind me, in his grief-thickened voice: 'She's going away from me. She promised to stay here if I did what she told me. She promised to be my girl—'

'Shut up, stupid.' Her voice cut like a lash, and Donny gasped as if the lash had been laid across his back.

'What did she tell you to do, Donny? Tell me just what you did.'

'When she checked in last night with the fella from Detroit, she made a sign I wasn't to let on I knew her. Later on she left me a note. She wrote it with a lipstick on a piece of paper towel. I still got it hidden, in the kitchen.'

'What did she write in the note?'

He lingered behind me, fearful of the gun in the girl's hand, more fearful of her anger.

She said: 'Don't be crazy, Donny. He doesn't know a thing, not a thing. He can't do anything to either of us.'

'I don't care what happens, to me or anybody else,' the anguished voice said behind me. 'You're running out on me, breaking your promise to me. I always knew it was too good to be true. Now I just don't care any more.'

'I care,' she said. 'I care what happens to me.' Her hazel eyes shifted to me, above the unwavering gun. 'I won't stay here. I'll shoot you if I have to.'

'It shouldn't be necessary. Put it down, Fern. It's Bartolomeo's gun, isn't it? I found the shells to fit it in his glove compartment.'

'How do you know so much?'

'I talked to Angel.'

'Is he here?' Panic whined in her voice.

'No. I came alone.'

'You better leave the same way then, while you can go under your own power.'

'I'm staying. You need protection, whether you know it or not. And I need information. Donny, go in the kitchen and bring me that note.'

'Don't do it, Donny. I'm warning you.'

His sneakered feet made soft indecisive sounds. I advanced on the girl, talking quietly and steadily.

'You conspired to kill a man, but you don't have to be afraid. He had it coming. Tell the whole story to the cops, and my guess is they won't even book you. Hell, you can even become famous. The government wants you as a witness in a tax case.'

'What kind of a case?'

'A tax case against Angel. It's probably the only kind of rap they can pin on him. You can send him up for the rest of his life like Capone. You'll be a heroine, Fern.'

'Don't call me Fern. I hate that name.' There were sudden tears in her eyes. 'I hate everything connected with that name. I hate myself.'

'You'll hate yourself more if you don't put down the gun. Shoot me and it all starts over again. The cops will be on your trail, Angel's troopers will be gunning for you.'

Now only the cot was between us, the cot and the unsteady gun facing me above it.

'This is the turning-point,' I said. 'You've made a lot of bum decisions and almost ruined yourself, playing footsie with the evillest men there are. You can go on the way you have been, getting in deeper until you end up in a refrigerated drawer, or you can come back out of it now, into a decent life.'

'A decent life? Here? With my father married to Mabel?'

'I don't think Mabel will last much longer. Anyway, I'm not Mabel. I'm on your side.'

Ella made a decision. I could tell a mile away what she was going to do. She dropped the gun on the blanket. I scooped it up and turned to Donny:

'Let me see that note.'

He disappeared through the kitchen door, head and shoulders drooping on the long stalk of his body.

'What could I do?' the girl said. 'I was caught. It was Bart or me. All the way up from Acapulco I planned how I could get away. He held a gun in my side when we crossed the border, the same way when we stopped for gas or to eat at the drive-ins. I realised he had to be killed. My father's motel looked like my only chance. So I talked Bart into staying there with me overnight. He had no idea who the place belonged to. I didn't know what I was going to do. I only knew it had to be something drastic. Once I was back with Angel in the desert, that was the end of me. Even if he didn't kill me, it meant I'd have to go on living with him. Anything was better than that. So I wrote a note to Donny in the bathroom, and dropped it out the window. He was always crazy about me.'

Her mouth had grown softer. She looked remarkably young and virginal. The faint blue hollows under her eyes were dewy. 'Donny shot Bart with Bart's own gun. He had more nerve than I had. I lost my nerve when I went back into the room this morning. I didn't know about the blood in the bathroom. It was the last straw.'

She was wrong. Something crashed in the kitchen. A cool draught swept the living-room. A gun spoke twice, out of sight. Donny fell backwards through the doorway, a piece of brownish paper clutched in his hand. Blood gleamed on his shoulder like a red badge.

I stepped behind the cot and pulled the girl down to the floor with me. Gino came through the door, his two-coloured sports shoe stepping on Donny's labouring chest. I shot the gun out of his hand. He floundered back against the wall, clutching at his wrist.

I sighted carefully for my second shot, until the black bar of his eyebrows was steady in the sights of the .38. The hole it made was invisible. Gino fell loosely forward, prone on the floor beside the man he had killed.

Ella Salanda ran across the room. She knelt, and cradled Donny's head in her lap. Incredibly, he spoke, in a loud sighing voice:

'You won't go away again, Ella? I did what you told me. You promised.'

'Sure I promised. I won't leave you, Donny. Crazy fool.'

'You like me better than you used to? Now?'

'I like you, Donny. You're the most man there is.'

She held the poor insignificant head in her hands. He sighed, and his life came out bright-coloured at the mouth. It was Donny who went away.

His hand relaxed, and I read the lipstick note she had written him on a piece of porous tissue:

'Donny: This man will kill me unless you kill him first. His gun will be in his clothes on the chair beside the bed. Come in and get it at midnight and shoot to kill. Good luck. I'll stay and be your girl if you do this, just like you always wished. Love. Ella.'

I looked at the pair on the floor. She was rocking his lifeless head against her breast. Beside them, Gino looked very small and lonely, a dummy leaking darkness from his brow.

Donny had his wish and I had mine. I wondered what Ella's was.

2

COPS AND G-MEN

Stories of the Law Officers

THE HUNTING OF HEMINGWAY

MacKinlay Kantor

The man who played a major role in introducing the tough cop into hardboiled fiction as a central figure was William J. Flynn, who had been a lawman himself for years as the former head of the United States Secret Service. Just as Joseph T. Shaw had given special prominence to hardboiled dicks in the pages of Black Mask, *so the thickset, pugnacious Flynn encouraged writers to his pulp magazine (which started publication as* Flynn's *in 1924 and then became* Detective Fiction Weekly *in 1928) to write about lawmen who were a match for gangsters and every bit as tough as the private eyes. It was a theme he had begun to explore himself as early as 1922, with a series entitled 'Peabody Smith, the Famous Investigator of the US Secret Service', obviously based on his own experiences, and it was one that clearly appealed to several of the writers whose contributions began to reach his desk—the versatile Max Brand, Arthur B. Reeve (creator of the Scientific Detective, Craig Kennedy), Cornell Woolrich (of whom more later) and MacKinlay Kantor.*

'Mac' Kantor, who was destined to win a Pulitzer Prize for his Civil War novel Andersonville *(1955) and acclaim as a Hollywood scriptwriter, is also credited with a landmark in the hardboiled genre by writing one of the first cop series in the pulps. The stories were about two brothers, Nick and Dave Glennan, who worked for the New York Police Department. Dave, the elder of the two, was a hard-nosed detective, effective but rather set in his ways, while Nick, fifteen years his junior, was quicker-thinking and more direct in his style. The tales about these two and their investigations into murders, robberies and the activities of the city's criminals appeared in* Detective Fiction Weekly *during the early Thirties and, despite their popularity, have rarely been reprinted since.*

MacKinlay Kantor (1904–) was born in Iowa and began his career as a journalist on the Daily News *in Webster City, followed by a spell as a columnist on the* Des Moines Tribune. *In 1930 he moved to New York where he worked on his early novels and contributed with increasing success to* Detective Fiction Weekly. *He also had several brushes with the very policemen he was writing about. On the first occasion, he was driving his car, still bearing its Iowa licence plates, when he was stopped by a group of New Jersey cops on the look-out for a number of mid-western gangsters on the run, including the notorious John Dillinger. A year later the same thing happened—although Kantor confessed this time that he* had *been speeding—and he found himself facing two of the same men. Fortunately they recognised him—and also the fact that he was a writer they enjoyed reading in* Detective Fiction Weekly. *Instead of a ticket, he was invited back to the precinct station so that the whole group could regale him with cases for future plots. A third occasion, when he was actually seeking inspiration for a story about the Glennan brothers, proved far more disturbing, as he later explained: 'Once on the outskirts of Westfield I parked in a quiet lane near a deserted estate and went into a trance, trying to rustle up a plot for another* Weekly *story. The next thing I knew there were cops with drawn revolvers standing on both sides of the car. They wanted to know what I was doing there. I told them honestly, "Trying to think up a unique way of murdering a man," but I almost laughed on the other side of my face before I was through explaining!'*

Kantor, of course, later turned to novels of historical fiction, becoming one of the most widely read American writers with classics like The Voice of Bugle Ann *(1935),* Gettysburg *(1952) and* Story Teller *(1967)—in recognition of which he was made Consultant in American Letters to the Library of Congress in Washington. However, he always retained an affection for his pulp stories about the Glennan brothers, which he believed had 'a kind of sharpness and pungency'. Here is one of the best, in which he has apparently made use of his own brush with the law to recount the brothers' manhunt for a desperate gangster.*

*   *   *

Inspector Bourse looked very tired. He had been awake all night, and he was not as young as he had been in the days when he wore a grey helmet and sported a walrus-moustache.

The two young men and the two blowsy, over-dressed women crowded close around him as he sat crouched in the deep, gaudily upholstered chair.

Bourse asked, 'How's your watch, Ricardi? And yours, Nick Glennan?'

Coonskin cuffs slid back from two husky wrists, and for a moment there was silence.

'Eight-eight, sir.'

'That's me, Inspector. Eight-eight.'

'You ladies'—he slurred the word—'got your guns in your pocket-books?'

'Yes, sir.'

'Then,' said old Inspector Bourse, 'I'd like to know what's keeping you. Go to it. Don't give 'em a break. They never gave a break in their lives, least of all Hemingway. And remember them vests. Shoot 'em in the kisser.'

Said one of the women, whose name was Cohen, 'That reminds me—'

'Shoot him in the pants,' nodded the old chief, 'the coat and vest is mine. All right, gentlemen.'

They went out through the kitchen, and a uniformed patrolman opened the rear door. They went down two flights of bleak stairway and crowded into a red and black taxicab which had been waiting at the alley entrance with idling motor. Nobody said anything. The driver seemed very husky for a taxi driver—he should have been able to command an occupation more fitting to one who scaled two hundred and eight pounds and whose shoulders were all steel and wire.

At the Balmoral Street end of the alley, the taxicab turned left, and left a second time at Dorchester Avenue; now it was heading east and parallel to the alley where it had stood waiting a moment before. This block was lined almost solidly with apartment buildings of the less-than-first-class variety, though here and there an old residence stood out solidly, resisting the cheap encroachment of red and yellow brick walls.

'Right here,' said the youngest, handsomest man, and the cab slowed to the kerb in front of Number 1441.

The street looked innocent enough. It was then about eight-thirteen of an ordinary weekday morning, and Dorchester Avenue was an ordinary weekday street if ever there was one. A milk truck was parked ahead of the taxicab, and an express delivery van across the street. Protruding from a nearby delivery lane was the rear end of an Eclipse Laundry truck, and its driver was nowhere in sight. Apparently he had taken his little collapsible cart and vanished within the nearest building, where no doubt he was gathering loads of soiled linen or distributing the unsoiled variety. From behind the flimsy, opaque curtains of an opposite apartment, Inspector Bourse looked down at all these things and called them good.

He knew, as well, that behind 1441 Dorchester Avenue a junkman was driving through the main alley and was just about to have an altercation with a city garbage truck which blocked his way. He knew that not all the tenants of 1441 were still asleep or sitting over early breakfasts. No, at least a dozen of those tenants had taken occupancy during the previous day and night—slyly, carefully, silently—and just now they would have firearms ready to hand.

In the stupid four-and-a-half storey building which was numbered 1441, a young man sat in the tiny sun parlour of Apartment 327. He would have been exceedingly interested had he known that Inspector Bourse was watching his windows. He was not a nice young man. His face was the colour of the paper in which your butcher wraps meat, and his mouth had come down directly from a remote ancestor who served as a torturer for a Louis.

He was twenty-seven years old; he had killed men in Chicago, Dallas, Saginaw, Fort Wayne, Kansas City, Tulsa and in the town where he now sat. Mail trucks and banks had been levied upon, women had been forced to bestow their caresses upon him, and strangely enough some of them didn't have to be forced. The man's name was Chester Hemingway, and he had a personal cash estate of three hundred and fifteen thousand dollars.

The young man was chewing something. His thin jaws worked knowingly, cruelly, and not with the comfortable carelessness of the habitual gum-chewer. They went crunching up and down, pulverising some mysterious food between their gleaming white teeth. It was horrible, but forever fascinating, to watch Chet Hemingway chew. He was always chewing.

'Chet,' came a voice from the next room.

Without turning his head, Hemingway said, 'Yeah?' There was a scowl upon his face whenever he spoke.

'What's down there?'

'Cab. Couple of broads with two college boys in coon coats.'

'They were making a lot of noise. I just wondered—'

Chet Hemingway told his companion, 'Well, I'll do all the wondering that's done around here. Sure they're making a lot of noise. Anybody's making a lot of noise that's fried. These folks are fried—especially the two broads.' He leaned an inch closer to the window and his icy green eyes stared down at the gay party advancing towards the court entrance directly below. 'And broad is the word,' he muttered to himself. 'I like mine thinner than that.'

He thought of Lily.

'Tomsk,' he called, 'where's Lil?'

'Still asleep, I guess.'

'I wish to hell she'd get up and get us some breakfast. Tell her to get up.'

He heard Tomsk mutter to Heras, and Heras went padding down the short hall to knock at a bedroom door. 'Hey, Lil. Get up. Chet says for you to get up.' Lil's fretful voice came back after a moment: 'Oh, for God's sake!' She yawned. 'Oh, all right,' she said, 'I'm comin', tell him.'

Hemingway smiled. If one of those monkeys ever made a pass at Lily, he'd shoot his teeth out of his ears. Really, he must be getting fond of Lil—fonder than he'd ever been of anybody. That wouldn't do, to get fond of her. One of these days he'd have to get rid of her, one way or another. But for the present—

He heard the party of four—coonskin college boys and fat, painted women, come lumbering up the stairway. His hand went to his belly-gun, then away from it. Drunks. Hell-raising punks with a couple of alley-cats they'd picked up during a night of revelry. Nobody to be alarmed about . . . Two Railway Express deliverymen came across the street, carrying a heavy box between them. Far down the hallway, a milkman clinked his bottles. There was the mutter of rubber tyres close at hand—that laundryman was coming down the hall, knocking on doors as he came.

The radio mourned: '*Laaaast Round-Up* . . .'

Chet chewed and swallowed, swallowed and chewed. To the next room he called, 'Hey, Tomsk. I hear the laundry guy coming. Tell Lil to get ready to go to the door. You scram, you and Heras.' With sullen boredom, he lifted his eyes to the ceiling above his head. How long, how long would they have to stay in this damn building, this damn town? But it was too hot to try for South America, yet. Maybe another month—

At that moment, he had the first notion that it might be a good idea to take Lil along with him when he went. He had meant to ditch her in New Orleans—give her a roll, if he felt she was safe, but ditch her.

If he felt she wasn't safe, he could always put a hole through her and drop her off a bridge with an old steam radiator wired to her neck and legs. That had happened before, too. But not to Lil. That was Jenny. Jenny had never turned up again, either—the quicksands down deep in the river took care of that. It was one rap they'd never have against him.

Actually, Chet Hemingway was falling in love with Lil, and didn't realise it. It was funny: after all these weeks, and on this day when she was to be killed, that he should fall in love with her.

'Git along, little dogies, git along, little dogies—'

In the short stairway between the second and third floors, Detective Nick Glennan said to Detective Pete Ricardi, 'Okay. Dave will be opposite that little service door in the side hall. Horn will go down there as soon as we pick up the Tom-gun.'

One of the women, whose name was Cohen, gave a shrill and alcoholic laugh. He shone in the annual police vaudeville, did Benny Cohen. The other woman, whose name was Detective Barney Flynn, laughed even louder. But it was a coarse bellow; Flynn didn't make as good a woman as Cohen.

'You'll be bringing them out here, armed to the teeth,' muttered Nick Glennan. 'You sound like a hippopotamus, Barney. Okay,' he said again, as they reached the third floor. Nick wasn't a sergeant yet, but he was commanding this squad, and if nothing went wrong he might very soon be a sergeant.

Detective Horn came trundling his laundry cart down the hallway. He bestowed one solemn wink on the inebriated college boys and their blowsy companions; his face was rather pale. Ricardi leaned forward and lifted a Thompson submachine gun from under the pile of soft blue bags in the little cart. His coonskin coat slid from his shoulders; his slim hands moved capably from drum to trigger and back again; Ricardi was the best machine gunner in the department.

The women were doing things to themselves. Their coats and henna wigs vanished—the dresses were brief and sketchy and wouldn't bother them much, though they lost their rhinestone-buckled shoes in a hurry. They emerged from their disguises looking like nothing on land or sea, but they had .38s in their hands.

All this conversation, whispered as it was, and all this hasty disrobing and assembling of armature, took about three jerks. Horn ambled ahead, laundry cart and all, and vanished around the turn into the side hall where Sergeant Dave Glennan, Nick's fat brother, would be waiting inside the door of the opposite kitchen.

It didn't look like Hemingway and Tomsk and Scummy Heras had much of a chance. Across the street, Inspector Bourse and Chief of Detectives Moore were having a severe case of the jitters. Another minute, another two minutes—

The two Railway Express men dumped their box inside the vestibule on the opposite side of the court, and turning, drew their guns. In the alley at the rear, three detectives on an odoriferous garbage truck and two more detectives on a junkman's wagon, all became embroiled in a vituperative argument, which made it necessary for them to descend and gather opposite the back stairways.

A milkman came along the hall. He wore white and had an account-book, but his name was Detective Kerry. Silently the four other officers crept down the hall beside him. Kerry jangled bottles in the little wire basket he carried. '*Git along, little dogies,*' said Chet Hemingway's radio, '*git along—*'

They were on each side of the door of apartment 327. Nick Glennan pressed the little pearly button; Ricardi motioned for Kerry to jangle his bottles again, and under cover of the musical tinkle he made ready with his machine gun.

They heard a distant blatting of the kitchen buzzer; that was Horn.

'Milkman,' chanted Detective Kerry.

'Laun-dry . . .' droned Detective Horn, far around the corner.

'. . . *Laaast Round-Up . . . git along, little dogies . . .*' Somewhere inside there was a woman's voice, and a man replied.

'Who's there?'

'Milk-mannn . . .'

The door opened a crack. Cohen reached up with his foot and shoved it back; the man inside was Two-faced Tomsk, and if indeed he had possessed two faces he couldn't have looked any more surprised.

'Stick 'em up, Tomsk,' whispered Glennan. 'You haven't got a chance.'

They heard Sergeant Dave Glennan's voice from the kitchen door: 'Look out, Horn!' and they heard the sharp report of a small automatic. Lil wasn't taking any chances, either—she must have carried a gun with her when she went to the door.

Two-faced Tomsk threw himself forward in a dive, wrenching out his revolver as he came. Scummy Heras had been lying flat on the high-backed davenport, out of sight, but he came up with a .45 in each hand.

Tomsk had fired once and his bullet went between Kerry's arm and the side of his body, and then Tomsk continued forward to the floor with two of young Nick Glennan's Police Positive souvenirs in his head.

Scummy Heras was more of a problem. The stool pigeon hadn't lied when he talked about bullet-proof vests. Ricardi's machine gun dusted the davenport in a quick staccato, but all it did was bruise Heras' ribs. One of the gangster's guns was empty by that time; he had put a bullet through Barney Flynn's chest, and a lot more too close for anybody's comfort.

Through the kitchenette and little hallway, Sergeant Dave Glennan and Laundryman Horn came roaring in a flank attack. 'Drop it, Scummy,' they were yelling, but Scummy didn't mind worth a cent. He was backed against the French windows, and he kept going as long as he could. A fistful of slugs from Dave's sawn-off mashed him back against the yielding windows—the panes went crackling to bits, and Heras' body dropped, turning and twisting, to the paved court three storeys below.

But where was Mr Chester Hemingway, who had slain men in Chicago, Kansas City and points east and west? When the screaming roar of exploded cartridges died down, the little radio was still mourning about the lonesome prairies, but Chet Hemingway wasn't around. Nick Glennan tripped over an upset chair and raced on into the sun parlour; his brother and Horn were diving into bedrooms, and from every stair-way came a thunder of feet as the squads converged on apartment 327. But Chet Hemingway was not at home to receive them.

Nick flashed one baffled glance around the sun parlour. There was the radio, and there was Chet's half-burned cigarette already scorching the carpet, and there was— Nick swore, heartily. He climbed up on the table and stepped from there on top of the radiator. A square hole had been sawn in the ceiling, and through that hole it was evident that Hemingway had gone soaring.

'Two apartments,' Nick sobbed to himself. 'Two! And nobody had an idea about it—327—427, right upstairs—to hell with that stool pigeon—'

He thrust his hands through the ragged opening and found solid wood still warm and slippery from the clutch of Chet Hemingway's hands. He hauled himself up into apartment 427. A scraping sound, somewhere—and, sure, he might have had a bullet through his head if Chet Hemingway had lingered to give it to him . . .

The apartment was furnished, like the one below, but it was evident at a glance that no one lived here. They had rented it for only one purpose—the very purpose which it had served. With a little more warning, the whole gang would have climbed through that square hole and disappeared.

The door into the hallway was wide open—Nick ground his teeth. A ladder stood against the wall at the end of the hall, and a trap in the roof was opened. To think that those devils would have anticipated the whole thing—ladder and all! He paused only to bellow at the men below him, and then swarmed up the ladder.

He came out into a glare of cold sunlight, and a bullet screeched beside the trap door. Nick Glennan growled, and raised his gun. On the next roof but one, a slim figure in white shirt and black pants was vaulting over a three-foot barrier. Nick had one unexploded shell left in his cylinder. He spread his feet wide apart and took careful aim; the gun banged. The distant figure fell forward, recovered its balance, and sprinted ahead with torn shirt fluttering.

'Those *vests*,' sighed Nick, 'those inventions of the devil . . . and to think he wore it under his shirt . . .' All this time he was racing across the gravel and jumping narrow chasms and leaping low walls, like a runaway maniac. He came to the last building of the row, and looked over the edge to see that mocking figure dropping from the last rung of the fire escape. Nick whistled; he yelled and beckoned to the other cops who were swarming out of the distant trap door; he threw a perfectly good gun which smashed on the pavement, missing Chet Hemingway's head by six inches.

But it was all too late, now. Hemingway went up on one side of a taxicab; he thrust his gun against the driver . . . The detectives started after him one minute later, but that minute made about a mile's difference. And in crowded city streets, a mile is a mile. Still chewing and swallowing, Hemingway rode out of the detectives' lives. Temporarily . . .

For all the secrecy with which this coup was planned, there had been a leak somewhere in the department. The press had been tipped off, and for once the press had not gummed things up. Men from the *News Detail* and *Tribune* came swarming eagerly into the building from Dorchester Avenue; already flashlight bulbs were flashing in the dim courts and alleyways, and reporters were clamouring.

Inspector Bourse and Chief of Detectives Moore fought their way through the crowd and up to apartment 327. With grim satisfaction they contemplated the prone body of Two-faced Tomsk and the shattered window where Scummy Heras had taken his last tumble. But when they looked around, hopefully, for another corpse—and found it—they were not so pleased. Miss Lily Denardo was the other corpse.

'Well,' said the old Inspector. He looked down at the pretty white face and the ridiculous folds of stained crêpe-de-chine which swathed the slim figure. 'How'd this happen?'

Sergeant Dave Glennan's jowls trembled slightly. 'I don't know. I'm afraid it was me.'

'Had a gun, eh?' Bourse's foot touched the little automatic. 'I don't think we'll be blaming you for this, Dave me boy.'

The sergeant said, 'That wasn't it. She did take a crack at Horn and me, but her gun jammed or something. Just one shot and no more. She started in here—Scummy was shooting at the whole world, and I ups with my shotgun—'

Bourse looked at him. 'And kills the girl with a .45 calibre bullet?' he asked calmly.

Glennan blinked. 'Thank Heaven for that! I never realised, sir. Yes, that hole does look like a .45. I—thought—'

'Never mind what you thought. Let's find the bullet.'

'Here it is, sir,' said Horn.

The bullet had driven through Miss Lily Denardo's heart, with the sad artistry of which that calibre is capable at close range, and had lodged in the wall. They dug it out.

'Who was shooting .45s?' barked the Inspector.

Kerry scratched his torn sleeve. 'Nobody except the Tom-gun—Ricardi. We all had regulation guns. And Ricardi's bullets would have had to ricky-shay to hit her where she was a-standing. No, sir—take a look at Scummy's guns. There's one on the floor, and I guess he took the other with him when he went through the window.'

The ballistics expert established it later in the day; Scummy Heras had shot Lily, by design or accident. They never knew just how or why. It didn't matter. All the detectives were glad that none of them had killed her. She was too pretty.

'And so,' Inspector Bourse grunted, at three o'clock that afternoon, 'you let him get away. The meanest devil this side of hell, and you let him slide through your fingers.'

Every man who had taken part in the Dorchester Avenue raid—except Flynn, who lay in the hospital—was in Inspector Bourse's office.

'Mind,' he said, 'I'm blaming not a mother's son of you—individually. You all worked hard and had your nerve with you. Young Nick Glennan especially. I'll say that. When he went kiting through that hole in the ceiling, he took a mighty chance.'

Nick sat there and looked at his shoes. He felt his cheeks burning.

'But nevertheless, there you are. We had the best shots of the Bureau up there this morning, and we had the edge on that gang. And we let Hemingway get away. Sure, we didn't know about that apartment upstairs. Nobody did. The stool pigeon didn't. But our job was to get Chet Hemingway, more than any of the rest. We didn't get him. *Your* job was to get Chet Hemingway. *You* didn't get him. There it is. Eat it up; may it make you sick at the stomach.'

His desk telephone jangled. Slowly, Bourse reached down and lifted the bracket. 'I told you not to bother me,' he growled at the operator. 'I—What? ... All right,' he said, 'connect me.'

He looked at the rows of faces across his desk. 'A man,' he said. 'Claims he has something important about this morning.'

A new voice came on the wire. The eyes of Inspector Bourse froze bitterly as he listened.

'This,' said the voice, 'is Chet Hemingway—'

'Yes,' said Bourse. His voice crackled. His hand slid across the transmitter as he snapped at Ricardi, who sat directly in front of him, 'Get on a phone. Trace this call! ...'

'You didn't get me this morning,' came Hemingway's voice, 'and I'm still in town. Listen, you dirty flatfoot—you had to kill that little frail—she was a peach of a kid—she—'

Bourse said, 'We didn't kill her, Hemingway. Scummy did it.'

'Yeah?' snarled Chet. 'Listen—I'm not going to stay here long enough for you to trace this call. But I read the papers. Every damn sheet in town was shouting the praises of the noble detectives you had up there—and by *name*—get that? By name. I'm going to stay in town until I get every last guy who was in on that job. And you, too! I'll get you all.'

There was a click.

Bourse leaped to his feet. 'Did you get it?' he roared through the open door where Ricardi had gone.

No, no. There hadn't been enough time ...

Briefly and pointedly, Bourse told the men what Hemingway had said. They weren't much impressed; most of them had heard that story before. 'Go out and get Hemingway,' said the old man in dismissal. And they went, hopefully.

But it wasn't so funny an hour later. Chief of Detectives Moore came in, with no ceremony. 'Ricardi's dead,' he cried. 'He was crossing the street at Comanche and Main, and a car came past and hit him. Head on. Dragged him three hundred feet.'

Bourse kneaded the cigar-stub in his fingers. 'Must have been an accident,' he muttered. But in his heart he knew that it wasn't any accident. He turned round and looked at the window.

'Hit-and-run?' he asked, over his shoulder.

'Yes,' said Moore. 'Hit-and-run. They got the car ten minutes later. It was a hot car. But the driver was gone.'

The Inspector sat in silence for a time, drumming on the desk with his fingers. 'We traced Hemingway how far?'

'Well, he took the taxi driver's coat and cap, and made him get out of the cab at Fourth and Mississippi. They found the cab about eleven o'clock on Mulberry Street. It had only been run nine miles in all, according to a check. We can't say definitely that we traced him to Mulberry Street, as we don't know what happened in between—'

Bourse nodded. 'I'm thinking I'd better talk to my stool pigeon.'

'It may mean his life, now,' said the chief of detectives.

'So it may. His name is Adamic. Know him?'

'No. Who is he?'

'A pawnbroker and loan-shark down in the Delta. On Sage Street.'

Moore wagged his head. 'I remember, now. George Adamic. A small, grey fellow with black eyes.'

'Yes. It seems that he knew Two-faced Tomsk from 'way back, and had disposed of some bonds for him after that Western Savings stick-up. Adamic is as close as the tomb. We could never have sweat nothing out of him; he came to me voluntarily, and made me swear—' Bourse made a wry face. 'We both belong to the same lodge, and it's one to which you belong as well. He made me swear I wouldn't turn him in.'

Moore asked, 'Why was he singing about Hemingway?'

'He knew they was in apartment 327 at 1441 Dorchester Avenue, and that was all he knew, except that they had a young arsenal and wore vests. Moore, it seems that Hemingway pushed over a man named Kolchak in Chicago last month. And Kolchak was George Adamic's brother-in-law. Family ties—nothing less. That's the only reason he talked.'

'You'd best talk to Adamic now,' nodded Moore.

Bourse took up his phone.

'If he's still alive,' added Moore, softly.

And when George Adamic didn't answer the telephone which rang so long and stridently in his narrow little shop, Inspector Bourse sent Squad Sixteen whistling in that direction. Sergeant Dave Glennan and Detectives Horn and Kerry found the store unlocked, and it was a wonder that folks in that scrubby neighbourhood hadn't looted the place of every last thing. Only their inherited terror of George Adamic and the power he wielded over their sad little lives had kept them from raiding his shop, unguarded and defenceless as it was.

Detective Horn it was who found George Adamic in a dark washroom behind the rows of second-hand overcoats. Adamic was shot through the heart and the medical examiner estimated that he had been dead since about nine o'clock that morning.

Nick Glennan's handsome face was a bit drawn. Inspector Bourse's harsh accusation was still ringing in his ears; he felt that he had failed, miserably enough, when circumstances demanded the most of him. And now, to be sent for—private and special—. Maybe old Bourse was going to ask him to turn in his gun and badge. And after being promoted to plainclothes only last fall! When, heaven knew that he must have deserved it.

'Sit down, Nick,' said the old inspector.

'Begging your pardon,' murmured Nick. 'I'll take it standing up.'

There was a sudden, misty twinkle in the older man's eyes. He saw that his door was locked and the heavy shade drawn over the window, and then he sat down behind his desk and looked at Nick. Distantly a chiming clock announced that it was five-thirty.

'Glennan,' asked Bourse, 'do you know why I sent for you?'

'I'm afraid I do. But I hope I don't.'

Bourse grinned wearily. 'Pshaw, why are you a-worrying? That was a bad break.' He smoked in silence for a moment. 'Nick, you're young—'

'Yes, sir. I'll be getting over it as rapidly as possible.'

'You've got nerve.'

'I hope so, sir.'

'And brains.'

'Well,' said Nick.

'Every man in my department has nerve, and most of them have got a brain or two. But you have something else. You showed it when you was a rookie cop and helped clean out that gang on Acola Street; and you showed it when you ran down those Kentucky gorillas that had us all stumped, in the fall. That's the reason you're wearing plainclothes. You have that strange and fortunate thing which you have through no fault of your own: instinct, my boy. A nose for it.'

Bourse wrinkled his own pug nose in demonstration. 'Your big brother Dave is a good sergeant; I wouldn't be asking for none better. But he ain't got the hunch that you have—the kind of natural, hound-dog notion of being a good detective—smelling things out. Nick, did any of your ancestors, rest their souls, have second sight?'

Nick wriggled. 'I've heard that my father was the seventh son of a seventh son, sir. But I'm only the second son of a seventh son.'

'However that may be, what would you do about Hemingway?'

'I'd like to get him, sir.'

'I want you to tell me, me boy.'

Nicholas Glennan stood looking at the carpet for a while. 'We haven't much to go on, sir.'

'Mulberry Street is right near Adamic's place. You know about Adamic? Very good. Hemingway must have ditched his cab, walked in there, shot Adamic, and walked out again.'

'Yes, sir. But not in taxi clothes.'

'What would he have done?'

'At least he would have put on a good suit and hat, and maybe taken a suitcase or travelling bag. The store was full of 'em, and some not half bad. Hemingway's always been one to take life easy and comfortable, sir, or so his record shows. Probably he had money on him. Maybe a belt, under that bullet-proof vest.'

Bourse nodded slightly. 'I'm 'way ahead of you, boy. But he wouldn't show that face around town—not with the papers full of it, and a million people gasping for the reward.'

'But he wouldn't have had time for much disguise, sir. Not a hair-bleach or nothing like that. It would have to be quick and simple.'

'The usual? Glasses? Moustache?'

'That's my notion, Inspector. This loan-broker had whole cases full of bankrupt notions—glasses of various kinds, even false whiskers, perhaps.'

Bourse sighed. 'Blue goggles and green whiskers! I thought better of your perspicacity, me boy.'

'It's doing fine, sir. My per—what you said.'

Bourse played with a pen-holder. 'And then?'

'The witness to the killing of Ricardi said that a young man with glasses drove the car, sir.'

Bourse hunched his shoulders, as if expecting a bullet to come through the window behind him. 'Do you think he'll make good his boast, and stay around town long enough to get every one of us, as he promised?'

'No,' said Nick, promptly, 'when he's cooled off he'll see that the average is ag'inst him. But he might try to get another one or two.'

'You feel certain of it?'

'He's a mad dog, they say. What the stories call a Lone Wolf. A red-hot killer, and always has been. And like all of them, he is what you call an ee-gow-ist. He'll want to write his name large before he leaves town.'

Bourse slammed up out of his chair. 'I'm afraid we're getting nowhere. What do you think is the best bet? What would you do if you had your choice and was playing a free hand? I've got men all over town, a-raiding here and a-raiding there, and every cop on every corner is on the lookout. But what would you like to do?'

'Begging your pardon,' whispered Nick, 'but I'd like to stick beside the man he's most likely to come after next.'

'And that's—'

'Yourself, sir.'

Chet Hemingway looked very dignified and circumspect. He did not look at all like a mad dog, although he might have answered up to Nick Glennan's characterisation as an egoist.

'Drive me,' he told the taxicab driver, 'to 561 Alamo Street.'

'Yes, sir.'

The minutes passed to the feeble ticking of the meter. Dusk was here, and the low-lit auto lights swished past on every side. Alamo Street was a narrow, quiet court a bare mile from the heart of town; it was here, at 558, that Inspector Bourse lived with his plump wife and his plump, old-maid daughter.

The driver set Hemingway down promptly enough in front of the old apartment building numbered 561, and Hemingway paid the bill. He tipped not extravagantly or penuriously, but in an ordinary fashion; it was not well for the taxi driver to have a too clear memory of his passenger. Then Hemingway stepped into the lobby of the building and examined mail boxes until the cab drove away.

He walked back out to the kerb and glanced to the east and west.

Couldn't be better. There were only two cars parked in the entire block, and between Number 561 and the next building ran a narrow sluice which led to a rear alley—he could see the lights back there glistening on the lids of garbage cans. Inspector Bourse lived straight across the street. If he had come home before this, he would be going out again. Hemingway's mouth slid back in a bitter smile, his killing grin, as he reasoned how stupid the motive which had prompted Inspector Bourse to have his address and telephone number listed in the directory.

Chet Hemingway leaned among the shadows near the opening of the areaway, and waited. He could wait without jumping nerves or too eager mind; he had spent a good share of his life waiting for men to come, waiting for mail trucks and bank watchmen. Once he had even waited eighteen months in a penitentiary before his chance came. But whenever the opportunity appeared, the opportunity for which Chet happened to be waiting, no one could grasp it any quicker than he. That was how he happened to have more than three hundred thousand dollars stowed in various corners of the country, and a good fifteen thousand dollars fastened next to his skin, under his expensive silk undershirt.

Two girls passed; an old man; a plump woman; solitary young men. Homegoing folks, bound for dinner and quiet evenings in their apartments. Only one person entered the building at 558, and that was a young girl—stenographer, probably. Idly, Hemingway wondered whether she knew Bourse. He put his hand into his coat pocket, took out his usual food, and began to crack it between his teeth.

He thought of Lily. Sentimental and superstitious, like most of his kind, he began to think of Lily as a swell dame—a kind of saint—now that she was dead. 'I'll get the dirty louse, kid,' he told her. This would look good in the tabloids. *Lone Wolf Killer Avenges Murder of Sweetheart Slain by Cops.* It was pretty good stuff.

He stiffened. Here was a cop, a big, stupid patrolman, lumbering down the street with idly-swinging club. He might flash a light into the narrow path between the two buildings, and it wouldn't be safe to hide there. Chet didn't want to bump off a cop. He wanted to bump off Inspector Bourse.

So he bent forward and peered into the gloom. 'Kitty,' he began to call, softly, 'here, kitty-kitty.' The cop came closer. Hemingway still called to his cat. The heavy feet ambled past.

'Oh, officer,' Chet said.

The man stopped. 'Yeh?'

'If you see a black kitten down the block anywhere, would you mind sticking it in the vestibule here at 561? My kid's cat. Run away ... Here, kitty-kitty-kitty.'

'Sure.' The cop lumbered away. Chet stared after him with narrowed eyes. Like to let him have it. Now he hoped that Bourse wouldn't appear on the doorstep until the cop was around the next corner.

The patrolman had just disappeared when a big car hummed into Alamo Street from the avenue. Its brakes crunched; it stopped in front of 558 ... A department car; yes, Hemingway could see a gong above the running-board. Bourse got out.

Chet swallowed the last tiny morsel in his mouth. He brought out his gun; the belly-gun from inside his trousers—he had two, now—and one had been taken from Adamic's shop that morning. Wait until the car was at least half a block up the street. The old devil would still be fooling with his door key, or at least standing in the vestibule, plainly visible from outside. The men in the car would either have to turn it, or else jump out and run back; that was all the start Hemingway would need.

'Nine o'clock.'

'You bet, sir.'

A cab was coming from the direction of the avenue, coming slowly, as if hunting for an address. The big department car moved away from the kerb—screeched into second gear—went purring away down the block. Chet's left hand went to the automatic, Adamic's gun, and brought it out. He would have to stop that cab before it interfered, though experience had taught him to fear nothing from the terrorised bystanders at such a scene.

Inspector Bourse's portly body was sharply outlined against the vestibule lights. Oh, you old Mick, thought the bandit, I've seen you more than once before this ... His belly-gun began to stutter. Bourse fell against the door. Those were soft-nosed bullets, and they would play hell with any man's ribs. With his left hand, Hemingway turned his automatic towards the advancing taxicab. One shot in the radiator or windscreen—he wasn't particular—

A long, bright smear came from the side of the cab, and something tore at the skirt of Chet Hemingway's coat. He snarled, and stepped back into the narrow court between the buildings. He had fixed old Bourse, but he wasn't expecting this. Bullets squirted all around him, flattening among the bricks. He let his whole clip speed towards the taxicab, then he turned and ran. In his heart he was cursing savagely.

Those damn fly-cops—they were half a block or more away, and out of the picture. But this cab—. Who in—

A bullet screamed from the concrete beside him, and still he could feel that wrenching blow which had torn at his coat. Just that close ... He sprinted twenty yards down the alley, dodged between a line of garages, and sped out into the street beyond. It was a through street, and there were plenty of cars, parked or moving. In the distance behind him he heard yells and pounding feet. At the first entrance he found, he dodged inside. Luck. Plenty of it. He needed it.

It was an office building with an L-shaped vestibule opening on the side street and on the avenue as well. Over here the humming traffic had drowned all the affray on Alamo Street. Chet strolled round the corner of the corridor, trying to still the hammering heart inside his body. The one elevator man on duty nodded at him.

Hemingway glanced at the directory on the wall. The little white lines of names were swimming. He picked one out ... Jacobson, Rudolph. 420. He turned to the elevator man.

'Is Mr Jacobson gone?' His gasping lungs pushed up against his throat, but he fought them back.

'Yes, sir. It's after six. Most everybody's gone.'

'Okay.'

He went out to the avenue. A row of waiting taxicabs blurred before his eyes, and distantly he could hear a siren whining. These folks would think it was a fire truck. Well, it wasn't any fire truck.

He stepped into the first cab. 'Let's go downtown,' he said.

'Yes, sir.'

They went towards the bridge, through the evening crush of cars, and Chet Hemingway had the pleasure of watching traffic cops clear the north-bound lanes to make passage for a rocketing squad car which hooted its way towards Alamo Street. He fumbled for a cigarette, and found a torn paper of matches ground into the hole in his coat pocket. The bullet of the would-be avenger had come just that close. He swore. But there was his food—a little of it, still left to him. Chet began to chew it.

He'd better get out of town as soon as possible. One way or another. They'd have picked men at every station, and the highways wouldn't be very safe. He'd have to think.

He arrived at his hotel safely enough and went without further incident to his room. But during the next hour, when he sat munching, enjoying a cigarette or two and coldly re-enacting the finish of Inspector

Bourse, his leaping brain would have turned to jelly had it visualised the steel net which was closing in on him.

Bourse drew a long breath. 'Glennan,' he said to Nick, 'what was that about your being the seventh son of a seventh son?'

'It wasn't me. It was the old man.'

'Nevertheless—'

'Heras will be hotter than ever in hell, sir, when he realises that you was wearing his bullet-proof vest.'

The old inspector rubbed his sore body and examined the shreds in his clothing. 'It's a wonderful vest, boy. I don't see why hoods always have these things better than the cops, but they do. At least nobody could ever blame you for not dropping Hemingway, up there on the roof.'

'I should have drilled him through the head, sir.'

Bourse fingered a tiny scrap of limp, gilded cardboard which he held in his hands. 'At least you drilled this out of his pocket.'

'Yes, but it's twice in one day that I had him under my gun and let him get away.'

They stood there together in front of a gleaming spotlight while officers swarmed through every nook and cranny along Alamo Street. Bourse turned to Sergeant Dave Glennan. 'No use, Dave. He's gone. But he left his calling card.'

The fat sergeant waddled over to the shaft of light. 'I'll take you on, sparrow cop,' he told his younger brother, 'at any shooting gallery in the Palace Amusement Park, when it opens in warm weather.'

'You go to hell,' whispered Nick.

'Shut up your big gab, Dave,' added the inspector, kindly. 'Nick was shooting from a moving taxicab, into the dark—shooting at gun-flashes—and anyway, if it hadn't been for him you'd be getting your shoes shined for an inspector's funeral.'

He offered the torn scrap of cardboard. 'This was over there across the street where he stood, when we looked for bloodstains.'

Dave turned the fragment between his big fingers. He spelled aloud, 'Diamond Match Com ... E ... L. And what's this that looks like the west end of a spider?'

'It's a coat-of-arms, Owl Eyes,' snarled his brother, 'and that is by way of being his stopping place. You don't recognise the souvenir matches of high-priced hotels, but the inspector does. He says that is part of a fold of matches from the Aberdeen Hotel.'

'Just because you found it there—'

'If you look close, Owl Eyes, you can see the fuzz of lead along one side. The luck of Nicholas Glennan was working; I ripped open his pocket, and half the torn paper of matches comes out.'

'But,' cried Dave, 'that's no sign he's there!'

'He took a suit from Adamic's store, or I don't know where else. And do them second-hand guys leave matches lying around in the pockets of their suits? No, Macushla. He gathered that up today since he's been on the loose. And not in no one-arm restaurant, but likely enough in a hotel room.'

The inspector said, 'Get your squad together, Dave. Tell Rhineheimer to get his.'

'Yes, sir. But—God—you can't raid the whole hotel. It's got twenty-two hundred rooms!'

'We cannot. But we can soon get a list of the folks who registered today, and their room numbers. And after that, in case we run up against a snag, your kid brother that once was a sparrow cop in a park—well, he's got an idea. And I've observed that his ideas are apt to be good.'

'What is this idea that he has, inspector?'

For reply, Nick displayed some very small, silvery fragments in the palm of his big hand. They were egg-shaped bits crusted with a strange and frosty deposit, and none of them was longer than three-quarters of an inch. 'Over there on the sidewalk, beside that alley,' his polite voice announced.

'Them!' snorted Dave Glennan. '*Them!* What the hell! What's the worth of those? Nicholas, why don't you turn in your badge and gun, and become a member of the white wings? You scavenger, you.'

'Well,' said Nick, 'I've seen them before. And many of them.' He dropped the fragments into his vest pocket.

'We're wasting time,' Inspector Bourse announced.

The chambermaid—Number Seventy-two, she was, of the Aberdeen Hotel—had plenty of nerve. Really she didn't need a lot of nerve, since she wasn't compelled to place herself within range of direct gunfire. When Nicholas Glennan tapped softly upon the door of Room 1661, and an answering bark came from inside, the woman controlled her quivering throat adequately.

She crouched close beside the thick wall and said, 'Chambermaid.'

The man inside the room seemed waiting for something. Finally he spoke in a voice full of annoyance. 'I don't need you, girlie. Trot along.'

For a fatal moment there was silence in the hall, and inside the room. 'Just to clean up your room, sir.'

There had been people outside the door, up there in Dorchester Avenue—milkman, laundryman—the door had been opened, and the law had come. Chet Hemingway wasn't taking a chance in the world. He snarled, 'Run along and peddle yourself some place else!'

Gently, Nick Glennan drew the frightened chambermaid round the corner, past the house detectives and the group of hard-faced officers from headquarters. 'What he says is good advice, lady,' he murmured. 'You'd better go.' There was a tense shuffling of feet on the thick rug.

Glennan looked coolly into the eyes of a brother detective. 'It's him?'

'Sure. His voice. I was a witness in KC when they had him up for trial. Know it anywhere.'

'Okay,' breathed Nick Glennan.

He said, 'Hemingway. Are you going to come out, or do you want to be carried? Last fall we said that to some hoods, and they decided to stay. We carried them out and embalmed them. What do you say?'

In 1661, Chet Hemingway took out his two guns and turned towards the door. He fancied how it would look, in the headlines. 'I say come and get me, if you're man enough!' He put a heavy slug through the door.

'I am,' responded Nick, 'and here—I—come.'

A machine gun was lifted, but Nick's gesture stayed the ready finger. 'No,' he muttered, 'I missed him—twice. This time it's me or him.'

He took care of the lock with his first three bullets, and heavy pebbles of lead gouged whole strips out of the veneer as he kicked against the wrecked door . . . Inside, there was the distant slam of the bathroom door, so Glennan braced his whole body against the big slice of wood which blocked his way. He crashed to the floor, the sundered hinges flying wide. The bathroom door opened a crack, and in that crack was a jet of dancing flame . . . turned out the lights . . . well, one of them, there in the dark.

Flat on the floor, with the air splitting beside his ears, he took steady aim at a point above the flashes, and scattered his three remaining bullets there. There was sudden silence—a cough, and then the sound of a body falling into a bathtub.

They switched on the lights, and sniffed in the doorway.

'He got Glennan.'

'The hell he got Glennan,' said Nick. He climbed to his feet and pushed the bathroom door wide. For one in Hemingway's messy condition, the bathtub was a very good place for him to be sprawled.

Inspector Bourse looked at the corpse.

'You must have second sight,' he muttered.

'No indeed, sir. It was the shells.'

He found them in his vest pocket, and juggled them in his hands.

'Pistachio nuts,' somebody said.

Nick Glennan nodded, soberly. After all, Hemingway had been a man and now he wasn't anything. Rest his soul, if possible ... 'The nut shells was all over the sun parlour, up on Dorchester Avenue,' he said. 'They was also scattered on the sidewalk tonight where he waited for the inspector. He was a pig for them, it would seem. When the bell-boy said that the man in Room 1661 of this hotel had sent twice for pistachio nuts during the day, it had to be Hemingway and no other. Probably he's feeding on them this minute, wherever he's gone.'

'I'll answer that,' remarked his brother, grimly. 'If Hemingway is eating pistachio nuts this minute, he's eating roasted ones.'

DEAD ON HER FEET

Cornell Woolrich

Although Cornell Woolrich, who also wrote for Detective Fiction
Weekly, *had no brushes with the law like those of his fellow contributor
MacKinlay Kantor, he had a very different opinion of New York's cops,
and a recurring feature in his stories is the attempts by policemen to
fix evidence, to subvert justice and to use brutality to intimidate both
the innocent and the guilty. Writing of this, Woolrich's biographer,
Francis M. Nevins, has said, 'The overall impression he creates is of
a human power just as brutal and malignant as the dark powers above,
indeed their earthly counterpart—and the characteristic means of evok-
ing this impression is by portraying incredible police brutality and its
casual acceptance as completely natural by everyone, including the
victims.' There are, in fact, dozens of such stories to be found among
the hundreds that Cornell Woolrich wrote for the pulps—for example,
'The Body Upstairs' in which some officers stick lighted cigarettes
under a suspect's armpits; 'Graves for the Living' where a man being
questioned has acid tipped over him; and the terrifying 'Detective William Brown' who beats a prisoner almost senseless and then taunts
him with a glass of water which he pours gloatingly onto the floor just
in front of the man. A similar kind of casual violence is also to be found
in his novel* The Bride Wore Black *(1940), in the person of the homicide
cop, Lew Wanger. Even the environment in which these men work—
especially the sparse and dingy back rooms of the precinct stations—
is portrayed in a style that is unique among the pulp writers.*

*The life of Cornell Woolrich (1903–1968) was every bit as bizarre
as his stories. His childhood was spent being shuttled backwards and
forwards between his mining engineer father who worked in Latin
America and his New York socialite mother. He began writing while
still at college, and his first published work,* Cover Charge *(1926), was
an attempt at a Jazz Age novel in the style of his literary hero, F. Scott
Fitzgerald. This provided him with an entrée to Hollywood where he*

was briefly married to the daughter of the veteran producer, J. Stuart Blackton. The marriage apparently lasted only two weeks and was allegedly unconsummated; whereupon Woolrich, who may well have been homosexual, fled back to New York. Here he was to spend the rest of his life, closeted in one hotel room after another with his overbearing mother. Although this strange bond undoubtedly contributed to Woolrich becoming a recluse, he wrote prodigiously and soon earned himself a reputation in the eyes of a number of critics for being able to create 'an atmosphere of terror equalled only by that of Edgar Allan Poe'. After the death of his mother in 1958, his own health collapsed and in his last years he was both a diabetic and an alcoholic. When he, too, died, a lonely and embittered man confined to a wheelchair by his infirmities, he left an estate in excess of a million dollars.

Woolrich's literary reputation has grown with every passing year through film, radio and television adaptations of his work—the Alfred Hitchcock version of his story, Rear Window *(1954), long ago attained classic status. Here is one of his stories of police brutality written in 1935, in which a tough, wisecracking rookie cop investigates the death of a girl at a marathon dance and demonstrates a malicious lack of feeling for either the victim or her luckless partner. The contrast between Nick Glennan and Woolrich's young Smitty could not be more striking . . .*

* * *

'And another thing I've got against these non-stop shindigs,' orated the chief to his slightly bored listeners, 'is they let minors get in 'em and dance for days until they wind up in a hospital with the DTs, when the whole thing's been fixed ahead of time and they haven't a chance of copping the prize anyway. Here's a Missus Mollie McGuire been calling up every hour on the half-hour all day long, and bawling the eardrums off me because her daughter Toodles ain't been home in over a week and she wants this guy Pasternack arrested. So you go over there and tell Joe Pasternack I'll give him until tomorrow morning to fold up his contest and send his entries home. And tell him for me he can shove all his big and little silver loving-cups—'

For the first time his audience looked interested, even expectant, as they waited to hear what it was Mr P. could do with his loving-cups, hoping for the best.

'—back in their packing-cases,' concluded the chief chastely, if somewhat disappointingly. 'He ain't going to need 'em any more. He has promoted his last marathon in this neck of the woods.'

There was a pause while nobody stirred. 'Well, what are you all standing there looking at me for?' demanded the chief testily. 'You, Donnelly, you're nearest the door. Get going.'

Donnelly gave him an injured look. 'Me, Chief? Why, I've got a red-hot lead on that payroll thing you were so hipped about. If I don't keep after it it'll cool off on me.'

'All right, then you Stevens!'

'Why, I'm due in Yonkers right now,' protested Stevens virtuously. 'Machine-gun Rosie has been seen around again and I want to have a little talk with her—'

'That leaves you, Doyle,' snapped the merciless chief.

'Gee, Chief,' whined Doyle plaintively, 'gimme a break, can't you? My wife is expecting—' Very much under his breath he added: '—me home early tonight.'

'Congratulations,' scowled the chief, who had missed hearing the last part of it. He glowered at them. 'I get it!' he roared. 'It's below your dignity, ain't it! It's too petty-larceny for you! Anything less than the St Valentine's Day massacre ain't worth going out after, is that it? You figure it's a detail for a bluecoat, don't you?' His open palm hit the desk-top with a sound like a firecracker going off. Purple became the dominant colour of his complexion. 'I'll put you all back where you started, watching pickpockets in the subway! I'll take some of the high-falutinness out of you! I'll—I'll—' The only surprising thing about it was that foam did not appear at his mouth.

It may have been that the chief's bark was worse than his bite. At any rate no great amount of apprehension was shown by the culprits before him. One of them cleared his throat inoffensively. 'By the way, Chief, I understand that rookie, Smith, has been swiping bananas from Tony on the corner again, and getting the squad a bad name after you told him to pay for them.'

The chief took pause and considered this point.

The others seemed to get the idea at once. 'They tell me he darned near wrecked a Chinese laundry because the Chinks tried to pass him somebody else's shirts. You could hear the screeching for miles.'

Doyle put the artistic finishing touch. 'I overheard him say he wouldn't be seen dead wearing the kind of socks you do. He was asking me did I think you had lost an election bet or just didn't know any better.'

The chief had become dangerously quiet all at once. A faint drumming sound from somewhere under the desk told what he was doing with his fingers. 'Oh he did, did he?' he remarked, very slowly and very ominously.

At this most unfortunate of all possible moments the door blew open and in breezed the maligned one in person. He looked very tired and at the same time enthusiastic, if the combination can be imagined. Red rimmed his eyes, blue shadowed his jaws, but he had a triumphant look on his face, the look of a man who has done his job well and expects a kind word. 'Well, Chief,' he burst out, 'it's over! I got both of 'em. Just brought 'em in. They're in the back room right now—'

An oppressive silence greeted him. Frost seemed to be in the air. He blinked and glanced at his three pals for enlightenment.

The silence didn't last long, however. The chief cleared his throat. '*Hrrrmph.* Zat so?' he said with deceptive mildness. 'Well now, Smitty, as long as your engine's warm and you're hitting on all six, just run over to Joe Pasternack's marathon dance and put the skids under it. It's been going on in that old armoury on the west side—'

Smitty's face had become a picture of despair. He glanced mutely at the clock on the wall. The clock said four—a.m., not p.m. The chief, not being a naturally hard-hearted man, took time off to glance down at his own socks, as if to steel himself for this bit of cruelty. It seemed to work beautifully. 'An election bet!' he muttered cryptically to himself, and came up redder than ever.

'Gee, Chief,' pleaded the rookie, 'I haven't even had time to shave since yesterday morning.' In the background unseen nudgings and silent strangulation were rampant.

'You ain't taking part in it, you're putting the lid on it,' the chief reminded him morosely. 'First you buy your way in just like anyone else and size it up good and plenty, see if there's anything against it on moral grounds. Then you dig out one Toodles McGuire from under, and don't let her stall you she's of age either. Her old lady says she's sixteen and she ought to know. Smack her and send her home. You seal everything up tight and tell Pasternack and whoever else is backing this thing with him it's all off. And don't go 'way. You stay with him and make sure he refunds any money that's coming to anybody and shuts up shop good and proper. If he tries to squawk about there ain't no ordinance against marathons just lemme know. We can find an ordinance against anything if we go back far enough in the books—'

Smitty shifted his hat from northeast to southwest and started reluctantly towards the great outdoors once more. 'Anything screwy like this that comes up, I'm always It,' he was heard to mutter rebelliously. 'Nice job, shooing a dancing contest. I'll probably get bombarded with powder-puffs—'

The chief reached suddenly for the heavy brass inkwell on his desk, whether to sign some report or to let Smitty have it, Smitty didn't wait to find out. He ducked hurriedly out of the door.

'Ah me,' sighed the chief profoundly, 'what a bunch of crumbs. Why didn't I listen to me old man and join the fire department instead!'

Young Mr Smith, muttering bad language all the way, had himself driven over to the unused armoury where the peculiar enterprise was taking place.

'Sixty cents,' said the taxi-driver.

Smitty took out a little pocket account-book and wrote down—*Taxi-fare—$1.20.* 'Send me out after nothing at four in the morning, will he!' he commented. After which he felt a lot better.

There was a box-office outside the entrance but now it was dark and untenanted. Smitty pushed through the unlocked doors and found a combination porter and doorman, a black gentleman, seated on the inside, who gave him a stub of pink pasteboard in exchange for fifty-five cents, then promptly took the stub back again and tore it in half. 'Boy,' he remarked affably, 'you is either up pow'ful early or up awful late.'

'I just is plain up,' remarked Smitty, and looked around him.

It was an hour before daylight and there were a dozen people left in the armoury, which was built to hold two thousand. Six of them were dancing, but you wouldn't have known it by looking at them. It had been going on nine days. There was no one watching them any more. The last of the paid admissions had gone home hours ago, even the drunks and the Park Avenue stay-outs. All the big snow-white arc lights hanging from the rafters had been put out, except one in the middle, to save expenses. Pasternack wasn't in this for his health. The one remaining light, spitting and sizzling way up overhead, and sending down violet and white rays that you could see with the naked eye, made everything look ghostly, unreal. A phonograph fitted with an amplifier was grinding away at one end of the big hall, tearing a dance-tune to pieces, giving it the beating of its life. Each time the needle got to the end of the record it was swept back to the beginning by a sort of stencil fitted over the turntable.

Six scarecrows, three men and three girls, clung ludicrously together in pairs out in the middle of the floor. They were not dancing and they were not walking, they were tottering by now, barely moving enough to keep from standing still. Each of the men bore a number on his back. *3*, *8*, and *14* the numbers were. They were the 'lucky' couples who had outlasted all the others, the scores who had started with them at the bang of a gun a week and two days ago. There wasn't a coat or vest left among the three men—or a necktie. Two of them had replaced their shoes with carpet-slippers to ease their aching feet. The third had on a pair of canvas sneakers.

One of the girls had a wet handkerchief plastered across her forehead. Another had changed into a chorus-girl's practice outfit—shorts and a blouse. The third was a slip of a thing, a mere child, her head hanging limply down over her partner's shoulder, her eyes glazed with exhaustion.

Smitty watched her for a moment. There wasn't a curve in her whole body. If there was anyone here under age, it was she. She must be Toodles McGuire, killing herself for a plated loving-cup, a line in the newspapers, a contract to dance in some cheap honky-tonk, and a thousand dollars that she wasn't going to get anyway—according to the chief. He was probably right, reflected Smitty. There wasn't a thousand dollars in the whole set-up, much less three prizes on a sliding scale. Pasternack would probably pocket whatever profits there were and blow, letting the fame-struck suckers whistle. Corner-lizards and dance-hall belles like these couldn't even scrape together enough to bring suit. Now was as good a time as any to stop the lousy racket.

Smitty sauntered over to the bleachers where four of the remaining six the armoury housed just then were seated and sprawled in various attitudes. He looked them over. One was an aged crone who acted as matron to the female participants during the brief five-minute rest-periods that came every half-hour. She had come out of her retirement for the time being, a towel of dubious cleanliness slung over her arm, and was absorbed in the working-out of a crossword puzzle, mumbling to herself all the while. She had climbed halfway up the reviewing stand to secure privacy for her occupation.

Two or three rows below her lounged a greasy-looking counterman from some one-arm lunchroom, guarding a tray that held a covered tin pail of steaming coffee and a stack of wax-paper cups. One of the rest-periods was evidently approaching and he was ready to cash in on it.

The third spectator was a girl in a dance dress, her face twisted with pain. Judging by her unkempt appearance and the scornful bitter look in her eyes as she watched the remaining dancers, she had only just recently disqualified herself. She had one stockingless foot up before her and was rubbing the swollen instep with alcohol and cursing softly under her breath.

The fourth and last of the onlookers (the fifth being the man at the door) was too busy with his arithmetic even to look up when Smitty parked before him. He was in his shirt-sleeves and wore blue elastic armbands and a green celluloid eye-shade. A soggy-looking stogie protruded from his mouth. A watch, a megaphone, a whistle, and a blank-cartridge pistol lay beside him on the bench. He appeared to be computing the day's receipts in a pocket notebook, making them up out of his head as he went along. 'Get out of my light,' he remarked ungraciously as Smitty's shadow fell athwart him.

'You Pasternack?' Smitty wanted to know, not moving an inch.

'Naw, he's in his office taking a nap.'

'Well, get him out here, I've got news for him.'

'He don't wanna hear it,' said the pleasant party on the bench.

Smitty turned over his lapel, then let it curl back again. 'Oh, the lor,' commented the auditor, and two tens left the day's receipts and were left high and dry in Smitty's right hand. 'Buy yourself a drop of schnapps,' he said without even looking up. 'Stop in and ask for me tomorrow when there's more in the kitty—'

Smitty plucked the nearest armband, stretched it out until it would have gone around a piano, then let it snap back again. The business manager let out a yip. Smitty's palm with the two sawbucks came up flat against his face, clamped itself there by the chin and bridge of the nose, and executed a rotary motion, grinding them in. 'Wrong guy,' he said and followed the financial wizard into the sanctum where Pasternack lay in repose, mouth fixed to catch flies.

'Joe,' said the humbled side-kick, spitting out pieces of ten-dollar-bill, 'the lor.'

Pasternack got vertical as though he worked by a spring. 'Where's your warrant?' he said before his eyes were even open. 'Quick, get me my mouth on the phone, Moe!'

'You go out there and blow your whistle,' said Smitty, 'and call the bally off—or do I have to throw this place out in the street?' He turned suddenly, tripped over something unseen, and went staggering halfway across the room. The telephone went flying out of Moe's hand at one end and the sound-box came ripping off the baseboard of the wall at the other. '*Tch, tch*, excuse it please,' apologised Smitty insincerely. 'Just when you needed it most, too!'

He turned back to the one called Moe and sent him headlong out into the auditorium with a hearty shove at the back of the neck. 'Now do like I told you,' he said, 'while we're waiting for the telephone repairman to get here. And when their dogs have cooled, send them all in here to me. That goes for the black guy and the washroom dame, too.' He motioned towards the desk. 'Get out your little tin box, Pasternack. How much you got on hand to pay these people?'

It wasn't in a tin box but in a briefcase. 'Close the door,' said Pasternack in an insinuating voice. 'There's plenty here, and plenty more will be coming in. How big a cut will square you? Write your own ticket.'

Smitty sighed wearily. 'Do I have to knock your front teeth down the back of your throat before I can convince you I'm one of these old-fashioned guys that likes to work for my money?'

Outside a gun boomed hollowly and the squawking of the phonograph stopped. Moe could be heard making an announcement through the megaphone. 'You can't get away with this!' stormed Pasternack. 'Where's your warrant?'

'Where's your licence,' countered Smitty, 'if you're going to get technical? C'mon, don't waste any more time, you're keeping me up! Get the dough ready for the pay-off.' He stepped to the door and called out into the auditorium: 'Everybody in here. Get your things and line up.' Two of the three couples separated slowly like sleepwalkers and began to trudge painfully over towards him, walking zig-zag as though their metabolism was all shot.

The third pair, Number 14, still clung together out on the floor, the man facing towards Smitty. They didn't seem to realise it was over. They seemed to be holding each other up. They were in the shape of a human tent, their feet about three feet apart on the floor, their faces and shoulders pressed closely together. The girl was that clothes-pin, that stringbean of a kid he had already figured for Toodles McGuire. So she was going to be stubborn about it, was she? He went over to the pair bellicosely. 'C'mon, you heard me, break it up!'

The man gave him a frightened look over her shoulder. 'Will you take her off me please, Mac? She's passed out or something, and if I let her go she'll crack her conk on the floor.' He blew out his breath. 'I can't hold her up much longer!'

Smitty hooked an arm about her middle. She didn't weigh any more than a discarded topcoat. The poor devil who had been bearing her weight, more or less, for nine days and nights on end, let go and folded up into a squatting position at her feet like a shrivelled Buddha. 'Just lemme stay like this,' he moaned, 'it feels so good.' The girl, meanwhile, had begun to bend slowly double over Smitty's supporting arm, closing up like a jackknife. But she did it with a jerkiness, a deliberateness, that was almost grisly, slipping stiffly down a notch at a time, until her upside-down head had met her knees. She was like a walking doll whose spring has run down.

Smitty turned and barked over one shoulder at the washroom hag. 'Hey you! C'mere and gimme a hand with this girl! Can't you see she needs attention? Take her in there with you and see what you can do for her—'

The old crone edged fearfully nearer, but when Smitty tried to pass the inanimate form to her she drew hurriedly back. 'I—I ain't got the stren'th to lift her,' she mumbled stubbornly. 'You're strong, you carry her in and set her down—'

'I can't go in there,' he snarled disgustedly. 'That's no place for me! What're you here for if you can't—'

The girl who had been sitting on the sidelines suddenly got up and came limping over on one stockingless foot. 'Give her to me,' she said. 'I'll take her in for you.' She gave the old woman a long hard look before which the latter quailed and dropped her eyes. 'Take hold of her feet,' she ordered in a low voice. The hag hurriedly stooped to obey. They sidled off with her between them, and disappeared around the side of the orchestra-stand, towards the washroom. Their burden sagged low, until it almost touched the floor.

'Hang onto her,' Smitty thought he heard the younger woman say. 'She won't bite you!' The washroom door banged closed on the weird little procession. Smitty turned and hoisted the deflated Number 14 to his feet. 'C'mon,' he said. 'In you go, with the rest!'

They were all lined up against the wall in Pasternack's 'office', so played-out that if the wall had suddenly been taken away they would have all toppled flat like a pack of cards. Pasternack and his shill had gone into a huddle in the opposite corner, buzzing like a hive of bees.

'Would you two like to be alone?' Smitty wanted to know, parking Number 14 with the rest of the droops.

Pasternack evidently believed in the old adage, 'He who fights and runs away lives to fight, etc.' The game, he seemed to think, was no longer worth the candle. He unlatched the briefcase he had been guarding under his arm, walked back to the desk with it, and prepared to ease his conscience. 'Well folks,' he remarked genially, 'on the advice of this gentleman here' (big pally smile for Smitty) 'my partner and I are calling off the contest. While we are under no legal obligation to any of you' (business of clearing his throat and hitching up his necktie) 'we have decided to do the square thing, just so there won't be any trouble, and split the prize money among all the remaining entries. Deducting the rental for the armoury, the light bill, and the cost of printing tickets and handbills, that would leave—'

'No you don't!' said Smitty. 'That comes out of your first nine days' profits. What's on hand now gets divvied without any deductions. Do it your way and they'd all be owing you money!' He turned to the doorman. 'You been paid, feller?'

'Nossuh! I'se got five dolluhs a night coming at me—'

'Forty-five for you,' said Smitty.

Pasternack suddenly blew up and advanced menacingly upon his partner. 'That's what I get for listening to you, know-it-all! So New York was a sucker town, was it! So there was easy pickings here, was there! Yah!'

'Boys, boys,' remonstrated Smitty, elbowing them apart.

'Throw them a piece of cheese, the rats,' remarked the girl in shorts. There was a scuffling sound in the doorway and Smitty turned in time to see the lamed girl and the washroom matron each trying to get in ahead of the other.

'You don't leave me in there!'

'Well I'm not staying in there alone with her. It ain't my job! I resign!'

The one with the limp got to him first. 'Listen, mister, you better go in there yourself,' she panted. 'We can't do anything with her. I think she's dead.'

'She's cold as ice and all stiff-like,' corroborated the old woman.

'Oh my God, I've killed her!' someone groaned. Number 14 sagged to his knees and went out like a light. Those on either side of him eased him down to the floor by his arms, too weak themselves to support him.

'Hold everything!' barked Smitty. He gripped the pop-eyed doorman by the shoulder. 'Scram out front and get a cop. Tell him to put in a call for an ambulance, and then have him report in here to me. And if you try lighting out, you lose your forty-five bucks and get the electric chair.'

'I'se pracktilly back inside again,' sobbed the terrified man as he fled.

'The rest of you stay right where you are. I'll hold you responsible, Pasternack, if anybody ducks.'

'As though we could move an inch on these howling dogs,' muttered the girl in shorts. Smitty pushed the girl with one shoe ahead of him. 'You come and show me,' he grunted. He was what might be termed a moral coward at the moment; he was going where he'd never gone before.

'Straight ahead of you,' she scowled, halting outside the door. 'Do you need a road-map?'

'C'mon, I'm not going in there alone,' he said and gave her a shove through the forbidden portal.

She was stretched out on the floor where they'd left her, a bottle of rubbing alcohol that hadn't worked uncorked beside her. His face was flaming as he squatted down and examined her. She was gone all right. She was as cold as they'd said and getting more rigid by the minute. 'Overtaxed her heart most likely,' he growled. 'That guy Pasternack ought to be hauled up for this. He's morally responsible.'

The cop, less well-brought-up than Smitty, stuck his head in the door without compunction.

'Stay by the entrance,' Smitty instructed him. 'Nobody leaves.' Then, 'This was the McGuire kid, wasn't it?' he asked his feminine companion.

'Can't prove it by me,' she said sulkily. 'Pasternack kept calling her Rose Lamont all through the contest. Why don't-cha ask the guy that was dancing with her? Maybe they got around to swapping names after nine days. Personally,' she said as she moved towards the door, 'I don't know who she was and I don't give a damn!'

'You'll make a swell mother for some guy's children,' commented Smitty following her out. 'In there,' he said to the ambulance doctor who had just arrived, 'but it's the morgue now, and not first-aid. Take a look.'

Number 14, when he got back to where they all were, was taking it hard and self-accusing. 'I didn't mean to do it, I didn't mean to!' he kept moaning.

'Shut up, you sap, you're making it tough for yourself,' someone hissed.

'Lemme see a list of your entries,' Smitty told Pasternack.

The impresario fished a ledger out of the desk drawer and held it out to him. 'All I got out of this enterprise was kicks in the pants! Why didn't I stick to the sticks where they don't drop dead from a little dancing? Ask me, why didn't I!'

'Fourteen,' read Smitty. 'Rose Lamont and Gene Monahan. That your real name, guy? Back it up.' 14 jerked off the coat that someone had slipped around his shoulders and turned the inner pocket inside out. The name was inked onto the label. The address checked too. 'What about her, was that her real tag?'

'McGuire was her real name,' admitted Monahan, 'Toodles McGuire. She was going to change it anyway, pretty soon, if we'dda won that thousand'—he hung his head—'so it didn't matter.'

'Why'd you say you did it? Why do you keep saying you didn't mean to?'

'Because I could feel there was something the matter with her in my arms. I knew she oughtta quit, and I wouldn't let her. I kept begging her to stick it out a little longer, even when she didn't answer me. I went crazy, I guess, thinking of that thousand dollars. We needed it to get married on. I kept expecting the others to drop out any minute, there were only two other couples left, and no one was watching us any more. When the rest-periods came, I carried her in my arms to the washroom door, so no one would notice she couldn't make it herself, and turned her over to the old lady in there. She couldn't do anything with her either, but I begged her not to let on, and each time the whistle blew I picked her up and started out from there with her—'

'Well, you've danced her into her grave,' said Smitty bitterly. 'If I was you I'd go out and stick both my feet under the first trolley-car that came along and hold them there until it went by. It might make a man of you!'

He went out and found the ambulance doctor in the act of leaving. 'What was it, her heart?'

The AD favoured him with a peculiar look, starting at the floor and ending at the top of his head. 'Why wouldn't it be? Nobody's heart keeps going with a seven- or eight-inch metal pencil jammed into it.'

He unfolded a handkerchief to reveal a slim coppery cylinder, tapering to needle-like sharpness at the writing end, where the case was pointed over the lead to protect it. It was aluminium—encrusted blood was what gave it its copper sheen. Smitty nearly dropped it in consternation—not because of what it had done but because he had missed seeing it.

'And another thing,' went on the AD. 'You're new to this sort of thing, aren't you? Well, just a friendly tip. No offence, but you don't call an ambulance that long after they've gone, our time is too val—'

'I don't getcha,' said Smitty impatiently. 'She needed help; who am I supposed to ring in, potter's field, and have her buried before she's quit breathing?'

This time the look he got was withering. 'She was past help hours ago.' The doctor scanned his wrist. 'It's five now. She's been dead since three, easily. I can't tell you when exactly, but your friend the medical examiner'll tell you whether I'm right or not. I've seen too many of 'em in my time. She's been gone two hours anyhow.'

Smitty had taken a step back, as though he were afraid of the guy. 'I came in here at four-thirty,' he stammered excitedly, 'and she was dancing on that floor there—I saw her with my own eyes—fifteen, twenty minutes ago!' His face was slightly sallow.

'I don't care whether you saw her dancin' or saw her doin' double-hand-springs on her left ear, she was dead!' roared the ambulance man testily. 'She was celebrating her own wake then, if you insist!' He took a look at Smitty's horrified face, quieted down, spit emphatically out of one corner of his mouth, and remarked: 'Somebody was dancing with her dead body, that's all. Pleasant dreams, kid!'

Smitty started to burn slowly. 'Somebody was,' he agreed, gritting his teeth. 'I know who Somebody is, too. His number was Fourteen until a little while ago; well, it's Thirteen from now on!'

He went in to look at her again, the doctor whose time was so valuable trailing along. 'From the back, eh? That's how I missed it. She was lying on it the first time I came in and looked.'

'I nearly missed it myself,' the intern told him. 'I thought it was a boil at first. See this little pad of gauze? It had been soaked in alcohol and laid over it. There was absolutely no external flow of blood, and the pencil didn't protrude, it was in up to the hilt. In fact I had to use forceps to get it out. You can see for yourself, the clip that fastens to the wearer's pocket, which would have stopped it halfway, is missing. Probably broken off long before.'

'I can't figure it,' said Smitty. 'If it went in up to the hilt, what room was there left for the grip that sent it home?'

'Must have just gone in an inch or two at first and stayed there,' suggested the intern. 'She probably killed herself on it by keeling over backwards and hitting the floor or the wall, driving it the rest of the way in.' He got to his feet. 'Well, the pleasure's all yours.' He flipped a careless salute, and left.

'Send the old crow in that had charge in here,' Smitty told the cop.

The old woman came in fumbling with her hands, as though she had the seven-day itch.

'What's your name?'

'Josephine Falvey—Mrs Josephine Falvey.' She couldn't keep her eyes off what lay on the floor.

'It don't matter after you're forty,' Smitty assured her drily. 'What'd you bandage that wound up for? D'you know that makes you an accessory to a crime?'

'I didn't do no such a—' she started to deny whitely.

He suddenly thrust the postage-stamp of folded gauze, rusty on one side, under her nose. She cawed and jumped back. He followed her retreat. 'You didn't stick this on? C'mon, answer me!'

'Yeah, I did!' she cackled, almost jumping up and down, 'I did, I did—but I didn't mean no harm. Honest, mister, I—'

'When'd you do it?'

'The last time, when you made me and the girl bring her in here. Up to then I kept rubbing her face with alcohol each time he brought her back to the door, but it didn't seem to help her any. I knew I should of gone out and reported it to Pasternack, but he—that feller you know—begged me not to. He begged me to give them a break and not get them ruled out. He said it didn't matter if she acted all limp that way, that she was just dazed. And anyway, there wasn't so much difference between her and the rest any more, they were all acting dopey like that. Then after you told me to bring her in the last time, I stuck my hand down the back of her dress and I felt something hard and round, like a carbuncle or berl, so I put a little gauze application over it. And then me and her decided, as long as the contest was over anyway, we better go out and tell you—'.

'Yeah,' he scoffed, 'and I s'pose if I hadn't shown up she'd still be dancing around out there, until the place needed disinfecting! When was the first time you noticed anything the matter with her?'

She babbled: 'About two-thirty, three o'clock. They were all in here—the place was still crowded—and someone knocked on the door. He was standing out there with her in his arms and he passed her to me and whispered, "Look after her, will you?" That's when he begged me not to tell anyone. He said he'd—' She stopped.

'Go on!' snapped Smitty.

'He said he'd cut me in on the thousand if they won it. Then when the whistle blew and they all went out again, he was standing there waiting to take her back in his arms—and off he goes with her. They all had to be helped out by that time, anyway, so nobody noticed anything wrong. After that, the same thing happened each time—until you came. But I didn't dream she was dead.' She crossed herself. 'If I'da thought that, you couldn't have got me to touch her for love nor money—'

'I've got my doubts,' Smitty told her, 'about the money part of that, anyway. Outside—and consider yourself a material witness.'

If the old crone was to be believed, it had happened outside on the dance floor under the bright arc lights, and not in here. He was pretty sure it had, at that. Monahan wouldn't have dared try to force his way in here. The screaming of the other occupants would have blown the roof off. Secondly, the very fact that the floor had been more crowded at that time than later, had helped cover it up. They'd probably quarrelled when she tried to quit. He'd whipped out the pencil and struck her while she clung to him. She'd either fallen and killed herself on it, and he'd picked her up again immediately before anyone noticed, or else the Falvey woman had handled her carelessly in the washroom and the impaled pencil had reached her heart.

Smitty decided he wanted to know if any of the feminine entries had been seen to fall to the floor at any time during the evening. Pasternack had been in his office from ten on, first giving out publicity items and then taking a nap, so Smitty put him back on the shelf. Moe, however, came across beautifully.

'Did I see anyone fall?' he echoed shrilly. 'Who didn't! Such a commotion you never saw in your life. About half-past two. Right when we were on the air, too.'

'Go on, this is getting good. What'd he do, pick her right up again?'

'Pick her up! She wouldn't get up. You couldn't go near her! She just sat there swearing and screaming and throwing things. I thought we'd have to send for the police. Finally they sneaked up behind her and hauled her off on her fanny to the bleachers and disqualified her—'

'Wa-a-ait a minute,' gasped Smitty. 'Who you talking about?'

Moe looked surprised. 'That Standish dame, who else? You saw her, the one with the bum pin. That was when she sprained it and couldn't dance any more. She wouldn't go home. She hung around saying she was framed and gypped and we couldn't get rid of her—'

'Wrong number,' said Smitty disgustedly. 'Back where you came from.' And to the cop: 'Now we'll get down to brass tacks. Let's have a crack at Monahan—'

He was thumbing his notebook with studied absorption when the fellow was shoved in the door. 'Be right with you,' he said offhandedly, tapping his pockets, 'soon as I jot down—. Lend me your pencil a minute, will you?'

'I—I had one, but I lost it,' said Monahan dully.

'How come?' asked Smitty quietly.

'Fell out of my pocket, I guess. The clip was broken.'

'This it?'

The fellow's eyes grew big, while it almost touched their lashes, twirling from left to right and right to left. 'Yeah, but what's the matter with it, what's it got on it?'

'You asking me that?' leered Smitty. 'Come on, show me how you did it!'

Monahan cowered back against the wall, looked from the body on the floor to the pencil, and back again. 'Oh no,' he moaned, 'no. Is that what happened to her? I didn't even know—'

'Guys as innocent as you rub me the wrong way,' said Smitty. He reached for him, hauled him out into the centre of the room, and then sent him flying back again. His head bonged the door and the cop looked in enquiringly. 'No, I didn't knock,' said Smitty, 'that was just his dome.' He sprayed a little of the alcohol into Monahan's stunned face and hauled him forward again. 'The first peep out of you was, "I killed her." Then you keeled over. Later on you kept saying, "I'm to blame, I'm to blame." Why try to back out now?'

'But I didn't mean I did anything to her,' wailed Monahan, 'I thought I killed her by dancing too much. She was all right when I helped her in here about two. Then when I came back for her, the old dame whispered she couldn't wake her up. She said maybe the motion of dancing would bring her to. She said, "You want that thousand dollars, don't you? Here, hold her up, no one'll be any the wiser." And I listened to her like a fool and faked it from then on.'

Smitty sent him hurling again. 'Oh, so now it's supposed to have happened in here—with your pencil, no less! Quit trying to pass the buck!'

The cop, who didn't seem to be very bright, again opened the door, and Monahan came sprawling out at his feet. 'Geez, what a hard head he must have,' he remarked.

'Go over and start up that phonograph over there,' ordered Smitty.

'We're going to have a little demonstration—of how he did it. If banging his conk against the door won't bring back his memory, maybe dancing with her will do it.' He hoisted Monahan upright by the scruff of the neck. 'Which pocket was the pencil in?'

The man motioned towards his breast. Smitty dropped it in point-first. The cop fitted the needle into the groove and threw the switch. A blare came from the amplifier. 'Pick her up and hold her,' grated Smitty.

An animal-like moan was the only answer he got. The man tried to back away. The cop threw him forward again. 'So you won't dance, eh?'

'I won't dance,' gasped Monahan.

When they helped him up from the floor, he would dance.

'You held her like that dead, for two solid hours,' Smitty reminded him. 'Why mind an extra five minutes or so?'

The moving scarecrow crouched down beside the other inert scarecrow on the floor. Slowly his arms went round her. The two scarecrows rose to their feet, tottered drunkenly together, then moved out of the doorway into the open in time to the music. The cop began to perspire.

Smitty said: 'Any time you're willing to admit you done it, you can quit.'

'God forgive you for this!' said a tomb-like voice.

'Take out the pencil,' said Smitty, 'without letting go of her—like you did the first time.'

'This is the first time,' said that hollow voice. 'The time before—it dropped out.' His right hand slipped slowly away from the corpse's back, dipped into his pocket.

The others had come out of Pasternack's office, drawn by the sound of the macabre music, and stood huddled together, horror and unbelief written all over their weary faces. A corner of the bleachers hid both Smitty and the cop from them; all they could see was that grisly couple moving slowly out into the centre of the big floor, alone under the funereal heliotrope arc light. Monahan's hand suddenly went up, with something gleaming in it; stabbed down again and was hidden against his partner's back. There was an unearthly howl and the girl with the turned ankle fell flat on her face amidst the onlookers.

Smitty signalled the cop; the music suddenly broke off. Monahan and his partner had come to a halt again and stood there like they had when the contest first ended, upright, tent-shaped, feet far apart, heads locked together. One pair of eyes was as glazed as the other now.

'All right break, break!' said Smitty.

Monahan was clinging to her with a silent, terrible intensity as though he could no longer let go.

The Standish girl had sat up, but promptly covered her eyes with both hands and was shaking all over as if she had a chill.

'I want that girl in here,' said Smitty. 'And you, Moe. And the old lady.'

He closed the door on the three of them. 'Let's see that book of entries again.'

Moe handed it over jumpily.

'Sylvia Standish, eh?' The girl nodded, still sucking in her breath from the fright she'd had.

'Toodles McGuire was Rose Lamont—now what's your real name?' He thumbed at the old woman. 'What are you two to each other?'

The girl looked away. 'She's my mother, if you gotta know,' she said.

'Might as well admit it, it's easy enough to check up on,' he agreed. 'I had a hunch there was a tie-up like that in it somewhere. You were too ready to help her carry the body in here the first time.' He turned to the cringing Moe. 'I understood you to say she carried on like nobody's never-mind when she was ruled out, had to be hauled off the floor by main force and wouldn't go home. Was she just a bum loser, or what was her grievance?'

'She claimed it was done purposely,' said Moe. 'Me, I got my doubts. It was like this. That girl the feller killed, she had on a string of glass beads, see? So the string broke and they rolled all over the floor under everybody's feet. So this one, she slipped on 'em, fell and turned her ankle and couldn't dance no more. Then she starts hollering blue murder.' He shrugged. 'What should we do, call off the contest because she couldn't dance no more?'

'She did it purposely,' broke in the girl hotly, 'so she could hook the award herself! She knew I had a better chance than anyone else—'

'I suppose it was while you were sitting there on the floor you picked up the pencil Monahan had dropped,' Smitty said casually.

'I did like hell! It fell out in the bleachers when he came over to apolo—' She stopped abruptly. 'I don't know what pencil you're talking about.'

'Don't worry about a little slip-up like that,' Smitty told her. 'You're down for it anyway—and have been ever since you folded up out there just now. You're not telling me anything I don't know already.'

'Anyone woulda keeled over; I thought I was seeing her ghost—'

'That ain't what told me. It was seeing him pretend to do it that told me he never did it. It wasn't done outside at all, in spite of what your old lady tried to hand me. Know why? The pencil didn't go through her dress. There's no hole in the back of her dress. Therefore she had her dress off and was cooling off when it happened. Therefore it was done here in the restroom. For Monahan to do it outside he would have had to hitch her whole dress up almost over her head in front of everybody—and maybe that wouldn't have been noticed!

'He never came in here after her; your own mother would have been the first one to squawk for help. You did, though. She stayed a moment after the others. You came in the minute they cleared out and stuck her with it. She fell on it and killed herself. Then your old lady tried to cover you by putting a pad on the wound and giving Monahan the idea she was stupefied from fatigue. When he began to notice the coldness, if he did, he thought it was from the alcohol-rubs she was getting every rest-period. I guess he isn't very bright anyway—a guy like that, that dances for his coffee-and. He didn't have any motive. He wouldn't have done it even if she wanted to quit, he'd have let her. He was too penitent later on when he thought he'd tired her to death. But you had all the motive I need—those broken beads. Getting even for what you thought she did. Have I left anything out?'

'Yeah,' she said curtly, 'look up my sleeve and tell me if my hat's on straight!'

On the way out to the Black Maria that had backed up to the entrance, with the two Falvey women, Pasternack, Moe and the other four dancers marching single file ahead of him, Smitty called to the cop: 'Where's Monahan? Bring him along!'

The cop came up mopping his brow. 'I finally pried him loose,' he said, 'when they came to take her away, but I can't get him to stop laughing. He's been laughing ever since. I think he's lost his mind. Makes your blood run cold. Look at that!'

Monahan was standing there, propped against the wall, a lone figure under the arc light, his arms still extended in the half-embrace in which he had held his partner for nine days and nights, while peal after peal of macabre mirth came from him, shaking him from head to foot.

NICE WORK

Peter Cheyney

The hardboiled story took several years to cross the Atlantic and find a substantial following in Britain. Initially, the gaudy, violent covers of the pulp magazines, with their illustrations of leering gunmen and terrified females, were viewed as unsuitable for British readers: those titles that did reach the country tended to arrive as ballast in cargo ships and were then sold in cut-price chain stores. However, when the top writers like Daly, Hammett, Chandler and Gardner began to enjoy hardcover publication, their fiction took on a kind of respectability and started to be published in Britain as well. Here the more astute and less easily shocked crime fans soon realised that the genre was going through a radical change. Finally, a few British writers began to imitate the Americans' hardboiled style, most prominent among them a former songwriter, journalist and owner of an investigation agency named Peter Cheyney, of whom the detective story historian H. R. F. Keating has written in his Whodunit? A Guide to Crime Fiction *(1982), 'Best known for his Lemmy Caution books which brought the feel of the hard-nosed private eye novel to a London setting, Cheyney was accused of being sadistic, spurious and fascist in his writings. His books were certainly tough and excitingly different from most contemporaneous British crime writing.'*

Lemmy Caution was a G-man based in New York, who spoke in crisp, staccato sentences, never backed away from violence and took the fight against crime to the criminals themselves. He tackled with equal vigour cases against gangsters, drug-dealers and those who ran vice and protection rackets. British critics decided immediately after his first appearance in September 1936, in This Man is Dangerous, *that he was 'a very tough egg'. Lemmy had been created by Cheyney partly from his own knowledge of the workings of the London criminal underworld and partly from his enthusiasm for American gangster films, especially those based on the work of W. R. Burnett. Four more novels and a number of short stories about the irascible G-man followed, quickly establishing Peter Cheyney as Britain's first star member of the hardboiled school. In 1938, in* The Urgent Hangman, *he also introduced a private detective, Slim Callaghan, and for the next decade he was one of the biggest-selling crime authors in the country. In 1940 Lemmy Caution became the star of a BBC radio series which was very popular throughout the war years, to be followed by a series of eight films starring Eddie Constantine and culminating in the surreal* Alphaville *(1965), directed by Jean-Luc Godard, in which Lemmy found himself in a mechanised police state of the future.*

Peter Reginald Evelyn Cheyney (1896–1951) first tried writing while still at school—remembering years later that even at that time he loved using 'machine gun phrases'—and then worked for a while as a solicitor's clerk and composer for the stage. After military service in the First World War (where he was shot in the stomach in the same manner as many of Lemmy Caution's adversaries), he embarked on a career in journalism and founded 'Cheyney's Research and Investigations', which brought him into contact with the criminal elements of London and thereby the raw material for his books. Although there were those who objected to what they saw as the excessive violence in his fiction, Cheyney's work undoubtedly represented another landmark in the story of hardboiled fiction. 'Nice Work' is a typical Lemmy Caution tale and was originally published in 1936.

*   *   *

The guy in the dirty grey fedora looked like he might have come out of the Bellevue Morgue—off a slab. He was big and his jaw jutted over the edge of his upturned coat collar. His eyes shifted all over as if he was waiting for somebody to pick up any time. His shoes were broken and the upper of one had gone rotten with wet. Each time he took a step it squelched.

He had four days' growth of hair on his face and he kept in the shadow of the wall. His fingers, inside his coat pocket, were clasped round the butt of a .38 police Positive that had once been issued to a copper who got himself cited for bravery in the line of duty the day after they buried him.

The guy hadn't got a collar or a shirt. Under the overcoat was a cotton undervest. The pant-legs showing under the overcoat were too short and the cuffs at the bottom were grimed with mud that never came from New York.

Every time he passed a store or somewhere where it was light he stuck his head down into his coat collar. Once he saw a kid carrying some bread, and he licked his lips like a hungry dog. His nose was bothering him. He hadn't a handkerchief and it was sore. If you've ever tried blowing your nose on newspaper you'll know what I mean.

He turned off Bowery at Kenmare. He was limping. He had a blister on his right foot where the shoe was broken. He hastened his steps with an effort. On Mott he saw the newsboy.

The boy was standing on the edge of the sidewalk looking around. When he saw the guy in the dirty grey fedora he crossed the street and stood in the shadow. Further down the limping guy crossed and slowed up. Then he looked around, too, and worked up slowly towards the boy.

The boy made a play of selling him a news-sheet. The limping guy took it. On the front page he could see his own picture, and across the top of the sheet was a banner caption—'Fremer Breaks Jail—Kills Two Guards'.

That was him.

He spoke to the boy through the side of his mouth. He licked his lips before he spoke.

'Talk quick,' he said. 'Where's that blonde of Franchini's?'

The boy grinned at him. 'You're in luck, mug,' he said. 'She's in Moksie's dive. She's hangin' around there plenty. An' is she drinkin' or is she? She's the rye queen an' toppin' off with rum. Does she get high!'

The limping guy swore quietly.

'Where's she gettin' the dough, kid?' he asked.

The newsboy spat graphically.

'She ain't,' he said. 'Moksie's puttin' it on the cuff.' He dropped his voice. 'Seen that in the sheet about you?' he muttered. 'They're offerin' five grand for you, dead or alive. How'd you like that, pal?'

But the man was gone. The newsboy looked after him as he disappeared into the shadows and spat once more.

The guy limped towards the waterfront. He stood up under a light in an alley and read the paper. What the kid had said was true. They were offering five grand for him dead or alive. He licked his lips and grinned—like a wolf. Then he began to walk.

It was midnight when he dragged himself down the stairs at Moksie's speak on the waterfront. The place was near empty. Moksie was leaning over the bar reading a news-sheet. The limping guy walked over slowly and looked at Moksie.

'Keep your trap shut, and like it, sucker,' he said. 'I've gotta gun in my pocket that's liable to go shootin' itself off supposin' somebody starts to do anything that even looks screwy. Where's Franchini's girl?'

Moksie nodded his head towards the far corner. The guy looked over and saw her. There was a measure of rye at Moksie's elbow. He picked it up and drained it. Then he limped over to the woman.

She was twenty-eight and still pretty. She was pretty high, and a half-bottle of rotgut with a fake bacardi label stood in front of her. Her eyes were heavy and her last perm had gone haywire on her. Her skin was good and her hands were trembling. She kept tapping on the floor with a four-inch heel.

The guy slumped into a chair opposite her. She looked at it and then him.

'So what?' she said. She grinned cynically. 'You ain't the only guy worth five grand,' she said. 'Feelin' good, I suppose, because you broke out. Well ... maybe they'll get you, sucker. They do get 'em, you know. An' what do you want anyhow?'

He leaned towards her.

'Listen, kid,' he said. 'I gotta talk fast an' you gotta listen. I been on my feet for forty-eight hours, an' unless I get under cover they'll pick me up and fry me. I'm nearly through. I'm soaked an' hungry, an' I could use liquor'—she pushed the bacardi towards him and he took a swig from the bottle—'but I gotta contact Franchini. I tell ya I gotta. Now, don't give me that stuff about not knowin' where he is. I know all about it. They're offering five grand for him, too, ain't they? An' you're his girl, ain't you? Well ... so you *gotta* know.'

She jerked up her head and looked at him. A gleam of faint interest showed in her eyes.

'I contacted Marelli tonight,' he went on. 'He says that he can get Franchini an' me away if I can lay under cover for two days. Well, where's Franchini hidin'? Join me up with him. Another two hours an' they'll have me. Marelli will get us outa this burg in two days, an' I can fix to get him paid an' he knows it. Well ... I'll do a trade.

'Get me along to his hide-out. I got no dough—nothin' except an empty gun an' a cough. Fix me some eats an' contact Marelli. He'll get us out of here on Thursday. I'm tradin' my lay-up with Franchini for the getaway for him. Well . . . do we deal?'

She smiled. Her teeth were white and even.

'What a fine pair of killers youse two are,' she said. 'Takin' it on the lam both of you an' both scared stiff.' She looked at the paper. 'So you bust out up the river,' she said. 'How'dya get down here? Hi-jacked a car?'

He nodded. 'I bumped a guy in a Ford,' he said. 'I think I done him too. He took two slugs. They got plenty on me now . . .'

She took another drink and passed the bottle back to him.

'D'ya meet a guy called Lloyd Schrim in the big house?' she said. 'A young kid—about twenty-three. He got life for a killin'.'

He nodded. 'I know,' he said. 'He got it for rubbin' out Gerlin' at the Polecat Road-house. He told me he never done it. He said he took the rap for some other guy. He's not a bad kid. He's ill. He's got no dough, so they got him workin' in the jute mill. He's got TB—they get that way in the mill. I reckon he was played for a sucker by the guy who did the job, but he wouldn't talk. That's why they're ridin' him an' makin' it tough. I don't reckon he'll last much longer.'

She looked at him.

'Why don't he try a break?' she asked. 'You done it. Why can't he?'

He grinned. 'I got friends outside,' he said, 'friends with dough. You can make a break, but it costs dough. It cost some pals of mine seven grand to get me out.'

She grinned.

'Ain't you the expensive baby?' she said. 'Seven grand to get you out and the cops offerin' five for you. You oughta feel swell.'

He coughed. Underneath the table she heard his shoe squelch.

'Listen, kid,' she said, 'I'll fix it. I'll trade puttin' you up with Franchini until Marelli can get you both away. Franchini ain't got no pals like you with dough and contacts, an' he can't put his nose outside the dump. They're offering five grand for him, too.

'Now, listen. I'm going outside to grab a cab. Pull your hat down an' get in so the driver don't see you. Get him to drop you on Tide Alley at Parata Wharf. Down the bottom is a bust-in warehouse. Franchini's on the top floor, but be careful. He's liable to shoot anybody he don't know.

'I'll be along in half an hour. When I come you tell me where I contact Marelli, an' we'll fix the job. So long—killer!'

*

Franchini opened the door and looked at the limping guy. Franchini was tall and thin and dirty. He hadn't shaved for a week, and his mouth was still twitching from cocaine.

He grinned. 'Come in,' he said. 'You're Fremer. The dame 'phoned me. I reckon the idea of gettin' out of this hell-broth looks good to me. I'm for Canada.'

The other grinned. 'Me too,' he said.

He closed and bolted the door behind him, and took a swig at the bottle on the table. Beside it was an automatic. There was another in Franchini's hand.

Franchini put the second gun down beside the first and sat at the table with the two guns in front of his hands, which lay on the table behind them.

'You gotta gun?' he asked.

Fremer pulled the police pistol out of his pocket and threw it on the table.

'No shells,' he said laconically. 'There was only two in it, an' I used 'em on the guy in the Ford I came down in.'

Franchini nodded.

'OK,' he said. 'We'll wait for the dame.'

They sat there waiting, taking swigs from the bottle on the table.

It was quiet. Franchini was just taking a wallop at the bottle when they heard a car grind round the corner outside. Fremer, who had his fingers under the table ledge, suddenly uptilted the table. Franchini's guns crashed to the floor. Simultaneously Fremer went across the table top at Franchini.

The door smashed open. Half a dozen cops under a police lieutenant burst in with their guns showing.

'Stick 'em up, boys,' said the lieutenant. 'We got a date for you two with the hot seat. Take it easy now.' He snapped the steel cuffs on Franchini and turned towards Fremer with another pair.

Fremer kept his hands up.

'OK, lieutenant,' he said. 'Just feel in the lining of my coat and you'll find my badge. I'm Lemmy Caution, New York "G" Division. We played it this way to get Franchini. I guessed the dame would come and spill the works to you.'

The lieutenant found the badge. Caution dropped his hands. Franchini began to be sick in the corner.

'You're a mug, Franchini,' said the 'G' man. 'You oughta know that dame of yours was always stuck on Lloyd Schrim. We reckoned that if we planted a fake story about some guy called Fremer bustin' out of the big house an' taking it on the lam to New York, and splashed his picture on the front page, she would fall for the set-up.

'How the hell do you expect a woman to be in love with a guy and have two killers bottled up in a room and not squeal when she's just been told that her boy friend was dyin' of TB through workin' in the jute mill; that they was ridin' him for not talkin' over a job that she knew durn well that he never pulled?

'She reckoned that the ten grand she'd get for turnin' us in would fix an escape for him. I thought she would, an' took a chance on it. Take him away, boys.'

The 'G' man limped down the steps at Moksie's. He walked over to the bar and ordered rye. Moksie pushed the bottle over the bar.

The 'G' man picked it up and walked over to the corner table where the woman was slumped. Her head was between her arms. She was crying.

He sat down opposite her and put the bottle on the table. He put his hand under her chin and pushed her head up. She fell back in the chair.

'Cut it out, sister,' he said. 'It can be tough. I suppose they told you that there wasn't goin' to be no reward, huh? That it was a frame-up? Well, that's the way it goes. Have a drink an' stop the waterworks. It annoys the customers.'

She took a drink from the bottle.

'You're funny, ain't you, copper?' she said. 'It's a big laugh, ain't it? You pull a fast one on me, an' I shoot my mouth an' wise you up to where Franchini is hidin' out, an' you get him fried and I'm left on the heap.'

The 'G' man grinned.

'Listen, sweetheart,' he said. 'This act wasn't so easy to put on. I ain't had any food for two days an' I walked on this broken shoe so as to give myself an honest to goodness blister.

'Another thing, it ain't so bad as it looks. You see, I handled that Polecat Inn shootin' a long time ago. I never believed that your boy friend pulled it. As a matter of fact, Franchini did it, an' Lloyd took the rap for him an' wouldn't talk. When Franchini bumped that last mug an' scrammed, an' we couldn't find where he was, I thought this little act up an' it worked.

'Have another drink an' then let's go and eat. There's a guy waitin' for you down at Centre Street by the name of Lloyd Schrim. I had him sprung this mornin'. He reckons he wants to marry you or something like that.

'An' there ain't no need to ask a lotta questions. He never worked in no jute mill an' he ain't got TB.

'Say, do you know what's good for a blister?'

THE LADY SAYS DIE!

Mickey Spillane

The English crime fiction historian, H. R. F. Keating, has called Mickey Spillane's most famous character, Mike Hammer, 'perhaps the nastiest hardboiled dick ever to stalk the pages, a great kicker in the groin, shooter in the belly, breaker of bones, gouger out of eyes and burner up of baddies in general'. Even the American magazine Time *takes a similar view, having declared in a feature about the man and his creator, 'The forces of law, order and decency prove no match for Mickey Spillane's private eye, whose impatience with these virtues amounts to a crusade.' Such views have, however, done nothing to diminish the popularity of the Hammer novels, beginning with* I, the Jury, *published in 1947, which have sold by the million ever since. Certainly, few other hardboiled dicks have been able to match the sales of Spillane's books which have nevertheless been condemned for their sexual content— although by today's standards the descriptions are pretty tame. The author has admitted that his inspiration for Mike Hammer was the genre's 'founding father', Race Williams, a comment which prompted pulp historian Ron Goulart to observe somewhat grudgingly, 'Hammer can be seen as a sort of bloated caricature of Williams, even though he lacks Williams' inadequate attempts to explain.'*

As a result of the success of the Mike Hammer books, Frank Morrison (Mickey) Spillane (1918–) was one of the world's most popular novelists during the Fifties and Sixties, a far cry from his upbringing in a tough neighbourhood of New Jersey. His early writing was for comic books and he was one of the originators of Captain Marvel and Captain America. After serving as a pilot in the American Air Force during the Second World War, when he flew many combat missions, Spillane was employed for a time by the FBI and helped to break up a narcotics ring. The violence and gunshot wounds he suffered during this operation provided him with much of the first-hand physical and emotional experience which he used to such effect in the Hammer novels and his other series of books about a lone espionage agent, Tiger Mann.

Cops and lawmen tend to play secondary roles in most of Spillane's novels, and it is only in his short stories that any of them move to the centre of the stage. Among the most interesting of these law officers is Inspector Early, a sharp, no-nonsense cop who becomes embroiled in a case of murder and high finance in 'The Lady Says Die!' The story is making its first anthology appearance since it was published in Manhunt Detective Story Monthly *in October 1953 and offers something of a new dimension to what is generally perceived as the Spillane tradition.*

*   *   *

The stocky man handed his coat and hat to the attendant and went through the foyer to the club's main lounge. He stood in the doorway for a scant second, but in that time his eyes had seen all that was to be seen: the chess game beside the windows, the foursome at cards and the lone man at the rear of the room sipping a drink.

He crossed between the tables, nodding briefly to the card players, and went directly to the back of the room. The other man looked up from his drink with a smile. 'Afternoon, Inspector. Sit down. Drink?'

'Hello, Dunc. Same as you're drinking.'

Almost languidly, Dunc made a motion with his hand. The waiter nodded and left. The inspector settled himself in his chair with a sigh. He was a big man, heavy without being given to fat. Only his high shoes proclaimed him for what he was. When he looked at Chester Duncan he grimaced inwardly, envying him his poise and manner, yet not willing to trade him for anything.

Here, he thought smugly, *is a man who should have everything yet has nothing. True, he has money and position, but the finest of all things, a family life, was denied him.* And with a brood of five in all stages of growth at home, the inspector felt that he had achieved his purpose in life.

The drinks came and the inspector took his, sipping it gratefully. When he put it down he said, 'I came to thank you for that, er . . . tip. You know, that was the first time I've ever played the market.'

'Glad to do it,' Duncan said. His hands played with the glass, rolling it around in his palms. His eyebrows shot up suddenly, as though he was amused at something. 'I suppose you heard all the ugly rumours.'

A flush reddened the inspector's face. 'In an offhand way, yes. Some of them were downright ugly.' He sipped his drink and tapped a cigarette on the side of the table. 'You know,' he said, 'if Walter Harrison's death hadn't been so definitely a suicide, you might be standing an investigation right now.'

Duncan smiled slowly. 'Come now, Inspector. The market didn't budge until after his death, you know.'

'True enough. But rumour has it that you engineered it in some manner.' He paused long enough to study Duncan's face. 'Tell me, did you?'

'Why should I incriminate myself?'

'It's over and done with. Harrison leaped to his death from the window of a hotel room. The door was locked and there was no possible way anyone could have gotten in that room to give him a push. No, we're quite satisfied it was suicide and everybody that ever came in contact with Harrison agrees that he did the world a favour when he died. However, there's still some speculation about you having a hand in things.'

'Tell me, Inspector, do you really think I had the courage or the brains to oppose a man like Harrison, and force him to kill himself?'

The inspector frowned, then nodded. 'As a matter of fact, yes. You *did* profit by his death.'

'So did *you*,' Duncan laughed.

'Ummmm.'

'Though it's nothing to be ashamed about,' Duncan added. 'When Harrison died the financial world naturally expected that the stocks he financed were no good and tried to unload. It so happened that I was one of the few who knew they were as good as gold and bought while I could. And, of course, I passed the word on to my friends. Somebody had might as well profit by the death of a rat.'

Through the haze of the smoke Inspector Early saw his face tighten. He scowled again, leaning forward in his chair. 'Duncan, we've been friends quite a while. I'm just cop enough to be curious and I'm thinking that our Harrison was cursing you before he died.'

Duncan twirled his glass around. 'I've no doubt of it,' he said. His eyes met the inspector's. 'Would you really like to hear about it?'

'Not if it means your confessing to murder. If that has to happen I'd much rather you spoke directly to the DA.'

'Oh, it's nothing like that at all. No, not a bit, Inspector. No matter how hard they tried, they couldn't do a thing that would impair either my honour or my reputation. You see, Walter Harrison went to his death through his own greediness.'

The inspector settled back in his chair. The waiter came with drinks to replace the empties and the two men toasted each other silently.

'Some of this you probably know already, Inspector,' Duncan said . . .

'Nevertheless, I'll start at the beginning and tell you everything that happened. Walter and I met in law school. We were both young and not too studious. We had one thing in common and only one. Both of us were the products of wealthy parents who tried their best to spoil their children. Since we were the only ones who could afford certain—er—pleasures, we naturally gravitated to each other, though when I think back, even at that time there was little true friendship involved.

It so happened that I had a flair for my studies whereas Walter didn't give a damn. At examination time, I had to carry him. It seemed like a big joke at the time, but actually I was doing all the work while he was having his fling around town. Nor was I the only one he imposed upon in such a way. Many students, impressed with having his friendship, gladly took over his papers. Walter could charm the devil himself if he had to.

And quite often he had to. Many's the time he talked his way out of spending a weekend in jail for some minor offence—and I've even seen him twist the dean around his little finger, so to speak. Oh, but I remained his loyal friend. I shared everything I had with him, including my women, and even thought it amusing when I went out on a date and met him, only to have him take my girl home.

In the last year of school the crash came. It meant little to me because my father had seen it coming and got out with his fortune increased. Walter's father tried to stick it out and went under. He was one of the ones who killed himself that day.

Walter was quite stricken, of course. He was in a blue funk and got stinking drunk. We had quite a talk and he was for quitting school at once, but I talked him into accepting the money from me and graduating. Come to think of it, he never did pay me back that money. However, it really doesn't matter.

After we left school I went into business with my father and took over the firm when he died. It was that same month that Walter showed up. He stopped in for a visit and wound up with a position, though at no time did he deceive me as to the real intent of his visit. He got what he came after and in a way it was a good thing for me. Walter was a shrewd businessman.

His rise in the financial world was slightly less than meteoric. He was much too astute to remain in anyone's employ for long, and with everybody talking about Harrison, the Boy Wonder of Wall Street, in every other breath, it was inevitable that he open up his own office. In a sense, we became competitors after that, but always friends.

Pardon me, Inspector, let's say that I was his friend; he never was mine. His ruthlessness was appalling at times, but even then he managed to charm his victims into accepting their lot with a smile. I for one know that he managed the market to make himself a cool million on a deal that left me gasping. More than once he almost cut the bottom out of my business, yet he was always in with a grin and a big hello the next day as if it had been only a tennis match he had won.

If you've followed his rise then you're familiar with the social side of his life. Walter cut quite a swath for himself. Twice, he was almost killed by irate husbands, and if he had been, no jury on earth would have convicted his murderer. There was the time a young girl killed herself rather than let her parents know that she had been having an affair with Walter and had been trapped. He was very generous about it. He offered her money to travel, her choice of doctors and anything she wanted—except his name for her child. No, he wasn't ready to give his name away then. That came a few weeks later.

I was engaged to be married at the time. Adrianne was a girl I had loved from the moment I saw her and there aren't words enough to tell how happy I was when she said she'd marry me. We spent most of our waking hours poring over plans for the future. We even selected a site for our house out on the island and began construction. We were timing the wedding to coincide with the completion of the house and if ever I was a man living in a dream world, it was then. My happiness was complete, as was Adrianne's, or so I thought. Fortune seemed to favour me with more than one smile at the time. For some reason my own career took a sudden spurt and whatever I touched turned to gold, and in no time the Street had taken to following me rather than Harrison. Without realising it, I turned several deals that had him on his knees, though I doubt if many ever realised it. Walter would never give up the amazing front he affected.'

At this point Duncan paused to study his glass, his eyes narrowing. Inspector Early remained motionless, waiting for him to go on.

'Walter came to see me,' Duncan said. 'It was a day I shall never forget. I had a dinner engagement with Adrianne and invited him along.

Now I know that what he did was done out of sheer spite, nothing else. At first I believed that it was my fault, or hers . . .

Forgive me if I pass over the details lightly, Inspector. They aren't very pleasant to recall. I had to sit there and watch Adrianne captivated by this charming rat to the point where I was merely a decoration in the chair opposite her. I had to see him join us day after day, night after night, then hear the rumours that they were seeing each other without me; then discover for myself that she was in love with him.

Yes, it was quite an experience. I had the idea of killing them both, then killing myself. When I saw that that could never solve the problem I gave it up.

Adrianne came to me one night. She sat and told me how much she hated to hurt me, but she had fallen in love with Walter Harrison and wanted to marry him. What else was there to do? Naturally, I acted the part of a good loser and called off the engagement. They didn't wait long. A week later they were married and I was the laughing stock of the Street.

Perhaps time might have cured everything if things didn't turn out the way they did. It wasn't very long afterwards that I learned of a break in their marriage. Word came that Adrianne had changed and I knew for a fact that Walter was far from being true to her.

You see, now I realised the truth. Walter never loved her. He never loved anybody but himself. He married Adrianne because he wanted to hurt me more than anything else in the world. He hated me because I had something he lacked—happiness. It was something he searched desperately for himself and always found just out of reach.

In December of that year Adrianne took sick. She wasted away for a month and died. In the final moments she called for me, asking me to forgive her; this much I learned from a servant of hers. Walter, by the way, was enjoying himself at a party when she died. He came home for the funeral and took off immediately for a sojourn in Florida with some attractive showgirl.

God, how I hated that man! I used to dream of killing him! Do you know, if ever my mind drifted from the work I was doing I always pictured myself standing over his corpse with a knife in my hand, laughing my head off.

Every so often I would get word of Walter's various escapades, and they seemed to follow a definite pattern. I made it my business to learn more about him and before long I realised that Walter was almost frenzied in his search to find a woman he could really love. Since he was a fabulously wealthy man, he was always suspicious of a woman wanting him more than his wealth, and this very suspicion always was the thing that drove a woman away from him.

It may seem strange to you, but regardless of my attitude I saw him quite regularly. And equally strange, he never realised that I hated him so. He realised, of course, that he was far from popular in any quarter, but he never suspected me of anything else save a stupid idea of friendship. But having learned my lesson the hard way, he never got the chance to impose upon me again, though he never really had need to.

It was a curious thing, the solution I saw to my problem. It had been there all the time, I was aware of it being there, yet using the circumstance never occurred to me until the day I was sitting on my veranda reading a memo from my office manager. The note stated that Walter had pulled another coup in the market and had the Street rocking on its heels. It was one of those times when any variation in Wall Street reacted on the economy of the country, and what he did was try to undermine the entire economic structure of the United States. It was with the greatest effort that we got back to normal without toppling, but in doing so a lot of places had to close up. Harrison, however, had doubled the wealth he could never hope to spend anyway.

As I said, I was sitting there reading the note when I saw her behind the window in the house across the way. The sun was streaming in, deflecting the gold in her hair, making a picture of beauty so exquisite as to be unbelievable. A servant came and brought her a tray, and as she sat down to lunch I lost sight of her behind the hedges and the thought came to me of how simple it would all be.

I met Walter for lunch the next day. He was quite exuberant over his latest adventure, treating it like a joke.

I said, 'Say, you've never been out to my place on the island, have you?'

He laughed, and I noticed a little guilt in his eyes. 'To tell the truth,' he said, 'I would have dropped in if you hadn't built the place for Adrianne. After all . . .'

'Don't be ridiculous, Walter. What's done is done. Look, until things get back to normal, how about staying with me a few days? You need a rest.'

'Fine, Duncan, fine! Any time you say.'

'All right, I'll pick you up tonight.'

We had quite a ride out, stopping at a few places for drinks and hashing over the old days at school. At any other time I might have laughed, but all those reminiscences had taken on an unpleasant air. When we reached the house I had a few friends in to meet the fabulous Walter Harrison, left him accepting their plaudits and went to bed.

We had breakfast on the veranda. Walter ate with relish, breathing deeply of the sea air with animal-like pleasure. At exactly nine o'clock the sunlight flashed off the windows of the house behind mine as the servant threw them open to the morning breeze.

Then she was there. I waved and she waved back. Walter's head turned to look and I heard his breath catch in his throat. She was lovely, her hair a golden cascade that tumbled around her shoulders. Her blouse was a radiant white that enhanced the swell of her breasts, a gleaming contrast to the smooth, tanned flesh of her shoulders.

Walter looked like a man in a dream. 'Lord, she's lovely!' he said. 'Who is she, Dunc?'

I sipped my coffee. 'A neighbour,' I said lightly.

'Do you . . . do you think I can get to meet her?'

'Perhaps. She's quite young and just a little bit shy and it would be better to have her see me with you a few times before introductions are in order.'

He sounded hoarse. His face had taken on an avid, hungry look. 'Anything you say, but I have to meet her.' He turned around with a grin. 'By golly, I'll stay here until I do, too!'

We laughed over that and went back to our cigarettes, but every so often I caught him glancing back towards the hedge with that desperate expression creasing his face.

Being familiar with her schedule, I knew that we wouldn't see her again that day, but Walter knew nothing of this. He tried to keep away from the subject, yet it persisted in coming back. Finally he said, 'Incidentally, just who is she?'

'Her name is Evelyn Vaughn. Comes from quite a well-to-do family.'

'She here alone?'

'No, besides the servants she has a nurse and a doctor in attendance. She hasn't been quite well.'

'Hell, she looks the picture of health.'

'Oh, she is now,' I agreed. I walked over and turned on the television and we watched the fights. For the sixth time a call came in for Walter, but his reply was the same. He wasn't going back to New York. I felt the anticipation in his voice, knowing why he was staying, and had to concentrate on the screen to keep from smiling.

Evelyn was there the next day and the next. Walter had taken to waving when I did and when she waved back his face seemed to light up until it looked almost boyish. The sun had tanned him nicely and he pranced around like a colt, especially when she could see him. He pestered me with questions and received evasive answers. Somehow he got the idea that his importance warranted a visit from the house across the way. When I told him that to Evelyn neither wealth nor position meant a thing he looked at me sharply to see if I was telling the truth. To have become what he was he had to be a good reader of faces and he knew that it *was* the truth beyond the shadow of a doubt.

So I sat there day after day watching Walter Harrison fall helplessly in love with a woman he hadn't met yet. He fell in love with the way she waved until each movement of her hand seemed to be for him alone. He fell in love with the luxuriant beauty of her body, letting his eyes follow her as she walked to the water from the house, aching to be close to her. She would turn sometimes and see us watching, and wave.

At night he would stand by the window, not hearing what I said because he was watching her windows, hoping for just one glimpse of her, and often I would hear him repeating her name slowly, letting it roll off his tongue like a precious thing.

It couldn't go on that way. I knew it and he knew it. She had just come up from the beach and the water glistened on her skin. She laughed at something the woman who was with her said and shook her head back so that her hair flowed down her back.

Walter shouted and waved and she laughed again, waving back. The wind brought her voice to him and Walter stood there, his breath hot in my face. 'Look here, Duncan, I'm going over to meet her. I can't stand this waiting. Good Lord, what does a guy have to go through to meet a woman?'

'You've never had any trouble before, have you?'

'Never like this!' he said. 'Usually they're dropping at my feet. I haven't changed, have I? There's nothing repulsive about me, is there?'

I wanted to tell the truth, but I laughed instead.

'You're the same as ever. It wouldn't surprise me if she was dying to meet you, too. I can tell you this . . . she's never been outside as much as since you've been here.'

His eyes lit up boyishly. 'Really, Dunc. Do you think so?'

'I think so. I can assure you of this, too. If she does seem to like you, it's certainly for yourself alone.'

As crudely as the barb was placed, it went home. Walter never so much as glanced at me. He was lost in thought for a long time, then: 'I'm going over there now, Duncan. I'm crazy about that girl. By God, I'll marry her if it's the last thing I do.'

'Don't spoil it, Walter. Tomorrow, I promise you, I'll go over with you.'

His eagerness was pathetic. I don't think he slept a wink that night. Long before breakfast he was waiting for me on the veranda. We ate in silence, each minute an eternity for him. He turned repeatedly to look over the hedge and I caught a flash of worry when she didn't appear.

Tight little lines had appeared at the corner of his eyes and he said, 'Where is she, Dunc? She should be there by now, shouldn't she?'

'I don't know,' I said. 'It does seem strange. Just a moment.' I rang the bell on the table and my housekeeper came to the door. 'Have you seen the Vaughns, Martha?' I asked her.

She nodded sagely. 'Oh, yes sir. They left very early this morning to go back to the city.'

Walter turned to me. 'Hell!'

'Well, she'll be back,' I assured him.

'Damn it, Dunc, that isn't the point!' He stood up and threw his napkin on the seat. 'Can't you realise that I'm in love with the girl? I can't wait for her to get back!'

His face flushed with frustration. There was no anger, only the crazy hunger for the woman. I held back my smile. It happened. It happened the way I planned for it to happen. Walter Harrison had fallen so deeply in love, so truly in love that he couldn't control himself. I might have felt sorry for him at that moment if I hadn't asked him, 'Walter, as I told you I know very little about her. Supposing she is already married?'

He answered my question with a nasty grimace. 'Then she'll get a divorce if I have to break the guy in pieces. I'll break anything that stands in my way, Duncan. I'm going to have her if it's the last thing I do!'

He stalked off to his room. Later I heard the car roar down the road.

I went back to New York and was there a week when my contacts told me of Walter's fruitless search. He used every means at his disposal, but he couldn't locate the girl. I gave him seven days, exactly seven days. You see, that seventh day was the anniversary of the date I introduced him to Adrianne. I'll never forget it. Wherever Walter is now, neither will he.

When I called him I was amazed at the change in his voice. He sounded weak and lost. We exchanged the usual formalities; then I said, 'Walter, have you found Evelyn yet?'

He took a long time to answer. 'No, she's disappeared completely.'

'Oh, I wouldn't say that,' I said.

He didn't get it at first. It was almost too much to hope for. 'You . . . mean you know where she is?'

'Exactly.'

'Where? Please, Dunc . . . where is she?' In a split second he became a vital being again. He was bursting with life and energy, demanding that I tell him.

I laughed and told him to let me get a word in and I would. The silence was ominous then. 'She's not very far from here, Walter, in a small hotel right off Fifth Avenue.' I gave him the address and had hardly finished when I heard his phone slam against the desk. He was in such a hurry he hadn't bothered to hang up . . .'

Duncan stopped and drained his glass, then stared at it remorsefully. The inspector coughed lightly to attract his attention, his curiosity prompting him to speak.

'Then he found her?' he asked eagerly.

'Oh, yes, he found her. He burst right in over all protests, expecting to sweep her off her feet.'

This time the inspector fidgeted nervously. 'Well, go on.'

Duncan motioned for the waiter and lifted a fresh glass in a toast. The inspector did the same. Duncan smiled gently. 'When she saw him she laughed and waved. Walter Harrison died an hour later . . . from a window in the same hotel.'

It was too much for the inspector. He leaned forward in his chair, his forehead knotted in a frown. 'But what happened? Who was she? Damn it all, Duncan . . .'

Duncan took a deep breath, then gulped the drink down.

'Evelyn Vaughn was a helpless imbecile,' he said. 'She had the beauty of a goddess and the mentality of a two-year-old. They kept her well tended and dressed so she wouldn't be an object of curiosity. But the only habit she ever learned was to wave bye-bye . . .'

ACCIDENT REPORT

Ed McBain

The famous 87th Precinct which is ostensibly located on the island of Isola—although no one is in any doubt that it is a thinly disguised representation of teeming Manhattan in New York City—was evolved during the last years of the pulp era and is the setting for one of the best-known police procedural series in the world. The starkly realistic stories are all about terror and brutality at street level, yet are frequently relieved by a vein of slapstick comedy that makes them unique in crime fiction. The various characters of the Precinct, particularly tough Detective Steve Carella, the giant Detective Cotton Hawes and the unredeemed braggart Detective Andy Parker, have become household names thanks to the continuing series of books, plus half a dozen movies and television series, which started in 1956 with the novels Cop Hater and The Mugger. The saga developed from crime and detective stories that the author had been writing ever since the early Fifties, and followed hard on the heels of the huge success of The Blackboard Jungle (1954), a novel of violence and racial tension in New York schools which has become a classic and was made into the first movie in which the teenage craze of Rock 'n' Roll was featured. The riots perpetrated by young audiences in New York and London cinemas when the picture was first screened only added to the book's legendary status.

Ed McBain (1926–   ) is the pen-name of Evan Hunter who was born in New York and as a youngster and then a teacher in the city saw crime at first hand, especially the street gangs, drug pushers and petty criminals who would become the focus of his early stories for hardboiled magazines such as Adventure, Manhunt and Bloodhound. His affection for pulp fiction was clearly evident in one series he wrote under the name of Curt Cannon, with titles such as I Like 'em Tough (1958) and I'm Cannon—for Hire (1959). Told in the first person, these hardboiled cases were all about a tough former private eye who lived *in the Bowery and described himself as a derelict. Readers soon realised that here was a man with whom even the toughest of the other hardboiled dicks might find it hard to work, given to making statements such as 'I drink twenty-five hours out of twenty-four' and 'I sleep on park benches when I don't have the money for a bed'. The characters who work in the 87th Precinct may be a shade more sociable than Cannon, but certainly every bit as tough. Detective Sergeant Mike Jonas, the narrator of 'Accident Report' (from* Manhunt, 1953), *is a hard-nosed cop who tackles one of the most emotive cases any policeman can be faced with—the brutal killing of another member of the force.*

*   *   *

There was a blanket thrown over the patrolman by the time we got there. The ambulance was waiting, and a white-clad intern was standing near the step of the ambulance, puffing on a cigarette.

He looked up as I walked over to him, and then flicked his cigarette away.

'Detective-Sergeant Jonas,' I said.

'How do you do?' the intern answered. 'Dr Mallaby.'

'What's the story?'

'Broken neck. It must have been a big car. His chest is caved in where he was first hit. I figure he was knocked down, and then run over. The bumper probably broke his neck. That's the cause of death, anyway.'

Andy Larson walked over to where we were standing. He shook his head and said, 'A real bloody one, Mike.'

'Yeah.' I turned to the intern. 'When was he hit?'

'Hard to say. No more than a half-hour ago, I'd guess offhand. An autopsy will tell.'

'That checks, Mike,' Andy said. 'Patrolman on the beat called it in about twenty-five minutes ago.'

'A big car, huh?'

'I'd say so,' the intern answered.

'I wonder how many big cars there are in this city?'

Andy nodded. 'You can cart him away, Doc,' he said. 'The boys are through with their pictures.'

The intern fired another cigarette, and we watched while he and an attendant put the dead patrolman on a stretcher and then into the ambulance. The intern and the attendant climbed aboard, and the ambulance pulled off down the street. They didn't use the siren. There was no rush now.

A cop gets it, and you say, 'Well, gee, that's tough. But that was his trade.' Sure. Except that being a cop doesn't mean you don't have a wife, and maybe a few kids. It doesn't hurt any less, being a cop. You're just as dead.

I went over the accident report with Andy.

ACCIDENT NUMBER 46A-3
FIRST NAME AND INITIALS James C.
PRECINCT NO. 032
AIDED NUMBER 67-4
SEX M
SURNAME Benson
ADDRESS 1812 Crescent Ave.
AGE 28

My eyes skipped down the length of the card, noting the date, time, place of occurrence.

NATURE OF ILLNESS OR INJURY Hit and run
FATAL ✓
SERIOUS
SLIGHT
UNKNOWN

I kept reading, down to the circled items on the card that told me the body had been taken to the morgue and claimed already. The rest would have been routine in any other case, but it was slightly ironic here.

TRAFFIC CONTROLLED BY OFFICER?
NAME Ptm. James C. Benson
SHIELD NO. 3685
TRAFFIC CONTROLLED BY LIGHTS? Yes
COMMAND Traffic Division
LIGHTS IN OPERATION? Yes

I read the rest of the technical information about the direction of the traffic moving on the lights, the police action taken, the city involved, and then flipped the card over. Under the NAMES AND ADDRESSES OF WITNESSES (IF NONE, SO STATE) the single word 'None' was scribbled.

The officer who'd reported the hit and run was Patrolman P. Margolis. He'd been making the rounds, stopped for his usual afternoon chat with Benson, and had found the traffic cop dead in the gutter. There were skid marks on the asphalt street, but there hadn't been a soul in sight.

'How do you figure it, Andy?' I asked.

'A few ideas.'

'Let's hear them.'

'The guy may have done something wrong. Benson may have hailed him for something entirely different. The guy panicked and cut him down.'

'Something wrong like what?'

'Who knows? Hot furs in the trunk. Dead man in the back seat. You know.'

'And you figure Benson hailed him because he was speeding, or his windscreen wiper was crooked? Something like that?'

'Yeah, you know.'

'I don't buy it, Andy.'

'Well, I got another idea.'

'What's that? Drunk?'

Andy nodded.

'That's what I was thinking. Where do we start?'

'I've already had a check put in on stolen cars, and the lab boys are going over the skid marks. Why don't we go back and see if we can scare up any witnesses?'

I picked my jacket off the back of the chair, buttoned it on, and then adjusted my shoulder clip. 'Come on.'

The scene of the accident was at the intersection of two narrow streets. There was a two-family stucco house on one corner, and empty lots on the other three corners. It was a quiet intersection, and the only reason it warranted a light was the high school two blocks away. A traffic cop was used to supplement the light in the morning and afternoon when the kids were going to and coming from school. Benson had been hit about ten minutes before classes broke. It was a shame, because a bunch of home-bound kids might have saved his life—or at least provided some witnesses.

'There's not much choice,' Andy said.

I looked at the stucco house. 'No, I guess not. Let's go.'

We climbed the flat, brick steps at the front of the house, and Andy pushed the bell button. We waited for a few moments, and then the door opened a crack, and a voice asked, 'Yes?'

I flashed my buzzer. 'Police officers,' I said. 'We'd like to ask a few questions.'

The door stayed closed, with the voice coming from behind the small crack. 'What about?'

'Accident here this afternoon. Won't you open the door?'

The door swung wide, and a thin young kid in his undershirt peered out at us. His brows pulled together in a hostile frown. 'You got a search warrant?' he asked.

'What have you got to hide, sonny?' Andy asked.

'Nothing. I just don't like cops barging in like storm troopers.'

'Nobody's barging in on you,' Andy said. 'We want to ask a few questions, that's all. You want to get snotty about it, we'll go get a goddamned search warrant, and then you'd better hold onto your head.'

'All right, what do you want?'

'You changed your song, huh, sonny?'

'Leave it be, Andy,' I said. 'Were you home this afternoon, son?'

'Yeah.'

'All afternoon?'

'Yeah.'

'You hear any noise out here in the street?'

'What kind of noise?'

'You tell me.'

'I didn't hear any noise.'

'A car skidding, maybe? Something like that?'

'No.'

'Did you *see* anything unusual?'

'I didn't see anything. You're here about the cop who was run over, ain't you?'

'That's right, son.'

'Well, I didn't see anything.'

'You live here alone?'

'No. With my mother.'

'Where is she?'

'She ain't feeling too good. That's why I've been staying home from school. She's been sick in bed. She didn't hear anything, either. She's in a fog.'

'Have you had the doctor?'

'Yeah, she'll be all right.'

'Where's your mother's room?'

'In the back of the house. She couldn't have seen anything out here even if she was able to. You're barking up the wrong tree.'

'How long you been out of school, son?'

'Why?'

'How long?'

'A month.'

'Your mother been sick that long?'

'Yeah.'

'How old are you?'

'Fifteen.'

'You better get back to school,' Andy said. 'Damn fast. Tell the city about your mother, and they'll do something for her. You hear that?'

'I hear it.'

'We'll send someone round to check tomorrow. Remember that, sonny.'

'I'll remember it,' the kid said, a surly look on his face.

'Anybody else live here with you?'

'Yeah. My dog. You want to ask him some questions, maybe?'

I saw Andy clench his fists, so I said, 'That'll be all, son. Thanks.'

'For what?' the kid asked, and then he slammed the door.

'That lousy snot-nose,' Andy said. 'That little son of a . . .'

'Come on,' I said. We started down, and I looked at the empty lots on the other corners. Then I turned back to take a last look at the house. 'There's nothing more here,' I said. 'We better get back.'

There were thirty-nine cars stolen in New York City that day. Of the bigger cars, two were Buicks, four Chryslers, and one Cadillac. One of the Chryslers was stolen from a neighbourhood about two miles from the scene of the accident.

'How about that?' Andy asked.

'How about it?'

'The guy stole the buggy and when Benson hailed him, he knew he was in hot water. He cut him down.'

'*If* Benson hailed him.'

'Maybe Benson only stuck up his hand to stop traffic. The guy misunderstood, and crashed through.'

'We'll see,' I said.

We checked with the owner of the Chrysler. She was a fluttery woman who was obviously impressed with the fact that two policemen were calling on her personally about her missing car.

'Well, I never expected such quick action,' she said. 'I mean, *really*.'

'The car was a Chrysler, ma'm?' I asked.

'Oh, yes,' she said, nodding her head emphatically. 'We've never owned anything but a Chrysler.'

'What year, ma'm?'

'I gave all this information on the phone,' she said.

'I know, ma'm. We're just checking it again.'

'A new car. 1960.'

'The colour?'

'Blue. A sort of robin's egg blue, do you know? I told that to the man who answered the phone.'

'Licence number?'

'Oh, again? Well, just a moment.' She stood up and walked to the kitchen, returning with her purse. She fished into the purse, came up with a wallet, and then rummaged through that for her registration. 'Here it is,' she said.

'What, ma'm?'

'7T 8458.'

Andy looked up. 'That's a Nassau County plate, ma'm.'

'Yes. Yes, I know.'

'In the Bronx? How come?'

'Well . . . oh, you'll think this is silly.'

'Let's hear it, ma'm.'

'Well, a Long Island plate is so much more impressive. I mean— well, we plan on moving there soon anyway.'

'And you went all the way to Nassau to get a plate?'

'Yes.'

Andy coughed politely. 'Well, maybe that'll make it easier.'

'Do you think you'll find the car?'

'We certainly hope so, ma'm.'

We found the car that afternoon. It was parked on a side street in Brooklyn. It was in perfect condition, no damage to the front end, no blood anywhere on the grille or bumper. The lab checked the tyres against the skid marks. Negative. This, coupled with the fact that the murder car would undoubtedly have sustained injuries after such a violent smash, told us we'd drawn a blank. We returned the car to the owner.

She was very happy.

*

By the end of the week, we'd recovered all but one of the stolen cars. None of them checked with what we had. The only missing car was the Cadillac. It had been swiped from a parking lot in Queens, with the thief presenting the attendant with a ticket for the car. The m.o. sounded professional, whereas the car kill looked like a fool stunt. When another Caddy was stolen from a lot in Jamaica, with the thief using the same *modus operandi*, we figured it for a ring, and left it to the Automobile Squad.

In the meantime, we'd begun checking all auto body and fender repair shops in the city. We had just about ruled out a stolen car by this time, and if the car was privately owned, the person who'd run down Benson would undoubtedly try to have the damage to his car repaired.

The lab had reported finding glass slivers from a sealbeam embedded in Benson's shirt, together with chips of black paint. From the position of the skid marks, they estimated that he'd been hit by the right side of the car, and they figured the broken light would be on that side, together with the heaviest damage to the grille.

Because Andy still clung to the theory that the driver had been involved in something fishy just before he hit Benson, we checked with the local precinct squads for any possibly related robberies or burglaries, and we also checked with the Safe, Loft and Truck Squad. There'd been a grocery store holdup in the neighbouring vicinity on the day of the hit and run, but the thief had already been apprehended, and he was driving a '50 Ford. Both headlights were intact, and any damage to the grille had been sustained years ago.

We continued to check on repair shops.

When the Complaint Report came in, we leaped on it at once. We glossed over the usual garbage in the heading, and skipped down to the DETAILS:

Telephone message from one Mrs James Dailey, owner and resident of private dwelling at 2389 Barnes Avenue. Dispatched Radio Motor Patrol # 761. Mrs Dailey returned from two-week vacation to find picket fence around house smashed in on north-west corner. Tyre marks in bed of irises in front yard indicate heavy automobile or light truck responsible for damage. Black paint discovered on damaged pickets. Good tyre marks in wet mud of iris bed, casts made. Tyre size 7.60-15.4-ply. Estimated weight 28 pounds. Further investigation of tread marks disclosed tyre to be Sears,

Roebuck and Company, registered trademark Allstate Tyres. Catalogue number 95K 01227K. Case still active pending receipt of reports and further investigation.

'You can damn well bet it's still active,' Andy said. 'This may be it, Mike.'

'Maybe,' I said.

It wasn't. The tyre was a very popular seller, and the mail order house sold thousands of them every year, both through the mails and over the counter. It was impossible to check over-the-counter sales, and a check of mail-order receipts revealed that no purchases had been made within a two-mile radius of the hit and run. We extended the radius, checked on all the purchasers, and found no suspicious-looking automobiles, although all of the cars were big ones. There was one black car in the batch—and there wasn't a scratch on it.

But Mrs Dailey's house was about ten blocks from the scene of the killing, and that was too close for coincidence. We checked out a car and drove over.

She was a woman in her late thirties, and she greeted us at the door in a loose housecoat, her hair up in curlers.

'Police officers,' I said.

Her hand went to her hair, and she said, 'Oh, my goodness.' She fretted a little more about her appearance, belted the housecoat tighter around her waist, and then said, 'Come in, come in.'

We questioned her a little about the fence and the iris bed, got substantially what was in the Complaint Report, and then went out to look at the damage. She stayed in the house, and when she joined us later, she was wearing tight black slacks and a chartreuse sweater. She'd also tied a scarf around her hair, hiding the curlers.

The house was situated on a corner, with a side street intersecting Barnes Avenue, and then a gravel road cutting into another intersection. The tyre marks seemed to indicate the car had come down the gravel road, and then backed up the side street, knocking over the picket fence when it did. It all pointed to a drunken driver.

'How does it look?' she asked.

'We're working on it,' Andy said. 'Any of your neighbours witness this?'

'No. I asked around. No one saw the car. They heard the crash, came out and saw the damaged fence, but the car had gone already.'

'Was anything missing from your house or yard?'

'No. It was locked up tight. We were on vacation, you know.'

'What kind of a car does your husband drive, ma'm?'

'A '58 Olds. Why?'

'Just wondering.'

'Let's amble up the street, Mike,' Andy said. 'Thank you very much, ma'm.'

We got into the car, and Mrs Dailey watched us go, striking a pretty pose in the doorway of her house. I looked back and saw her wave at one of her neighbours, and then she went inside.

'Where to?' I asked Andy.

'There's a service station at the end of that gravel road, on the intersection. If the car came up that road, maybe he stopped at the station for petrol. We've got nothing to lose.'

We had nothing to gain, either. They'd serviced a hundred big black cars every day. They didn't remember anything that looked out of line. We thanked them, and stopped at the nearest diner for some coffee. The coffee was hot, but the case sure as hell wasn't.

It griped us. It really griped us.

Someone had a black car stashed away in his garage. The car had a damaged front end, and it may still have had blood stains on it. If he'd been a drunken driver, he'd sure as hell sobered up fast enough—and long enough to realise he had to keep that car out of sight. We mulled it over, and we squatted on it, and we were going over all the angles again when the phone rang.

I picked it up. 'Jonas here.'

'Mike, this is Charlie on the desk. I was going to turn this over to Complaint, but I thought you might like to sit in on it.'

'Tie in with the Benson kill?'

'Maybe.'

'I'll be right down.' I hung up quickly. 'Come on, Andy.'

We went downstairs to the desk, and Charlie introduced us to a Mr George Sullivan and his daughter Grace, a young kid of about sixteen. We took them into an empty office, leaving Charlie at the desk.

'What is it, Mr Sullivan?' I asked.

'I want better protection,' he said.

'Of what, sir?'

'My child. Grace here. All the kids at the high school, in fact.'

'What happened, sir?'

'You tell him, Grace.'

The kid was a pretty blonde, fresh and clean-looking in a sweater and skirt. She wet her lips and said, 'Daddy, can't . . .'

'Go on, Grace, it's for your own good.'

'What is it, Miss?' Andy asked gently.

'Well . . .'

'Go on, Grace. Just the way you told it to me. Go on.'

'Well, it was last week. I . . .'

'Where was this, Miss?'

'Outside the high school. I cut my last period, a study hour. I wanted to do some shopping downtown, and anyway a study hour is nowhere. You know, they're not so strict if you cut one.'

'Yes, Miss.'

'I got out early, about a half-hour before most of the kids start home. I was crossing the street when this car came around the corner. I got onto the sidewalk, and the car slowed down and started following me.'

'What kind of a car, Miss?'

'A big, black one.'

'Did you notice the year and make?'

'No. I'm not so good at cars.'

'All right, what happened?'

'Well, the man driving kept following me, and I started walking faster, and he kept the car even with me all the time. He leaned over towards the window near the kerb and said, "Come on, sweetheart, let's go for a ride." ' She paused. 'Daddy, do I have to . . .'

'Tell them all of it, Grace.'

She swallowed hard, and then stared down at her saddle shoes.

'I didn't answer him. I kept walking, and he pulled up about ten feet ahead of me, and sat waiting there. When I came up alongside the car, he opened the door and got out. He . . . he . . . made a grab for me and . . . and I screamed.'

'What happened then?'

'He got scared. He jumped into the car and pulled away from the kerb. He was going very fast. I stopped screaming after he'd gone because . . . because I didn't want to attract any attention.'

'When was this, Miss?'

'Last week.'

'What day?'

'It was Wednesday,' Mr Sullivan put in. 'She came home looking like hell, and I asked her what was wrong, and she said nothing. I didn't get the story out of her until today.'

'You should have reported this earlier, Miss,' Andy said.

'I . . . I was too embarrassed.'

'Did you notice the licence plate on the car?'

'Yes.'

'Did you get the number?'

'No. It was a funny plate.'

'How do you mean funny?'

'It was a New York plate, but it had a lot of lettering on it.'

'A lot of lettering? Was it a suburban plate? Was the car a station wagon?'

'No, it wasn't.'

'A delivery truck?'

'No, it was a regular car. A new one.'

'A new car,' I repeated.

'Are you going to do something about this?' Mr Sullivan asked.

'We're going to try, sir. Did you get a good look at the man, Miss?'

'Yes. He was old. And fat. He wore a brown suit.'

'How old would you say, Miss?'

'At least forty.'

Mr Sullivan smiled, and then the smile dropped from his face. 'There should be a cop around there. There definitely should be.'

'Would you be able to identify the man if we showed him to you?'

'Yes, but . . . do I have to? I mean, I don't want any trouble. I don't want the other kids to find out.'

'No one will find out, Miss.'

'This wouldn't have happened if there was a cop around,' Mr Sullivan said.

'There was a cop,' I told him. 'He's dead.'

When they left, we got some coffee and mulled it over a bit more.

'A new car,' Andy said.

'With a funny plate. What the hell did she mean by a funny plate?'

'On a new car.'

I stood up suddenly. 'I'll be dipped!' I said.

'What?'

'A new car, Andy. A funny plate. A New York plate with lettering on it. For Christ's sake, it was a *dealer's* plate!'

Andy snapped his fingers. 'Sure. That explains how the bastard kept the car hidden so well. It's probably on some goddamned garage floor, hidden behind the other cars in the showroom.'

'Let's go, Andy,' I said.

It wasn't difficult. It's tough to get a dealer's franchise, and there aren't very many dealers in any specific neighbourhood. We tried two, and we hit the jackpot on the third try.

We spotted the car in one corner of the big garage. We walked over to it, and there was a mechanic in grease-stained overalls working on the right headlight.

'Police,' I told him. 'What's wrong there?'

He continued working, apparently used to periodic checks from the Automobile Squad. 'Sealbeam is broken. Just replacing it.'

'What happened to the grille?'

'Oh, a small accident. Damn shame, too. A new car.'

Andy walked round to the back and saw the paint scratches on the trunk. He nodded when he came around to me again.

'Back's all scratched, too,' he said to the mechanic.

'Yeah, this goddamn car's been a jinx ever since we got it in.'

'How so?'

'Got a headache with this one. The day we took it out for a test, the fool driver ran it into a ditch. Sliced hell out of both rear tyres, and we had to replace them. All this in the first week we had this pig.'

'Did you replace with Allstate?' I asked.

The mechanic looked up in surprise. 'Why, yeah. Say, how did you know?'

'Where's your boss?' Andy asked.

'In the front office.' The mechanic got up. 'Hey, what's this all about?'

'Nothing that concerns you, Mac. Fix your car.'

We went to the front office, a small cubicle that held two desks and two leather customer chairs. A stout man was sitting at one desk, a telephone to his ear. I estimated his age at about forty-two, forty-three.

He looked up and smiled when we came in, nodded at us, and then continued talking.

'Yes ... well, okay, if you say so. Well look, Sam, I can't sell cars if I haven't got them ... You just do your best, that's all. Okay, fine.' He hung up without saying goodbye, got out of his chair and walked over to us.

'Can I help you gentlemen?'

'Yes,' Andy said. 'We're interested in a car. Are you the owner of this place?'

'I am.'

'With whom are we doing business?'

'Fred Whitaker,' he said. 'Did you have any particular car in mind?'

'Yes. The black Buick on the floor.'

'A beautiful car,' Whitaker said, smiling.

'The one with the smashed grille and headlight,' I added.

The smile froze on his face, and he went white. 'Wh . . . what?'

'Did you smash that car up?'

Whitaker swallowed hard. 'No . . . no. One of my mechanics did it.'

'Who?'

'I've . . . I've fired him. He . . .'

'We can check this, Whitaker.'

'Are . . . are you policemen?'

'We are. Come on, let's have it all. We've got a girl to identify you.'

Whitaker's face crumbled. 'I . . . I guess that's best, isn't it?'

'It's best,' Andy said.

'I didn't mean to run him down. But the girl screamed, you know, and I thought he'd heard it. He stuck up his hand, and I . . . I got scared, I suppose, and there was no one around, so I . . . I knocked him . . . I knocked him down. Is he all right? I mean . . .'

'He's dead,' I said.

'Dead?' Whitaker's eyes went wide. 'Dead . . .'

'Was it you who smashed that picket fence?' Andy asked.

Whitaker was still dazed.

'Wh . . . what?' he said, very slowly after a pause.

'The picket fence. On Barnes.'

'Oh. Yes, yes. That was afterwards. I was still scared. I . . . I made a wrong turn, and I saw a police car, and I wanted to get away fast. I . . . I backed into the fence.'

'Why'd you bother that little girl, Whitaker?'

He collapsed into a chair. 'I don't know,' he said. 'I don't know.'

'You're in a jam,' Andy said. 'You'd better come along with us.'

'Yes, yes.' He stood up, took his hat from a rack in the corner, and then started for the door. At the door he stopped and said, 'I'd better tell my mechanics. I'd better tell them I'll be gone for the day.'

I looked at Whitaker, and I thought of Benson. My eyes met Andy's, and I put it into words for both of us.

'You'll be gone a lot longer than that, Whitaker.'

FREAKY DEAKY

Elmore Leonard

Some of the toughest cops in contemporary fiction are to be found in the hardboiled novels of Elmore Leonard, who has been keeping the old tradition alive for the last two decades as well as attracting an ever-increasing readership with each new book. His heroes are men like Ray Cruz, in the violent story City Primeval: High Noon in Detroit *(1981), who takes the law into his own hands to bring the killer of a judge to justice; Bryan Hurd, who pits his wits against a demented Florida millionaire in* Split Images *(1983); Vincent Mora and his doomed love affair with a prostitute who is murdered in* Glitz *(1985); and Marshal Raylan Givens, the lawman with a penchant for cowboy boots and shooting first, who features in both* Pronto *(1993) and* Riding the Rap *(1995). Their antagonists are equally colourful street people, whose violent ways and profane language Elmore Leonard captures brilliantly—characters such as the sleazy robbers Ernest 'Stick' Stickley and Frank J. Ryan in* Swag *(1976); the ex-informer Ed Rosen, on the run from three hitmen, in* The Hunted *(1978); Chilli Palmer, the loan shark who dreams of being a film mogul in* Get Shorty *(1990) and Bobby 'The Pruner' Deogracias, one-time bounty hunter, part-time gardener and full-time psycho who features in* Riding the Rap *and was described by the* Daily Telegraph *reviewer as being 'as nasty as anything Leonard has dreamed up'. Of all these people, Stephen Amidon added in the* Sunday Times, *'The hoods, low-lifes and con artists who populate Elmore Leonard's world are as American as apple pie.'*

Elmore Leonard (1925–), recently described by Time Out *as 'the king of crime fiction who has elevated pulp to an art form with his hard-boiled thrillers', was a copywriter and then advertising agency executive before becoming an author in the Fifties. His early work was almost entirely Westerns, highlighted by* 3.10 to Yuma, *which in 1957 was made into a classic film with Van Heflin and Glenn Ford. Although his books sold well enough on both sides of the Atlantic, it was when he switched to crime novels that he became a cult figure. Leonard, who is known to his friends as 'Dutch', often sets stories in Detroit where he lives and has every opportunity to study the idiom and mannerisms of the local minor league gangsters, petty thieves and hustlers. It is they who turn up, suitably disguised, as the weird characters in his books to confront the equally unforgettable cops, in exploits which blend violence and riotous humour in a unique way. 'Freaky Deaky' (written in 1988) is also set in Detroit, where cop Chris Mankowski finds himself on the trail of a group of small-time criminals who have become terrorists and are on a bombing spree across the city.*

* * *

Chris Mankowski's last day on the job, two in the afternoon, two hours to go, he got a call to dispose of a bomb.

What happened, a guy by the name of Booker, a 25-year-old super-dude twice-convicted felon, was in his Jacuzzi when the phone rang. He yelled for his bodyguard Juicy Mouth to take it. 'Hey, Juicy?' His bodyguard, his driver and his houseman were around somewhere. 'Will somebody get the phone?' The phone kept ringing. The phone must have rung 15 times before Booker got out of the Jacuzzi, put on his green satin robe that matched the emerald pinned to his left earlobe and picked up the phone. Booker said: 'Who's this?' A woman's voice said, 'You sitting down?' The phone was on a table next to a green leather wingback chair. Booker loved green. He said, 'Baby, is that you?' It sounded like his woman, Moselle. Her voice said, 'Are you sitting down? You have to be sitting down for when I tell you something.' Booker said, 'Baby, you sound different. What's wrong?' He sat down in the green leather chair, frowning, working his butt around to get comfortable. The woman's voice said, 'Are you sitting down?' Booker said, 'I *am*. I have sat the fuck down. Now you gonna talk to me, what?' Moselle's voice said, 'I'm supposed to tell you that when you get up, honey, what's left of your ass is gonna go clear through the ceiling.'

When Chris got there a uniform let him in. There were 13th Precinct cars and a Tactical station wagon parked in front of the house. The uniform told Chris that Booker had called 911. They radioed him here and when he saw who it was he called Narcotics and they jumped at it, a chance to go through the man's house wide open with their dog.

A guy from Narcotics who looked like a young vagrant told Chris that Booker was a success story: had come up through the street-dealing organisations, Young Boys Incorporated and Pony Down, and was now on about the third level from the top. Look around, guy 25 living in a home on Boston Boulevard, a mansion, originally owned by one of Detroit's automotive pioneers. The guy from Narcotics didn't remember which one. Look how Booker had fucked up the house, painted all that fine old oak panelling puke green. He asked Chris how come he was alone.

Chris said most of the squad was out on a run, picking up illegal fireworks, but there was another guy coming, Jerry Baker. Chris said, 'You know what today is?' And waited for the guy from Narcotics to say no, what? 'It's my last day on the Bomb Squad. Next week I get transferred out.' He waited again.

The guy from Narcotics said, 'Yeah, is that right?'

He didn't get it.

'It's the last time I'll ever have to handle a bomb, if that's what we have, and hope to Christ I don't make a mistake.'

The guy still didn't get it. He said, 'Well, that's what Booker says it is. He gets up, it blows up. What kind of bomb is that?'

'I won't know till I look at it,' Chris said.

'Booker says it's the fucking Italians,' the guy from Narcotics said, 'trying to tell him something. It makes sense, otherwise why not shoot the fucker? Like we know Booker's done guys we find out at Metro in long-term parking. Guy's in the trunk of his car, two in the back of the head. Booker's a bad fucking dude, man. If there was such a thing as justice in the world we'd leave his ass sitting there, let him work it out.'

Chris said, 'Get your people out of the house. When my partner gets here, don't stop and chat, okay? I'll let you know if we need Fire or EMS, or if we have to evacuate the houses next door. Now where's Booker?'

The guy from Narcotics took Chris down the hall towards the back of the house, saying, 'Wait'll you see what the spook did to the library. Looks like a fucking tent.'

It did. Green-and-white striped parachute cloth was draped on four sides from the centre point of the high ceiling to the top of the walls. The Jacuzzi bubbled in the middle of the room, a border of green tile around it. Booker sat beyond the sunken bath in his green leather wingback. He was holding on to the round arms, clutching them, fingers open. Behind him, French doors opened onto a backyard patio.

'I been waiting,' Booker said. 'You know how long I been waiting on you? I don't know where anybody's at, I been calling—you see Juicy Mouth?'

'Who's Juicy Mouth?'

'Supposed to be guarding my body. Man, I got to go to the toilet.'

Chris walked up to him, looking at the base of the chair. 'Tell me what the woman said on the phone.'

'Was the bitch supposed to be in love with me?'

'What'd she tell you?'

'Say I get up I'm *blown* up.'

'That's all?'

'Is that *all*? Man, that's final, that's all there is all, nothing else.'

Chris said, 'Yeah, but do you believe it?'

'Asshole, you expect me to stand up and find out?'

Chris was wearing a beige tweed sports coat, an old one with sagging pockets. He brought a Mini-Mag flashlight out of the left side pocket, went down flat on the floor and played the light beam into the four-inch clearance beneath the chair. The space was empty. He came to his knees, placed the Mini-Mag on the floor, brought a stainless Spyder-Co lockback pocket-knife from the right side pocket and flicked open the short blade with one hand in a quick practised motion.

Booker said, 'Hey,' pushing back in the chair.

'Cover yourself,' Chris said. 'I don't want to cut anything off by mistake.'

'Man, be careful there,' Booker said, bringing his hands off the chair arms to bunch the skirts of the robe between his bare legs, up tight against his crotch.

'You feel anything under you?'

'When I sat down it felt . . . like, different.'

Chris slit open the facing of the seat cushion, held the edges apart and looked in. He said, 'Hmmmmmmmmmm.'

Booker said, 'What you mean hmmmmmmm? Don't give me no hmmmmmmmmm shit. What's in there?'

Chris looked up at Booker and said, 'Ten sticks of dynamite.'

Booker was clutching the chair arms again, his body upright, stiff, telling Chris, 'Get that shit out from under me, man. Get it out, get it out of there!'

Chris said, 'Somebody doesn't like you, Booker. Two sticks would've been plenty.'

Booker said, 'Will you pull that shit *out*? Do it.'

Chris sat back on his heels, looking up at Booker. 'I'm afraid we have a problem.'

'What problem? What are you talking about?'

'There's something in there that looks like an inflatable rubber cushion, fairly flat, lying on top of the dynamite.'

'So pull the shit out, man. You see it, pull it out.'

'Yeah, but what I don't see is what makes it go bang. It must be in the back part, where the cushion zips open.'

'Then open the motherfucker.'

'I can't, you're sitting on it. It's probably a two-way pressure switch of some kind. I can't tell for sure, but that'd be my guess.'

Booker said, 'Your *guess*? You telling me you don't know what you doing?'

'We get all kinds,' Chris said. 'I have to see it before I know what it is . . . or whether or not I can disarm it. You understand?'

'Wait a minute now. You saying *if* you can take it apart?'

'And the only way to get to it,' Chris said, 'is to cut through the back of the chair.'

'Then cut it, cut it, I don't give a shit about the chair.'

'You run into the frame, all that heavy wood and springs . . .' Chris paused. He said, 'I don't know,' shaking his head.

Booker said, 'Look, motherfucker. You get this shit out from under me. You cut, you do what you have to do, you get it out.'

'On the other hand,' Chris said, 'it might not be a bomb at all. Just the dynamite in there. You know, to scare you, keep you in line. I mean, is there a reason anybody'd want to take you out?'

Booker said, 'You mean like just the shit, but no way to blow it?'

'Yeah.'

'Like they telling me look what could happen?'

'Maybe.'

'Say I could just get up, was all bullshit what they made her say to me? On the phone?'

'That's possible,' Chris said, 'but I don't think I'd take the chance. Let's see what my partner says, when he gets here.'

Booker said, 'Man, I got to go the toilet, bad.'

Chris watched Jerry Baker taking in the size of the house as he came up the walk, away from the uniforms and the blue Detroit Police radio cars blocking both sides of the boulevard. It was Jerry's day off. He wore a black poplin jacket and a Detroit Tigers baseball cap: a tall man, bigger and older than Chris, 25 years on the force, 15 as a bomb tech. He remembered what day this was and said to Chris, 'You shouldn't be here.'

Standing inside the doorway, Chris told him about the green leather chair Booker was sitting in.

And Jerry said it again, looking at his watch. 'No, you shouldn't be here. Forty minutes, you'll be through.'

He looked outside at the guy from Narcotics waiting on the porch, waved him over and told him to call for Fire and EMS and get everybody away from the house. The guy from Narcotics said, 'Can't you guys handle this one?'

Jerry said, 'You'll hear it if we can't.' Walking down the hall to the Jacuzzi room he said to Chris, 'If we save this asshole's life, you think he'll appreciate it?'

Chris said, 'You mean will he say thank you? Wait'll you meet him.'

They entered the room, Jerry gazing up at the green-and-white tenting, and Booker said, 'Finally, you motherfuckers decide you gonna do something?'

Chris and Jerry took time to look at each other. They didn't say anything. Jerry got down to inspect the sliced-open seat cushion between Booker's muscular legs and said, 'Hmmmmmmmmm.'

Booker said, 'Another one, goes hmmmmmmmmm. I'm sitting here on high explosives the motherfucker goes hmmmmmmmmmm.'

Jerry stood up, looking at Chris again. 'Well, he's cool. That's a good thing.'

Chris said, 'Yeah, he's cool.'

As Jerry walked around to the back of the green leather chair, Booker, sitting upright, raised his head.

'Hey, I got to go the toilet, man, bad.'

Jerry reached over the backrest to put his hand on Booker's shoulder. 'You better wait. I don't think you can make it.'

'I'll tell you what I have to make. I mean it.'

Jerry said, over Booker to Chris, 'The boy looks fast.'

'Used to run from the Narcs in his Pony joggers, one of those Pony Down delivery boys,' Chris said. 'Yeah, I imagine he's fast.'

Booker was still upright with his head raised. 'Wait now. What're we saying here if I'm fast? Bet to it, man, I'm fast.'

Chris said, 'We don't want you to get the idea you can dive out of your chair into your little swimming-pool and make it.'

Booker said, 'In the Jacuzzi? I get in there I be safe?'

'I doubt it,' Chris said. 'If what you're sitting on there, if it's wired and it's not one of your friends being funny . . .'

Jerry said, 'Or if it's not a dud.'

Booker said, 'Yeah, what?'

Chris said, 'If it's a practical joke—you know, or some kind of warning—then there's nothing to worry about. But if it's wired, you raise up and it goes . . .'

'I couldn't get in the Jacuzzi quick enough, huh?'

'I doubt it.'

'His feet might stay on the floor,' Jerry said, 'remain in the house.'

Chris agreed, nodding. 'Yeah, but his ass'd be sailing over Ohio.'

Jerry moved from behind the chair to the French doors. 'We better talk about it some more.'

Booker's head turned to follow Chris. 'Where you going? Hey, motherfucker, I'm talking to you!'

Chris stepped out and closed the door. He moved with Jerry to the far edge of the slate patio before looking back at the French doors in the afternoon sunlight. They could hear Booker in there, faintly. They crossed the yard, Jerry offering Chris a cigarette. He took one and Jerry gave him a light once they reached the driveway and were standing by the three-car garage, alone in the backyard. Jerry looked up at the elm trees. He said, 'Well, they're finally starting to bud. I thought winter was gonna run through May.'

Chris said, 'That's my favourite kind of house. Sort of an English Tudor, before Booker got hold of it.'

Jerry said, 'Why don't you and Phyllis buy one?'

'She likes apartments. Goes with her career image.'

'She must be jumping up and down, finally got her way.'

Chris didn't say anything.

'I'm talking about your leaving the squad.'

'I know what you meant. I haven't told her yet. I'm waiting till I get reassigned.'

'Maybe Homicide, huh?'

'I wouldn't mind it.'

'Yeah, but would Phyllis?'

Chris didn't answer. They smoked their cigarettes and could hear fire equipment arriving. Jerry said, 'Hey, I was kidding. Don't be so serious.'

'I know what you're saying,' Chris said. 'Phyllis is the kind of person that speaks out. Something bothers her, she tells you about it.'

'I know,' Jerry said.

'There's nothing wrong with that, is there?'

'I'm not saying anything against her.'

'What it is, Phyllis says things even some guys would like to but don't have the nerve.'

'Yeah, 'cause she's a woman,' Jerry said, 'she doesn't have to worry about getting hit in the mouth.'

Chris shook his head. 'I don't mean putting anybody down or being insulting. Like we're at a restaurant, one of those trendy places the waiter introduces himself? This twinkie comes up to the table, he goes, "Hi, I'm Wally, I'm gonna be your waitperson this evening. Can I get you a cocktail?" Phyllis goes, "Wally, when we've finished dinner, you gonna take us out and introduce us to the dishwasher?" She goes, "We really don't care what your name is as long as you're here when we want something."'

Jerry grinned, adjusting his Tiger baseball cap. 'That's good, I can appreciate that. Those guys kill me.'

They drew on their cigarettes. Chris looked at his, about to say something, working the butt between his thumb and second finger to flick it away, and the French doors and some of the windows on this side of the house exploded out in a billow of grey smoke tinged yellow. They stood looking at the shattered doorway, at the smoke and dust thinning, settling over the glass and wood fragments, shreds of blackened green-and-white debris on the patio, silence ringing in their ears now. After a few moments they started down the drive, let the people waiting in front know they were okay.

Chris said, 'Yeah, the twink comes up to the table, says he's gonna be our waitperson. But you have to understand, Phyllis wasn't trying to be funny, she was serious. That's the way she is.'

3

THE HOODS

Tales of the Criminal Fraternity

TRAVELLING LIGHT

W. R. Burnett

*The first and arguably still best-known gangster in hardboiled fiction
was Cesare Bandello, known as Rico, the tough little Chicago hood
whose profound influence on the crime genre and movies was apparent
for many years after he first appeared in 1929, in W. R. Burnett's novel*
Little Caesar. *The book itself was also the first important piece of fiction
about the power of the underworld, and has been described as one of
the most famous of all realistic crime novels. In Rico, the small-time
crook who ruthlessly gains control of the Chicago underworld by elimin-
ating all his rivals, writers everywhere were provided with the prototype
gangster, and his shade is much in evidence in later hardboiled fiction.
Although* Little Caesar *was an immediate best-seller, it was the film
made the following year, with Edward G. Robinson as Rico, that established both the star's name and the novel's legendary status. The story,
which provided a wholly convincing picture of gangster life, marked
another milestone in that it was told largely from the point of view of
the criminal. This was a device that many other writers would copy.*

The success of Little Caesar *had been hard-earned by William Riley
Burnett (1899–1982) who had written five novels, several plays and a
large number of short stories during the late Twenties, all of which he
had tried unsuccessfully to get published before moving from his home
town of Springfield, Ohio, to Chicago. It was here, in the era of Al
Capone, that he found the inspiration for his hardboiled gangster novel
and the genre which would make him famous. Following this success,
he wrote several more crime novels and short stories, most of which
were also filmed—*Scarface *(based on the life of Capone and made in
1932 with Paul Muni),* High Sierra *(starring Humphrey Bogart in 1941)
and* The Asphalt Jungle *(first filmed in 1950 with Sterling Hayden and
Marilyn Monroe and later adapted for a very popular TV series with
Jack Warden). For twenty years Burnett was also one of the highest-
paid scriptwriters in Hollywood, working on productions such as* This

Gun for Hire, *based on Graham Greene's story,* The Racket *(1951)* *and* Sergeants Three *(1962). He received several Oscar nominations* *for this work and was awarded the O. Henry Memorial prize in 1930* *for his short story 'Dressing Up'. In 1980 the Mystery Writers of* *America made him a Grand Master.*

'Travelling Light', his story reprinted here, was first published in *1935 and, because of its storyline of a young man who falls into the* *company of two bank robbers on the run from the law, may just have* *been a trial run for his famous novel* High Sierra, *written five years* *later, in which a former convict, also heading west, becomes involved* *in an abortive robbery and finds himself trapped by the police.*

* * *

Johnny ate slowly, relishing the good hot coffee and the combination sandwich. He had intended getting a plain ham sandwich, as he wanted to conserve his money, but the smell of cooking had been too much for him.

The counterman leaned on his elbow and stared past Johnny at the broad macadam highway in the glare of the Arizona winter sun. To the counterman Johnny was just another weary hitch-hiker. Hordes of them passed every day; some of them headed for California, some of them headed East. Only one thing about Johnny interested him: he was wearing an old football sweater, and the numeral 7 could still be made out on the faded fabric across his shoulders, though the number itself had been ripped off long ago. The counterman turned from the road to stare languidly at Johnny.

'Come a long way?'

'Only from Ohio,' Johnny grinned feebly.

The counterman whistled. 'Football sweater you're wearing, ain't it?'

'Yeah. Freshman team at Ohio State.'

'Make the varsity?'

'Yeah. I played my sophomore year. Halfback. But my old man ran out of dough.'

'Hitting for Southern Cal?'

'Yeah,' Johnny answered. 'Los Angeles.'

'Everybody is.'

There was a loud shriek of tyres and a big, expensive-looking sedan turned suddenly from the highway and stopped at the filling station with a jerk. Two men got out. One was big and broad-shouldered and redheaded; the other was small and frail-looking with a narrow face and black hair.

'Fill 'er up, Cap,' called the big man. 'We chow. Back in a minute.'

'Boy,' said the counterman, 'that car's been places. Look at the dust all over it.'

The men came in and sat down at the counter. Their well-cut clothes were covered with dust; their eyes were bloodshot and they both looked haggard and done in, the small one especially.

'Hey, pal,' said the big one, 'we want two club sandwiches and a couple o' coffees. And make it fast, will you?'

The counterman went to make the sandwiches. The little man stared at Johnny for a moment; then he leaned forward and whispered something to the redhead, who turned, stared briefly, then said:

'Hiya, kid. Hoofing?'

'Yeah.'

'How'd you like to drive a couple guys to El Portal?'

'That's right on my way.'

'Okay,' said the big man. 'Eats, if any, and transportation; maybe a little dough if you give us service. We're in a hurry.'

'I'll do my best.'

Red smiled.

'Buddy, you'll have to push that hack to hit the road like we want to hit it.'

'Yeah,' said the little man, 'my wife's sick over in El Portal. We got a telegram saying they thought maybe she might kick off, so I want to get there and get there quick.'

'I'm sorry,' said Johnny. 'I'm not afraid to open a car up.'

'Good,' said the big man. 'Let's get acquainted. Call me Red; that's practically the only name I got. My skinny friend here is George. What's your name?'

'Johnny.'

'Okay, Johnny. As soon as we chow we start.'

The counterman came with their sandwiches. They wolfed them down, then gulped down their coffee. The counterman watched them with raised eyebrows: never in his life had he seen anybody eat so fast. They got up. Red threw a dollar on the counter.

'Okay?' he asked.

'You got some change coming.'

'Keep it. Go out to a good restaurant and get your lunch.'

The two men walked so fast Johnny could hardly keep up with them.

Red paid for the gasoline, then he and George got into the back seat. Johnny jumped in and started the motor with a roar; this was a real hack; he hadn't driven one like it since his freshman year in college, when the real estate business was good and his dad was in the big money.

The counterman was standing in the door of the barbecue joint when Johnny drove past.

'Luck, eh?' he called.

'You tell it,' said Johnny.

In a few moments Johnny had left the little Arizona town and the barbecue joint far behind. In the rear-view mirror he could see Red and George, leaning back against the cushions, their hats over their eyes, their legs stretched out. Those two birds were certainly worn out, all right; they were already half asleep.

Once Red sat up suddenly and, leaning forward, looked at the dashboard.

'Atta stuff, buddy,' he said. 'George was right about you. He said you looked like you wasn't scared of no blowout. Don't worry. These tyres are good. Keep moving.'

Johnny nodded and Red lay back. They passed through some Mexican villages and Johnny slowed down. At several places they saw Indian hogans with fat squaws sitting in front of them. There were no towns in this desolate region: only a handful of Mexicans and Indians lost in this gigantic flat valley, hemmed in by gigantic lavender mountains.

For some reason traffic was very light on this national highway and when Johnny saw a car running slowly ahead of him he slackened his pace a little, then gradually slowed down almost to a stop. George didn't miss a beat in his snoring, but Red sat up at once.

'Keep moving,' he said harshly.

But Johnny pointed. A girl hitch-hiker in brown slacks and a green sweater was struggling with two men who were trying to pull her into their car. A third man was inching the car along, keeping up with them as the girl pushed her way forward, trying to get away.

'She's doing all right,' said Red. 'A little ride will do her good. Keep moving.'

'No,' said Johnny, jamming on the brakes. 'I won't keep moving.' He turned and looked straight into Red's chill grey eyes. He saw Red clench his fists; he saw the huge muscles rippling under his coat sleeve, but he wasn't intimidated. That girl needed help and she was going to get it.

'Okay,' said Red wearily, turning away. Then he grinned and said: 'It's your party, Johnny, old sock. Let's see you go to work.'

Johnny jumped out of the car and ran towards the struggling girl. The men let loose of her when they saw Johnny coming, and one of them drew back his fist.

'Stay out of this, partner, if you know what's good for you,' said one of them. 'This is my gal and she's trying to beat it.'

Johnny hesitated. The men looked tough. The girl didn't; quite the contrary. She reminded him of some of the girls he had gone to school with back in Ohio.

'What about it, sister?' he demanded.

'I never saw these men before.'

'It's a lie.'

'Okay,' said Johnny. 'You guys leave this girl alone. Beat it.'

'Sez you!' said the man in the car.

The two men, who had been struggling with the girl, jumped Johnny. One of them hit him behind the ear and turned him half around; the other kicked him hard three times. In a moment one of them hit him on the jaw and he went down. But he was boiling now and came up fighting. The third man jumped from the car and got into the fight. Johnny had never seen so many fists before in his life, but finally he landed a good solid blow and one of the men moved out of the fight, holding his stomach. Johnny went down again. Dazed, he sat looking up at the blazing blue sky. Much to his surprise, Red, with a broad grin on his freckled face, moved into his line of vision.

'You ain't doing so good, Johnny,' he said. Then he turned to the two men who were waiting for Johnny to get up: 'Now, now; you boys are getting too rough. Mustn't play rough.' Then he threw back his head and laughed.

The men looked at each other uneasily. This redheaded guy was big as an ox and looked plenty tough.

'You, baby,' said Red, turning to the girl, 'give us the lowdown quick. Family affair?'

'I never saw these men before.'

'Wouldn't like to go bye-bye with 'em?'

'Of course not.'

'No use, boys. Get in your kiddie car and shove off.'

'Sez you,' one of the men said feebly.

Suddenly Red reached out and, taking the men by their coat collars, jammed their faces together. They both staggered back, dazed.

'Sez me.'

The man who had been hit in the stomach was already sitting at the wheel; the other two climbed in beside him groggily. The car moved off.

Johnny was still a little dazed; he stood rubbing his jaw. The girl came over to him and put her hand on his arm.

'Thanks. I'm glad you came along.'

'Don't mention it.'

Red looked on, smiling sardonically; then he said:

'Sister, we're going as far as El Portal and we're going fast. Hop in, we ain't got all night.'

'Well, I . . .' She looked at Johnny for a long time, then she said: 'All right.'

When they got back to the car, Johnny held the door open for her.

'Wouldn't like to ride back here with old Red, would you?' Red demanded.

The girl said nothing. She didn't know just what to say. She climbed in with Johnny.

Johnny drove in silence for a long time. In a few minutes he picked up the car with the three men in it and went past them blowing the horn. The girl glanced at the speedometer. It read 76.

'Do you have to drive that fast?' she demanded.

'Yes,' said Johnny. 'The little one's wife is very sick. Afraid she'll die. She's in El Portal.'

'The little one?' She turned to look. 'That's a funny way to . . . aren't these men friends of yours?'

'No. I'm hitch-hiking to sunny Cal. I'm just the chauffeur. They drove all night and are worn out.'

She turned again and Red grinned at her.

'I didn't thank you,' she said. 'Thanks.'

'Just routine,' said Red. 'I always go round fighting over dames. Or else they're fighting over me. You know how it is. Like to come back here?'

'Nix,' said George. 'Let the kid alone.'

'Can't I have any fun?'

'You just had your fun. Beating up guys is your fun.' George groaned and lay back. 'I'm tired! Only clucks use their fists. You always was a cluck, Red.'

Red yawned and, lying back, put his hat over his eyes.

There was a long silence. The monotonous, burned country rushed past. Suddenly the girl leaned forward and began to cry.

'Excuse me,' she said, 'but I've had about all I can stand. I hitched from Texas. It's my first time. I never had any idea things would be so bad.'

Johnny patted her on the shoulder. She tried to stifle her sobs. Red leaned forward.

'Johnny,' he cried, 'let that girl alone. Where was you brung up? Look at the state you got her in.'

Johnny turned slightly.

'Listen ... I ...'

Red burst out laughing, delighted, then he leaned back and put his hat over his face.

'What a man!' said Johnny, shaking his head. To the girl, who was calmer now: 'Going far?'

'El Portal.'

'That's where we're going.'

'I know. I could hardly believe my ears.'

'Live there?'

'Yes. My boy friend lives there, too. He's a lawyer, trying to get a start.'

'It's tough now for anybody to get a start.'

'We were going to get married but we had a row. I wanted to go to work. He wasn't making enough for us to get married on. Oh, we had a beautiful row, and I ran away.'

Johnny turned to look at her.

'Yeah? You wanted to go to work and he wouldn't let you? I'd like to see that guy.'

'He wins. I give up,' said the girl, smiling slightly. 'But I'll never let him know what a time I've had.'

Turning, Johnny glanced out of the corner of his eye at the girl. She was mighty pretty with her wavy light brown hair, her blue eyes, and her clear-cut, refined face. He began to envy the lawyer.

They were nearing the California line now and were getting into a true desert region. Great drifts of sand rose on either side of them; they went for miles at a time without seeing any vegetation. It was early afternoon and the sun was beating down with almost summer intensity.

George was sleeping peacefully, but Red had had a good rest, he said, although he had seemed to sleep but little, and was sitting up with his legs crossed, smoking a cigarette and whistling.

From time to time the girl looked out across the mile after mile of dazzling wasteland, which stretched unbroken to the enormous lavender mountains to the north. Finally she shuddered:

'What an idiot I was to think I could hike through this place. It's awful.'

'Pretty bad,' said Johnny, nodding.

'It gives me the creeps. There ought to be a law.'

'Too many laws now,' said Red, leaning forward. 'You never know when you're going to break one. Eh, baby?'

'My name's Edna,' said the girl. 'I don't like to be called "baby".'

'Don't you, baby? That's tough, baby. I always call my babies baby.'

The girl turned and looked straight into Red's eyes.

'Why don't you be nice?'

Red lowered his head and made his shoulders shake.

'George,' he said, punching his companion, 'she's appealing to my better nature. Now that touches me ... Say, Johnny, what're we making?'

'Little over sixty.'

'Slow down till this copper goes past.'

Johnny saw a motorcycle cop coming towards them from the opposite direction. He slowed the car gradually. Glancing into the rear-view mirror, he saw that George was sitting up, alert now; Red's face was hard and menacing. The cop looked at them sharply as they passed him.

'He's turning,' said Red. 'Outrun him, Johnny.'

'They sting you here for speeding,' said Johnny.

'You're feeling so good, Red,' George sneered. 'Take the wheel.'

'No time,' said Red, leaning forward. 'Outrun him, kid. You heard me. Fifty bucks if you outrun him.'

'That's different.'

Johnny pushed the accelerator to the floorboard and the car shot away, roaring over the black macadam.

The girl touched his arm.

'Do you think? ...'

'Right now for fifty bucks I'd climb a tree in this hack.'

'Now you're talking,' said Red. 'Give her the gun, boy.'

Mile after mile the cop trailed them; there'd be a dip in the road and they'd lose him, but when they got on the flat again, there he'd be. The strain was beginning to tell on Johnny; little pains began to run up and down his back and his accelerator foot was numb and he could feel the heat of the engine through his shoe.

'Curve,' cried Red. 'He's gaining a little. We may lose him here.'

Just as Red spoke, the cop's motorcycle began to wobble; he had either blown a tyre or had hit a stone in the road; the motorcycle slewed round, then rolled end over end, throwing the cop in a long arc over into the mesquite.

'Yow!' yelled Red. 'A nose dive. Nice work, Johnny.'

'But, good heavens . . .' the girl began. Johnny nudged her with his elbow. He knew they were in a spot. Red and George were real bad ones; he was sure of it now.

'Keep her moving,' said Red. 'We shook that rat off but he might get up.'

Johnny glanced at the girl. He could see that she was very nervous. He laughed to cover up, and said the first thing that came into his head:

'That boy friend of yours expecting you?'

The girl started.

'No. It's a surprise. He thinks I'm still in Dallas.'

'Oh, just a little surprise. Well, we'll soon be in. I wish you luck.'

'Thanks. Going to stay in El Portal a while?'

'Maybe I'll stay the night. I've got to get on to Los Angeles.'

'Good luck to you, too.'

'Thanks.'

They were close to El Portal now. The girl saw the familiar ragged line of hills to the north and smiled. They had left the desert and the lavender mountains behind.

George said: 'All right, Red. You take the wheel—we're getting in close.'

Johnny slowed down as they passed through a little village on the outskirts. Red started over the seat and Johnny, still holding the wheel and keeping his foot on the accelerator, moved over out of his way. The girl made room for them.

Just as Red took the wheel, they heard the roar of motors. Turning, Johnny saw a couple of squad cars skidding into the main highway from a side road.

'It's a trap,' yelled George. 'Give her the gun, Red.'

The girl screamed. George was knocking the glass out of the back window with the butt of an automatic. Gasping, Johnny pushed the girl into a kneeling position on the floor.

'Stay there, honey,' he cried. 'We're in for it.'

They were getting into the suburbs. Cars swerved to the side of the road as the huge sedan bore down on them at eighty miles an hour.

Red had his jaw set and the accelerator to the floorboard; with a slight twist of the wheel he miraculously avoided car after car. Behind them the sirens were going full blast.

George pulled up the back seat and took out a sub-machine gun; then, kneeling, he poked it through the back window.

'Where does this next road go, baby?' yelled Red, reaching down and slapping the girl.

She looked up.

'I . . .'

'You're a great help. If we don't get off this main highway we'll be right in the centre of town.'

The girl looked over the car door.

'Turn right, next road,' she said. 'It's a straight shoot to San Diego.'

'Atta girl.'

Scarcely slacking speed, Red whipped the car around in a wide turn; the tyres shrieked wildly and the car careened and skidded, but righted itself. George was thrown violently to the floor.

'Call your shots, you lug!' he cried, getting up groggily.

Looking back, Johnny saw one of the squad cars go over as it tried to make the turn, saw a man thrown clear and into a field at the side of the road. But the second car came on. George began to fire out the back window with the machine gun.

'Guy shooting with a rifle,' said George calmly.

A bullet whined past them, then another. Suddenly they heard a loud metallic ping; then there was a terrific explosion.

'Good night,' said George. 'Church is out.'

The man with the long-range rifle had hit a rear tyre. The car turned half round, careened wildly, then jumped the road and rolled over into a field.

When Johnny came to they were carrying him into the county jail on a stretcher. Looking up, he saw Red, handcuffed, walking beside him. Red grinned.

'Nice party, eh?'

Johnny saw the stern faces of the deputy sheriffs. An old man with a tobacco-stained moustache was staring down at him.

'Okay, sonny?' he asked, smiling.

'I guess so. Where's the girl?'

'They just took her in. What she's doing with you, I don't know. She used to be a mighty nice girl. Knew her father.'

Johnny sat up.

'Listen here . . .'

'Never mind, son,' said the sheriff. 'It'll all come out later.'

Red and Johnny had been put into the first cell in the corridor and, pressing their faces against the bars, they could see what was going on in the sheriff's office at the front of the jail. George was in the cell next to them. Beyond George was the tank, where some drunks were shouting and laughing. The girl had been put into a cell at the far end of the L-shaped cell block and they could not see her.

The sheriff's office was jammed all afternoon: lawyers, deputies, city officials of all kinds, newspapermen and photographers milled about, and there was so much noise that George got up from time to time and yelled to them to be quiet, as he was trying to rest.

The cell block was not partitioned off from the sheriff's office but was a continuation with a low railing dividing it from the front hallway. All afternoon men crowded to the railing to stare in at the famous bank robbers: Red Hammond and George (Gloomy) Cooke.

Johnny sat on his bunk, staring at the floor.

'Red,' he said, 'why don't they let the girl and me go? You told them all about us.'

'Fat chance,' said Red. 'They're all scared. Two to one you both stand trial. 'Course I'll testify for you; I like to testify. So will George and he can make any prosecuting attorney look like a deuce. He's smart, that guy. You'll get off, don't worry. But you may stand trial.'

'I'm surprised the girl's boy friend hasn't turned up.'

'How'd you like it, if she was your girl, not knowing all the facts?'

Johnny said nothing.

Red turned from the bars and came over to the bunk.

'What's up?' asked Johnny.

'Nothing. I thought it was the chief of police again. It's just one of the process servers. Didn't you get a bang out of that chief of police? Boy, we got friends in this place. All the big shots want us to come and stay with them. The chief sure would've liked to get us in his new escape-proof jail. Boy, didn't the old whittler swell up, though? We was his prisoners. Hot-cha!'

'Pipe down, Red,' called George.

'Okay.' Red sat down and lit a cigarette.

'That sheriff's all right,' said Johnny. 'He doesn't treat you like you were dirt, like all the others.'

'No, he's friendly,' said Red with a laugh; then he added: 'God bless his dear old heart of gold.'

Johnny said nothing.

'I told you to pipe down. That mouth of yours will get you in trouble some day,' called George.

Red jumped up.

'Look here—' he said.

A matron was coming down the corridor with the girl. Johnny ran up to the front of the cell. He saw a tall, thin, light-haired young man standing at the railing, waiting for the girl.

'Her boy friend,' said Johnny.

'I lose,' said Red.

The girl turned and smiled wanly at Johnny. Then she went up to the young man. His face was stern. He began shouting at her. She started back, bewildered, then lowered her head. Johnny and Red strained their ears, trying to hear. From time to time they caught a phrase: '... You weren't satisfied to stay here ... all the way to Texas ... mixed up with gangsters ... what will everybody say? ... how do I know you were hitch-hiking ... getting in with three strange men ... I'd have sent you the money ... no, I can't help you now ... you asked for it, now you've got it ... disgracing all my people ...'

Red laughed and shouted:

'What a baboon you turned out to be! Say, that gal's on the square.'

'Some of your friends, I see,' said the young man, then he turned and went out.

The girl followed the matron back along the corridor.

'Stiff upper lip,' Johnny called after her.

'You got yourself a girl,' said Red. 'Right on the good old bounce. See? She's right in your lap.'

Johnny sat down on the bunk. He felt better now, much better. After a while, without realising it, he began to whistle.

After they had eaten and the turnkey had taken the tin plates away, the sheriff came down the corridor and stopped before the first cell.

'How you doing, boys?' he asked, smiling at them. He had his coat off, as it was a rather hot evening, and they saw that he had a big revolver in a shoulder holster in addition to the automatic on his hip.

'Two-gun man, eh, sheriff?' said Red, grinning.

'Used to be,' she sheriff replied. 'I can remember the days of the gun-fanners. Well, boys, sleep tight. Food okay? We aim to please.'

They saw him go into the front part of the jail, where his office was, and sit down at his desk. Near him a clerk was working at a typewriter, painfully typing a letter with one finger. A new turnkey came on duty and sat for a while on the sheriff's desk, talking to him, then disappeared.

George had been looking out the window of his cell ever since he had eaten.

'What's up?' Red demanded.

'Squad car cruising this district. Sort of making regular rounds. The chief of police's not taking any chances, I guess. Time is it?'

Red pressed his face against the bars and stared out into the front office.

'Ten after six.'

Johnny watched them. They seemed excited. He was almost certain they were up to something; what, he couldn't imagine. Of course Red had boasted that they had friends in El Portal, but Johnny thought that he might be joking. After all, 'friends', if any, don't storm jails. But why had they been in such a hurry to get to El Portal? Were they running away from something or towards it? Johnny watched, while Red walked back and forth slowly.

'How many left now?' George asked suddenly.

'Three,' said Red, 'but the clerk don't count and I can't see the turnkey.'

There was a long silence, then Red gave a jump and whispered:

'Okay, George.'

Pressing his face against the bars, Johnny saw three well-dressed men walk quickly into the jail. The sheriff, who had been reading a newspaper, jumped up. But the men were already holding guns on him. A dapper little man in a tight blue suit seemed to be the leader.

'Well, Buffalo Bill,' he said, 'stick up your paws. Reach for the ceiling.'

The sheriff stood with his mouth open, his hands shaking.

'Where are you, boys?' yelled one of the men.

'Right back here,' yelled Red. 'Get the turnkey.' In his excitement Red began to rattle the cell door. He had forgotten all about Johnny, who still had his face pressed to the bars.

'Where is he?'

'Look around for him. He can't be far.'

The man in the blue suit shouted at the sheriff: 'Where's the turnkey?'

'Don't know.'

'Remember quick.'

Johnny held his breath.

'I won't tell you.'

'Look for him, look for him,' cried Red.

The man in the blue suit hit the sheriff over the head with the barrel of his revolver, and when the sheriff didn't fall, he hit him again.

Johnny gritted his teeth.

Staggering, the sheriff went for his gun. A man in a brown suit jumped forward suddenly and hit the sheriff in the mouth with his fist. The sheriff fell back into his chair. In spite of his bravado, you could see that he was a very old man; his hat had fallen off and his sparse grey hair was standing up all over his head. The man in the brown suit disarmed him, then leaned forward and hit him again with his fist.

'Talk, you old goat!'

But the man in the blue suit shouted:

'There's the turnkey.'

Johnny heard the turnkey cry out.

Then he saw two of the men pulling him up the corridor. The clerk had fainted and had fallen forward across his desk, upsetting an inkwell. Johnny saw the ink dripping to the floor.

The turnkey, pale as death, goaded by the visitors, who were nervous now, fumblingly unlocked the door of Red's cell, then George's. Red leaped out into the corridor. The man in the blue suit handed Red an automatic, then turned and hit the turnkey over the head with the barrel of his revolver. The turnkey fell limp. George grabbed a Thompson gun from one of the men and they all started down the corridor. The man in the blue suit turned.

'What about this monkey?' he demanded, jerking his thumb at Johnny.

'Don't pay no attention to him,' cried Red, 'he's a softie. Let's get going.'

Johnny stood at the door of the cell, not knowing what to do. He was trembling with excitement and rage. Those dirty, lowdown brutes, treating a nice old guy like that; it was just ignorance and viciousness; absolutely unnecessary; they could have managed the jailbreak much better with a little less violence.

The man in the brown suit amused himself by slapping the sheriff's face several times very hard. Johnny saw the old man recoil; his nose began to bleed. Johnny lost his head. Rushing down the corridor, he tackled George from behind, and when they fell, he grabbed George's machine gun and got to his knees. George was knocked out by the fall onto the cement floor and lay groaning.

'Beat it,' yelled the man in the blue suit. 'Ain't that a siren I hear?'

Red glanced at George, then he fired twice at Johnny, two snap shots that went wide. The machine gun cut loose in Johnny's hands. Scared half to death, and amazed by the violent recoil of the gun, Johnny tried to stop it; he was firing high, spattering lead all over the walls and ceiling of the jail. The men ran out, shouting. Red turned and fired again, missing; then he ran out. The gun slipped from Johnny's grasp, kicked him in the stomach, knocking him over; then it subsided.

He heard the screaming of sirens and the roar of a powerful motor on the getaway, then he got groggily to his feet and walked over to the sheriff.

'Are you all right?' he cried.

'Well,' said the sheriff, trying to smile, 'I wouldn't go as far as to say that, but I'm still here.'

The judge leaned forward and looked at Johnny and the girl, who were a little nervous and kept glancing at each other. The judge was a young man with the face of a humorist.

'Case dismissed,' he said, then he shook his finger at them. 'Now I could say, let this be a lesson to you. But I know it won't. Nothing is ever a lesson to anybody, and if that sounds like philosophy, make the most of it. It was a mighty nice thing you did, standing up for old Jim Hughes, but why couldn't you have used a revolver! It's going to cost us five hundred dollars to fix up that jail and we may take it out of your share of the reward.'

A bailiff turned to the sheriff and winked, then they both burst out laughing.

'Order in the court,' said the judge. 'Another thing, if Jim Hughes was a Democrat I'd like him better, but I guess he just got started wrong. As I said before, case dismissed.'

'Thanks, your Honour,' said Johnny, grinning.

The sheriff got between Johnny and the girl and put his arms around them.

'Don't suppose you want to go over and see your friends in the new city jail, eh?' He laughed, then he groaned and rubbed his jaw. 'That one fellow surely had a hard hand. Must have done some honest work before he started using a gun. You kids come and have lunch with me and the missus. She wants to meet you. How about it?'

'Well,' said Johnny, 'I've got to see a fellow first.'

'What fellow?' asked the girl.

'Why,' said Johnny, 'that boy friend of yours. I feel like I'm responsible for getting you in this jam, so I thought I would—'

'Going to ask him to take me back?'

'Well, I thought . . .'

The sheriff stood looking at them, smiling slightly.

'What an idiot you are!' said the girl, then she turned to the sheriff. 'Yes, we'll come for lunch.'

PASTORALE

James M. Cain

*One writer to develop W. R. Burnett's concept of telling stories from
the criminal's viewpoint was James M. Cain, another genuine original
in the field of hardboiled fiction, whose first novel,* The Postman Always
Rings Twice, *published in 1934, also guaranteed his enduring fame.
The story of a young drifter who lusts after the wife of an ageing café
proprietor, as a result of which both plan the old man's murder, was
another instant best-seller and soon afterwards filmed. Where Cain
differed from his predecessors—and especially from Dashiell Hammett
and Raymond Chandler with whom reviewers persisted in comparing
him—was in making most, if not all, of his characters genuinely
unpleasant people and revealing through their emotions and actions
how they could ultimately commit murder. As Chris Steinbrunner and
Otto Penzler have explained in* Encyclopedia of Mystery and Detection
*(1976), 'Whereas Hammett and Chandler wrote about good-bad, soft-
tough detectives who tried to unravel the mess that someone else caused
by a violent or greedy act, Cain created two-dimensional characters
interested in themselves and motivated by their lust for money or sex
or some form of snobbery. They are flawed characters because they
are too thoroughly evil and Cain shows them no mercy.' The author's
biographer, David Maddern, has gone even further and called Cain
'the twenty-minute egg of the hardboiled school'.*

*James Mallahan Cain (1892–1977) seemed destined for any career
rather than that of a 'poet of tabloid murder', as the critic Edmund
Wilson later described him. His own youthful ambition was to be an
opera singer, but instead his parents encouraged him to be a teacher
and he taught mathematics and English for several years before opting
for journalism. He became an outspoken columnist on the* Baltimore
Sun *and then the* New York World, *but various editorial restrictions
so infuriated him that he turned instead to fiction. The success of* The
Postman Always Rings Twice *(which was filmed in 1946 with John*

Garfield and Lana Turner) gave him freedom of expression and the opportunity to influence significantly the development of the hardboiled genre. He was himself as tough as the people he wrote about, as H. R. F. Keating has commented: 'Cain was a bigger than life man, as hot-headed and tough-minded as any of his characters. He was a fighter for what he believed to be right and a man to have on your side in a fight.' Like W. R. Burnett, Cain was recruited by Hollywood to write scripts and also saw two of his subsequent novels, Double Indemnity *(1943) and* Mildred Pierce *(1945), turned into box office hits. Until only a couple of years before his death he continued writing his own brand of hardboiled fiction with its unique slant on human nature. 'Pastorale', despite its deceptive title, should not fool the reader, for it is a tale of sex and murder in typical Cain style which he wrote in 1945. It is fascinating, too, because of its undoubted similarities to that ground-breaking novel,* The Postman Always Rings Twice, *which he had written over a decade earlier.*

* * *

Well, it looks like Burbie was going to get hung. And if he does, what he can lay it on is, he always figured he was so dam smart.

You see, Burbie, he left town when he was about sixteen year old. He run away with one of them travelling shows, 'East Lynne' I think it was, and he stayed away about ten year. And when he come back he thought he knowed a lot. Burbie, he's got them watery blue eyes what kind of stick out from his face, and how he killed the time was to sit around and listen to the boys talk down at the poolroom or over at the barbershop or a couple other places where he hung out, and then wink at you like they was all making a fool of theirself or something and nobody didn't know it but him.

But when you come right down to what Burbie had in his head, why it wasn't much. 'Course, he generally always had a job, painting around or maybe helping out on a new house, like of that, but what he liked to do was to play baseball with the high-school team. And they had a big fight over it, 'cause Burbie was so old nobody wouldn't believe he went to the school, and them other teams was all the time putting up a squawk. So then he couldn't play no more. And another thing he liked to do was sing at the entertainments. I reckon he liked that most of all. 'Cause he claimed that a whole lot of the time while he was away he was on the stage, and I reckon maybe he was at that, 'cause he was pretty good, specially when he dressed hisself up like a old-time Rube and come out and spoke a piece what he knowed.

Well, when he come back to town he seen Lida and it was a natural. 'Cause Lida, she was just about the same kind of a thing for a woman as Burbie was for a man. She used to work in the store, selling dry goods to the women, and kind of making hats on the side. 'Cepting only she didn't stay on the dry goods side no more'n she had to. She was generally over where the boys was drinking Coca Cola, and all the time carrying on about did they like it with ammonia or lemon, and could she have a swallow outen their glass. And what she had her mind on was the clothes she had on, and was she dated up for Sunday night. Them clothes was pretty snappy, and she made them herself. And I heard some of them say she wasn't hard to date up, and after you done kept your date why maybe you wasn't going to be disappointed. And why Lida married the old man I don't know, lessen she got tired working at the store and tooken a look at the big farm where he lived at, about two mile from town.

By the time Burbie got back she'd been married about a year and she was about due. So her and him commence meeting each other, out in the orchard back of the old man's house. The old man would go to bed right after supper and then she'd sneak out and meet Burbie. And nobody wasn't supposed to know nothing about it. Only everybody did, 'cause Burbie, after he'd get back to town about eleven o'clock at night, he'd kind of slide into the poolroom and set down easy like. And then somebody'd say, 'Yay, Burbie, where you been?' And Burbie, he'd kind of look around, and then he'd pick out somebody and wink at him, and that was how Burbie give it some good advertising.

So the way Burbie tells it, and he tells it plenty since he done got religion down to the jailhouse, it wasn't long before him and Lida thought it would be a good idea to kill the old man. They figured he didn't have long to live nohow, so he might as well go now as wait a couple of years. And another thing, the old man had kind of got hep that something was going on, and they figured if he throwed Lida out it wouldn't be no easy job to get his money even if he died regular. And another thing, by that time the Klux was kind of talking around, so Burbie figured it would be better if him and Lida was to get married, else maybe he'd have to leave town again.

So that was how come he got Hutch in it. You see, he was afeared to kill the old man hisself and he wanted some help. And then he figured it would be pretty good if Lida wasn't nowheres around and it would look like robbery. If it would of been me, I would of left Hutch out of it. 'Cause Hutch, he was mean. He'd been away for a while too, but him going away, that wasn't the same as Burbie going away. Hutch was sent. He was sent for ripping a mail-sack while he was driving the mail-wagon up from the station, and before he come back he done two year down to Atlanta.

But what I mean, he wasn't only crooked, he was mean. He had a ugly look to him, like when he'd order hisself a couple of fried eggs over to the restaurant, and then set and eat them with his head humped down low and his arm curled around his plate like he thought somebody was going to steal it off him, and handle his knife with his thumb down near the tip. Nobody didn't have much to say to Hutch, and I reckon that's why he ain't heared nothing about Burbie and Lida, and et it all up what Burbie told him about the old man having a pot of money hid in the fireplace in the back room.

So one night early in March, Burbie and Hutch went out and done the job. Burbie, he'd already got Lida out of the way. She'd let on she had to go to the city to buy some things, and she went away on No. 6, so everybody knowed she was gone. Hutch, he seen her go, and come running to Burbie saying now was a good time, which was just what Burbie wanted. 'Cause her and Burbie had already put the money in the pot, so Hutch wouldn't think it was no put-up job. Well, anyway they put twenty-three dollars in the pot, all changed into pennies and nickels and dimes so it would look like a big pile, and that was all the money Burbie had. It was kind of like you might say the savings of a lifetime.

And then Burbie and Hutch got in the horse and wagon what Hutch had, 'cause Hutch was in the hauling business again, and they went out to the old man's place. Only they went around the back way, and tied the horse back of the house so nobody couldn't see it from the road, and knocked on the back door and made out like they was just coming through the place on their way back to town and had stopped by to get warmed up, 'cause it was cold as hell. So the old man let them in and give them a drink of some hard cider what he had, and they got canned up a little more. They was already pretty canned, 'cause they both of them had a pint of corn on their hip for to give them some nerve.

And then Hutch he got back of the old man and crowned him with a wrench what he had hid in his coat.

*

Well, next off Hutch gets sore as hell at Burbie, 'cause there ain't no more'n twenty-three dollars in the pot. He didn't say nothing. He just set there, first looking at the money, what he had piled up on the table, and then looking at Burbie.

And then Burbie commences soft-soaping him. He says hope my die he thought there was a thousand dollars anyways in the pot, on account the old man being rich like he was. And he says hope my die it sure was a big surprise to him how little there was there. And he says hope my die it sure does make him feel bad, on account he's the one had the idea first. And he says hope my die it's all his fault and he's going to let Hutch keep all the money, dam if he ain't. He ain't going to take none of it for hisself at all, on account of how bad he feels. And Hutch, he don't say nothing at all, only look at Burbie and look at the money.

And right in the middle of while Burbie was talking, they heared a whole lot of hollering out in front of the house and somebody blowing a automobile horn. And Hutch jumps up and scoops the money and the wrench off the table in his pockets, and hides the pot back in the fireplace. And then he grabs the old man and him and Burbie carries him out the back door, hists him in the wagon, and drives off. And how they was able to drive off without them people seeing them was because they come in the back way and that was the way they went. And them people in the automobile, they was a bunch of old folks from the Methodist Church what knowed Lida was away and didn't think so much of Lida nohow and come out to say hello. And when they come in and didn't see nothing, they figured maybe the old man had went in to town and so they went back.

Well, Hutch and Burbie was in a hell of a fix all right. 'Cause there they was, driving along somewheres with the old man in the wagon and they didn't have no more idea than a bald-headed coot where they was going or what they was going to do with him. So Burbie, he commence to whimper. But Hutch kept a-setting there, driving the horse, and he don't say nothing.

So pretty soon they come to a place where they was building a piece of county road, and it was all tore up and a whole lot of tool-boxes laying out on the side. So Hutch gets out and twists the lock off one of them with the wrench, and takes out a pick and a shovel and throws them in the wagon. And then he got in again and drove on for a while till he come to the Whooping Nannie woods, what some of them says has got a ghost in it on dark nights, and it's about three mile from the old man's farm. And Hutch turns in there and pretty soon he come to a kind of a clear place and he stopped. And then, first thing he's said to Burbie, he says,

'Dig that grave!'

So Burbie dug the grave. He dug for two hours, until he got so dam tired he couldn't hardly stand up. But he ain't hardly made no hole at all. 'Cause the ground is froze and even with the pick he couldn't hardly make a dent in it scarcely. But anyhow Hutch stopped him and they throwed the old man in and covered him up. But after they got him covered up his head was sticking out. So Hutch beat the head down good as he could and piled the dirt up around it and they got in and drove off.

After they'd went a little ways, Hutch commence to cuss Burbie. Then he said Burbie'd been lying to him. But Burbie, he swears he ain't been lying. And then Hutch says he *was* lying and with that he hit Burbie. And after he knocked Burbie down in the bottom of the wagon he kicked him and then pretty soon Burbie up and told him about Lida. And when Burbie got done telling him about Lida, Hutch turned the horse around. Burbie asked then what they was going back for and Hutch says they're going back for to git a present for Lida. So they come back to the grave and Hutch made Burbie cut off the old man's head with the shovel. It made Burbie pretty sick, but Hutch made him stick at it, and after a while Burbie had it off. So Hutch throwed it in the wagon and they get in and start back to town once more.

Well, they wasn't no more'n out of the woods before Hutch takes hisself a slug of corn and commence to holler. He kind of raved to hisself, all about how he was going to make Burbie put the head in a box and tie it up with a string and take it out to Lida for a present, so she'd get a nice surprise when she opened it. Soon as Lida comes back he says Burbie has got to do it, and then he's going to kill Burbie. 'I'll kill you!' he says. 'I'll kill you, dam you! I'll kill you!' And he says it kind of sing-songy, over and over again.

And then he takes hisself another slug of corn and stands up and whoops. Then he beat on the horse with the whip and the horse commence to run. What I mean, he commence to gallup. And then Hutch hit him some more. And then he commence to screech as loud as he could. 'Ride him, cowboy!' he hollers. 'Going East! Here come old broadcuff down the road! Whe-e-e-e-e!' And sure enough, here they come down the road, the horse a-running hell to split, and Hutch a-hollering, and Burbie a-shivering, and the head a-rolling around in the bottom of the wagon, and bouncing up in the air when they hit a bump, and Burbie dam near dying every time it hit his feet.

After a while the horse got tired so it wouldn't run no more and they had to let him walk, and Hutch set down and commence to grunt. So Burbie, he tries to figure out what the hell he's going to do with the head. And pretty soon he remembers a creek what they got to cross, what they ain't crossed on the way out 'cause they come the back way. So he figures he'll throw the head overboard when Hutch ain't looking. So he done it. They come to the creek, and on the way down to the bridge there's a little hill, and when the wagon tilted going down the hill the head rolled up between Burbie's feet, and he held it there, and when they got in the middle of the bridge he reached down and heaved it overboard.

Next off, Hutch give a yell and drop down in the bottom of the wagon. 'Cause what it sounded like was a pistol shot. You see, Burbie done forgot that it was a cold night and the creek done froze over. Not much, just a thin skim about a inch thick, but enough that when that head hit it it cracked pretty loud in different directions. And that was what scared Hutch. So when he got up and seen that head setting out there on the ice in the moonlight, and got it straight what Burbie done, he let on he was going to kill Burbie right there. And he reached for the pick. And Burbie jumped out and run, and he didn't never stop till he got home to the place where he lived at, and locked the door, and climbed in bed and pulled the covers over his head.

Well, the next morning a fellow come running into town and says there's hell to pay down at the bridge. So we all went down there and first thing we seen was that head laying out there on the ice, kind of rolled over on one ear. And next thing we seen was Hutch's horse and wagon tied to the bridge rail, and the horse dam near froze to death. And the next thing we seen was the hole in the ice where Hutch fell through. And the next thing we seen, down on the bottom next to one of them bridge pilings, was Hutch.

So the first thing we went to work and done was to get the head. And believe me, a head laying out on thin ice is a pretty dam hard thing to get, and what we had to do was to lasso it. And the next thing we done was to get Hutch. And after we fished him out he had the wrench and the twenty-three dollars in his pockets and the pint of corn on his hip and he was stiff as a board. And near as I can figure out, what happened to him was that after Burbie run away he climbed down on the bridge piling and tried to reach the head and fell in.

But we didn't know nothing about it then and after we done got the head and the old man was gone and a couple of boys that afternoon found the body and not no head on it, and the pot was found, and them old people from the Methodist Church done told their story and one thing another, we figured out that Hutch done it, specially on account he must of been drunk and he done time in the pen and all like of that, and nobody ain't thought nothing about Burbie. They had the funeral and Lida cried like hell and everybody tried to figure out what Hutch wanted with the head and things went along thataway for three weeks.

Then one night down to the poolroom they was having it some more about the head, and one says one thing and one says another, and Benny Heath, what's a kind of a constable around town, he started a long bum argument about how Hutch must of figured if they couldn't find the head to the body they couldn't prove no murder. So right in the middle of it Burbie kind of looked around like he always done and then he winked. And Benny Heath, he kept on a-talking, and after he got done Burbie kind of leaned over and commence to talk to him. And in a couple of minutes you couldn't of heard a man catch his breath in that place, accounten they was all listening at Burbie.

I already told you Burbie was pretty good when it come to giving a spiel at a entertainment. Well, this here was a kind of a spiel too. Burbie act like he had it all learned by heart. His voice trimmled and ever couple of minutes he'd kind of cry and wipe his eyes and make out like he can't say no more, and then he'd go on.

And the big idea was what a whole lot of hell he done raised in his life. Burbie said it was drink and women what done ruined him. He told about all the women what he knowed, and all the saloons he's been in, and some of it was a lie 'cause if all the saloons was as swell as he said they was they'd of throwed him out. And then he told about how sorry he was about the life he done led, and how hope my die he come home to his old home town just to cut out the devilment and settle down. And he told about Lida, and how she wouldn't let him cut it out. And then he told how she done led him on till he got the idea to kill the old man. And then he told about how him and Hutch done it, and all about the money and the head and all the rest of it.

And what it sounded like was a piece what he knowed called 'The Face on the Floor', what was about a bum what drawed a picture on the bar room floor of the woman what done ruined him. Only the funny part was that Burbie wasn't ashamed of hisself like he made out he was. You could see he was proud of hisself. He was proud of all them women and all the liquor he'd drunk and he was proud about Lida and he was proud about the old man and the head and being slick enough not to fall in the creek with Hutch. And after he got done he give a yelp and flopped down on the floor and I reckon maybe he thought he was going to die on the spot like the bum what drawed the face on the bar room floor, only he didn't. He kind of lain there a couple of minutes till Benny got him up and put him in the car and tooken him off to jail.

So that's where he's at now, and he's went to work and got religion down there, and all the people what comes to see him, why he sings hymns to them and then he speaks them his piece. And I hear tell he knows it pretty good by now and has got the crying down pat. And Lida, they got her down there too, only she won't say nothing 'cepting she done it same as Hutch and Burbie. So Burbie, he's going to get hung, sure as hell. And if he hadn't felt so smart, he would of been a free man yet.

Only I reckon he done been holding it all so long he just had to spill it.

THE DEADLY CIRCLE
Samuel Fuller

*The name Samuel Fuller is not one readily associated with hardboiled
fiction, but rather with a controversial film-maker whose violent and
brutal films have made him a cult hero, especially in France where he
is now considered one of the most influential postwar directors. Yet
Fuller, who has written many of the screenplays for his pictures, began
his career writing short stories for the pulp magazines and published
several hardboiled novels, including the gruesome* Burn, Baby, Burn
*(1935). Though long out of print and difficult to trace, all these works
demonstrate his abiding fascination with people who are corrupt and
amoral—themes which also run through many of his pictures. As
Ephraim Katz has written in his* International Film Encyclopedia *(1980),
'Fuller's output, mostly action pictures of the B category, reflects in its
directness and brutal violence his experiences as a crime reporter,
a tramp and a soldier . . . while his crude political views, basically
conservative and chauvinistic, have alienated critics of both the extreme
Left and the extreme Right.' This said, few would disagree that Sam
Fuller has been a vital force in the American cinema, and critic Andrew
Sarris has called him 'an authentic American primitive', citing the
exciting visual style of his movies such as* Pickup on South Street *(1953),*
Underworld USA *(1961),* The Naked Kiss *(1965) and* The Klansman
(1974).

*Born in Worcester, Massachusetts, in 1911, Fuller began working at
the age of 12 as a copyboy on the* New York Journal *and at 17 was a
crime reporter for the* San Diego Sun. *During the Depression years he
was a hobo, wandering about the countryside, riding on freight trains
from place to place. He then began to use his natural talent as a
storyteller to contribute to the pulp magazines. His first tales appeared
in* Underworld, *a gaudy, all-action monthly which was published in
Springfield, Massachusetts, not far from his own home town, and whose
editor clearly shared Fuller's fascination with American low-life. Sup-*

ported by the income from these stories, he began to churn out pulp novels, then in 1936 decided to try his hand at film scripts and two years later collaborated on the notorious Gangs of New York *with James Cruze. During the years of the Second World War he was an exemplary soldier in the US Army, fighting in Europe and North Africa where he won several awards for bravery, including a Purple Heart. On his return to Hollywood he began the film career which has since made him so admired in many quarters and so reviled in others.*

Even in the days when he was writing pulp fiction, Fuller made full use of his first-hand experiences as a crime reporter and rolling stone— as his hardboiled story 'The Deadly Circle', written for Underworld *in May 1934, clearly shows. And in Mike Halpeny, the cruel and ruthless protagonist of the story, is the same kind of figure who would return time and again under different names in Sam Fuller's extraordinary movies . . .*

*   *   *

Mike Halpeny made an incongruous picture as he scurried down the grass-grown road which crossed the Canadian boundary from New York. The road he was on had been made by loggers and trappers nearly a century ago. It had then lapsed into a deer trail until American prohibition opened it again as an excellent route for smugglers. It meandered through a rugged, almost primeval forest from the Adirondacks far into Canada. Mike Halpeny, a New York gunman, was hurrying along this road, a half hour before sunset, dressed as he probably would have dressed for a stroll along Fifth Avenue, except that now he carried in his right hand a Winchester rifle of the latest model. This rifle was loaded and unlocked.

Mike had parked his car a quarter of a mile back.

Mike wanted to kill Jake Connti with one single shot. He knew old Jake fairly well.

He walked another quarter of a mile before coming to the selected spot. It was a place where the road dipped abruptly into a narrow valley at the bottom of which was a gorge, a mere crack in the earth. The second-growth birch and spruce, which crowded the old road elsewhere, here swayed back on both sides leaving a small open space which was covered with stunted shrubs and glacial rocks.

'A cinch,' he grinned. 'This is sure old Jake's spot.'

*

Old Jake Connti, whom Mike was stalking, had a strange racket. He was a bootlegger who smuggled American alcohol into Canada, selling it there at a modest two hundred per cent profit. He wasn't a gunman, not even a gangster. In fact he was rather a respectable, married man. His wife, Dolly, was much younger than he, and it was because of Dolly and a matter of several thousand dollars that Old Jake was now driving towards his death. Mike Halpeny had been a driver for Jake until a month before, when Jake had learned that the younger man had been stepping out with Dolly. Jake had led Mike into his warehouse and there had given him a most deliberate and exhaustive beating.

Mike Halpeny looked strange kneeling there behind the tree roots. His suit was light blue, his socks and tie a still lighter blue, and his shirt was white with fine blue stripes. He wore low shoes of black and white leather. He crouched in silence, but his appearance seemed to make a clamour amid the dignified stillness of the forest.

In a few minutes this stillness was rudely shattered by the noise of a motor.

The big truck came into sight on the opposite crest. It lumbered down the short slope, then almost stopped as Jake changed gears at the log bridge. Jake was bending over the wheel staring down at the rough bridge. He had a half of a black cigar in his mouth, and was talking to himself in a grumbling sort of way common to lonely men. He had almost crossed the bridge and had changed gears when suddenly a small black hole appeared as if by magic right in the middle of his forehead.

The truck acted as if it had been struck a vital blow. It lurched and went careening off the road. As it whirled to its side Jake's body went hurtling through the air, landed on the edge of the gorge and fell to the bottom.

Mike was cursing. Twenty feet below him he could see the dead body of Jake sprawled comfortably against the far side of the narrow gully. Jake had fallen so that he was leaning against the wall; his left arm had caught on a snag of rock, and this held his hand in an odd beckoning gesture which was lost upon the unimaginative Mike.

Mike had to run up the little valley nearly a hundred yards before he could get down to where Jake was, but once there the rest was easy. The roll of bills was in a chamois bag under Jake's left arm. He rifled through these rapidly, grinned with satisfaction, then turned and ran up the gully.

Now came the bright part of Mike's plan. It really was Dolly's idea. 'Put the gun where it will never be found,' she had said. So when Mike crawled out of the gully he went straight into the woods. He roamed around more or less aimlessly looking for a spot that would be easy to dig into. A little more than a hundred yards from the edge of the woods he found a tiny open space carpeted with soft, rotted leaves. Using his hands and the rifle he dug down a foot or more and carefully buried the weapon.

Then, flashing his light among the spectral trunks of the birches, he started to trot away. He wove back and forth among the trees, following the spot of light. In a little while he began to run. In less than five minutes he knew that he should have come to the road long ago. Well, the remedy was easy. He turned and ran the other way. It seemed to him that he ran that way for an hour. No road. He was becoming panicky.

Mike Halpeny was a very smart young man, but he did not know that a human being cannot walk in a straight line unless he has something to guide him or unless he is walking on a marked path, such as a city pavement. A man who doesn't know enough to walk towards two selected objects, keeping them in line, will walk in a circle or change his direction at every feature of the ground.

So Mike simply wandered. Once in the middle of the night he had sense enough to sit down and try to reason himself out of his position, but the more he thought the more frightened he became. He got up and started circling a tree, and counting. At ten he halted and started to run madly in the direction he was facing. He ran until he was exhausted. At this time, though he didn't know it, he was not twenty feet from the road and less than fifty from his car, but when he started again he went off at an angle to the right. After that he roamed at diverging angles and in steadily decreasing circles until dawn.

Just at sunrise he came out of the woods into a little open space. He didn't recognise the place, but just to be out of the woods was such a relief that he gave a hoarse cry and ran down the rough slope. Suddenly the ground seemed to open under him. He dove out headfirst into a rocky gorge.

Hours later Mike Halpeny awoke with the hot sun beating down on his bare head. He was lying among small, blood-covered rocks. He tried to say, 'Where am I?' but his lips wouldn't move. He tried to move his legs, but though he could see them, it was as if they weren't there at all. He couldn't even move a foot. He found that he could move his head slowly. To the left stretched the bottom of a dry gulch, covered with rocks. He saw a white butterfly floating about idly. He moved his head slowly to the right.

Within a few feet of him sat Jake Connti, his left arm still hanging to the snag and having that queer beckoning gesture.

Mike Halpeny had travelled the inevitable circle of the lost.

GET A LOAD OF THIS

James Hadley Chase

Sex, violence and gangsters were also the basic ingredients of the stories written by James Hadley Chase who, from 1939 until the early Eighties, was known as 'the unchallenged British champion of the American hardboiled school'. The title of Chase's début novel, No Orchids for Miss Blandish, *is today familiar to millions of people who may never even have heard his name—a fact which owes much to the notoriety the book earned on its publication just as the Second World War was breaking out. Several critics were so outraged by the story about a millionaire's daughter kidnapped by a brutal mob of gangsters who then torture and rape her, that they demanded it should be banned from sale. Even the outspoken George Orwell—who a few years later would write the controversial novel of the future,* 1984—*published an essay, 'Raffles and Miss Blandish', in which he called the work 'sordid and brutal', adding: 'The book contains eight full-dress murders, an unassessable number of casual killings and woundings, an exhumation (with a careful reminder of the stench), the flogging of Miss Blandish, the torture of another woman with red-hot cigarette ends, a strip-tease act, a third-degree scene of unheard of cruelty and much else of the same kind.'*

With such publicity, and the terrors inspired by the German bombing of Britain during the Blitz which made people eager for any form of escapism, it is perhaps not surprising that the book sold over a million copies in the next few months and had reached a grand (though by no means final) total of over five million by the end of the next decade. The trials of Miss Blandish became, in the words of another article, 'one of the best selling mysteries ever published' and assured its author's fame.

For all the seeming authenticity of this hardboiled novel and the 80 or so which followed it, the fact remains that James Hadley Chase, whose real name was René Lodge Brabazon Raymond (1906–1985), had never visited America or even come into contact with a genuine gangster when he began writing. Born in Ealing, West London, the son of an army officer, he was briefly a door-to-door encyclopaedia sales-man before becoming the distribution manager of a book wholesaler. It was here that he realised the demand among British readers for the thrillers of Hammett and Chandler, and after reading James M. Cain's The Postman Always Rings Twice *decided to write a hardboiled novel himself. A newspaper report he came across about the infamous Ameri-can Ma Baker and her killer sons is believed to have provided the inspiration, and after six weekends of intensive work, aided by an atlas of the United States, several guide books and a dictionary of American slang, he had completed* No Orchids for Miss Blandish *(a title that is said to have come to him while he was in the bath!). The success of this book led in 1942 to an adaptation for the London stage, and it was later filmed twice, in 1946 and 1971.*

Only two books appeared in the next four years, as Chase was conscripted into the RAF where he served with distinction, becoming a Squadron Leader. After the war he resumed a regular flow of similar titles, all of which enjoyed massive sales and enabled him to go and live in Switzerland. Back in England, a whole school of paperback writers cashed in on his success with gangster stories of their own, including Hank Janson (who was actually prosecuted for obscenity), Ben Sarto, Darcy Glinto, and the pseudonymous 'Griff'. All were very popular with post-war readers until the market collapsed in the Sixties, but none could match the success of Chase, which continued unabated in both hardcover and paperback.

James Hadley Chase created many memorable villains, including Eddie Schultz, the gangster in Miss Blandish; *Herman Radnitz, the evil tycoon with his hired killer, Lu Silk, in* This is For Real *(1965); and Rabener, the drug-dealer, in 'Get a Load of This' (1942) which is one of Chase's very few short stories. Like* Miss Blandish, *it also formed the basis of a London stage play which ran successfully at the London Hippodrome through the worst of the bombing.*

*   *   *

It sometimes happens that you meet a dame who's such a hot number that you want a second look. Maybe you're driving a car at the time of seeing her. Most likely you'll run up on the kerb or have a collision. Then, again, you may be walking along the street, and, turning your head as she passes, you bang into someone who starts bawling you out. Well, Fanquist was one of those take-a-second-look dames. You know what I mean, don't you? An all-metal blonde with a build-up that does things to you, and a figure that weakens your resistance.

I saw her for the first time when she was working for a guy called Rabener. This guy ran a smart restaurant-floor show on Broadway. I'd known Rabener off and on for several months. He was smart; maybe he was too smart. Anyway, I didn't like him. He was a cold, hard-faced guy, and I guess he had a mean streak somewhere. It always knocked me how the hell he ever made a success of his restaurant; but he did.

Fanquist acted as his secretary. Odd name that, but it came out after that it was just a glamour build-up. I've forgotten her real name, but it was something pretty terrible. Anyway, we don't have to bother with that.

As I was saying, I used to see quite a lot of her when I went to the restaurant. My work as a society columnist took me there most nights. It was as good a joint as any for meeting the sophisticated mob I wrote about. She didn't mix with the customers. I'd see her pass through from time to time on her way up to Rabener's office. Her appearance generally made the men splash soup on their shirt-fronts. She was that kind of a dame.

I played around with the idea of getting to know her, and I guess I wasn't the only one. Rabener wasn't having any. When I suggested that I'd like to meet her, he just looked at me as if I were something that'd crawled out of an exhaust pipe. So I actually never spoke to the broad. And what's more, after what happened, I don't suppose I ever shall.

You see, one evening she killed Rabener. It was quite a spectacular killing. It happened when Rabener was in the restaurant—slam bang in front of everyone.

Rabener had been hunting around for a publicity stunt for some time. He wasn't satisfied with the entertainment he was giving. He thought all the other night-spots were doing the same sort of thing, and of course he was right. He even asked me for a suggestion, but I didn't see why I should help to fill his pockets, so I played dumb. Well, he did hit on an idea. He staged one of those crazy thriller nights on us unexpectedly. You know the kind of thing. We were given a horrific ballet—a faked gun-fight, a guy pretending to be stabbed, someone punching his pal in the eye and other such harmless stuff which went down big with the moronic mob. The evening was nearly over when it happened, and the crowd was well oiled. There had been a great deal of shooting, and believe me it sold a lot of liquor.

Rabener came in and walked around the tables, having a word here and there with the customers. He could never unbend, but we were used to him by now, and we gave him a big hand for the fun and games he'd arranged for us.

I was sitting with a party near the stairs leading to the office. As Rabener was going round, Fanquist suddenly appeared at the head of the stairs. I forgot about Rabener and concentrated on her. Believe me, she certainly was the tops. There was just one little thing that had kept me from insisting on an introduction. She looked tough. When I say tough I mean she didn't look the type who'd give in without a fight. My time's so tied up that unless they give in quick I have to pass them up. It's too bad, but that's the way I live. Anyway, I should worry. There are still a lot of broads even today who do it for the joy of it.

Fanquist came slowly down the stairs. Her large eyes were like ice-blue chunks of sky. She passed close to me. I saw she had a small automatic in her hand, which she held by her side. For a moment I thought she had joined in the fun and games, but something about her made me think otherwise. I suppose I ought to have grabbed the gun, but I didn't. I was curious; I wondered what the hell she was going to do. I thought I was going to get a front-row seat at a first-rate news scoop. I was so sure that I grabbed the telephone that was plugged in at the table. I rang the night editor.

Rabener became aware of her when she was about twenty paces from him. He looked up and met her eye. He reacted like he had trodden on a rattlesnake. I guess that guy saw death staring him right in the face and did he sweat! His face went loose and yellow. His eyes stood out like toadstools.

Everyone sat watching. I don't suppose anyone in the room realised that this wasn't play-acting—but me!

She didn't take her eyes off Rabener. The gun came up slowly, and the little black muzzle stared Rabener right in the face. Just before she shot him, the night editor came through. I gave him a running commentary on the whole set-up. Boy! Was that guy shaken!

The gun made a vicious little crack. It startled us into a half-foot leap. A spot of blood appeared in the middle of Rabener's forehead. He swayed over with his hands pushed out, as if imploring her not to do it. Then he went down on his face.

She turned and walked back to the office without haste and without looking at anyone. It was the coolest killing of the century.

The uproar didn't start until she had disappeared. Then holy hell started popping.

I just sat there, feeding the night editor with the stuff while he slammed it down on paper. It was on the streets within half an hour.

Handling a murder like that gave me a reputation that I've been trying to live down ever since.

There was no bother about arresting the broad. She just sat in the office until the cops came. They didn't like to bust in on her at first. They were scared she'd start some more shooting. One of the braver ones went in at last. He found her smoking a cigarette as calm as a chink in a hop-dream.

When I got home I was as jumpy as a flea; even a couple of double ryes didn't do me any good. I just could not imagine what had made her do it. It wasn't as if it was in a jealous rage. It was all so utterly cold-blooded.

The stink the newspapers raised in the morning would have suffocated a skunk. They played it all over the front page. There were photos of Rabener; there were photos of Fanquist behind the bars. She looked as calm in jail as she did when she shot him. I guess nothing this side of hell would rattle that baby. But she wouldn't talk; she wouldn't say why she had shot Rabener. They worried her for hours in a nice way. That's one thing she had in her favour. She was such a dizzy-looking number that there was no cop strong enough to get tough. A week or so before the trial came on I ran into the local police captain. He was having a snack at Sammy's Bar. I spotted him through the window. I walked right in and parked on the next stool.

He looked at me with a cold eye that the cops reserve for newspaper guys and started bolting his food like he was in a hurry.

'Don't strangle yourself, Cap,' I said, 'I've got plenty of time and I won't run away.'

'I know,' he said, sticking a sandwich way down his throat. 'But I ain't got nothing for you.'

'Tell me one thing,' I returned, 'has she talked?'

'Not a word; not one goddam word.'

'OK, Cap. I won't worry you again.' I slid off the stool. 'That was a nice little red-head you were leading into temptation last night; I admire your taste. Well, Cap, I'll beat it.'

The Captain looked like he was going to have a stroke. His neck expanded and his eyes looked like poached eggs. 'Hey!' he said in a strangled voice. 'Where do you get that stuff?'

I paused. 'I didn't get any stuff, Cap,' I said, 'it was you who were doing the trafficking.'

'Now, listen,' he said feverishly, 'you've got to keep your trap shut about that. It was business—you understand?'

'You're of interest to the public,' I pointed out; 'it's got to go in the column. If your wife gets mad, what the hell do I care?'

He sat like an exploded balloon. 'OK,' he said bitterly. 'What do you want to know?'

I resumed my stool and ordered a club sandwich. 'Give me the dope, Cap. You're not telling me that you haven't unearthed a lot of stuff what would interest me. I won't print it until you say so. I've been in on this from the start, and I may as well finish it.'

It took me a little time to handle him, but the red-head threat worked like a charm.

Rabener, he told me, was the brain behind one of the biggest dope-rings in the country. He used the night-club as a front. He had to have some place where pedlars could come with safety each month to collect the dope. What better place than a well-established, busy night-club? Rabener was a killer too. Years ago he'd been a small-time heist man. His ruthlessness as a killer took him slowly to the top of the ladder of gangdom. He was smart. He always kept in the background. Whereas other big-shots were rounded up by the FBI, Rabener managed to keep clear. When repeal came in, he decided to go in for dope. So thorough were his preparations that no one had ever suspected the night-club to be the distributing centre of the dope-ring.

Somehow or other Fanquist fitted into this picture. The Captain wasn't quite sure where she did fit in. But they couldn't tie her up with the dope traffic. They could get nothing out of her. The smaller members of the ring had vanished. Fanquist was the only one who could enlighten the police, and she wouldn't talk.

'Maybe she thinks someone will knock her off if she squeals,' I suggested.

'Yeah, it might be that; but why did she kill Rabener?'

'I'd like to know too,' I returned. 'Think she'll get off?'

The Captain shrugged. 'I don't mind if she does,' he said. 'Nice-lookin' dish, ain't she?'

I agreed very heartily.

The trial was fixed at last, and the court-room was packed to the ceiling. Strong men trampled on weak women to get in; strong women gave up in despair. It was a real picnic for the men all right. They'd come to see Fanquist, and nothing on two legs would stop them.

The Judge was a dopey-looking old hound. The DA seemed nervous, but the defending counsel was as cocky as hell. There was not one woman on the jury. I thought that it was almost inevitable the Fanquist woman was going to get acquitted.

I had a front seat, a packet of sandwiches, and a flask of rye. No one was going to stampede me. Jackson, the night editor, was with me. We both felt that we had an interest in the case.

Fanquist looked good. She sat by her counsel, quiet, still and restful. Boy; how she could dress! Any young dope wanting to know what the female form looked like had only to step up and get an eyeful of Fanquist. He'd learn more in that glance than all the text-books on anatomy could teach him in a year.

'If I have to watch that dame all day,' the night editor grumbled, 'I shall go nuts.'

I understood how he felt even though he was a coarse-minded slob. I knew the court-room was steamed up to hell.

The DA got to his feet for his opening speech. It lacked the ginger and hate he usually worked into his openers.

'That guy,' the night editor grumbled, 'ain't got his mind on his job. If you ask me, he's worried by his lower nature.'

It didn't matter how much the DA played the killing down, the facts were undeniable. Fanquist had shot Rabener in front of a hundred witnesses. Even if the DA didn't want to be responsible for burning her nice little tail, he couldn't very well help himself.

The counsel for the defence rose to his feet. 'Your honour,' he said with a bland look on his face, 'before going further with this trial, I would like to ask the District Attorney a question.'

The Judge told him to go ahead.

The defence turned to where the DA was sitting. 'Can you assure me,' he asked, 'that the bullet found in Rabener's skull could have been fired from my client's automatic?'

You could have hung your hat on the silence that followed.

The DA went all colours of the rainbow. He got to his feet with a feeble, 'Your honour—I object!'

The Judge, who had been giving himself an eyeful of Fanquist, looked at him coldly. 'I think that is perfectly in order. In fact, I will go further and say it is a very proper question.'

The defence smiled. 'I take it that you are unable to do so,' he said blandly. 'In which case, I must ask for an adjournment while this point is verified.'

The Judge looked at him intently. 'Why have you raised this point?' he asked.

'Your honour,' the defence returned, 'my client did not kill Rabener. It will be found that the bullet in Rabener's skull could not possibly have been fired from a small automatic. The bullet, I should imagine, came from a Smith-Wesson revolver. Perhaps at this point I should wait until the bullet has been checked.'

So the Judge adjourned the Court for two hours.

It caused a sensation. There wasn't one person who left the building during those two hours' wait; the atmosphere was electric.

When the Court sat again, I think the only person in the room who wasn't worked up was Fanquist.

The Judge looked at the DA. 'Well,' he said, 'what are your findings?'

The DA looked a sick man. 'Your honour,' he returned, 'the defence is right. The bullet that killed Rabener was fired from an Army service revolver.'

When the uproar died down, the Judge scowled at the defence. 'Why was this case ever brought to trial?' he demanded.

The defence rose to his feet. 'I can explain, your honour, and will do so immediately. You will recall that on the night of the killing, Rabener had put on a special form of entertainment. The idea being that his usual floor-show was continually interrupted by faked shootings, thrills and so on. Rabener had arranged with Fanquist that she should participate in this publicity stunt. He thought it would be amusing if she pretended to murder him. She was given a gun loaded with blanks, and she carried out her instructions. She had no more idea that Rabener was killed when she fired than she had that someone, using a gun fitted with a silencer, had fired at the same time as she had at Rabener. She returned to the office. And when she was arrested she instantly thought that by some accident the gun had been loaded with live ammunition instead of blanks. The realisation that she had killed a man was such a shock to her that her reactions were slightly abnormal, which was only to be expected. Rabener was killed by a person unknown who used a silencer and an Army service revolver. This is pure supposition on my part, but I did take the trouble to examine the wound, and thought it very unlikely that so small a bullet could have made such a big hole in Rabener's head. The prosecution, having so many witnesses who actually saw my client apparently kill Rabener, did not think of checking the matter, or even of checking Fanquist's gun, which was only loaded with one blank round.'

There was a great deal of talk, but of course she got off. Who killed Rabener was never discovered. After all, he was an enemy of society, and the State didn't want to spend too much money tracking his killer down.

I've thought a lot about this since. It did strike me that if Fanquist had a lover who wanted, for some reason or other, to kill Rabener, this method was an exceedingly good one. Suppose this lover had suggested to Rabener to stage the crazy thriller night? Rabener never had those kind of ideas himself. Suppose this lover and Fanquist arranged that she should pretend to kill Rabener, whilst the lover, hidden somewhere, actually did the shooting, using a much heavier type of gun. While she was waiting the two months for her trial, the lover could have plenty of time to leave the country and set up somewhere, so that when it was over she could join him. It was obvious to me from the expression on Rabener's face that he certainly had not arranged for Fanquist to join in the fun. He knew all right when she shot him that he was going to die.

Of course, this is just my theory. I'm probably wrong; but you know how newspaper guys get when there's a story around. But I did hear that she had sailed for South America, and that spot is as good as the next if you're hiding from the cops. What do you think?

IT'S A WISE CADAVER

David Goodis

Cops who have gone wrong or been fired from the police force are a favourite theme in hardboiled novels. Many of these ex-officers are then forced to earn their living as private eyes or else throw in their lot with the gangsters and villains they once set out to catch. This theme particularly fascinated David Goodis, who was a prolific contributor to the pulps during the Thirties and Forties and now, after years of neglect, has been rediscovered: many of his novels are being republished on both sides of the Atlantic. Al Reid, who features in 'It's a Wise Cadaver' which Goodis wrote for New Detective *in July 1946, is typical of this breed. Kicked out of the New York force for an unspecified offence, he has formed his own small agency and even taken into partnership a fellow ex-cop named Renner who has also been thrown out, for punching a sergeant. In this story the pair are hired by a mobster named Calotta to find a con-man who has defrauded him of $10,000. Several other stories featuring the pair appeared in* New Detective, *as well as in the novel* Behold This Woman. *Reid in particular is an astute, wisecracking man with an eye for the main chance—whichever side of the law it may happen to be—and has a simple motto, 'Trust no one'.*

David Goodis (1917–1967) was born in New York and struggled to make a living in a variety of jobs. He was obsessed with writing and wrote his first novel when he was 21, entitling it The Ignited. *According to his own account he was dissatisfied with the result and 'threw it in the furnace', thereafter directing his attention to cracking the crime pulp magazines. These stories, many of which focused on criminals and low life, eventually got him work writing for the radio in New York and later producing scripts in Hollywood. In 1947 his novel* Dark Passage *was bought for the movies and, starring Humphrey Bogart and Lauren Bacall, became a box office hit. Four years later, another novel,* Nightfall, *was featured on television, and in 1960 his novella* False

Identity, *about two private eyes in New Orleans, was adapted for the popular ABC weekly series* Bourbon Street Beat, *starring Richard Long and Andrew Duggan. Four years before his death, Goodis received the accolade of having his work used by Alfred Hitchcock, as well as scripting an outstanding version of fellow hardboiled novelist Henry Kane's best-selling work,* An Out for Oscar, *for the* Alfred Hitchcock Hour.

'It's a Wise Cadaver' is a typical David Goodis story of the kind which would surely have helped earn him an even bigger reputation, had not his career been cut short by his early death. By being reprinted here for the first time it will help to cement his fame, along with the new editions of his novels, including the classic Dark Passage, Nightfall *and* Down There, *which were reprinted in 1993.*

* * *

It was on the desk, waiting for him. Renner cursed. He liked this habit that the boss had of going out on a case and leaving him nothing except one of these notes with a brief—too brief—description of the deal plus a few careless directions. Renner picked up the note, scowled at it.

On that Village kill—big dough involved. Believe it or not, I'm working for Calotta.

Al.

And then an address— Renner swore and walked heavily out of the little office, chewing imaginary gum.

Driving downtown he worried, as usual, about himself. There was no getting away from the fact that he had been a fool to punch a certain house sergeant in the mouth. The unfortunate incident had occurred little more than a year ago and it had resulted in his being toed off the force and into the lap of Al Reid. Reid, a wise guy, had been kicked out a year or so before that and had started his own little agency. Upon hearing of Renner's trouble, he had offered to take his ex-colleague in, on the premise that two could starve to death as cheaply as one.

He brought his sour speculations back to the present. *If Calotta is mixed up with us and if Reid is working for Calotta, then the pay-off has been reached.*

Calotta, in legal, technical parlance, had no visible means of support—but the technicality was only in force because the police from Miami to Manhattan assiduously kept their eyes shut. Five years earlier

Reid had engaged one of Calotta's boys in a gun duel and had killed him. A week later Al Reid had narrowly missed a trip to the morgue when somebody put a time bomb in his apartment—and if the two had become bosom pals and co-workers since, Renner hadn't heard about it.

However, time heals all wounds.

Renner's destination was a typical Greenwich Village tenement. A lot of kids on the street and a lot of noise and thick air. He saw a few loiterers in the doorway and muttered, 'Calotta,' figuring it would work as a password.

It did and he found himself taken inside, up a dark flight of steps, through a dark hallway, and into a room. Al was there, along with three frightened women, a frightened old man, a heavy-set man who looked sore and mean—and a corpse.

The corpse was stretched out on the floor and it was almost swimming in its own blood. The blood came from a big hole in the head and an axe leaning against a dirty bed told the rest of the story.

Al grinned at Renner and said, 'The guy on the floor is Dominic Varella. He is a very intelligent kid of twenty who got the idea that he could get rich quick. Imagine, in times like these!'

'Then what?'

'He was not very original, even alive. He told a lot of nice people that a boat loaded down with gold is sunk off the Asbury Park beach, and he is organising a diving expedition, and do they care to share in the box office receipts?'

'That is an old one,' Renner agreed.

'Quite true,' Al smiled, 'but Dominic had a new angle. He went to a printer and had a fake newspaper story made up. Then he had other literature prepared, including accounts of his success as a deep-sea diver on the Pacific Coast, together with photographs. Pretty smart and thorough, don't you think?'

'It wouldn't take me over,' Renner said.

'It took me,' Calotta snarled.

Renner looked him over. He and Calotta were about of a size—which was big. The other was forty if he was a day, and he had a low forehead, a heavy blue beard, a broken nose and thick lips. With a face like that, Renner thought, a man couldn't stay honest.

Al said, 'Yeah, what do you think of that? This Dominic actually hooked our Calotta for ten grand. Imagine that! And there are several more personages who have been taken over for even larger sums.'

Renner said, 'Who killed this guy?' He looked at Calotta and right away they parted friendship.

'Here's what I know,' Al said. 'Calotta called me down here. This is Dominic's room. He says that someone murdered Dominic and he wants me to find out who done it. He don't want the cops in on this deal because the cops are sore at him, and besides, he is sore at the cops. Is that right, Calotta?'

'Yeah,' the gangster said. 'I want to find out who killed Dominic, because whoever did it knows what I want to know.'

'And what's that?' Renner said.

'Use your head!' Al suddenly yelled. 'This Dominic has salted all the dough he took in on this swindle away somewhere and Calotta wants to know where it is. Do I have to draw you a picture?'

Renner shrugged. 'Well,' he said, 'what do we have to work on?'

Al gestured towards the three frightened women, the frightened old man. He said, 'These three girls are all tenants in this place. Our friend Dominic nicked them for a few hundred bucks apiece with his Asbury Park treasure story. The old guy is the printer who set up the phoney newspaper story.'

'That all?' Renner asked. 'Who found out about the printer?'

'I did,' Al said, 'and believe me, pal, it was a neat piece of work. No sooner does Calotta call me in on this case and show me the newspaper clippings, than I put two and two together and get four. I visit the three printers who are situated within convenient radius of this neighbourhood and one of them turns out to be this happy lad, who did the job for our friend Dominic.'

'Well, that's something,' Renner said, without the least glimmering idea of what he was talking about.

Al turned to Calotta. 'Tell you what,' he said. 'We'll need a little time to work on this. We'll go back to our office and figure on it. We ought to have an answer for you by tonight.'

'Okay,' Calotta said. There was a smart grin on his face. 'You go back to your office and figure the job out. I'll stay here and wait for you to come back. Of course you won't go to the cops?'

'Of course I won't go to the cops,' Al smiled.

He and Calotta grinned amiably at one another. Calotta's face reminded Renner of the hyenas he had seen at the Bronx Zoo.

In the coupé, before he kicked the car into motion, Renner said, 'We go to the cops, of course.'

'Yeah? And from there to the cemetery,' Al replied. 'You're a moron.'

'Why?'

'Because Calotta has more than dough wrapped up in this deal. That should have been obvious even to you. And he isn't taking any chances, particularly with us. Right now he has guys following us.'

Renner looked in the rear-view mirror and saw a big black convertible swing out as he pulled from the kerb. He swore uncomfortably and said, 'Look, Al, are you tryin' to kid me, or something?'

'How?'

'This thing all points to Calotta. What are you stalling with him for? Forget that car behind us. Go to the cops and tell them that Calotta killed a guy. That's all there is to it.'

'I called you a moron,' Al said. 'I wasn't kidding about that.'

'Have it your own way,' Renner said.

He drove the rest of the way in silence and parked the car a block away from the office.

Al said, 'Just act natural and dumb. We're going upstairs.'

They went into the office and Al shut the door and then he said, 'They're out in the hall and waiting for us. They'll want to know what we're doing, so they won't start anything unless they get suspicious.'

'That's nice,' Renner said. 'What do we do, stay here and wait until they do?'

'You stay,' Al said. 'In the meantime I'm taking a chance with the window. I'm going back to the Village. I just pulled this gag to get Calotta's boys out of the way. Now I'm going back there and finish the case. You sit here and talk out loud and argue with me.'

'But you won't be here,' Renner said.

'That's just the point,' Al smiled. 'I won't be here.'

He walked over to the window, opened it and looked down. Then he climbed out, and Renner heard him making his way down the fire escape.

The three frightened women were still there. So was the frightened man. So was the corpse. Calotta was master of ceremonies. He had a revolver in his hand. He was telling the four frightened people to keep quiet. That was when Al came in.

Calotta looked at Al and said, 'Well?'

'I got it figured out,' Al said. He looked at the revolver in Calotta's hand and he said, 'Play nice.'

'Don't stall,' Calotta said. He levelled the revolver at Al's chest.

'Put down the toy or I don't talk,' Al said. He sighed and then he added, 'You're not a very trusting employer, are you, Calotta? I'm telling you that I got this case all figured out and I'm ready to earn my pay cheque as soon as you put the revolver away.'

Calotta frowned and put the revolver back in his shoulder holster. As soon as he was sure that the rod was in its leather, Al jumped. He had to do this fast and he couldn't depend on his fists, because of Calotta's size. He kneed Calotta in the stomach and when the heavy man doubled, Al kneed him again in the chin. Calotta went up against the wall, but he didn't go out. He threw fists, cursing, spitting teeth and blood as Al jabbed fast. Then it was the knee again, and this time it caught Calotta on the point of the chin and knocked him cold.

While the three frightened women and the frightened old man were jabbering like peacocks in a typhoon, Al took the revolver from Calotta's shoulder holster. He waved the women out of the room. Then he brought his arm up slowly and aimed the rod at the frightened old man.

'You killed Dominic, didn't you?'

The frightened old man began to shiver. 'No—no—not me. I—'

'Aw, cut it out,' Al said. 'You oughta be glad I saved you from Calotta. You know what he would have done to you? He would have cut off your nose, and then he would have cut out your tongue, and then he would have cut your eyes out, and maybe he'll still do it, unless—'

'All right,' the frightened old man said. 'I'll tell you. I killed Dominic. I made an agreement with him. I would fix up the newspaper clippings, and in return he would give me a share of the money. It was my idea to start with. He told me that he had it in his room—'

'And you believed him,' Al said. 'You came up here with an axe and you killed him and then while you were looking for the money Calotta knocked on the door and you got away while the getting was good. You didn't know till then Calotta was mixed up in it. You went back to your print shop and you were minding your own business at the press when I came in.'

The frightened old man said, 'How—how can you know all this?'

'I'm a smart guy,' Al said. 'But it's easy when you take a good look at the axe. It's all red from Dominic's blood. But besides the red there's a lot of black on the blade and on the handle. It's printer's ink. You used the axe to crack open the lids of ink barrels. Then you were dumb enough to use the same axe to crack open Dominic's skull.'

The old man said, 'Dominic was no good—he betrayed an old man's trust. Calotta is a gangster—a murderer. If he goes free, he will do more harm than is left in me. Let me go.'

'Sure,' Al said, stepping aside. 'Still, there wasn't any real reason Dominic couldn't have told about your little deal—to his father.'

The old man started, looked at Al oddly with comprehending eyes, then stepped hurriedly past him.

Renner had been talking to himself for over an hour when the door opened, and Calotta was there. So was Al. And the sharp boys.

'What do you call this?' Renner said.

'It's payday,' Al said.

Calotta looked sore and mean, but as he walked into the office he took out a cheque book. As he made out a cheque for a thousand dollars he said, 'Any other guy I'd bump off, Reid. But I've always appreciated brains, and that's why I'm taking this the right way. I made a bargain with you and I'm keeping it. I told you to find out who killed Dominic. And I told you to keep the cops strictly out of this.'

'And the only way I could keep the cops out of it was to knock you cold before you got nasty with the gun,' Al said.

'That's right, Reid,' Calotta said. He handed Al the cheque. 'You found out who killed Dominic, and you kept the cops out of it, and I'm paying you off. But now, Reid, I'm going back there and I'm getting hold of the old guy!'

He went out and the sharp boys followed him.

Fifteen seconds after the door closed, Renner said, 'I don't get it.'

'It's what you call a fair bargain,' Al said. 'And now it's closed. But it's a shame that Calotta don't know about the old guy. He jumped out of that sixth-storey window just before Calotta came to.'

Renner shrugged. 'You can give me details later,' he said. 'Right now we better hurry and cash this cheque. I don't trust them crooks.'

THE FRIGHTENING FRAMMIS

Jim Thompson

The term 'grifting', to describe an American form of confidence-trickery—the art of living off gullible people—has become widely known recently due to the critically acclaimed movie The Grifters *(1990), starring Anjelica Huston, John Cusack and Annette Bening, which has also at last brought international recognition for another remarkable pulp writer, Jim Thompson. Ignored for years, his stories lost in old magazines and 29 ephemeral paperbacks, Thompson's work has now been rediscovered and largely republished, earning the most stunning accolades. Nigel Algar, introducing a tribute to the author at the National Film Theatre in 1990, declared, 'Jim Thompson did not so much transcend the genre of mystery fiction as shatter its conventions', while the* Sunday Times *felt he was 'a great American original'. Ian Penman of* The Independent *stated even more unequivocally that he was 'a king of pulp fiction'.*

Like The Grifters, *several of his other novels have been filmed—notably* Pop 1280, *about a corrupt, cowardly policeman who goes berserk, which Bertrand Tavernier made in France in 1972 as* Coup de Torchon *(the French having been among the first to recognise Thompson's talent);* The Killer Inside Me *(1975), with Stacey Keach, which Stanley Kubrick has called 'probably the most chilling and believable first-person story of a criminally warped mind that I have ever encountered'; and* The Kill-Off *(1989), starring Loretta Gross as an evil woman spreading a web of corruption in a shabby seaside resort with her malicious phone calls. The writer who was once dismissed as just another trashy exponent of the 'I-kicked-her, it-felt-good crime-writing school' (to quote the* Sunday Times *again) is now becoming the subject of academic theses, as well as being identified as a major source of inspiration for the current leaders of the hardboiled genre, Elmore Leonard, James Ellroy and Quentin Tarantino.*

James Thompson (1906–1977) was born in Anadarko, Oklahoma,

the son of an oil man who spent his money as fast as he earned it,
forcing young Jim to seek early employment. After a succession of jobs
including truck-driving, debt collecting, hotel bell-hop and doorman,
he decided like many others of his generation to try writing for the
pulps. He found receptive editors on a variety of magazines, ranging
in subject-matter from Westerns to Southern rural dramas and crime
fiction. It was not until he was 43 that Jim Thompson wrote his first
novel, Nothing More than Murder, *which was to prove his one and only*
hardback publication. Between 1949 and 1959 he produced the bulk of
his paperback fiction—including five novels in 1953 and the same
number the following year—as well as writing several film scripts,
including two with Stanley Kubrick, The Killing *(1956) and* Paths of
Glory *(1957), and episodes for TV series like* McKenzie's Raiders.

Since Thompson's death, not only has there been a resurgence of
interest in his work, but legends have grown about his drinking and
writing habits. (One such story maintains he wrote the classic Pop 1280
in two weeks to fit an already commissioned cover, and was paid a fee
of $1,000 which he promptly drank away in a protracted binge.) The
short story here first appeared in one of the early issues of Alfred
Hitchcock's Magazine *(February 1957) and features Mitch Allison, a*
cynical, hardbitten con man, who is as memorable in his way as any
other in Jim Thompson's unique gallery of low-life characters.

* * *

For perhaps the hundredth time that day, Mitch Allison squared his
shoulders, wreathed his face with an engaging grin and swung his thumb
in a gesture as old as hitch-hiking. And for perhaps the hundredth time
his appeal was rudely ignored. The oncoming car roared down on him
and past him, wiping the forced grin from his face with the nauseous
blast of its exhausts.

Mitch cursed it hideously as he continued walking, damning the car's
manufacturer, its owner and finally, and most fulsomely, himself.

'Just couldn't be satisfied, could you?' he grumbled bitterly. 'Sitting
right up on top of the world, and it wasn't good enough for you. Well,
how do you like this, you stupid dull-witted moronic blankety-blank-
blank!'

Mitch Allison was not the crying kind. He had grown up in a world
where tears were more apt to inspire annoyance than sympathy, and a
sob was likely to get you a punch in the throat. Still, he was very close

to weeping now. If there had been any tears in him, he would have bawled with sheer shame and self-exasperation.

Less than a day ago, he had possessed almost twenty thousand dollars, the proceeds from robbing his wife, swindling the madam of a parlour house and pulling an intricate double double-cross on several 'business' associates. Moreover, since it had been imperative for him to clear out of Los Angeles, his home town, he had had a deluxe stateroom on the eastbound Super Chief. Then . . .

Well, there was this elderly couple. Retired farmers, ostensibly, who had just sold their orange grove for a five-figure sum. So Mitch had tied into them, as the con man's saying is, suggesting a friendly little card game. What happened then was figuratively murder.

The nice old couple had taken him like Grant took Richmond. Their apparently palsied hands had made the cards perform in a manner which even Mitch, with all his years of suckering chumps, would have declared impossible. He couldn't believe his own eyes, his own senses. His twenty grand was gone and the supposed suckers were giving him the merry ha-ha in a matter of two hours.

Mitch has threatened to beat them into hamburger if they didn't return his dough. And that, of course, was a mistake, the compounding of one serious error with another. For the elderly couple—far more practised in the con than he—had impeccable references and identification, while Mitch's were both scanty and lousy.

He couldn't establish legitimate ownership to twenty cents, let alone twenty grand. Certainly, he was in no position to explain how he had come by that twenty grand. His attempts to do so, when the old couple summoned the conductor, had led him into one palpable lie after another. In the end, he had had to jump the train, sans baggage and ceremony, to avoid arrest.

So now, here he was. Broke, disgusted, footsore, hungry, hitch-hiking his way back to Los Angeles, where he probably would get killed as soon as he was spotted. Even if no one else cared to murder him, his wife Bette would be itching to do so. Still, a guy had to go someplace, didn't he? And having softened up Bette before, perhaps he could do it again. It was a chance—his only chance.

A hustling man needs a good front. Right now, Mitch looked like the king of the tramps.

Brushing the sweat from his eyes, he paused to stare at a sign attached to a roadside tree: Los Angeles—125 Miles. He looked past the sign into the inviting shade of the trees beyond it . . . The ocean would be over there somewhere, not too far from the highway. If he could wash up a little, rinse out his shirt and underwear . . .

He sighed, shook his head and walked on. It wasn't safe. The way his luck was running, he'd probably wade into a school of sharks.

In the distance, he heard another car approaching. Wearily, knowing he had to try, Mitch turned and swung his thumb.

It was a Cadillac, a big black convertible. As it began to slow down, Mitch had a feeling that no woman had ever given him such a going over and seemed to like so well what she saw as the one sitting next to the Cad's driver.

The car came on, slower and slower. It came even with him, and the woman asked, 'How far to El Ciudad?'

'El Ciudad?'—the car was creeping past him; Mitch had to trot along at its side to answer the question. 'You mean, the resort? About fifty miles, I think.'

'I see.' The woman stared at him searchingly. 'Would you like a ride?' she asked.

'Would I!'

She winked at Mitch, spoke to the man behind the wheel. 'All right, stupid. Stop. We're giving this guy a ride.'

The man grunted a dispirited curse. The car stopped, then spurted forward savagely as Mitch clambered into the back seat.

'What a jerk!' The woman stared disgustedly at her companion. 'Can't even give a guy a ride without trying to break his neck!'

'Dry up,' the man said wearily. 'Drop dead.'

'So damned tight you squeak! If I'd only known what you were like before I married you!'

'Ditto. Double you in spades.'

The woman took a pint of whiskey from the compartment, drank from it and casually handed it back to Mitch. He took a long thirsty drink and started to pass the bottle back. But she had turned away again, become engrossed in nagging at her husband.

Mitch was just a little embarrassed by the quarrel, but only a little. Mitch Allison was not a guy to be easily or seriously embarrassed. He took another drink, then another. Gratefully, he settled down into the deeply upholstered seat, listening disinterestedly to the woman's brittle voice and her husband's retorts.

'Jerk! Stingy! Selfish . . .' she was saying.

'Aw, Babe, lay off, will you? It's our honeymoon, and I'm taking you to one of the nicest places in the country.'

'Oh sure! Taking me there during the off-season! Because you're just too cheap and jealous to live it up a little. Because you don't want anyone to see me!'

'Now that isn't so, Babe. I just want to be alone with you, that's all.'

'Well, I don't want to be alone with you! One week in a lifetime is enough for me ...'

Mitch wondered what kind of chump he could be to take that sort of guff from a dame. In his own case, if Bette had ever talked that way to him—*pow!* She'd be spitting out teeth for the next year.

The woman's voice grew louder, sharper. The slump to her husband's shoulders became more pronounced. Incuriously, Mitch tried to determine what he looked like without those outsized sunglasses and the pulled-low motoring cap. But he didn't figure long. The guy straightened suddenly, swerved the car off into a grass-grown trail, and slammed on the brakes.

Mitch was almost thrown from the seat. The husband leapt from the car and went stomping off into the trees. She called after him angrily—profanely. Without turning, he disappeared from view.

The woman shrugged and looked humorously at Mitch. 'Some fun, huh, mister? Guess I rode hubby a little too hard.'

'Yeah,' said Mitch. 'Seems that you did.'

'Well, he'll be back in a few minutes. Just has to sulk a little first.'

She was red-haired, beautiful in a somewhat hard-faced way. But there was nothing hard-looking about her figure. She had the kind of shape a guy dreams about, but seldom sees.

Mitch's eyes lingered on her. She noticed his gaze.

'Like me, mister?' she said softly. 'Like to stay with me?'

'Huh?' Mitch licked his lips. 'Now, look, lady—'

'Like to have this car? Like to have half of fifty thousand dollars?'

Mitch always had been a fast guy on the uptake, but this babe was pitching right past him.

'Now look,' he repeated shakily. 'I-I-'

'You look,' she said. 'Take a good look.'

There was a briefcase on the front seat. She opened it and handed it back to Mitch. And Mitch looked. He reached inside, took out a handful of its contents.

The briefcase was filled, or at least half-filled, with traveller's cheques of one-hundred-dollar bills. They would have to be countersigned, of course, but that was—

'—a cinch,' the woman said intently. 'Look at the signature. No

curlicues, no fancy stuff. All you have to do is sign it plain and simple—
and we're in.'

'But—' Mitch shook his head. 'But I'm not—'

'But you could be Martin Lonsdale—you could be my husband. If
you were dressed up, if you had his identification.' Her voice faded at
the look Mitch gave her, then resumed again, sulkily.

'Why not, anyway? I've got a few rights, haven't I? He promised
me the world with a ring around it if I'd marry him, and now I can't
get a nickel out of him. I can't even tap his wallet because he keeps
all of his dough out of my hands with tricks like this.'

'Tough,' said Mitch. 'That's really tough, that is.'

He returned the cheques to the briefcase, snapped the lock on it and
tossed it back into the front seat. 'How could I use his identification
unless he was dead? Think he'd just go to sleep somewhere until I
cashed the cheques and made a getaway?'

The girl flounced around in the seat. Then she shrugged and got out.
'Well,' she said, 'as long as that's the way you feel . . .'

'We'll get hubby, right?' Mitch also got out of the car. 'Sure, we
will—you and me together. We'll see that he gets back safe and sound,
won't we?'

She whirled angrily, and stomped off ahead of him. Grinning, Mitch
followed her through the trees and underbrush. There was an enticing
roll to her hips—a deliberately exaggerated roll. She drew her skirt up
a little, on the pretext of quickening her stride, and her long, perfectly
shaped legs gleamed alluringly in the shade-dappled sunlight. Mitch
admired the display dispassionately. Admired it, without being in the
least tempted by it.

She was throwing everything she had at him, and what she had was
plenty. And he, Mitch Allison, would be the first guy to admit that she
had it. Still, she was a bum, a hundred and ten pounds of pure poison.
Mitch grimaced distastefully. He wished she would back-talk him a
little, give him some reason to put the slug on her, and he knew she
was too smart to do it.

They emerged from the trees, came out on the face of a cliff overlooking the ocean. The man's trail clearly led here, but he was nowhere
in sight. Mitch shot an enquiring glance at the girl. She shrugged, but
her face had paled. Mitch stepped cautiously to the edge of the cliff
and looked down.

Far below—a good one hundred feet at least—was the ocean: roiled,
oily-looking, surging thunderously with the great foam-flecked waves

of the incoming tide. It was an almost straight up-and-down drop to the water. About halfway down, snagged on a bush which sprouted from the cliff face, was a man's motoring cap.

Mitch's stomach turned sickishly. Then he jumped and whirled as a wild scream rent the air.

It was the girl. She was kneeling, sobbing hysterically, at the base of a tree. Her husband's coat was there, suspended from a broken off branch, and she was holding a slip of paper in her hands.

'I didn't mean it!' she wept. 'I wouldn't have done it! I was just sore, and—'

Mitch told her curtly to shut up. He took the note from her and read it, his lips pursed with a mixture of disdain and regret.

It was too bad, certainly. Death was always regrettable, whether brought on by one's own hand or another's. Still, a guy who would end his life over a dame like this one—well, the world hadn't lost much by the action and neither had he.

Mitch wadded the note and tossed it after the cliff. He frisked the coat and tossed it after the note. Then, briskly, he examined the wallet and personal papers of the late Martin Lonsdale.

There was a telegram, confirming reservations at El Ciudad Hotel and Country Club. There was a driver's licence, and a photostat of Martin Lonsdale's discharge from the army. Mitch examined the last two items with particular care.

Brown hair, grey eyes—yep, that was all right; that matched the description of his own eyes and hair. Weight one hundred and eighty—right on the nose again. Complexion fair—okay, also. Height six feet one inch . . .

Mitch frowned slightly. Lonsdale hadn't looked to be over five eight or nine, so—. So? So nothing. Lonsdale's shoulders had been slumped; he, Mitch, had only seen the man on his feet for a few seconds. At any rate, the height on these papers matched his own and that was all that mattered.

The girl was still on her knees, weeping. Mitch told her to knock it off, for God's sake, and when she persisted he kicked her lightly in the stomach. That stopped the tears, but it pulled the stopper on some of the dirtiest language he had ever heard.

Mitch listened to it for a moment, then gave her a stinging slap on the jaw. 'You've just passed the first plateau,' he advised her pleasantly. 'From now on, you won't get less than a handful of knuckles. Like to try for it, or will you settle for what you have?'

'You dirty, lousy, two-bit tinhorn.' She glared at him. 'I just lost my husband, and—'

'Which was just what you wanted,' Mitch nodded, 'so cut out the fake sob stuff. You wanted him dead. Okay, you got your wish, and with no help from me. So now let's see if we can't do a little business together.'

'Why the hell should I do business with you? I'm his widow. I've got a legal claim on the car and dough.'

'Uh-huh,' Mitch nodded judiciously. 'And maybe you can collect, too, if you care to wait long enough—and if there aren't any other claims against the estate. And if, of course, you're still alive.'

'Alive? What do you—'

'I mean you might be executed. For murder, you know. A certain tall and handsome young man might tell the cops you pushed Martin off of that cliff.'

He grinned at her. The girl's eyes blazed, then dulled in surrender.

'All right,' she mumbled. 'All right. But do you have to be so—so nasty, so cold-blooded? Can't you act like—uh—'

Mitch hesitated. He had less than no use for her, and it was difficult to conceal the fact. Still, when you had to do business with a person, it was best to maintain the appearance of friendliness.

'We'll get along all right, Babe.' He smiled boyishly, giving her a wink. 'This El Ciudad place. Is Martin known there?'

'He was never even in California before.'

'Swell. That strengthens my identification. Gives us a high-class base of operations while we're cashing the cheques. There's one more thing, though—' Mitch looked down at the telegram. 'This only confirms a reservation for Martin Lonsdale.'

'Well? It wouldn't necessarily have to mention his wife, would it? They have plenty of room at this time of year.'

Mitch nodded. 'Now, about the clothes. Maybe I'm wrong, but Marty looked quite a bit smaller than—'

'They'll fit you,' the girl said firmly. 'Marty bought his clothes a little large. Thought they wore longer that way, you know.'

She proved to be right. Except for his shoes, the dead man's clothes fitted Mitch perfectly.

Mitch retained only his own shoes and socks, and threw his other clothes into the ocean. Redressed in clean underwear, an expensive white shirt and tie and a conservative-looking blue serge suit, he climbed behind the wheel of his car. The girl, Babe, snuggled close to him. He backed out onto the highway and headed for El Ciudad.

'Mmmm . . .' Babe laid her head against his shoulder. 'This is nice, isn't it, honey? And it's going to be a lot nicer, isn't it, when we get to the hotel?'

She shivered deliciously. Mitch suppressed a shudder.

'We'll cash the cheques,' she murmured, 'and split on that. We'll divide everything, even-stephen, won't we, honey? . . . Well, won't we?'

'Oh, sure. Naturally,' Mitch said hastily. 'You just bet we will!'

And he added silently: *Like hell!*

El Ciudad is just a few miles beyond the outer outskirts of Los Angeles. A truly magnificent establishment during the tourist season, it was now, in midsummer, anything but. The great lawns were brown, tinder-dry. The long rows of palm trees were as unappetising as banana stalks. The tennis courts were half-hidden by weeds. Emptied of water and drifted almost full of dried leaves and rubble, the swimming pool looked like some mammoth compost pit. The only spots of brightness were the red and white mailbox at the head of the driveway and a green telephone booth at the first tee of the golf course.

Briefly, the exterior of the place was a depressing mess; and inside it was even less prepossessing. The furniture was draped with dust covers. Painters' dropcloths, lumber and sacks of plaster were strewn about the marble floor. Scaffolds reared towards the ceiling, and ladders were propped along the walls.

There was only a skeleton staff on duty; they were as dejected-looking as the establishment itself. The manager, also doubling as clerk, was unshaven and obviously suffering from a hangover. He apologised curtly for the disarray, explaining that the workmen who were refurbishing the place had gone on strike.

'Not that it makes much difference,' he added. 'Of course, we regret the inconvenience to you'—he didn't appear to regret it—'but you're our only guests.'

He cashed one of the hundred-dollar cheques for Mitch, his fingers lingering hungrily over the money. A bellboy in a baggy uniform showed 'Mr and Mrs Lonsdale' to their suite. It consisted of two rooms and a connecting bath. Mitch looked it over, dismissed the bellboy with a dollar tip and dropped into a chair in front of the air-conditioning vent.

'You know,' he told Babe, 'I'm beginning to understand your

irritation with Marty. If this is a sample of his behaviour, going to a winter resort in the middle of summer—'

'A double-distilled jerk,' Babe agreed. 'Scared to death that someone might make a play for me.'

'Mmm-hmmm,' Mitch frowned thoughtfully. 'You're sure that was his only reason? No matter how scared he was of competition, this deal just doesn't seem to make sense.'

'Well—' the girl hesitated. 'Of course, he probably didn't know it would be this bad.'

The kitchens and dining-room of El Ciudad were not in operation, but the bellboy made and served them soggy sandwiches and muddy coffee. He also supplied them with a bottle of whiskey at double the retail price. They had a few drinks and ate. Then, with another drink before him, Mitch sat down at the desk and began practising the signature of Martin Lonsdale.

For the one cheque—the one cashed by the manager—he had done all right. There was only a hundred dollars involved, and the manager had no reason to suspect the signature. But it would be a different story tomorrow when he began hitting the banks. Then, he would be cashing them with people whose business it was to be suspicious. His forgeries would have to be perfect, or else.

So he practised and continued to practise, pausing occasionally to massage his hand or to exchange a word with the girl. When, finally, he achieved perfection, he started to work on the cheques. Babe stopped him, immediately wary and alarmed.

'Why are you doing that? Aren't they supposed to be countersigned where they're cashed?'

Mitch shrugged. 'Not necessarily. I can write my name in front of the person who does the cashing. Just establish, you know, that my signature is the same as the one on the cheques.'

'Yes, but why—'

'To save time, dammit! This is a forgery job, remember? We hold all the cards, but it is forgery. Which means we have to hit and get—cash in and disappear. Because sooner or later, there's going to be a rumble. Now, if you're afraid I'm going to lam out with these things—'

'Oh, now, of course I'm not, honey.' But she stuck right with him until he had finished countersigning the cheques. She was quite prepared, in fact, to spend the rest of the night. Mitch didn't want that. He shoved the cheques back into the briefcase, locked it and thrust it into her hands.

'Keep it,' he said. 'Put it under your pillow. And now get out of here so I can get some sleep.'

He began to undress. The girl looked at him, poutingly.

'But, honey. I thought we were going to—uh—'

'We're both worn out,' Mitch pointed out, 'and there's another night coming.'

He climbed into bed and turned on his side. Babe left, reluctantly. She took the briefcase with her, and she locked the connecting door on her side of the bathroom.

Mitch rolled over on his back. Wide-eyed, staring into the darkness, he pondered the problem of giving Babe a well-deserved rooking. It was simple enough. After—and *if* he successfully cashed the cheques tomorrow, he had only to catch her off guard and put her on ice for the night. Bind and gag her, and lock her up in one of the clothes closets. From that point on, however, he wasn't sure what to do. Or, rather, he knew what to do, but he didn't know how the hell he was going to do it.

He couldn't scram in the Cad. A wagon like that would leave a trail a blind man could follow. For similar reasons, he couldn't zoom away in a taxi—if, that is, it was possible to get taxi service this far from the city.

How was he going to do it, then? Equally important, where would he hide out if he was able to do it? For he would sure as hell have to hide out fast after this caper. Babe would squawk bloody murder. It wouldn't make her anything, but she'd sure squawk. Her body was soft and lush but one look at that cast-iron mug of hers, and you knew she would.

So . . . ?

Mitch scowled in the darkness. Now Bette, his wife, had a nondescript car. She could get him away from here, and she could—but it was preposterous to think that she would. Not after that last stunt he'd pulled on her.

Yes, he'd planned on pleading for forgiveness before his meeting with Martin and Babe Lonsdale. But the situation had been different then. There wasn't any fifty grand at stake. There wasn't the risk of a long prison stretch. If he appealed to Bette, he'd have to give her the full pitch on this deal. Which meant, naturally, that he'd be completely at her mercy. And if she wasn't feeling merciful, if he couldn't fast-talk her into giving him a break, well, that would be the end of the sleigh ride.

Enter the cops. Exit Mitch Allison and fifty grand.

I'm going to have to stop crooking everyone, Mitch thought. *From now on I'm going to be honest, with at least one person.*

He fell asleep on this pious thought. Almost immediately, it seemed, it was morning and Babe was shaking him awake.

They headed into Los Angeles, stopping at a roadside diner for breakfast. As they ate, Mitch consulted the classified telephone directory, organising an itinerary for the day's operations. Because of the time factor, his targets—the banks—had to be separated by a discreet distance, lest he be spotted in going from one to another. Needless to say, it was also essential that he tackle only independent banks. The branch banks, with their central refer system, would nail a paper-pusher on his second try.

Babe watched Mitch work, admiration in her eyes—and increasing caution. Here was one sharp cookie, she thought. As sharp as she was tough. A lot sharper than she'd ever be. Being the kind of dame she was, she'd contemplated throwing a curve to win. Now she knew that wouldn't do it: she'd have to put the blocks to him before he could do it to her.

She was lingering in the background when he approached the teller's cage at the first bank. She was never more than a few feet away from him throughout the day, one of the most nerve-racking in Mitch Allison's career.

He began by pushing ten of the traveller's cheques, a thousand bucks at a time. A lead-pipe cinch with his appearance and identification. Usually a teller would do it on his own, or, if not, an executive's okay was a mere formality. Unfortunately, as Mitch soon realised, these thousand-dollar strikes couldn't get the job done. He was too short on time. He'd run out of banks before he ran out of cheques. So he upped the ante to two grand, and finally to three, and things really tightened up.

Tellers automatically referred him to executives. The executives passed him up the line to their superiors. He was questioned, quizzed, studied narrowly. Again and again, his credentials were examined—the description on them checked off, item by item, with his own appearance. By ten minutes of three, when he disposed of the last cheque, his nerves were in knots.

He and Babe drove to a nearby bar where he tossed down a few quick ones. Considerably calmer, then, he headed the car towards El Ciudad.

'Look, honey,' Babe turned suddenly in the seat and faced him. 'Why are we going to that joint, anyway? We've got the dough. Why not just dump this car for a price and beat it?'

'Just go off and leave our baggage? Start a lot of enquiries?' Mitch shook his head firmly.

'Well, no, I guess that wouldn't be so good, would it? But you said we ought to disappear fast. When are we going to do it?'

Mitch slanted a glance at her, deliberating over his reply. 'I can get a guy here in LA to shoot me a come-quick telegram. It'll give us a legitimate excuse for pulling out tomorrow morning.'

Babe nodded dubiously. She suggested that Mitch phone his friend now, instead of calling through El Ciudad's switchboard. Mitch said that he couldn't.

'The guy works late, see? He wouldn't be home yet. I'll call him from that phone booth out on the golf course. That'll keep anyone from listening in.'

'I see,' Babe repeated. 'You think of everything, don't you, darling?'

They had dinner at a highway drive-in. Around dusk, Mitch brought the car to a stop on El Ciudad's parking lot. Babe reached hesitantly for the briefcase. Mitch told her to go right ahead and take it with her.

'Just don't forget, sweetheart. I can see both entrances to the joint, and I've got the keys to this buggy.'

'Now, don't you worry one bit,' Babe smiled at him brightly. 'I'll be right inside waiting for you.'

She headed for the hotel, waving to him gaily as she passed through the entrance. Mitch sauntered out to the phone booth and placed a call to Bette. Rather, since she hung up on him the first two times, he placed three calls.

At last she stayed on the wire and he was able to give her the pitch. The result was anything but reassuring. She said she'd be seeing him— she'd be out just as fast as she could make it. And he could depend on it. But there was an ominous quality to her voice, a distinctly unwifely tone. Before he could say anything more, she slammed up the receiver for the third and last time.

Considerably disturbed, Mitch walked back across the dead and dying grass and entered the hotel. The manager-clerk's eyes shied away from him. The elevator-bellboy was similarly furtive. Absorbed in his worry over Bette, Mitch didn't notice. He got off at his floor and started down the hall, ducking around scaffolding, wending his way through a littered jungle of paint cans, plaster and wallpaper.

He came to the door of his room. He turned the knob, and entered. And something crashed down on his head.

It was dark when Mitch regained consciousness. He sat up, massaging his aching head, staring dizzily at the shattered glass on the floor—the remains of a broken whiskey bottle. Then he remembered; realisation came to him. Ripping out a curse, he ran to the window.

The Cad was still there on the parking lot. Yes, and the keys were still in his pocket. Mitch whirled, ran through the bath and kicked open the door to the other room.

It was empty, in an immaculate order, sans Babe and sans baggage. There was nothing to indicate that it had ever been tenanted. Mitch tottered back into his own room, and there was a knock on the door and he flung it open.

A man walked in and closed it behind him. He looked at Mitch. He looked down at the broken bottle. He shook his head in mild disapproval.

'So you are supposedly a sick man, Marty,' he said gutturally. 'So you have a great deal of money—my money. So drunk you should not get.'

'H-huh? W-what?' Mitch said. 'Who the hell are you?'

'So I am The Pig,' the man said. 'Who else?'

The name suited him. Place a pecan on top of a hen's egg and you've got a good idea of his appearance. He was perhaps five feet tall and he probably weighed three hundred pounds. His arms were short almost to the point of deformity. He had a size six head and a size sixty waistline.

Mitch stared at him blankly, silently. The Pig apparently misunderstood his attitude.

'So you are not sure of me,' he said. 'So I will take it from the top and give you proof. So you are The Man's good and faithful servant through all his difficulties. So The Man passes the word that you are to pay me fifty thousand dollars for services rendered. So you are a very sick man anyway, and have little to lose if detected while on the errand—'

'Wait a minute!' Mitch said. 'I—I'm not—'

'So you are to transport the money in small traveller's cheques. So you cannot be robbed. So they can be easily cashed without attracting unwanted attention. So you have had a day to cash them. So'—The Pig concluded firmly—'you will give me the fifty thousand.'

Mitch's mouth was very dry. Slowly, the various pieces of a puzzle

were beginning to add up. And what they added up to was curtains—
for him. He'd really stepped into something this time: a Grade A jam,
an honest-to-hannah, double-distilled frammis. The Pig's next words
were proof of the fact.

'So you know how I earned the fifty Gs, Marty. So you would not
like me to give you a demonstration. It is better to die a natural death.'

'N-now-now, listen!' Mitch stammered. 'You've got the wrong guy.
I'm not Martin Lonsdale. I'm—I'm . . . Look, I'll show you.' He started
to reach for his wallet. And groaned silently, remembering. He had
thrown it away. There was a risk of being caught with two sets of
identification, so—

'So?' The Pig said.

'I! Look! Call this Man whoever he is. Let me talk to him. He can
tell you I'm not—'

'So,' The Pig grunted, 'who can call Alcatraz? So—' he added, 'I
will have the money, Marty.'

'I don't have it! My wife—I mean the dame I registered in with—
has it. She had the room next to mine, and—'

'So, but no. So I checked the registry myself. So there has been no
woman with you.'

'I tell you there was! These people here—they're hungry as hell,
see, and she had plenty of dough to bribe them . . .' He broke off,
realising how true his words were. He resumed again, desperately: 'Let
me give you the whole pitch, tell you just what happened right from
the beginning! I was trying to thumb a ride, see, and this big Cadillac
stopped for me. And . . .'

Mitch told him the tale.

The Pig was completely unimpressed.

'So that is a fifty-grand story? So a better one I could buy for a
nickel.'

'But it's true! Would I make up a yarn like that? Would I come here,
knowing that you'd show up to collect?'

'So people do stupid things.' The Pig shrugged. 'So, also, I am a
day early.'

'But, dammit!—' There was a discreet rap on the door. Then it
opened and Bette came in.

This Bette was a honey, a little skimpy in the chin department,
perhaps, but she had plenty everywhere else. A burlesque house strip-
teaser, her mannerisms and dress sometimes caused her to be mistaken
for a member of a far older profession.

Mitch greeted her with almost hysterical gladness. 'Tell this guy, honey! For God's sake, tell him who I am!'

'Tell him . . . ?' Bette hesitated, her eyes flickering. 'Why, you're Martin Lonsdale, I guess. If this is your room. Didn't you send for me to—'

'N-nno!' Mitch burbled. 'Don't do this to me, honey! Tell him who I really am. Please!—'

One of The Pig's fat arms moved casually. The fist at the end of it smashed into Mitch's face. It was like being slugged with a brick. Mitch stumbled and fell flat across the bed. Dully, as from a distance, he heard a murmur of conversation . . .

'. . . had a date with him, a hundred-dollar date. And I came all the way out here from Los Angeles . . .'

'So Marty has another date. So I will pay the hundred dollars myself . . .'

There was a crisp rustle, then a dulcet, 'Oh, aren't you nice!' Then the door opened and closed, and Bette was gone. And The Pig slowly approached the bed. He had a hand in his pocket. There was a much bigger bulge in the pocket than a hand should make.

Mitch feigned unconsciousness until The Pig's hand started coming out of his pocket. Then Mitch's legs whipped up in a blur of motion. He went over backwards in a full somersault, landed on the other side of the bed, gripped and jerked it upward.

Speed simply wasn't The Pig's forte. He just wasn't built for it. He tried to get out of the way, and succeeded only in tripping over his own feet. The bed came down on him, pinning him to the floor. Mitch sent him to sleep with a vicious kick in the head.

Mitch realised he had been moving in a blur. But now his mind was crystal clear, sharper than it ever had been.

Where was Babe? Simple. Since she couldn't have ridden away from the place, she must have walked. And Mitch knew where she had walked to.

What to do with The Pig? Also simple. The materials for taking care of him were readily at hand.

Mitch turned on the water in the bathtub. He went out into the hall and returned with two sacks full of quick-drying plaster . . .

He left The Pig very well taken care of, sitting in plaster up to his chin. Then, guessing that it would be faster, he ran down the stairs and out to the Cadillac. Wheels spinning, he whipped it down the horseshoe driveway and out onto the highway.

He slowed down after a mile or two, peering off to his right at the weed-grown fields which lay opposite the ocean. Suddenly, he jerked the car onto the shoulder and braked it to a stop. He got out; his eyes narrowed with grim satisfaction.

He was approximately parallel now with the place where he had assumed the identity of Martin Lonsdale. The place where Martin Lonsdale had supposedly committed suicide. And out there in this fallow field was an abandoned produce shed.

From the highway, it appeared to be utterly dark, deserted. But as Mitch leaped the ditch and approached it, he caught a faint flicker of light. He came up on the building silently. He peered through a crack in the sagging door.

There was a small stack of groceries in one corner of the room, also a large desert-type water bag. Blankets were spread out in another corner. Well back from the door, a can of beans was warming over a Sterno stove. A man stood over it, looking impatiently at the food.

Mitch knew who he was, even without the sunglasses and cap. He also knew who he was *not*—for this man was bald and well under six feet tall.

Mitch kicked open the door and went in. The guy let out a startled 'Gah!' as he flung himself forward, swinging.

He shouldn't have done it, of course. Mitch was sore enough at him, as it was. A full uppercut, and the guy soared towards the roof. He came down, horizontal, landing amidst the groceries.

Mitch snatched him to his feet, and slapped him back into consciousness. 'All right. Let's have the story. All of it and straight, get me? And don't ask me what story or I'll—'

'I w-won't—I mean, I'll tell you!' the man babbled frantically.

'We—tied into Lonsdale at a motor-court. Figured he was carrying heavy, so Babe pulled the tears for a ride. We was just going to hold him up, you know. Honest to Gawd, that's all! But—but—'

'But he put up a fight and you had to bump him.'

'Naw! No!' the man protested. 'He dropped dead on us! I swear he did! I'd just pulled a knife on him—hadn't touched him at all—when he keeled over! Went out like a light. I guess maybe he must have had a bad ticker or something, but anyway . . .'

Mitch nodded judiciously. The Pig had indicated that Lonsdale was in bad health. 'So okay. Keep singing.'

'W-well, he didn't have hardly any dough in cash like we thought he would. Just that mess of cheques. But we'd pumped him for a lot

of info, and we figured if we could find the right kind of chump—
excuse me, Mister—I mean, a guy that could pass for Lonsdale—'

'So you did a little riding up and down the highway until you found
him. And you just damned near got him killed!'

He gave the guy an irritated shake. The man whimpered apologetic-
ally. 'We didn't mean to, Mister. We really figured we was doing you
a favour. Giving you a chance to make a piece of change.'

'I'll bet. But skip it. Where's Babe?'

'At the hotel.'

'Nuts!' Mitch slapped him. 'You were going to hole up here until
the heat was off! Now, where the hell is she?'

The man began to babble again. Babe hadn't known how soon she
could scram. There'd been no set time for joining him here. She had
to be at the hotel. If she wasn't, he didn't know where she was.

'Maybe run out on me,' he added bitterly. 'Never could trust her
around the corner, I don't see how she could get away, but—'

Mitch jerked a fist swiftly upward.

When the guy came to, he was naked and the room had been stripped
of its food, water and other supplies. His clothes and everything else
were bundled into one of the blankets, which Mitch was just lugging
out the door.

'Wait!' The man looked at him fearfully. 'What are you going to
do?'

He departed. A mile or so back up the road, he threw the stuff into
the ditch. He arrived at the hotel, parked and indulged in some very
deep thinking.

Babe had to be inside the joint. This money-hungry outfit was hiding
her for a price. But exactly where she might be—in which of its numerous rooms, the countless nooks and crannies, cellars and subcellars that
a place like this had—there was no way of telling. Or finding out. The
employees would know nothing. They'd simply hide themselves if they
saw him coming. And naturally he couldn't search the place from top to
bottom. It would take too long. Deliverymen—possibly other guests—
would be showing up. And then there was The Pig to contend with.
Someone must have driven him out here, and he would not have planned
to stay later than morning. So someone would be calling for him, and—

Well, never mind. He had to find Babe. He had to do it fast. And
since he had no way of learning her hiding-place, there was only one
thing to do. Force her out of it.

Leaving the hotel, Mitch walked around to the rear and located a rubbish pile. With no great difficulty, he found a five-gallon lard can and a quantity of rags. He returned to the parking lot. He shoved the can under the car's gas tank and opened the petcock. While it was filling he knotted the rags into a rope. Then, having shut off the flow of gasoline, he went to the telephone booth and called the hotel's switchboard.

The clerk-manager answered. He advised Mitch to beat it before he called the cops. 'I know you're not Lonsdale, understand? I know you're a crook. And if you're not gone from the premises in five minutes—'

'Look who's talking!' Mitch jeered. 'Go ahead and call the cops! I'd like to see you do it, you liver-lipped, yellow-bellied—'

The manager hung up on him. Mitch called him back.

'Now get this,' he said harshly. 'You said I was a crook. All right, I am one and I'm dangerous. I'm a crib man, an explosives expert. I've got plenty of stuff to work with. So send that dame out here and do it fast, or I'll blow your damned shack apart!'

'Really? My, my!' The man laughed sneeringly, but somewhat shakily. 'Just think of that!'

'I'm telling you,' Mitch said. 'And this is the last time I'll tell you. Get that dame out of the woodwork, or there won't be any left.'

'You wouldn't dare! If you think you can bluff—'

'In exactly five minutes,' Mitch cut in, 'the first charge will be set off, outside. If the dame doesn't come out, your building goes up.'

He replaced the receiver, went back to the car. He picked up the rags and gasoline, moved down the hall to the red-and-white mailbox. It stood in the deep shadows of the *porte-cochère* and he was not observed. Also, the hotel employees apparently were keeping far back from the entrance.

Mitch soaked the rag rope in the gasoline and tucked a length of it down inside the mailbox. Then he lifted the can and trickled its entire contents through the letter slot. It practically filled the box to the brim. The fluid oozed through its seams and dripped down upon the ground.

Mitch carefully scrubbed his hands with his handkerchief. Then, he ignited a book of matches, dropped them on the end of the rope. And ran.

His flight was unnecessary. For the 'bomb' was an almost embarrassing failure. There was a weak rumble, a kind of a growl—a hungry man's stomach, Mitch thought bitterly, would make a louder one. A few blasts of smoke, and the box jiggled a bit on its moorings. But that was the size of it. That was the 'explosion'. It wouldn't have startled a nervous baby. As for scaring those rats inside the joint, hell, they were probably laughing themselves sick.

Oh, sure, the box burned; it practically melted. And that would give them some trouble. But that didn't help Mitch Allison any.

From far down the lawn, he looked dejectedly at the dying flames, wondering what to do now. He gasped, his eyes widening suddenly as two women burst through the entrance of El Ciudad.

One—the one in front—was Babe, barelegged, barefooted, dressed only in her bra and panties. She screamed as she ran, slapping and clawing wildly at her posterior. And it was easy to see why. For the woman chasing her was Bette, and Bette was clutching a blazing blowtorch.

She was holding it in front of her, its long blue flame aimed straight at the brassy blonde's flanks. Babe increased her speed. But Bette stayed right with her.

They came racing down the lawn towards him. Then, Bette tripped and stumbled, the torch flying from her hands. And at practically the same instant, Babe collided head-on with the steel flagpole. The impact knocked her senseless. Leaving her to listen to the birdies, Mitch sat down by Bette and drew her onto his lap. Bette threw her arms around him, hugging him frantically.

'You're all right, honey? I was so worried about you! You didn't really think I meant the way I acted, did you?'

'I wouldn't have blamed you if you had,' Mitch said.

'Well, I didn't. Of course I was awfully mad at you, but you *are* my husband. I feel like murdering you myself lots of times, but I'm certainly not going to let anyone else do it!'

'That's my girl.' Mitch kissed her fondly. 'But—'

'I thought it was the best thing to do, honey. Just play dumb and then go get some help. Well—'

'Just a minute,' Mitch interrupted. 'Where's your car?'

'Over by the ocean,' Bette pointed, continued. 'Like I was saying, I found her listening out in the hall. I mean, she ducked away real fast, but I knew she had been listening. So I figured you'd probably be all right for a little while, and I'd better see about her.'

'Right,' Mitch nodded. 'You did exactly right, honey.'

'Well, she had a room just a few doors away, Mitch. I guess they had to move her nearby because they didn't have much time. Anyway, she went in and I went right in with her . . .'

She had asked Babe the score. Babe had told her to go jump, and

Bette had gone to work on her, ripping off her clothes in the process. Babe had spilled, after a time. Bette had learned, consequently, that there would be no help for Mitch unless she provided it.

'So I locked her in and went back to your room. But you were gone, and I guessed you must be all right from the look of things. That guy in the bathtub, I mean.' Bette burst into giggles, remembering. 'He looked so funny, Mitch! How in the world do you ever think of those stunts?'

'Just comes natural, I guess,' Mitch murmured modestly. 'Go on, precious.'

'Well, I went back to her room, and the clerk called and said you were threatening to blow up the place. But she wouldn't go for it. She said she was going to stay right there, no matter what, and anyway you were just bluffing. Well, I was pretty sure you were, too, but I knew you wanted to get her outside. So I went out in the hall again and dug up that big cigar lighter—'

Mitch chuckled and kissed her again. 'You did fine, baby. I'm really proud of you. You gave her a good frisk, I suppose? Searched her baggage?'

Bette nodded, biting her lip. 'Yes, Mitch. She doesn't have the money.'

'Don't look so down about it—' he gave her a little pat. 'I didn't figure she'd keep it with her. She's ditched it outside somewhere.'

'But, Mitch, you don't understand. I talked to her, and—'

'I know. She's a very stubborn girl.' Mitch got to his feet. 'But I'll fix that.'

'But, Mitch—she told me where she put the money. When I was chasing her with the torch.'

'Told you! Why didn't you say so? Where is it, for Pete's sake?'

'It isn't,' Bette said miserably. 'But it was.' She pointed towards the hotel. 'It was up there.'

'Huh? What are you talking about?'

'She . . . she mailed it to herself.'

Sick with self-disgust, Mitch climbed behind the wheel of Bette's car and turned it onto the highway. Bette studied his dark face. She patted him comfortingly on the knee.

'Now, don't take it so hard, honey. It wasn't your fault.'

'Whose was it, then? How a guy can be so stupid and live so long! Fifty grand, and I do myself out of it! I do it to myself, that's what kills me!'

'But you can't expect to be perfect, Mitch. No one can be smart all the time.'

'Nuts!' Mitch grunted bitterly. 'When was I ever smart?'

Bette declared stoutly that he had been smart lots of times. Lots and lots of times. 'You know you have, honey! Just look at all the capers you've pulled! Just think of all the people who are trying to find you! I guess they wouldn't be, would they, if you hadn't outsmarted them.'

'Well . . .' Mitch's shoulders straightened a little.

Bette increased her praise.

'Why, I'll bet you're the best hustler that ever was! I'll bet you could steal the socks off a guy with sore feet, without taking off his shoes!'

'You-uh-you really mean that, honey?'

'I most certainly do!' Bette nodded vigorously. 'They just don't make 'em any sneakier than my Mitch. Why—why, I'll bet you're the biggest heel in the world!'

Mitch sighed on a note of contentment. Bette snuggled close to him. They rode on through the night, moving, inappropriately enough, towards the City of Angels.

THE FIFTH QUARTER

Stephen King

There is no more famous admirer of Jim Thompson's work today than Stephen King, probably the biggest-selling author in the world. When a group of Thompson's books were republished in 1990 he wrote an enthusiastic endorsement to encourage new readers: 'Now, my friend, buckle your seatbelt and grab your gas-mask!' Although King is often categorised as a horror writer, his fiction has ranged across the spectrum from fantasy to crime and he is known to be a keen reader of hardboiled fiction. But having said this, 'The Fifth Quarter' is his only venture into the genre. It was written in 1972 and, interestingly, appeared in the raunchy American men's magazine Cavalier, *under the by-line of 'John Swithen'. Despite his prolific output, King has regularly used only one pseudonym, Richard Bachman, on a series of five titles published between 1977 and 1984 which an enterprising Washington bookstore clerk exposed after the appearance of the fifth title,* Thinner— *since when all have reappeared bearing the author's real name. 'John Swithen', on the other hand, has (to date) made only this one appearance, although there has been no attempt at subterfuge by King, who readily allowed 'The Fifth Quarter' to be reprinted in the February 1986 issue of* Twilight Zone *magazine. There it was headlined with a quote that might have come straight from the pages of any Thirties pulp: 'It's tough enough for four guys to split the pie. The fifth slice means murder.'*

Stephen King (1946–), who was born in Portland, Maine, had a number of jobs including that of janitor, mill-worker and library stacker before becoming a teacher and then a literary phenomenon following the publication of his first novel, Carrie, *in 1974. Many of his subsequent books have been filmed—most notably* The Shining *(1980),* Christine *(1983),* Firestarter *(1984) and* Pet Sematary *(1989)—and it has been estimated that he has already sold more than 100 million books worldwide. All a long way from his first published story with the very pulp title 'I Was a Teenage Graverobber' in* Comics Review! *King's sole hardboiled story which follows is very much in the Jim Thompson tradition and features a tough ex-convict, Flip Wilson, on the trail of some money from a bank robbery which is owed to a friend—now deceased.* Twilight Zone *rightly called it a 'swift, icy story' and it will surely remain in the reader's memory long after he has closed the pages of this book.*

*   *   *

I parked the heap around the corner from Keenan's house, sat in the dark for a moment, then turned off the key and got out. When I slammed the door, I could hear rust flaking off the rocker panels and dropping into the street. It wasn't going to be like that much longer.

The gun lay solidly against my chest as I walked. It was a .45, Barney's .45. It would do the job. And it gave the whole thing a sense of rough justice.

Keenan's house was an architectural monstrosity spread over half an acre of land, all slanting angles and steep-sloped roofs behind an iron fence. The gate was unlocked, as I'd hoped. The Sarge would be showing up later.

I walked to the driveway, staying close to the shrubbery and listening for any strange sound over the cutting whine of the January wind. There wasn't any. It was Thursday night, and Keenan's sleep-in maid would be out having a jolly time at somebody's Tupperware party. Nobody home but that bastard Keenan. Waiting for Sarge. Waiting for me.

The carport was open and I slipped inside. The ebony shadow of Keenan's Impala loomed. I tried the back door. It was open. I got in, sat down, and waited.

Now there was the faint sound of music. Jazz, very quiet, very good. Miles Davis, maybe. Keenan listening to Miles Davis and holding a gin fizz in one delicate hand. Nice for him.

It was a long wait. The hands on my watch crawled their way from eight-thirty to nine-thirty to ten. Time for a lot of thinking. I thought about Barney. About how he looked in that small boat when I found him on that day late last summer, staring up at me and making meaningless cawing noises. He'd been adrift for two days and looked like a boiled lobster. There was black blood encrusted across his midsection where he'd been shot.

He'd steered towards the cottage as best he could, but still it had been mostly luck. Lucky he'd gotten there, lucky he could still talk for a little while. I'd had a fistful of sleeping pills ready if he couldn't talk. I didn't want him to suffer. Not unless he could tell me something.

And he did. He told me almost all of it.

When he was dead, I went back to the boat and got his .45. It was hidden aft in a small compartment, wrapped in a waterproof pouch. Then I towed his boat out into deep water and sank it. If I could have put an epitaph on the square of piney woods where I buried him, it would have been Barnum's: 'There's one born every minute.' Instead, I went out to dig up what I could on the men who had done him. It had taken six months to get a file on two of them, and here I was.

At ten-twenty headlights splashed up the curving driveway and I hit the floor of the Impala. He drove into the carport, snuggling up close to Keenan's car. A VW by the sound. The little engine died and I could hear Sarge grunting softly as he got out of the little car. The overhead went on, and the sound of the side door clicking open came to me.

Keenan's voice: 'Sarge! You're late! Come on in and have a drink.'

'Scotch.'

I'd unrolled the window before. Now I stuck Barney's .45 through it, holding the stock with both hands. 'Stand still,' I said.

The Sarge was halfway up the cement steps. Keenan was looking down at him. They were both perfect silhouettes in the light spilling through from inside. I doubted if they could see much of me in the dark, but they could see the gun. It was a big gun.

'Who the hell are you?' Keenan asked.

'Flip Wilson,' I said. 'Move and you're dead. I'll put a hole in you big enough to graft a tv set in.'

'You sound like a kid,' Sarge said. He didn't move, though.

'Just don't move. That's all you've got to worry about.' I opened the Impala's back door and got out carefully. The Sarge was staring at me over his shoulder and I could see the glitter of his little eyes. One hand was spidering up the lapel of his 1943-model double-breasted suit.

'Get your hands up. '

The Sarge put his hands up. Keenan's already were. Instinct.

'Come down to the foot of the steps. Both of you.'

They came down, and out of the direct glare of the light I could see their faces. Keenan looked scared, but the Sarge was utterly composed. He was probably the one who had jobbed Barney.

'Face the wall,' I said. 'Both of you.'

'If you're after money—'

I laughed. It was a sound like cold clinkers being scraped out of a furnace. 'Yes, that's what I'm after. One hundred and eighty thousand dollars. Buried on a little island off Bar Harbor called Carmen's Folly.'

Keenan jerked as if he had been shot, but Sarge's concrete face never twitched. He turned around and put his hands on the wall, leaning his weight on them. Keenan followed suit, reluctantly. I frisked him first and got a cute little .32 with a brass-inlaid stock. I threw it over my shoulder and heard it bounce off one of the cars. Sarge was clean— and it was a relief to step away from him.

'We're going into the house. You first, Keenan, then Sarge, then me. Without incident, okay?'

We all walked up the steps and into the kitchen.

It was one of those germless tile and formica jobs that looks like it was spit whole out of some mass-production womb in Yokohama. A pony glass half full of brandy was sitting on the counter. I paraded them through into Keenan's living-room. It had apparently been done by some pansy decorator who never got over his crush on Ernest Hemingway. There was a flagstone fireplace with a moosehead mounted over it, staring at the mahogany bar across the room with eternally sparkling eyes. There was a buffet with a gunrack over it. The stereo had turned itself off.

I waved the gun at the couch. 'One on each end.'

They sat, Keenan on the right, Sarge on the left. The Sarge looked even bigger sitting down. There was an ugly, dented scar up in a crewcut that had grown too long. I put his weight at about two-seventy. I wondered why he owned a Volkswagen.

I grabbed an easy chair and dragged it over Keenan's quicksand-coloured rug until it was running distance from them. I sat down and let the .45 rest on my thigh. Keenan stared at it like a bird stares at a snake. The Sarge, on the other hand, was staring at me like I was a bird. 'Now what?' he asked flatly.

'Let's talk about maps and money,' I said.

'I don't know what you're talking about,' Sarge said. 'All I know is that little boys shouldn't play with guns.'

'How's Cappy MacFarland these days?' I asked casually.

It didn't get anything from the Sarge, but Keenan popped his cork. 'He knows. He knows, Sarge.' The words shot out of him like bullets.

'Shut up!' Sarge cracked at him. 'Shut up your goddamn mouth!'

Keenan shut his eyes and moaned a little. This was the part of the deal no one had told him about. I smiled. 'He's right, Sarge,' I said. 'I know. Almost all of it.'

'Who are you, kid?'

'No one you know. A friend of Barney's.'

'Don't know him,' Sarge said indifferently.

'He wasn't dead, Sarge. Not quite dead.'

Sarge turned a slow and murderous look on Keenan. Keenan shuddered and opened his mouth. 'Shut up,' Sarge said. 'I ought to break your goddamn neck.' Keenan's mouth shut with a snap. Sarge looked at me again. 'What does *almost* all of it mean?'

'Everything but the fine details. About the armoured car. The island. Cappy MacFarland. How you and Keenan and some bastard named Jagger killed Barney. And the map. I know about the map.'

'It wasn't the way he told you,' Sarge said. 'He was going to cross us.'

'He couldn't cross the street,' I said. 'He was just a patsy who could drive a car fast.'

He shrugged; it was like watching a minor earthquake. 'Okay. Be as dumb as you look.'

'I knew Barney had something on as early as last March. I just didn't know what. And then one night he had a gun. This gun. How did you connect with him, Sarge?'

'Someone who did time with him,' Sarge said. 'We needed a driver who knew eastern Maine and the Bar Harbor area. Keenan and I went to see him. He bought it.'

'I did time with him in South Portland,' I said. I smiled at Sarge. 'I liked him. He was dumb, but he was a good kid. He needed a keeper and it looked like I was elected. I didn't mind. We were thinking about a bank in Lewiston. He couldn't wait. So now he's underground.'

'Get me an onion,' Sarge said.

I picked up the gun and showed him the muzzle, and for the first time he was the bird and it was the snake. 'One more wisecrack and I'll put a bullet in your belly. Do you believe that?'

His tongue flickered in and out with startling quickness, lizardlike, and he nodded his head. Keenan was frozen. He looked like he wanted to retch but didn't quite dare.

'He told me it was big time, enough to last him ten years. That's all I could get. He took off on April third. Two days later four guys knock over the Portland-Bangor Brinks truck just outside of Carmel. All three guards dead. The newspapers said the robbers ran two roadblocks in a souped-up fifty-eight Ford. Barney had a fifty-eight Ford up on blocks, thinking about turning it into a stocker. I'm betting Keenan put up the front money for him to turn it into something a little better and a lot faster.'

I looked at them. No comment. Keenan's face was the colour of cheese.

'On May sixth I get a card postmarked Bar Harbor, but that doesn't mean anything—there are dozens of little islands that channel their mail through there. A mailboat picks it up. The card says: "Mom and family fine, store doing good. See you in July." It was signed with Barney's middle name. I leased a cottage on the coast, because Barney knew that would be the deal. July comes and goes, no Barney.'

I looked at them remotely. 'He showed up in early August. Courtesy of your buddy Keenan, Sarge. He forgot about the automatic bilge pump in the boat. You thought the chop would sink it quick enough, right, Keenan? But you thought he was dead, too. I had a yellow blanket spread out on Frenchman's Point every day. Visible for miles. Easy to spot. Still, he was lucky. He couldn't talk for long. You'd crossed him once already, right, Sarge? You didn't tell him the money was new, all the serial numbers recorded. Not even one of the syndicate boys would dare buy it for ten, maybe fifteen years.'

'That was for his own good,' Sarge rumbled. 'Ten years would make him thirty. Hell, I'll be sixty-one.'

'Did he buy Cappy MacFarland, too? Or was that just another surprise?'

'We all had to buy Cappy,' Sarge said. 'He was a good man. A professional. He got cancer last year. Inoperable. And he owed me a favour.'

'So the four of you went out to Cappy's island,' I said. 'Cappy buried the money and made a map.'

'It was Jagger's idea,' Sarge said. 'We couldn't hole up together for ten years. No one wanted to trust anyone else with knowing where the swag was—too much chance somebody'd go for the whole pie. And if we just split, somebody—your buddy, for instance—would get weak and spend some of it. If the cops put the arm on him, the guy might just cough up names. So we all went down to the beach for the afternoon. Cappy took care of it.'

'Tell me about the map.'

'I thought we'd get to that,' Sarge said with a wintry smile.

'Don't tell him!' Keenan cried out hoarsely. There was raw panic in his voice.

'Shut up,' Sarge said brutally. 'He knows it all, thanks to you. If he doesn't kill you, I will.'

'Your name's in a letter,' Keenan said wildly, 'if anything happens to me!'

'Cappy drew it good,' the Sarge said, as if Keenan were not there at all. 'He had some draughtsman training in Joliet Penitentiary. He cut the map into quarters. One for each of us. We were going to have a reunion on July 4, 1982. But there was trouble.'

'Yes,' I agreed. My voice sounded remote.

'If it makes you feel any better, it was Keenan's play. Solo. Had to be. Jagger and I took off in Cappy's boat. He was okay when we left.'

'You're a goddamn liar!' Keenan squealed.

'Who's got two hunks of map in his wall safe?' Sarge enquired. He looked at me again. 'It was still all right. Two quarters still wasn't enough. And maybe your buddy was better off out of the way. Three-way is better than four. Then Keenan called me. Gave me his address. Told me to come over and talk. Tonight. Of course, he had insurance. My name in an open-in-event-of-my-death letter that he'd sent his lawyer. His idea was that a two-way split would be even better than three. With three-quarters of the map, Keenan thought we might be able to dope it out.'

Keenan's face was like a moon drifting somewhere in a high stratosphere of terror.

'Where's the safe?' I asked him.

Keenan didn't say anything.

I had done some practising with the .45. It was a good gun. I liked it. I held it in both hands and shot Keenan in the forearm, just below the elbow. The Sarge didn't even jump. Keenan fell off the couch and curled up in a ball, holding his arm and screaming.

'Where's the safe?' I asked him.

Keenan continued to scream.

'I'll shoot you in the knee,' I said. 'The Sarge can carry you to the safe.'

'The print,' he gasped. 'The Van Gogh. Don't shoot me any more, huh?' He looked at me, grinning with pain and conciliation.

I motioned to Sarge with the gun. 'Stand facing the wall.'

The Sarge got up and looked at the wall, arms dangling limply.

'Now you,' I said to Keenan. 'Go open the safe.'

'I'm bleeding to death,' Keenan moaned.

I went over and stroked the butt of the .45 up the side of his cheek, laying back skin. 'Now you're bleeding,' I told him. 'Go open the safe or you'll bleed more.'

Keenan got up, holding his arm and blubbering. He took the print off its hooks with his good hand, revealing an office-grey wall safe. He threw a terrified glance at me and began to twiddle the dial. He made two false starts and had to go back. The third time he got it open. There were some papers and two wads of bills inside. He reached in, fumbled around, and came up with two squares of paper, about three inches square.

I had meant to tie him up and leave him. He was harmless enough; he wouldn't dare to come out of his house for a week. But it was like Sarge had said. He d'd have two.

And one of them had blood on it.

I shot him again, this time not in the arm. He went down like an empty laundry bag.

Sarge didn't flinch. 'I wasn't crapping you. Keenan jobbed your friend. They were both amateurs. Amateurs are stupid.'

I didn't answer. I looked down at the squares and shoved them into my pocket. Neither one had an X-marks-the-spot on it.

'What now?' Sarge asked.

'We go to your place.'

'What makes you think my piece is there?'

'I don't think you'd trust it any place else. But if it isn't, we'll go where it is.'

'You've got all the answers, huh?'

'Let's go.'

We went back to the garage. I sat in the back of the VW, on the side away from him. The size of the car made a surprise play on his part almost impossible. It would take him five minutes to get turned around. Two minutes later we were on the road.

It was starting to snow, big, sloppy flakes that clung to the windscreen and turned to instant slush when they struck the pavement. It was slippery going, but there wasn't much traffic.

After a half hour on Route 10, he turned off onto a secondary road. Fifteen minutes later we were on a rutted dirt track with snow-freighted pines staring at us on either side. Two miles along we turned into a short, trash-littered driveway.

In the limited sweep of the VW's headlights I could make out a rickety backwoods shack with a patched roof and a twisted tv aerial. There was a snow-covered old Studebaker in a gully to the left. Out in back was an outhouse and a pile of old tyres. Welcome to the Park-Sheraton.

'Home, sweet home,' Sarge said, and killed the engine.

'If this is a con, I'll kill you.'

He seemed to fill three-quarters of the tiny vehicle's front seat. 'I know,' he said.

'Get out.'

Sarge led the way up to the front door. 'Open it,' I said. 'Then stand still.'

He opened the door and stood still. I stood still. We stood there for about three minutes, and nothing happened. The only moving thing was a fat grey squirrel that had ventured into the middle of the yard to curse us.

'Okay,' I said. 'Let's go in.'

It was a rat warren. The one sixty-watt bulb cast a dingy glow over the whole room, leaving shadows like starved bats in the corners. Newspapers were scattered helter-skelter. Drying clothes were hung on a sagging rope. In one corner there was an ancient Videomaster tv. In the opposite corner was a rickety sink and a stark, rust-stained bathtub on claw feet. A hunting rifle stood beside it. A tremendously fat yellow tom was asleep on the kitchen table. The whole place smelled of wood-rot and sweat.

'It beats living raw,' Sarge said.

I could have argued the point, but didn't. 'Where's your quarter?'

'In the bedroom.'

'Let's go get it.'

'Not yet.' He turned around slowly, his concrete face hard. 'I want your word you ain't going to kill me when you get it.'

'How you going to make me keep it?'

He smiled, a slow, sleepy smile like a fissure opening in a glacier. 'No way at all. But I got you pegged.'

'Do tell.'

'The money isn't the only thing with you. If it was, I'd have tried for you before this. But you had to clean Barney's slate, too. Okay, it's clean. Keenan crossed him and Keenan's dead. If you want the bundle, too, okay. Maybe three-quarters will be enough—and mine has got a great big X on it. But you don't get it unless you promise what I'm paying for—my life.'

'How do I know you won't come after me?'

'I will, sonny,' the Sarge said softly. 'With a big gun. Because then it's going to be a new ball game.'

I laughed. 'All right. Throw in Jagger's address and you've got your promise. I'll keep it, too.'

The Sarge shook his head slowly. 'You don't want to play with Jagger, fella, Jagger will eat you up.'

I put the .45 on full cock.

'All right. He's in Coleman, Massachusetts. A ski lodge. Can you find it?'

'I'll find it. Let's get your piece, Sarge.'

The Sarge looked me over once more, closely. Then he nodded. We went into the bedroom.

A huge brass-railed bed, more newspapers, stacks of magazines—it was the living-room in spades. The walls were papered with pin-ups. A huge record player, the kind with the horn, sat on the floor.

The Sarge didn't hesitate. He picked up the lamp on the night-table and pried the base off it. His quarter of the map was neatly rolled up inside; he held it out wordlessly.

'Throw it,' I invited.

The Sarge smiled and tossed the tube of paper to me. 'There goes the money,' he said.

'I'm going to keep my promise,' I said. 'Consider yourself lucky. Out in the other room.'

Something cold flickered in his eyes. 'What are you going to do?'

'See that you stay in one place for a while. Move.'

We went out into the littered, madhouse kitchen again, a nifty little parade of two. The Sarge stood underneath the naked lightbulb, back to me, his shoulders hunched, anticipating the gunbarrel that was going to groove his head very shortly. I was just lifting the gun to clout him when the light blinked out.

The shack was suddenly pitch black.

I threw myself over to the right; Sarge was already gone. I could hear the thump and tumble of newspapers as he hit the floor in a flat dive. Then silence. Utter and complete.

I waited for my night vision, but when it came there was no help. The place was like a mausoleum in which a thousand dim shadows loomed. And the Sarge knew every one of them.

I knew about Sarge; material on him hadn't been hard to spade up. He had been a sergeant in World War II, and no one even bothered with his real name any more; he was just the Sarge, big and murderous and tough. He had been a commando in the Big War.

Somewhere in the dark he was moving in on me. He must have known the place like the back of his hand, because there wasn't a sound, not a squeaking board, not a foot scrape. But I could feel him getting closer and closer, flanking from the left or the right or maybe pulling a tricky one and coming in straight ahead.

The stock of the gun was very sweaty in my hand, and I had to control the urge to fire it wildly, randomly. I was very aware that I had three-quarters of the pie in my pocket. I didn't bother wondering why the lights had gone out. Not until the powerful flashlight stabbed in through the window, sweeping the floor in a wild, random pattern that just happened to catch the Sarge, frozen in a half-crouch seven feet to my left. His eyes glowed greenly in the bright cone of light, like cat's eyes.

He had a glinting razor blade in his right hand. I suddenly remembered the way his hand had been spidering up his coat lapel in Keenan's carport. He had gotten it out of his collar.

The Sarge said one word into the flash beam. 'Jagger?'

I don't know who got him first. A heavy-sounding pistol fired once behind the flashlight beam, and I pulled the trigger of Barney's .45 twice, pure reflex. The Sarge was thrown twistingly back against the wall with force enough to knock him out of one of his boots.

The flashlight snapped off.

I fired one shot at the window, but hit only glass. I lay on my side in the darkness and realised that Jagger was out there. And, although there were twelve rounds of ammunition back in my car, there was only one left in my gun.

Don't fool with Jagger, fella, the Sarge had said. *Jagger will eat you up.*

I had a pretty good picture of the room in my head now. I got up in a crouch and ran, stepping over Sarge's sprawled legs and into the corner. I got into the bathtub and poked my eyes up over the edge. There was no sound. No sound at all. Even the wood's noises seemed to have stopped. The bottom of the tub was gritty with flaked-off bathtub ring. I waited.

About five minutes went by. It seemed like five hours.

Then the light flicked on again, this time in the bedroom window. I ducked my head while the light bounced through the doorway. It probed briefly and clicked off.

Silence again. A long, loud silence. On the dirty surface of Sarge's porcelain bathtub I saw everything. Barney, with the clotted blood on his belly. Sarge, standing frozen in Jagger's flashlight beam, holding the razor blade professionally between thumb and first finger. And a dark shadow with no face. Jagger. The fifth quarter.

Suddenly there was a voice, just outside the door. It was soft and cultured, almost womanish, but not effete. It sounded deadly and competent as hell.

'Hey, you.'

I kept quiet. He wasn't getting my number without dialling a little.

When the voice came again it was by the window. 'I'm going to kill you, fella. I came to kill them. Now there's just you.'

A pause while he shifted position again. When the voice came, it came from the window just over my head—the one above the bathtub. My guts crawled up into my throat. If he flashed that light now—

'No fifth wheels need apply, fella. Sorry.'

I could barely hear him moving to his next position. It turned out to be back to the doorway. 'I've got my quarter with me, fella. You want to come and take it?'

I felt an urge to cough and repressed it.

'Come and get it, fella.' His voice was mocking. 'The whole pie. Come and take it away.'

But I didn't have to. He knew it. I was holding the chips. I could find the money now. With his single quarter, Jagger had no chance.

This time the silence really spun out. A half-hour, an hour, forever. Eternity squared. My body was going numb with stiffness. Outside, the wind was tuning up, making it impossible to hear anything but rattling snow against the walls. It was very cold. My feet had left me long ago. Now my legs were beginning to feel like blocks of wood.

Then, around one-thirty, a ghostly stirring sound like crawling rats in the darkness. I stopped breathing. Somehow Jagger had got in. He was right in the middle of the room—

Then I got it. *Rigor mortis*, hurried by the cold, was rearranging Sarge for the last time. I relaxed a little.

That was when the door rammed open and Jagger charged through, ghostly and visible in a mantle of white snow, tall and loose and gangling. I let him have it and the bullet punched a hole through the side of his head. And in the brief gunflash, I saw that what I had holed was a scarecrow with no face, dressed in some farmer's thrown-out pants and shirt. The burlap head fell off the broomstick neck as it hit the floor. Then Jagger was shooting at me.

He was holding a semi-automatic pistol, and the innards of the bathtub were like a great percussive hollow cymbal. Porcelain flew up, bounced off the wall, struck my face. Wood splinters rained on me.

Then he was charging, never letting up. He was going to shoot me in the tub like a fish in a barrel. I couldn't even put my head up.

It was Sarge who saved me. Jagger stumbled over one big, dead foot, staggered, and pumped bullets into the floor instead of over my head. Then I was on my knees. I pretended I was Vida Blue. I pegged Barney's big .45 at his head.

The gun hit him but didn't stop him. I stumbled over the rim of the tub getting out to tackle him, and Jagger put two groggy shots to the left.

The faint silhouette that was Jagger stepped back, trying to get a bead, one hand holding his ear where the gun had hit him. He shot me through the wrist. The second bullet ripped a groove in my neck. Then, incredibly, he stumbled over Sarge's feet again and fell backwards. He brought the gun up again and put one through the roof. It was his last chance. I kicked the gun out of his hand, hearing the wet wood sound of breaking bones. I kicked him in the groin, doubling him up. I kicked him again, this time in the back of the head, and his feet rattled a fast, unconscious tattoo on the floor. He was dead then, but I kicked him again and again, kicked him until there was nothing but pulp and strawberry jam, nothing no one could ever identify, not by teeth, not by anything. I kicked him until I couldn't swing my leg any more, and my toes wouldn't move.

I suddenly realised I was screaming and there was no one to hear me but dead men.

I wiped my mouth and knelt over Jagger's body.

My heap was just where I had left it, around the block from Keenan's house, but now it was just a ghostly hump of snow. I had left Sarge's VW about a mile back. I hoped my heater was still working. I was numb all over.

I got the door open and winced a little as I sat down inside. The crease in my neck had already clotted over, but my wrist hurt like hell.

The starter worked for a long time, and the motor finally cranked over. The heater was working, and the one wiper cleared away the snow on the driver's side. Jagger had been lying about his quarter, of course;

it wasn't on him, nor was it in the unobtrusive Studebaker Lark he had come in. But I had his wallet. And his address. If I needed it—and somehow I didn't think I would. Sarge's quarter was the one with the X.

I pulled out carefully. I was going to be careful for a long time. The Sarge had been right about one thing. Barney had been a dumb slob. The fact that he had also been my friend didn't matter any more. The debt had been paid.

I had a lot to be careful for.

THE WATCH

Quentin Tarantino

The phenomenal success of Quentin Tarantino's movie, Pulp Fiction, *released in 1994, has generated a whole new wave of interest in hard-boiled fiction. The film, set among Los Angeles low-life, features the violent misadventures of two hitmen (John Travolta and Sam Jackson) in a trio of episodes which could easily have been taken from the pages of a pulp magazine. Tarantino, who wrote the script of the picture, introduces elements of violence, robbery, drugs, corruption and gun play into the plot which won an Oscar for Best Original Screenplay and the Palme d'Or at the Cannes Film Festival. It made the young director a cult hero and confirmed that his earlier movie,* Reservoir Dogs *(1992), a gangster thriller about the aftermath of an ill-fated bank raid, had been no flash in the pan. What Tarantino did in both movies was to take a number of the cliché plot lines that had become familiar in the hardboiled pulps and breathe new life into them. Together, the pictures have encouraged a whole new generation to discover the works of many of the writers represented in the pages of this book—just as their director, himself a long-time fan of* noir *fiction, had hoped they would.*

Quentin Tarantino (1963–) was born in Knoxville, Tennessee, and named after the character Quint Asper, played by Burt Reynolds, in the popular Sixties TV show Gunsmoke. *Moving to Los Angeles with his mother in 1965, he was apparently unhappy at school but became fascinated with crime and horror movies and decided he wanted to be an actor and writer. While still in his teens, he wrote his first screenplay, 'Captain Peachfuzz and the Anchovy Bandit', and appeared briefly in a movie,* Golden Girls, *impersonating Elvis Presley! His first script to be filmed was* True Romance *in 1991, to be followed by the notorious* Natural Born Killers *which Oliver Stone directed. At 27 he made his own directorial début with* Reservoir Dogs—*and the rest is history. Tarantino's work mirrors his interest in the crime and gangster stories of the Thirties onwards, while his dialogue brilliantly captures the brutalised lives of his contemporary characters. 'The Watch' is a time-less piece of hardboiled fiction which, but for its Vietnam associations, might have been written at any time in the past half century yet is actually an episode from* Pulp Fiction *related by Captain Koons (Christopher Walken). It is yet another example of why the hardboiled genre is not only still flourishing, but surely destined to survive well beyond the century of its inception.*

*   *   *

Hi, little man. Boy, I sure heard a bunch about you.

See, I was a good friend of your Daddy's. We were in that Hanoi pit of hell over five years together.

Hopefully, you'll never have to experience this yourself. But when two men are in a situation like me and your Daddy were, for as long as we were, you take on certain responsibilities for each other.

If it had been me who had not made it, your Daddy would be talkin' right now to my son, Jim. But the way it worked out is I'm talkin' to you, Butch.

I got somethin' for ya.

This watch I got here was first purchased by your great-granddaddy. It was bought during the First World War in a little general store in Knoxville, Tennessee.

It was bought by Private Doughboy Ernie Coolidge the day he set sail for Paris. It was your great-granddaddy's war watch, made by the first company ever to make wristwatches. You see, up until then, people just carried pocket watches.

Your great-granddaddy wore that watch every day he was in the war. Then when he had done his duty, he went home to your great-grandmother, took the watch off his wrist and put it in an ol' coffee can.

And in that can it stayed 'til your grandfather Dane Coolidge was called upon by his country to go overseas and fight the Germans once again. This time they called it World War Two. Your great-granddaddy gave it to your granddad for good luck.

Unfortunately, Dane's luck wasn't as good as his old man's. Your granddad was a Marine and he was killed with all the other Marines at the Battle of Wake Island.

Your granddad was facing death and he knew it. None of the

boys had any illusions about ever leavin' that island alive.

So three days before the Japanese took the island, your 22-year-old grandfather asked a gunner on an Air Force transport named Winocki, a man he had never met before in his life, to deliver to his infant son, who he had never seen in the flesh, his gold watch.

Three days later, your grandfather was dead.

But Winocki kept his word. After the war was over, he paid a visit to your grandmother, delivering to your infant father his Dad's gold watch. This watch.

This watch was on your Daddy's wrist when he was shot down over Hanoi. He was captured and put in a Vietnamese prison camp.

Now he knew if the gooks ever saw the watch it'd be confiscated. The way your Daddy looked at it, that watch was your birthright. And he'd be damned if any slopeheads were gonna put their greasy yella hands on his boy's birthright.

So he hid it in the one place he knew he could hide somethin'. His ass.

Five long years he wore this watch up his ass. Then when he died of dysentery, he gave me the watch. I hid this uncomfortable hunk of metal up my ass for two years. Then, after seven years, I was sent home to my family.

And now, little man, I give the watch to you.

ACKNOWLEDGMENTS

Grateful acknowledgment is made to the following for
permission to reprint their copyrighted material:

Robert Leslie Bellem. "Dead Man's Head." Copyright by *Spicy Detective Stories,* 1935, and reprinted by permission of Walter Arundel.

W. R. Burnett. "Travelling Light." Copyright by *Harper's Magazine,* 1935, and reprinted by permission of H. N. Swanson Inc.

James M. Cain. "Pastorale." Copyright by *Ellery Queen's Mystery Magazine,* 1945, and reprinted by permission of Davis Publications Inc.

Raymond Chandler. "The Man Who Liked Dogs." Copyright by *Black Mask,* 1936, and reprinted by permission of Houghton Mifflin and Hamish Hamilton Ltd.

James Hadley Chase. "Get a Load of This." Copyright in *Get a Load of This,* 1942, and reprinted by permission of Robert Hale Ltd.

Peter Cheyney. "Nice Work." Copyright by *Sunday Dispatch,* 1936, and reprinted by permission of HarperCollins Ltd.

Carroll John Daly. "The Egyptian Lure." Copyright by *Black Mask,* 1928, and reprinted by permission of Mary A. Daly.

James Ellroy. "Torch Number." Copyright in *Justice for Hire,* 1990, and reprinted by permission of Dell Publishing.

Samuel Fuller. "The Deadly Circle." Copyright by *Underworld,* 1934, and reprinted by permission of Carwood Publishing Co Inc.

David Goodis. "It's a Wise Cadaver." Copyright by *New Detective,* 1946, and reprinted by permission of Scott Meredith Literary Agency.

Dashiell Hammett. "Arson Plus." Copyright by *Black Mask,* 1928 as by "Peter Collinson," and reprinted by permission of Harold Matson Company Inc.

MacKinlay Kantor. "The Hunting of Hemingway." Copyright by *Detective Fiction Weekly,* 1931, and reprinted by permission of Paul R. Reynolds Inc.

Stephen King. "The Fifth Quarter." Copyright by *Cavalier,* 1972 as by "John Swithen," and reprinted by permission of the author.

Elmore Leonard. "Freaky Deaky." Copyright in *Freaky Deaky,* 1988, and reprinted by permission of Viking Publishers Inc.